*Also by Hugh C. Rae and available in
Sphere Books*

THE MARKSMAN

The Shooting Gallery

HUGH C. RAE

SPHERE BOOKS LIMITED
30/32 Gray's Inn Road, London WC1X 8JL

First Published in Great Britain in 1972 by
Constable & Company Ltd

Copyright © 1972 by Hugh C. Rae
First Sphere Books edition 1973

TRADE
MARK

Printed in Great Britain by
Hazell Watson & Viney Ltd
Aylesbury, Bucks

ISBN 0 7221 7203 6

'Moments of melancholy, of distress, I think we all have them, more or less, and it is a condition of every *conscious* human life. It seems that some people have no self-consciousness. But those who have it, they may sometimes be in distress, but for all that they are not unhappy, nor is it something exceptional that happens to them.

And sometimes there comes relief, sometimes there comes new inner energy, and one rises up from it, till at last, some day, one perhaps doesn't rise up any more, *que soit*, but that is nothing extraordinary. . . .'

Vincent Van Gogh

'The bourgeois who call themselves "respectable citizens" do not become respectable as the result of contemplating moral values. Rather from the moment of their arising in the world they are thrown into a pattern of behaviour the meaning of which is respectability. Thus respectability acquires a being; it is not put to the question. Values are sown on my path as thousands of little real demands, like the signs which order us to keep off the grass. . . .

All these trivial passive expectations of the real, all these commonplace, everyday values, derive their meaning from an original projection of myself which stands as my choice of myself in the world. . . .

For the rest, there exist concretely alarm clocks, signboards, tax forms, policemen, so many guard rails against anguish.'

Jean-Paul Sartre

PART ONE

Red as a Christmas box, and squat, the buggy burst from
the curve by the crossroads wall. Bull-frog lamps glared
into the sullen darkness, shuddered, levelled and whipped
out, unleashed, into the long straight which carried the
highway past Ottersford Hospital. The road cut through
the forest like a river. October leaves pasted the buggy's
sleek fibreglass hull and churned up from the wheels in
sprays of pale colour which marked the landcraft's wake
through the haze of falling rain. Ranks of conifers and
oaks compressed the engine's sound and carried it thickly
ahead to trouble the ears of wakeful patients in the hospital's roadside wards. Car buffs, most of them in traction,
winced at the grinding gear-change and the wail of
brakes. When it came abreast of the gates, the buggy
changed direction as nimbly as a water-skipper, veered off
the blacktop and, canted on two stout wheels, entered the
hospital by the residents' quarters. The grounds were
deserted, empty squares ribbed with mesh-fences and
coldly lit, like a Stalagluft. Ambulance bays stood off to
the west, stark concrete shapes grey against the resinous
plantations. Prefabricated storerooms, low as bunkers,
spilled back over the shallow acres of the river basin. The
yard narrowed between them to a sudden wedge. The
buggy driver stamped hard on the brake and the wheels
bit and burned and slid out, spinning the machine full
circle, even as it came to rest. A tyre dangled over the
verge of the matron's lawn, still spinning madly, even
when the engine sounds faded out into silence. For a single
moment it was very quiet, breathlessly quiet, as if every
bird, beast and human creature in the quadrant had been
rendered voiceless by the arrival of the squat, red machine,
and its strange unexpected cargo.

Detective Inspector Ryan had the misfortune to live
close to Ottersford Hospital. The temptation was too much
for the muster clerk on the switchboard at County Head-

quarters in the town of Thane; thus Ryan found himself alone at the scene not ten minutes after the buggy's wheel had stopped its ponderous rotation and well in advance of the arrival of the Crime Squad caravan, fellow officers and Chief Superintendent McCaig, his boss. Though he'd lived close to it, Ryan had never been in the hospital before. The sight of it didn't impress him. He knew it to be a wartime military establishment which had grown too useful to be scrapped. Somewhere inside its walls was an ultra-modern surgical unit, but what went on there was all a bit mysterious even to a ranking police officer.

Ryan filed his Cortina into the back lot, parked, got out and walked over to the buggy. It took no great effort of his deductive powers to connect it with the scant report he'd received over the telephone. The novelty of being alone sharpened his senses, but, somehow, he couldn't quite rouse himself to urgency or associate the vehicle with any crime recorded in his memory-banks. It was a smooth, ugly contraption with bulging tyres and the name – *Ayer Sabre* – flamboyantly painted across its snout. Ryan had never heard of the breed. He examined it carefully but found no clues as to the identity of the owner and no signs of violence or struggle, other than the alarmingly unstable position on the edge of the lawn. That it had come in fast was obvious; the intractable hulk must be a bitch to drive at speed on a greasy road surface, demanding lightning reflexes and some measure of physical strength too. He would have covered it to protect the evidence from the rain but he could find no hood and had no sheet large enough in the boot of his Cortina. He looked round; the stillness and the silence, the absence of rubber-necking nurses and orderlies was bewildering. If the Sabre had housed the carcass of some young punter shivved in a pub brawl and whisked here by a mate to be yanked back from death by a medical miracle then the poor bastard would have been right out of luck. Bleeding to death in the back yard of the finest surgical unit in the country would be a nice touch of irony. Imagined ironies didn't turn Ryan on. He decided it was high time to plant a few individual paw-marks on the case before the boss showed up and accused him of malingering.

He walked a flagged path to the main block and presented himself at the reception desk. The foyer too was deserted, except for an elderly night porter barricaded inside his circular desk. Without showing the least interest in Ryan or his credentials the porter directed him down a long shabby corridor to a waiting room. As he walked down the endless ribbon of linoleum Ryan had the uncomfortable sensation of being watched. Behind the blank ward doors would be restive patients, each listening to the unfamiliar creak of his shoes and wondering who he was and what tragedy had brought him here at such an hour.

In the waiting room, Ryan found a young houseman. The short white jacket made him look like a Spanish waiter, an impression abetted by a swarthy complexion and a drooping moustache.

'Are you the fuzz?'

Ryan nodded.

'I'm Crammond. I found him.'

'Found who?'

'Don't you know?'

'Not yet. Tell me.'

'Is this a statement?'

'No, you'll do the formal shortly,' said Ryan. 'Give it to me briefly.'

'I was round the back of the morgue with a student nurse – that's me up to the foreskin in hot water for a start.'

'Where's the nurse now?'

'Locked in matron's office I shouldn't wonder. Very careful about the moral welfare of their lovely little nurses they are in this place.'

'What happened,' said Ryan, 'round the back of the morgue.'

'Nothing indecent, just necking.'

'And?'

'Well, we heard this roaring noise. I looked round the corner just in time to see this Ayer Sabre hammering in the bloody gate, doing about a hundred.'

'That fast?'

'Sixty, anyway,' said Crammond. 'I swear to God I thought the beast was going to have the most fantastic shunt. The guy got it stopped, though, just on the edge of the grass. Rosy and I ran out to it, of course.'

'How many occupants?'

'Two, a driver and a passenger. The driver didn't hang around, though. As soon as the buggy stopped, he vaulted right out of the seat and charged off across the lawn. I went after him, but Rosy called me back to attend to the guy still left in the buggy.'

'Finish about the driver,' said Ryan.

'He ran across the lawn and leaped over the fence into the trees and that's the last I saw of him. Ask Rosemary.'

'I will,' said Ryan. 'The driver, what did he look like?'

'I hardly saw him. He was about middle height, and wrapped up in a bright orange thing.'

'Thing?'

'Oilskin, or anorak. You know.'

'Did you notice anything else about him?'

'No, sorry.'

'Go on.'

'Well, initially I thought the guy in the buggy was pissed, though there was no smell of liquor. I gave him an examination, then sent Rosy to fetch the matron.'

'Why the matron?'

'When anything goes wrong you automatically send for the matron. A bitch she may be, but she is efficient. Inside two minutes, matron was back, bringing Doctor Lorimer with her. I'd concluded my examination by this time, and I, personally, was willing to swear that the guy was dead.'

'He was wounded, injured?'

'Not a scratch on him,' said Crammond. 'Except for the perforations on his arm.'

'Perforations?'

'Needle marks,' Crammond answered. 'The guy was a junkie.'

'I see,' said Ryan. 'What did Lorimer do?'

'Dredged him out of the buggy and hustled him over to the special block.'

'Special block. Why is it special?'

'It's the holy of holies,' Crammond said. 'Surgical and revivification units.'

'How long is it since all this took place?'

'Fifteen, maybe twenty minutes.'

'Did Lorimer think he was dead?'

Crammond shrugged. 'I'm not the confidant of the top surgeons. Anyhow, the Lazarus bit's so common round here, a guy can be dead one minute and sitting up begging for steak and chips the next.'

'Can you take me to the special block?'

'Now?'

'Yes.'

'I'm not supposed to go in there.'

Ryan put his hand on the houseman's shoulder. 'Tell them that horrible copper twisted your arm.'

From the outside the block appeared to be identical with its neighbours. Internally it was the last word in sterilised luxury. All floors were coated in a green substance which absorbed all sounds and vibrations, and the lights were set behind broad frosted diffusers which ate up all shadow. The temperature and humidity would remain static throughout the shift of the seasons and the daily fluctuations which weather imposed on the outside world. Ryan felt like a figure in a surreal fantasy and was relieved when Crammond led him to the matron. His relief didn't last long.

The woman was starched and prim, the epitome of authority. Ryan recognised the syndrome, though the form was extreme. She was the guardian of the medical grail, and puffed up with her own importance in the stewardship of life and death. Well, Ryan had seen many deaths in his time too, and more than a little of life, even if he was just a middle-aged detective with thinning hair, the onset of a paunch and an air of sympathetic remoteness which stemmed from being too long in the backwoods of Scottish policework. Her very glance told him that she considered him the acolyte of a vulgar order. He opened his mouth to explain his business, but she cut him off at once.

'I don't care who you are, you've no right to be in this building.'

'Where's the emergency admitted half an hour ago?' said Ryan.

'I'm not at liberty to divulge that.'

They were standing at the intersection of two long corridors, Crammond hanging sheepishly back. Ryan put on his toughest expression, and stared hard at the woman. Though she was probably no older than his wife, Jean, she had lost every shred of femininity. McCaig would enjoy crushing her underfoot. But McCaig wasn't on hand yet.

'Where is he?' Ryan said. 'Where's the patient?'

'With Doctors Lorimer and Mackenzie.'

'Where are they?'

11

'You can't . . .'

'I didn't ask if I could. I asked where you'd taken the patient.'

'To the revivification unit.'

'Is he still alive, then?'

'Doctor Lorimer is the only person authorised to hand out that sort of information.'

'All right. Where's Lorimer?'

'I *told* you. *Doctor* Lorimer is with the patient.'

Ryan looked round, saw light from an inshot office, and beyond it, at the nether end of the intersection, swing doors set with ports of fish-eye glass. Stepping swiftly round the matron, he started off up the corridor. She yelled at him, but he paid no attention. She grabbed his elbow, and a short undignified struggle might have followed, if, at that moment, the doors of the theatre hadn't swung open and two doctors robed in sage-green coveralls stepped out. Stripping off their gloves and masks, they came towards Ryan. Beyond, in the chamber, the inspector could make out nurses clad too in the green silky stuff. Gloved, masked and made bald by skintight skullcaps, the girls seemed as sexless as salamanders.

'Who is this . . . gentleman?'

The taller of the doctors had bushy grey hair and the habit of grooming it incessantly with the flat of his hand.

'A policeman,' the matron answered. She made it sound like a deadly plague.

'I'm Detective Inspector Ryan.'

'Yes, of course. I'm Lorimer.'

'Is the patient dead?'

'That, I'm afraid, is the case,' said Lorimer. 'We did everything possible to restore life, but . . .'

Stilted phrases clicked out in a tone of diffidence. Death didn't count for this man, who neither feared nor respected it in any of its countless manifestations. Ryan had watched coppers go the same sad way, and prayed to God it wouldn't happen to him.

Mackenzie, the assistant medico, was older and less chilly in his manner. Ruffs of fat swelled pinkly under his jowls and he seemed almost interested in Ryan.

Gravel-voiced, he said, 'The boy was virtually dead when he came to us. Too far gone.'

'He didn't come round at all?' asked Ryan.

12

'Not a flicker that the eye could see.'

'What killed him?'

'Cerebral shock engendered by intravenous injections of a narcotic compound,' said Mackenzie. 'Your own police surgeon will be able to embellish our report, no doubt.'

'Can you tell – even roughly – how long since the dose was administered?'

'I'm no pathologist.' Mackenzie shrugged. 'I'd hazard a guess at a couple of hours. Death occurred twelve minutes ago – technically, that is.'

Ryan wondered at the difference between technical death and the common or garden variety. He asked if he might be allowed to see the body, was given grudging permission, and went on into the unit.

The nurses had gone, their part played.

The chamber was a perfect hemisphere, like a soap-bubble sliced in half; light sources diffuse, colours bleached out, still, shadowless. Drained of colour too, the boy's naked body lay on a table. His expression was serene, his lips slightly parted. Reddish gold hair spilled tidily across his forehead and a tussock, slightly darker in hue, protected the soft bunch of his genitals. His legs were laid out straight, arms straight by his sides, palms uppermost, open. The crescent vein at the crease of his left elbow was pocked with tiny purple marks as if an insect had bitten him. Banked behind the table was an awesome range of equipment. Ryan scanned the bland enamel surfaces, found the gauge of the cardiac recorder and saw that it was thoroughly blank. Skeins of tubing and fine wires trailed from the corpse to the machines, leads tabbed with Scotch tape to the boy's chest and flanks. It seemed to Ryan as if the lad had never lived at all, as if he was an artificial creation waiting to be spurted with the stuff of life and begin his history as a person there and then, at a few minutes past midnight on Sunday, October sixteenth.

McCaig materialised by Ryan's side.

The Chief's sudden soundless entrance didn't startle Ryan, who hardly even bothered to look up from his contemplation of the victim – if victim he was. For a moment or two, the men stood together by the table, saying nothing.

At length Ryan murmured, 'He's dead.'

'I know,' said McCaig. 'Narcotics.'

'Poor wee bastard.'

'Have you identified him, Harry?'

'Not yet.'

'His name's McDowell.'

Ryan glanced up. 'Are you sure, Chief?'

'Yes,' McCaig said. 'Unfortunately I know his father.'

'Not *that* McDowell?'

'Yes, *that* McDowell.'

McCaig carefully hung up his raincoat and planted his hat on the hook. Though it would take only minutes to prepare the body for transfer, minutes were precious. He had conned the matron into lending him the use of her office. The desk was spotless and uncluttered. A single carnation was stuck in a dry test-tube in a brushed steel clamp. To house a flower in that sterile environment seemed like profanity. McCaig seated himself on a rigid metal chair and took out his radio, tuning in short-wave to the Crime Squad caravan which was parked by the buggy on the back lot.

Firstly he reeled off a list of preliminary instructions to Sellars, the inspector delegated to act as liaison officer. He told the young officer to arrange a pantechnicon to transport the Sabre intact to the garages under Central Headquarters and to alert experts capable of making an examination. He had no need to outline the basic routines; Sellars already had them in hand, the photographer, the fingerprint crew, the taking of statements from Crammond and the nurse, a search of the lawn and fences and the fringe of the woods into which the buggy's driver had vanished.

'Who's the local blue?' asked McCaig.

'Constable Millar, Ottersford village substation,' Sellars replied.

'Have Millar check out the dwellings north and south of the hospital, all along the bottom road. Like as not he'll know most of the folk. I want to establish the Sabre's exact line of approach. He can have a go at the filling stations too. See if he can piece together a description of the driver.'

'The fuel tank's near empty,' said Sellars.

McCaig swore, and Sellars comforted him by confessing that a tracer was already on its way to the computer room in Scottish Police Records. McCaig thanked the inspector, switched out and lifted the telephone on the desk. A moment later he was in direct contact with the duty sergeant in the Operations Room in the main county building.

'Is Sergeant Blair on the premises?' McCaig said.

'Just gone off home, sir.'

'Who is there, then? An older man?'

'Sergeant Lindsay, sir.'

'He'll do,' said McCaig. 'Put him on.'

'Lindsay, sir.' The voice was softened by the remnants of a West Highland accent.

McCaig said, 'Sergeant, I've a dirty job, and I want you to handle it.'

'Chief.'

'You'll have heard of Frank McDowell?'

'The councillor?'

'That's the one. His son's just got the chop. I want you to take a car up to the McDowell house in Mossburn and break the news to the parents. If they're not at home, track them down.'

'Aye, Chief.'

'But listen, don't inform them that the lad's dead. Just tell them he's met with an accident. Play it close and observe the parental reaction.'

'What am I to look for?'

'The McDowell boy appears to have been a narcotics addict.'

'Drugs?'

'Yes, drugs. Now, if he'd been on the habit for a while his parents are bound to know of it, and might have an inkling as to his source.'

'I've got the drift, Chief.'

'Another thing, I want you to swear out a warrant on the McDowell house. I hope we won't need it, but it's Frank McDowell we're dealing with and you never know how he'll react. He might start shouting about his legal rights, and if he does I want to be prepared to stuff the law down his bloody throat. Any questions?'

'No, Chief.'

'Right.'

McCaig dipped the receiver, held it against the buttons for a second then dialled a direct number. He waited, without obvious impatience, while the tone rang out.

After several minutes the line cleared and a girl's voice said, 'Sheila Summerfield.'

'Did I get you out of bed?'

'No, Chief, out of the bath.'

'Sorry to disturb you, Sheila, but we've been hit by something unusual and I need you back at the office. Can you make it?'

'How soon?'

'I'll send a car.'

'Ten minutes.'

'Fine,' said McCaig. 'What chance of pushing out a press release at this hour?'

'The Sundays will have gone out,' the girl told him. 'You won't get a newsprint until Monday.'

'TV?'

'Flashes, or a bulletin report?'

'Both.'

'Can do,' the girl said.

'Arrange a press conference for 06.00 hours.'

'Six o'clock on a Sunday morning?'

'If the bastards show signs of coming round, you can feed them some bumph about drugs . . .'

'Cannabis?'

'The hard stuff.'

'That'll bring them running, Chief.'

'You know the drill?'

'I should do.'

'Right,' said McCaig. 'Will you also get in touch with Edgar Pomfret of Customs Special Branch. Handle him gently. We need his help. Tell him we've had what looks like a surfacing of narcotics, and ask him if he'd be willing to advise me and brief my staff, since nobody north of the city line has much of a clue about this particular scene. Flatter him; he's pompous. Are you taking this down?'

'Yes, Chief.'

'Keep writing. Rouse Willy Rudkin, tell him to trot on down to the mortuary with his blades. If Willy's off fishing, pin down the new assistant.'

'Jebb?'

'That's the fellow. I'll want a cut made as soon as I can wangle the necessary papers, and just as soon as the parents have made formal identification. By the way, Lindsay will be bringing the parents down to the mortuary.

After they've gone through it, show them directly into my office and keep them there – unless they're too shattered and need medical attention. If any snags crop up, Sheila, put them on the slate and let me have them before I go in.'

'All clear, Chief,' the girl said. 'Who's dead?'

'Councillor McDowell's boy.'

'Good God!'

'Aye,' said McCaig. 'Ironic, isn't it?'

'Terrible.'

'Off you go, then, lass. Don't catch cold.'

'No,' the girl said. She sounded distant now and detached, thinking of McDowell, perhaps, and feeling pity for him and his wife.

McCaig replaced the receiver and sat back.

His mind was suddenly empty, his mouth dry and all the juices of his body pricking the surface of his skin in rank salt sweat. Though the connection was slight, the link with McDowell made him think of his own wife and filled him with the bewildered realisation that he hadn't really thought of her at all for days now. It was easy to forget, to push the personal side of his life completely to one side, not to fret about Muriel, or his son Derek. They were both gone. He was still married to Muriel, and neither of them had so far even mentioned the possibility of divorce. In all ways except the legal, though, they were no longer man and wife. In her last letter, she'd told him that she was well and happy, and he was not so selfish that the news was not good news. She'd found herself a job as a buyer in a Blackpool clothing store and would continue to live with her sister in Lytham St. Anne's.

He was sweating heavily. The bloody office was overheated and claustrophobic. He stuffed the radio into his pocket and pushed himself to his feet. His palm left a damp print on the polished surface of the desk. He wiped it with his sleeve, but only spread the stain. Gathering his will-power he pushed all thoughts of his wife right to the back of his mind. Her connection with the case which was opening at his feet was highly tenuous and best left dormant like so many other things in the past. Lifting his hat and coat from the hook, he groped for the panel of the plate-glass door. For the last ten minutes he'd been acting with eclectic spontaneity, like a computer spitting out all that had ever been fed into it. Now he was obliged to start thinking like a man again, and tread the tightrope to the end of a case which, no matter what the records said, he would treat as one of murder.

Procedurally it was wrong of him to make snap judgements, but it seemed too obvious to ignore the fact that the driver of that red beach-buggy was the key needed to unlock the mystery of McDowell's suppliers and provide a concrete lead to the pusher. Having gunned up on legal precedents, he would frame a charge and construct a case tight enough to put the bastards up for a maximum. So far, the peddling and misuse of drugs had been a very minor problem in the county. In a rural community rape, drunkenness, the game and drought laws seemed of much more import; no ostrich, though, McCaig was well aware that the problem of narcotic-trading would reach him soon enough – and that this might be it, the tip of the iceberg. All the free publicity and propaganda which the media tipped into youngsters' empty minds was bound to have its effect. He had anticipated a rash of arrests for possession of brown drugs and amphetamines – but not this, not a straight leap into the lethal whites. He hoped to Christ that young McDowell might turn out to be an isolated miscreant, that his source would be in another officer's bailiwick, in Glasgow or Edinburgh, say, where all manner of corruption was already known to flourish.

Strange, he could generate very little genuine anger at what had happened to Frank McDowell's boy. It wasn't malice, a deeply buried seed in his psyche; not that, only a tainting of the general public's apathy to killings which had no outward signs of violence and no spicy sexual connotations. At his age and in his position, he should know better.

Depressed, he lingered in the office until the corridor was no longer empty.

Swaddled in nylon, the body glided past, pale in the opaque passageway, like a length of plastic being carried downstream on a gentle current. A male orderly pushed the trolley; nurse, matron and doctors followed soberly in its wake. Last of all came Harry Ryan, carrying the boy's clothing and effects in two large plastic bags.

Hat in hand, McCaig watched the little procession pass by. The thick glass made it seem distant and remote. He slid open the door, stepped into the corridor and took his place behind Ryan. Soundlessly the entourage rolled over green rubber under cold lights towards the welcome darkness of the night outside where an ambulance waited to transport the boy back to town. Past elbows and hips, McCaig could just make out the shape of the lad's head under its shroud. The contours of the face bore a marked resemblance to his father's strong features – or was it only imagination?

Thinking again of Frank McDowell, so long an enemy, McCaig discovered an unexpected nugget of pity in the bedrock of his character. It bothered him considerably. Facing up to McDowell would be difficult enough without sentiment. No matter how grief took him, McDowell's involvement meant trouble.

Ignoring the man in uniform who stood like a sentinel at the office doorway, McDowell shoved past him and kicked the door shut with his heel.

The girl, McCaig's tart, a public expense-account whore, peered at him through thick-lensed spectacles and shook a strand of lank blonde hair from her face. She stood by the desk with a bunch of files pressed to her breasts as if he'd caught her naked and sly. Before he was more than a couple of paces into the office, the girl backed out through a door hidden between two towering filing cabinets.

McCaig was seated behind the big desk.

Stepping stiffly forward, McDowell planted his fists on the desk and leaned hard into them.

'McCaig.'

'I'm sorry, McDowell.'

'You knew all along he was dead.'

'I considered it advisable to break it to you gently.'

'You call that gently!'

'Sit down.'

'Answer me, McCaig.'

'Can I fetch you something – brandy, tea, coffee?'

'*Answer me.*'

'Answer you what?'

'You knew Tom was dead when you sent that highland copper to . . .'

'Look, you'd best sit down.'

'I tell you, I'm perfectly all right.'

Though he wasn't perfectly all right, he couldn't bring

19

himself to expose the depth of his shock to McCaig. When the chair edge brushed the backs of his knees, the joints buckled involuntarily and he found himself seated. His hands on the desk seemed to belong to a stranger.

McCaig was close.

The blonde appeared from between the cabinets.

She held a tumbler of brandy.

He never drank brandy; whisky was what he wanted.

The girl put the glass on the desk.

He resisted the impulse to reach out for it. The effort of will would be more bracing than the effects of the alcohol. In any guise, in any measure, he needed all the control he could muster right now.

McCaig's shoulders were too imposing for a man of only middle height, but under the bulk was a quickness, an alertness, and an arrogance too, which transformed McDowell's anguish into rage.

'Is Mrs McDowell . . . ?'

'She's being taken care of,' McDowell snapped.

An hour ago he had been as omnipotent in his own home as McCaig was here in his office, just a good-humoured host entertaining a few friends.

McCaig was smoking a cigarette.

To his astonishment, McDowell found a cigarette in his fingers too, and the taste of smoke in his mouth. Gaps, lapses of awareness; he shuddered.

McCaig hoisted his buttocks on to the edge of the desk. In an ashtray a spent match uncoiled a wisp of waxen smoke. McDowell sucked on the cigarette.

'Look, I can wait until tomorrow,' said McCaig. 'Postpone . . .'

'Postpone what?'

'I have some questions about . . . Tom.'

'Why?'

'Questions are necessary because of the manner of his death.'

McDowell remembered his glimpse of the body, Tom's body. It had been so whole, so perfect and unimpaired. His lashes cut off light, his cheeks screwed up. When he opened his eyes again everything seemed much brighter than before. Tom hadn't died in the wreckage of the Sabre after all; nobody, no bloody copper, had thought to tell him that, and the evidence of his eyes hadn't registered in his brain. McCaig was intent on hammering away all the props of his control.

'How did he . . . ?'

'Drugs,' McCaig said. 'Tom died as the result of a massive overdose of drugs.'

Now he understood; it was all just a conspiracy to ruin him and smash his reputation. That spark did not ignite, though, and instantly he saw the vanity of it, recognised just how tiny and insignificant his power-world was matched against this event.

'Tom didn't kill himself,' he told McCaig.

'We're not sure just how it happened. We do know, however, that the drug used was either heroin or cocaine.'

'*Liar!*'

'I'm sorry, McDowell, but it's the truth.'

McCaig said more, lots more. McDowell didn't listen. He was thinking about Tom, as much as he dared to think about Tom. Tom had deceived them all, effected a transformation in the end which, publicly at least, would make him appear to be what he was not. It occurred to McDowell that he may not have known his son at all; then, just as abruptly, the thought came to him that it was not wickedness but a quirk of circumstances which had contrived to kill the boy in this weird manner, not anything for which *he* could be seriously blamed. He didn't hear a word of McCaig's monologue. It was as if his mind had slipped down into the quiet black regions of sleep.

The girl disturbed him.

She brought in a tray with coffee cups and two white tablets.

McDowell wakened.

McCaig said, 'You haven't heard a word, have you?'

The girl placed the cup on the desk beside the brandy glass and held the aspirin in the hollow of her palm. She had a long narrow hand, dry-skinned, almost elegant, wore no rings or other ornaments. The cuff of her cardigan was dust-soiled, the blouse-sleeve fastened with two mis-matched buttons. The only means of being rid of her was to do what she wanted. He took the tablets, slung them over his throat and washed them down with coffee. The liquid was hot and bitter. He put the cigarette back in his mouth. Even at this time the taste buds did not cease to operate and he felt that his appreciation of the blend of coffee and tobacco was a callous betrayal of the state of his mind.

'Why should I listen, McCaig, when I *know* you're telling me a pack of lies?'

'I think you should throw in the towel and go on home.'

'Trying to get rid of me?'

'I had hoped you might be able to answer a few simple questions, but . . . forget it. It doesn't matter.'

'It matters to me.'

'Fine,' said McCaig, tightly. He leaned on his elbows, torso twisted, seams of his clothing strained. Every word was emphasised by a rap of knuckles on the desk, and the responding chime of glass and cup.

Carefully McDowell picked up the glass and drained it. The sensual response was muted; he hardly tasted the liquor.

'Surely you understand,' McCaig said, 'that if Tom *was* an addict then I must trace his source of supply immediately.'

'You can buy the damned stuff in any chemist's.'

'That's a fable. Heroin's hard to acquire, even on prescription, and . . . never mind.'

'No, no, go on, go on.'

'Where did Tom get the buggy?'

'What?'

'The Ayer Sabre?'

'From me. A gift. He was nineteen.'

McDowell's gullet closed. He reached for the glass. It was empty. McCaig did not seem inclined to send out for more. He took the cup instead and swilled the black liquid into his mouth. Robbed of his flair for articulate argument, the talent which had made him a councillor, he was utterly devoid of usable pretences.

'When did you buy him the buggy?'

'Last month.'

'September?'

'No, August.'

'An expensive gift.'

'I got it for an old song,' McDowell said. Vestigial pride in the transaction warmed him briefly. The truth was that he had derived more pleasure from the red beast than Tom ever had. He had spotted it, fully built, in a garage, had wanted to own it, had bought it for the boy. He had driven

22

it too, and enjoyed the experience thoroughly. 'Four hundred. A reconditioned Ford V6 under the hood.'

'Hard to handle?'

'Not once you get used to it.'

'You've driven it?'

'Of course.'

'Must be about the only one of its kind in the country?'

'Part of its attraction.'

'Did Tom's mates drive it too?'

'I really couldn't say.'

He couldn't fix the image of the Sabre clearly. It slithered and slipped out of his thoughts like an ice-cube. All he had in its place was the recollection of the thing under the folds of the linen sheet, and the rubber glove lifting.

McCaig said, 'Tom was a student?'

McDowell nodded; he wasn't really listening. He was engrossed in a scrutiny of the executive desk. It had an imperfection on the working of the bevel, a quirk in the tooling, a slip of the artisan's hand. He stared at it so hard that he almost expected the varnish to blister and bubble. While he was staring at the desk the anticipation of what McCaig might do came to him, bringing a deluge of anxiety.

'Where did he study?'

'New College, Thane,' said McDowell dully. 'Architecture. Second year.'

Silence: McCaig was waiting. McDowell's sustaining anger evaporated in the heat of that peculiar anxiety, peculiar because it hadn't occurred to him before. He squinted up into the cloud of light. McCaig stubbed out his cigarette and stuffed his hands into his jacket pockets, toying with coins or a key-chain, chinking, waiting. McDowell could not define the expression which lurked in the policeman's face; it might have been calculation and it might have been pity.

'Did Tom, to your knowledge, take drugs?'

'No.'

'To your knowledge did he keep drugs in the house?'

'No.'

'I'd like permission to search.'

'Search?'

'Your house.'

'My permission?'

'Yes.'

'Certainly not; under no circumstances.'

'I can furnish a search warrant – if necessary.'

'Search for what?'

'Drugs.'

'In *my* house !'

'I'm sure you understand that I must have the house searched.'

Cold fear coiled inside him, brandy and whisky in the chemistry too.

'Your wife won't be disturbed, I promise you,' said McCaig.

McDowell had forgotten about Mildred. How would he ever get her to believe that the truth was not just another elaborate slander against the character of her precious son? Anyway, Mildred would not be in Mossburn. She'd be in Armitage with the Menzies, lying in the narrow guest bedroom under the stairs, poleaxed by Dent's injections. With luck Dent would have pumped her so full of gloop that he would not have to face her until tomorrow. It would be better, in fact, if she did not waken again, slept forever with her illusions about Tom intact.

'Permission to search . . .' McCaig was insisting.

McCaig would search. McDowell knew what he would find. He couldn't allow it; couldn't prevent it. He was trapped. At least he had some pride left. Was there a hint in the arrogant bastard's eyes? Did he guess already? Lifting his shoulders he tried to suck air into the inflexible parts of his body, contracting his belly. How could he be expected to defend himself at a time like this? How could he be asked to explain his callousness – especially to McCaig? He reached to push the chair away, but the weakness in his legs had become alarming, worming up the marrow of his bones. Of course he could still fight it, but it hardly seemed worth the enormous effort. The bastard already had the warrant, didn't need permission. McCaig would not yield him a single minute's privacy, that necessary lull in which to be rid of the boxes. McCaig would be at his side from now until the search was completed. The policeman had left him no avenue of escape. Pressures of frustration and other emotions shot into his skull like lava from a volcano. McCaig grabbed at him but missed. He landed on the sisal carpeting, sprawled on his belly.

In the void above were people and voices, on the cinnamon carpeting a foxtrot of shoes.

McCaig was shouting, 'Sheila, Sheila, bring . . .'

That was all McDowell heard for quite a while.

By the time he came round and they got him back to Mossburn, the search was over.

They didn't find the boxes.

The boxes were no longer there.

Somebody had beaten McCaig to it.

Somebody had taken them away.

By mid-Sunday morning the McDowell case seemed to be losing its momentum. It was like that with some cases; they quickly bogged down in a tangle of dead-ends and unsatisfactory conclusions. The apparent answers which police deductive methods came up with often proved more baffling than useful. McCaig was tired and bored, though he would not admit to the last heresy. Sellars and Ryan had crawled off home to catch up on lost sleep and he should sensibly do likewise. Wheels were in motion and he knew that he could contribute no more until fresh evidence accumulated or until the Sabre's driver was brought to book. Something untoward in the nature of the lad's death disturbed him deeply, though; for his own comfort, he still classed pushers and addicts with the horde of petty criminals who would dive for a bolt-hole rather than saddle up and head for distant horizons. Edgar Pomfret agreed with him. Pomfret had put on a good show that morning. The head of Customs Special Branch was a good old-fashioned eccentric; there weren't many of them in law enforcement any more. Pomfret had exhibited his whole bag of tricks to the assembled officers and men of the Thane County Police Force, demonstrating the various types of drugs in circulation in underground markets, methods of administering the compounds, and, aided by an interesting collection of slides, had conducted an hour-long teach-in on procedures of search and arrest. McCaig did not grudge the time spent on this instruction and was grateful to Pomfret not only for the tutorial but for his promise of direct assistance in tracing possible sources of supply which might exist within the boundaries of the city.

His pre-dawn encounter with the boys of the press had been less satisfactory, and he hadn't given them enough to appease their appetite for hot scandal. Sheila had managed to place news with the local television stations, however, and he was just naïve enough to hope that out of the welter of crank calls and false sightings which would follow the transmissions, he might find a lead to the driver.

The rest of the facts were assembled in a large folder which lay open on the desk before him. The summary of the various reports and official statements wasn't terribly encouraging. According to the medical officer, Jebb, Tom McDowell had 'died of an overdose of heroin or cocaine at approximately midnight. Jebb's detailed analyses of organ contents and tissue textures hadn't been helpful. Nothing there to latch on to, or to compound the simple fact that McDowell had shot himself full of junk and died of it. No bruising; no breakages. Jebb claimed that McDowell was not an addict, however, and trotted out a sheaf of reasons for this interesting statement. McCaig was oddly gratified to have his own personal guess confirmed.

He leafed over another page of the file.

If Jebb's news had been largely uninteresting, the rest was positively depressing. The search of the grounds and the plantations round Ottersford Hospital had yielded only one item of value, the print of a shoe of sufficiently uncommon design to furnish a possible lead to the vanishing driver. The plaster-cast was of the toe and sole of the right foot, and came from an indentation on the soft muddy grass at the bottom of the lawn, close to the fence. The cast indicated that the shoe was a lightweight sports model, of the sort favoured by athletes; mathematical calculations put it as a standard size 8 filled by a man of approximately 5 feet 8 inches in height and of slender build.

Better than nothing, McCaig supposed.

Besides he was still short of several reports, and might find connections in them which would help him pad out his spectral portrait.

At a minute short of 14.00 hours Sheila reminded him that the first newscast was scheduled. He wheeled a portable Sony from a cupboard and watched the presentation. It lasted ninety seconds and came across like a series preview, a piece of fiction. Even to McCaig it didn't seem particularly pertinent, even real. He buried the Sony in the cupboard again, lay back in his chair and fell asleep.

The blipping of the intercom wakened him. He was thick, bleary and worth nothing.

He flipped the switch. 'What is it, Sheila?'

'Chief?'

'What's the time?'

'Ten past three.'

'Bloody hell!'

'A Constable Millar from Ottersford station wants to see you, sir. Shall I send him in?'

'I suppose you'd better,' said McCaig.

He sat up and tidied his collar and ran a comb through his sparse black hair, generally tried to appear keen and alert, like McCaig. The vanity made him think of Frank McDowell. It had been unpleasant, almost shocking, to witness the total disintegration of the man, a man who had always presented an air of absolute self-possession and emotional toughness, not to mention smooth grooming. To watch Frank McDowell collapse and writhe about on the office carpet hadn't given him any malicious kick at all, just made him wonder if there was any blow that life could administer which would make him go like that. It hadn't even been necessary to push McDowell; the questioning and the subsequent house search had provided no clues at all. McDowell had nothing to hide, except his anguish, and he wasn't making much of a go of hiding that, not so far.

The constable knocked deferentially on the inner door. McCaig told him to enter.

Millar was a big fresh-faced youngster with fair hair, an excellent advertisement for a generation reared on the bounties of a welfare state. Rainwater laced his oilskins and dripped from the hat in his hand.

'Still pouring?' asked McCaig.

'Yes, sir.'

'Have you being chasing that damned buggy all night long?'

'I have, sir.'

'Any luck?'

'Yes, sir; a bit.'

'Park yourself, then, and tell me what you found.'

Tentatively Millar lowered himself on to the chair before the Chief's desk. Even his trousers were damp, and must be cold too, pressing against his rump. McCaig

27

watched sympathetically as the youngster dug a regulation notebook from under his cape and carefully opened it.

He said, 'I found out where the Sabre came from, sir. I've a certain amount of description of the driver too.'

'Good.'

'Will I . . .'

'Please do.'

'The buggy came from town, sir, from Thane. It travelled out to Ottersford via the Laurieston Street bypass and Grange Road Service Station. It passed the service station at 23.40 hours. One of the garage hands noticed it particularly because it was travelling at such a lick. He didn't see the driver. The Sabre was spotted next outside the Kettles public house. D'you know the Kettles, sir?'

'Not well, no.'

'Used to be just a country pub, but it got a supper licence lately and runs dances and functions now. The Sabre was noticed by the resident piano-player when he was out for a breather. He's sure of the time to within five minutes, and put it at 23.45. The next sighting was at the road end of Donaldson's farm. The Thane-Lannerburn bus was pulled up there to let off one of the Donaldson girls. She and the bus driver both noticed the buggy but not the driver.'

'What about the piano-player. Didn't he see the driver?'

'Just the flash of an orange garment, sir.'

'Go on.'

'Next witness was a chap by the name of Pirie. An . . . itinerant worker.'

'A what?'

'A tinker, sir,' said Millar. 'They're camped up the dump behind the Eswick woods, working the tottie shaws for Donaldson. Pirie's the uncle of the tribe. He'll be in his fifties, I'd guess.'

'Was he sober?'

'Aye, he was sober,' said Millar, grinning. 'The crafty old bugger was at the poaching.'

'When did you visit the camp?'

'At about seven this morning, sir.'

McCaig laughed. 'Bet that put the breeze up their kilts.'

'It did that, sir.'

'How the devil did you winkle information out of tinkers?'

'Well, I . . .'

'Trade secrets, Constable?'

'Sir.'

'We all have them,' said McCaig. 'Anyhow, Pirie saw the Sabre.'

'He's not certain of the time, but he got a good look at the driver. Pirie's not a type I'd normally trust, sir, but his report seems to match with what we do know, so it's like as not accurate. The buggy near knocked him down. He was just louping the stile from the strath . . .'

'The gamekeeper's stile?'

'Aye,' said Millar. 'You can't beat a tinker for bold brass neck. I'm certain he'd have a salmon up his jook, or maybe a pheasant for the pot out of the estate properties. Told me he was just out for a wee stroll before bed. He stepped over the stile, and the Sabre came rocketing out of the bend and missed him by a whisker. Swerving and shunting all over the road, it was, Pirie says.'

'We'll come back to the driver. What happened next?'

'Well, that was the last positive sighting, sir. Couple of old folk in the cottage at the Smiddy thought they heard it, but they're too doddery to be wholly reliable.'

'No matter,' said McCaig. 'It's a straight run from the gamekeeper's stile to the hospital, near enough. What's your estimate of the vehicle's speed?'

'Averaging eighty, sir. Must've been hitting it hard on the straights, though.'

'Good. How about the driver?'

'He was fair, with a thin face, and young. Wore an orange or yellowish-red garment, like mountain-climbers wear, a Cagoule it's called. The hood was up, but there was a blue sweater, or, maybe, a scarf under it. Pirie saw gloves on his hands.'

'We knew that,' McCaig said. 'What else?'

'That's all, sir. I'm sorry it's so scant.'

'Can't be helped,' McCaig said. 'You've done well.'

'There's just one other thing, sir.'

'Oh!'

'I followed the Sabre back into town.'

'Did you now,' said McCaig. 'Any special reason?'

'Just a . . . a feeling, sir.'

'A hunch?'

'Yes, sir. I found where the Sabre came from.'

McCaig sat up straight at the desk. Feeding the note-book through his large fingers, Millar cocked his wrist so that the Chief could read the page. He'd written the address in huge block capitals on a blank leaf, knowing that it was important.

'It came from this address, sir, at approximately 23.30 hours on Saturday. I couldn't fine the time down further.'

McCaig leaned over the desk and squinted at the page.

'Sources?' he said.

'Neighbours, sir. I went up there hoping to . . .'

'You know who lives at 7, Rodale Avenue, of course?'

'The deceased, Thomas McDowell.'

'Some hunch!'

'And that's all, sir.'

'It's enough,' McCaig said.

Brian Menzies scratched his fluffy beard and blinked at his wife with bewildered pleading. One hand covered the mouthpiece of the instrument and he was drawn away from it, the cord taut, the receiver itself at arm's length.

'It's him,' he said.

'Who?' Laura wiped her hands on her apron.

'Frank.'

'Then talk to him.'

'No, I . . . I mean, you talk to him.'

'Give it here,' Laura said.

Menzies handed her the phone, glanced briefly behind him at the closed door of the guest room, then lumbered quickly up the corridor of the hallway and vanished into his den. Laura watched him until he was out of sight, immured behind the oak door. She knew that the death of the McDowell boy had upset him, but that the after-math, the good neighbour gesture of sheltering the bereaved in time of stress, was really too much for her husband. Brian was too direct and simple a soul to be comfortable and steadfast in moments of emotional stress. His strength was of another order, better suited to sudden crises, to action. He had always been a little bewildered by McDowell, though they had been friendly for several years. Now he was rendered unsure of the man's reaction. Willingly Brian had rescued Mildred from the horrible atmosphere of the police station. He would give her pro-tection in the physical sense just as long as she felt she needed it, but Frank was another can of beans. Frank would be liable to demonstrations of rage and bitterness too far from Brian's boyish nature to be anything but disturbing and unwelcome. She wasn't awed by Frank; how could she be?

She put the mouthpiece close to her lips. 'Frank, it's Laura.'

The first words he said were, 'The stuff's gone.'

Laura said nothing for a moment. He should, after all, have stayed with them. Frank wouldn't have it. He'd gone back to Rodale Avenue. He sounded normal, though, except for a huskiness in his throat, like the whisper of lust, or as if he'd been shouting to chase ghosts out of the empty rooms. It was bad for him to be alone. She could see some sense in it, however; so much might come out in the wash of the police investigation which would not be beneficial to anyone, and wouldn't help the poor kid anyway; best if they kept apart. Besides, Mildred was in the house. She had known that he would call, of course; it came as no surprise.

'Laura, did you hear me?'

'Yes.'

'You know what I mean?'

'The police, perhaps?'

'No,' McDowell said. 'Perhaps, perhaps Tom . . .'

It was a wicked game. Mention of the boy's name left her no stomach to sustain it further. 'I've got them.'

'Thank God!' She heard him sigh, almost, but not quite, like a sob. The relief in his tone sickened her. 'How did you get in? Was it open?'

'I reckoned McCaig would want to search, so I had Brian drive me round there while Dent was attending to Mildred. I made the excuse that I wanted to collect some clothes for Mildred.'

'But how did you find the stuff?'

'I guessed where you might hide it.'

'Thank God,' he said again. 'Where is it now?'

'Here.'

'Hidden?'

'Don't be ridiculous, Frank. Do you imagine I'd leave it lying around.'

'Destroy it.'

'I can't, not just now, not with Brian in the house.'

31

'You can take them out,' McDowell said. 'Wait! Is Brian liable to be on the extension?'

'Are you mad? You know he's not like that.'

'Listen, then, do what you can to be rid of that stuff. Jesus, I should never have bought it in the first place.'

'I don't see the relationship,' Laura said; but she did see the relationship. She wanted his answer.

He was quiet for a moment, breathing wheezily, then said, 'You're right, Laura, hang on to it, all of it. Provided it's not here, it's safe enough, I suppose.'

'Frank.'

'What?'

'You haven't asked about Mildred.'

'Yes,' he said, dutifully solemn. 'How is she?'

'Heavily sedated.'

'That's . . . yes, I'll call round tomorrow.'

'If you can spare the time.'

'What?'

'Yes, do call tomorrow, Frank.'

'Laura?'

'I'm here.'

'Thanks. Thanks for every . . .'

Laura Menzies hung up.

'You won't intimidate me, McCaig.'

'Look, McDowell, I don't give a damn about you. I'm sorry for your wife, if that's any comfort, but I'm not here to bully you. I'm doing my job, that's all.'

'I'm in no position to argue.'

'For once!' said McCaig. 'Is Mrs McDowell fit to be questioned yet?'

'She's with friends.'

'You're here alone?'

'Yes.'

'How are you?'

'Pardon?'

'Are you better?'

'I'd prefer it if you'd forget about this morning. I'd had too much to drink.'

'Right; so now you're fit to talk to me intelligently and without duress?'

'Have I any choice?'

'Generally,' said McCaig, through his teeth, 'relatives

and friends of criminal victims are only too willing to co-operate with the police, to see that justice is done.'

'Platitudes, McCaig; platitudes.'

'Unless, that is, the relatives have something to hide.'

'Now what the hell do you mean by that?'

McCaig gave no answer. All pity quenched, he stared at McDowell. Though McDowell was a year or two younger than he was, the ageing process had been skilfully disguised. One thing money could buy for you, if you were vain enough to use it to that end, was the similitude of youth, if not its resilience. Would he have been vain enough to shave and groom himself on the evening of the day Derek, his own lad, died? Copper or not, flint-hearted bastard or not, he seriously doubted it.

'Who tidied up?'

'The cleaning woman, of course,' McDowell retorted. 'I asked her to come in special today. Under the circumstances she could hardly refuse.'

McDowell tucked his hands under the tails of the bespoke jacket of hand-stitched heather tweed. In the pocket of the vest was a leather cigar case and a gold fountain pen, insignia of prosperity. The success which the clothes and trappings represented seemed brazen, untarnished even by the tragic loss of a son. There was no evidence of party debris in the lounge. The room was as well groomed and as trim as the man; a handsome room, with diamond-paned windows, a granite hearth and antique furniture. A log fire burned in the grate, spouts of ventilation from ducts under the iron-work blowing smoke into the chimney's throat. It was a far cry from the acrid palls and splutters McCaig got when he bothered to bank unpeeled timber into the fire at home. Light came from a single fluted lamp and, McCaig noticed, the walls were dotted with control panels of polished mahogany to operate the fashionable electronic devices which were incorporated into the fabric of the house. Personally he had never cared much about creature comfort. Maybe that had been one of the shoals on which his marriage foundered.

'Tom had a room of his own?'

'Naturally,' said McDowell.

'May I see it?'

'Your lackeys have already . . .'

'*Look,* don't push me too hard, McDowell. I can do this

33

myself, or I can ship round a regiment of big burly constables, the dumbest I can find. Now, what's it to be?'

'Upstairs.'

'Show me.'

'No, McCaig, it's not a guided tour. Top of the stairs, the door facing you. The light's on.'

McCaig went into the hallway. The man closed the door behind him. Neither of them had a right to be hostile at a time like this; but he hadn't started it, not then and not before. Groping, McCaig found a switch and lit the hall light. He took off his overcoat and draped it on a table by a vase of long-stemmed roses. He crossed to the telephone console and examined the extensions which led off to various parts of the house. The directory was clamped into a morocco binder. Quickly he scanned the special numbers listed in the front; all written in a neat quick hand – probably the wife's – and giving no information that he could latch on to.

He went upstairs.

Tom's room lay to the rear of the house. Two long windows made it as light and airy as a painter's studio; fitted carpets in warm tan, built-in closets, long polished pinewood table with a miniature draughtsman's board clamped to it; a single bed with a padded leather headboard and a Spanish spread – a bed that wouldn't be slept in again, like as not. Bedside table, with small lamp and alarm clock. In the room's centre was a Danish-style armchair, a mammoth black leather boxing-glove strapped to a tubular steel frame. It was a grand foundation on which a young man could build himself a lair fashioned to his own identity. Oddly, though, the place was as neat and formal as the downstairs lounge. It didn't lack comfort, only tokens of habitation, individuality; no posters, pin-ups, photographs. The mantelshelf was bare and the library shelves empty. The books had been pulled down and bound in bundles which stood now behind the door. Curious, McCaig scanned the spines; an average lot, thrillers of the less sensational variety, and many textbooks, some obviously left over from his schooldays. Straightening again, McCaig slid open the wardrobe doors. Hooks and hangers were empty. Drawers of the dressing table? Empty too. The desk was cleaned down to joints and sanded wood. God! By tomorrow little or no trace of Tom McDowell would linger here.

Frowning, the chief went out on the landing.

A drone of choral singing rose from the stairwell.

He walked softly along the passage to another door, turned the painted china knob and let the door swing open. He peered into the gloom.

The fourposter's frond-like drapes were illuminated by the thin shaft of light from the passageway, giving the huge bed an ethereal quality in the darkness. A tiny clenching sensation took McCaig's gut. It had not occurred to him before that his marriage had begun to founder in this house. The sight of the bed reminded him, put into his head the notion that maybe McDowell had sped the process of disintegration which had budded and broken out like a rank weed three years back. Though, until that moment, McCaig had been sure of his wife's integrity, the sureness was now gone. He could not quite bring himself to imagine her, attractive in her prime, sprawled on that bed, full, not of a lover's pleasure, but of a mean wrangling sort of envy of the fine house, of the material things in it.

It had been a bad year for them all. He'd been on detachment with Glasgow C.I.D., working long unpredictable shifts. Derek had just gone up to the Academy and was in process of discovering that he was a person in his own right, shaking off the velvet ties of security and parental need. The boy had been Muriel's companion for thirteen years and she missed his company badly. She was bored, discontented. McCaig could sympathise, but could not offer her simple solutions. She would accept no easy compromises. Though she could not clearly define what she expected him to do, short of giving up his job, none of his suggestions hit the mark and were turned against him as evidence to substantiate her unspoken charges of neglect and disaffection. It was about then that she became friendly with Mildred McDowell. He had listened with relief, but not wholehearted attention, as she prattled on about the McDowells, the women's little rituals of tea and coffee mornings, and to anthems about the grand house in Mossburn. He knew that Muriel was jealous, ashamed of the villa in the coopers' lane; he thought that phase might pass. He never did get to meet Mildred McDowell. He knew Frank casually, as a habitué of the pub round the corner from headquarters. McDowell was just beginning to make his way in the county, then; had one shop, though a good one, was up for election to the Rotary Club and, within a year, would be a member of the County Council. Muriel's friendship with Mildred lasted only a few months, then died – suddenly. Up to the neck in policework, McCaig never did discover the reason. Two months went past before he heard the first rumour. It wasn't much of a rumour. Muriel had been seen in McDowell's new Vanden Plas, alone with McDowell. McCaig did not know what to make of it. It wasn't scandal even, just a murmurous rumour. He couldn't feel shocked or angry or indignant; in a way he was almost relieved. At thirty-eight, Muriel was still an attractive woman. Besides, if there had been some trivial relationship between herself and the councillor, it had obviously terminated. Once more Muriel was shuttered by her own routines, bent on making him suffer for her malaise. No doubt, he would have forgotten the whole sad little episode, if McDowell himself hadn't stirred it up by his inexplicable behaviour.

The shop-keeper's progress up the monkey-puzzle tree of local politics was unnervingly rapid. Before his first term was out, he was a member of no less than three influential sub-committees, and seemed determined to make himself the self-elected voice of public conscience. His special target turned out to be McCaig. McDowell had no authority to do real damage to the standing of the Force but, as McCaig graduated from the ranks of inspector to Assistant Head of the County's Criminal Investigation Department, the councillor's sniping became personal, intensive and often almost slanderously vicious. In the Force McDowell's attacks were lightly shrugged off; for a while he became a standing joke, a bogyman. In effect he was powerless, a loud mouth, a wee thorn in the flesh of police public relations. With the personal incident so close in the past, though, McCaig could not afford the risk of taking up cudgels against him, nor could he bring himself to treat the man's animosity lightly. Never had he asked Muriel for an explanation, and never had she offered one. For close to a decade doubt had lain fallow in him. Now Muriel was gone, probably for good, and McDowell's only child lay dead on a slab in the town mortuary. A confluence of evil circumstances had pitched them together at last.

McCaig did not enter the room. He stared at the fourposter from the doorway. The air was warm, lavendered, laundered. Unanswered questions skipped across his mind like spiders over a stagnant pool. He uttered a small irate grunt, stepped back and impatiently closed the bedroom door.

The premises had already been combed. McCaig was not so puffed up with his own importance as to assume that exalted rank automatically conferred deductive genius. He wasn't going to find anything which his officers had missed. He returned to the ground-floor lounge. The Sunday choir had gone from the screen. Bette Davis glared pop-eyed out of the box and mouthed an ominous line of dialogue. Recalling the film, McCaig waited for Bogart to fill the curved glass with his inimical numbing menace. Cigar fitted into his mouth, attention riveted on the set, McDowell perched on the edge of an armchair.

'What have you done with the rest of Tom's effects?' McCaig asked.

'Packed them away.'

'Why?'

'I want to be rid of them.'

'Why?'

McDowell breathed a shallow mouthful of smoke from the wet panatella. 'My prerogative.'

'I want the clothing and all personal belongings held for forensic examination.'

'That isn't necessary, McCaig.'

'Telling me my job?'

'For how long must I keep them?'

'At least until after the inquest.'

'How long will that be?'

'A week; perhaps longer.'

'And just when, may I ask, will I be given permission to bury my son?'

McCaig closed his fingers in his palms. He came closer to the armchair. Gelid light from the screen bleached all the colour from McDowell's face, making him seem as flat and as dated as the characters in the melodrama.

'You're bloody anxious to be rid of him, aren't you?' McCaig said.

'I can do nothing for Tom now.'

'Not even . . . not even grieve for him a bit?'

'Grief is as grief does.'

McCaig bit off an abrasive retort, and got the bile to back down by carefully lighting a cigarette. McDowell was watching the movie again.

'You had a party here last night?' McCaig said.

'You know I did.'

'Was Tom here at any time during it?'

'No.'

'Not at any time?' pressed McCaig.

'I didn't see Tom at all on Saturday.'

'I didn't ask that; I asked if he came home yesterday evening.'

'No.'

'Where was he?'

'No idea.'

'Would your wife know?'

'I greatly doubt it.'

'What did Tom normally do with himself at weekends?'

'I tell you, McCaig. I have no earthly idea.'

'Did he take the Sabre?'

'It wasn't in the garage when I got home.'

'When did you get home?'

'Around seven – in the evening.'

'You were out all day?'

'All day.'

'Where?'

'In Edinburgh, on business.'

'So you wouldn't know when Tom left home on Saturday?'

'You're right; I wouldn't.'

McCaig was almost angry enough to hope that he could whittle away the bastard's unnatural self-confidence again and reduce him to the whimpering wreck who'd crawled over the office carpet earlier that day. It wouldn't be possible now, not with the man rested and sober. He seemed to have some sinister sort of therapy going for him, immunising him to any emotion deeper than arrogance.

'Mrs McDowell was home most of the day?' asked McCaig.

'I assume so.'

'Alone?'

'The cleaning woman would be here.'

'What's the woman's name?'

'Harrison.'

'Local?'

'From the Riverside district. Mildred will know the address.'

'Was this a dinner party?'

'Buffet supper.'

'In honour of anything special?'

'No, just the usual get-together. We split up for bridge for a couple of hours, then ate and chatted.'

'And drank.'

'In moderation.'

'Did anyone have a drop too much?'

'If they did, they didn't show it.'

'How many guests?'

'Six.'

'Six, plus you and your wife?'

'Yes.'

'I'd like a list of those present.'

'Your lackey made a note of all the names this morning.'

'Did he get them from you?'

'No,' said McDowell. 'I wasn't . . . I . . . no, not from me, from Laura Menzies.'

'Who were the guests?'

'The Menzies, the Binghams, George Johnston, and a young lady by the name of Dinwiddie.'

'How young?'

'Thirty, I would say. She's recently divorced. I hardly know her. The Menzies brought her along as a bridge partner for George.'

'Johnston's a bachelor?'

'Yes.'

'You didn't hear Tom come home at any time in the evening?'

'Must I tell you again, McCaig. Tom did *not* come home.'

'He had a key of his own?'

'Of course,' said McDowell. 'But he couldn't have slipped into the house without my hearing him.'

'In spite of the chatter and the booze?'

'McCaig . . .'

'The Sabre was seen coming out of your driveway at half past eleven last night. I've four reliable witnesses,' McCaig stepped round the chair and pushed the switch which killed the TV transmission. A cold steel-grey pupil remained suspended in the centre of the screen for a moment, then it too dwindled into glassy greyness.

'How?' said McDowell. 'How *can* you have witnesses to something which didn't happen?'

'Your neighbours are well enough acquainted with the Sabre. You told me yourself there isn't another like it in the town. That being the case, how do you explain the fact that three sets of neighbours, four people in all, saw it come out of the drive of this house last night at half past eleven?'

McDowell said nothing for fully a minute.

'I can't.'

'Do you still claim that Tom didn't come home last night?'

'I do,' said McDowell. 'Emphatically.'

'The garden,' said McCaig. 'What's in the garden?'

'Pardon?' said McDowell. 'If you mean what do we grow, I keep a gardener for . . .'

'Building-wise. Sheds?'

'Only the garage.'

'By the side of the house?'

'Yes.'

'All right,' McCaig said. 'Show me Tom's effects.'

The news had dented McDowell's plating; he was less certain and less aggressive. Stubbing out the panatella, he led McCaig from the lounge and through the house to the kitchen and laundry room. Cartons were piled in a corner behind the Bendix, packed with the boy's clothing but not sealed. The room was bright with neon and as warm as the lounge had been. It didn't even smell of soap and dampness.

'Did you check the pockets?' asked McCaig.

'I did. I found nothing but a few coins.'

'In a wallet?'

'Loose.'

'No wallet, or pocketbook?'

'No.'

'A diary?'

'No.'

'What about material from the desk upstairs. Surely he kept some personal papers there?'

'No, none.'

McCaig lifted off the top carton and put it on the board over the rinsing sinks. He opened the flaps and dug out a suit; expensive and formal, pin-stripe. He examined it, then laid it to one side, drew out a sports jacket. 'Tom must have had a wallet somewhere?'

'I'm not hiding it,' said McDowell.

'Have you seen him with a wallet?'

'Yes, yes, I have.'

'But it isn't here now?'

'I just assumed you lot had it with his . . .'

'We haven't,' said McCaig. 'It wasn't on him when he was found.'

'Robbery?'

'Who knows?' said McCaig. 'What will you do with all this stuff?'

'I haven't decided.'

'Destroy it?'

'God, no! Give it to the Salvation Army, like as not.'

The second carton contained shirts, underwear, socks, shoes. The third was thick with sweaters and overcoats. McCaig's examination was perfunctory. He stopped and swung round abruptly on McDowell.

'Just what the hell is this?' he demanded. 'What's going on here?'

'I beg your pardon?'

'Why the inordinate, indecent haste to get rid of your boy's belongings? Thinking of renting his room?'

McDowell snarled, then, quickly, brought his temper to heel. He turned away, leaned on the sink board and stared out of the narrow gridded window across the dark back lawns. Naked trees were limned with a pearly opalescence from the street lamps on the far side of the hill.

'Mildred,' said McDowell. 'Mildred will want to keep the lot; everything. She won't part with so much as a cuff-link, a pencil-stump. I know her; I know what she'll do.'

'I see.'

McDowell wheeled again. 'I doubt it. In any case, what's it got to do with how he died? How will it help you to find the person responsible?'

'What about his mates? Who were they? Where did he meet them?'

'I can't tell you anything about his personal life.'

'Come on,' said McCaig. 'You must know how he passed the time. What did he do with himself – play tennis,

41

squash, chess, go to the local hops, strum a guitar; *something?*

'No.'

'What do you mean : no?'

'He didn't do any of those things to any degree.'

'Then what *did* he do?'

McDowell looked at him without expression, at a loss. Suddenly McCaig understood the exact nature of McDowell's dilemma. He wasn't being intentionally evasive after all; truth was, he hardly knew the boy. McCaig was well placed to appreciate such a situation; Derek had been a stranger to him, too, for most of his life. Guilt and pride, mingled in McDowell, made a highly volatile mixture. The paucity of information he could yield up now must increase his hurt.

'I want all this stuff cleared out before she comes home,' McDowell said. He nodded to confirm his decision to himself. 'I won't give her the opportunity to . . . to set up a damned shrine. I won't have it. It's unhealthy.'

'Have you told your wife how Tom died?'

'Not yet.'

'How long can you keep it from her?'

'As long as possible.'

'Are you being fair?'

'Fair!' McDowell cried. 'Listen, for twenty bloody years Mildred's hardly given me a serious thought. I'm not exaggerating; I mean it. Twenty years. From the day Tom was born, she's thought of nothing but *his* welfare.' He made a sweeping backhand with his arm, a gesture which took in the Bendix, the sinks, the heaters, the neon-strips, the cartons, the entire house. 'I haven't always lived like this. Don't you believe it! It's only in the last six or seven years I've been able to afford the cleaner and the gardener and the part-time cook. Before that, Mildred did it all herself. She insisted on making a martyr of herself; but not for *me,* not to appease *me.* She crucified herself for her boy. I wouldn't have minded in the least if she'd been competent and proficient; she wasn't. She'd no talent for domestic organisation. This house was a pigsty filled with . . . with shit. The meals she served weren't fit for pigs. I only put up with it, stuck it out, because of him. I reckoned he was entitled to a stable home and some of the spoiling I never got when I was a kid.'

'McDowell . . .'

'No, listen,' the man went on. 'I didn't mind it too much, and I improved on it, when I earned the bread. But Tom's dead now, and *I'm* still alive. I'm damned if I'll give up what I've grabbed out of the mess to help her perpetuate a memory.'

'He was your son, McDowell.'

'Yes, but Tom wasn't . . . well, he wasn't the stuff that legends are made of.'

'At nineteen?' said McCaig.

'At twenty, at thirty, forty.' McDowell appeared anxious to make the policeman understand. 'He just wasn't . . . inspired. I mean, he didn't have any drive.'

'How did he fare at college?'

'Oh, he'd have muddled through the course and might even have come out as some kind of architect, but he wouldn't have been much better than mediocre. I knew him, McCaig, I knew him better than anybody. I saw him clearly. Listen, I was a better architect than he would ever have been – and I couldn't make the grade.'

'I didn't know you . . .'

'Oh, yes! That's how I started, as a student of architecture. But I got out, turned to keeping shop instead.'

'Maybe Tom's trouble was that he didn't have to fight to make his opportunities.'

'I could have understood it if he'd been a bit of a lad, a . . . a swinger, you know. But he was so damned *ordinary*.'

'Look how he died.'

'I just don't understand it.'

'There may have been more to your son than you realised.'

McDowell braced the small of his back against the sink and rubbed his forefinger over the edge of the leather cigar case. McCaig waited in silence, but McDowell had said all that he felt impelled to say, for the time being.

'Hang on to the contents of the cartons,' McCaig said, at last. 'You can hide them away if you like, but don't dispose of them.'

'What importance can they have now?'

'Perhaps none at all,' said McCaig. 'The minute your doctor friend . . .'

'Dent.'

'The moment Dent indicates that Mrs McDowell is fit to

43

answer a few questions, I'd be grateful if you'd contact me.'

'Very well.'

McCaig nodded and went out into the hall to collect his coat. He somehow didn't expect McDowell to play host, but the man followed him, opened the main door. The night air was damp and pleasantly cool after the overheated interior. Confident, formal, himself again, McDowell offered his hand.

He said, 'I appreciate what you're doing for me, McCaig. I'd like you to know that I'm grateful, and do understand your position.'

Ignoring the hand, McCaig tipped his hat. 'I'd do exactly the same for anyone,' he said, and walked down the path towards the Daimler.

Behind him the door slammed loudly.

Ryan tossed the morning paper over his shoulder into the back seat of the Cortina and lobbed his cigarette stub out of the open quarter-light. The press hadn't been kind to old McCaig after all, hadn't given him the kind of boost he'd planned. In the drug scene every snot-nosed cub considered himself an expert, and by-line journalists were howling like wolves, declaring that they'd known all along that vice was rife in the county. Finding a whipping boy was no problem – McCaig was always handy. Ryan could not understand the mentality of editors who peddled such distortions of the truth. He looked out of the window. Rain had piddled out overnight, leaving the sky still shored with cloud, slabbed like ferro-concrete up on the horizon. College brick had soaked up rain enough to turn dark red, like unfired earthenware. Lights of workshops and lecture rooms showed clear yellow through the glazed façades. For a costly modern educational establishment, Thane New College bore a distressing resemblance to a government plant. Against the windscreen Ryan propped a hand-written notice declaring the owner of the Cortina to be an officer of the law, then got out of the car. Carefully he locked all the doors, and checked the latch of the boot. Ever since he'd had a Murder Bag half-inched from the car in a parking lot he'd been nervous about its security. He looked aimlessly at the bands of students wending up the long avenue. A person expert in the mores of the generation would probably be able to distinguish the members of each course, but surely

44

only a biologist would be able to differentiate between the sexes. Boys and girls sported indiscriminate combinations of the same basic rig : bleached levis, shrunken corduroys, tie-dyed cottons and, since the weather wasn't quite Californian, thigh-length oilskins which would not have been out of place on a trawler's deck on the Dogger Bank. Harry, this is it! he thought. Intolerance; first intimation of the vulgar disease called middle-age.

Lindsay was wading fast through the crowd, with the clumping lope of a highland stalker, as if the genetic legacy of his ancestors had sunk to his feet like lead shot. Envying the sergeant his fitness, Ryan lit another cigarette.

'Sorry, I'm late.'

'You're not late,' Ryan said. 'I'm early.'

Side by side, doubly conspicuous, the detectives went through the gates and crossed the open court towards wide steps and the glass entrance doors. Except for a few cool glances the coppers incurred no excitement or resentment, though the students of New College must be aware of the nature of their business that morning. Mock marble paved the ground-floor concourse. Steps went up like a salmon ladder to a half landing on which stood two lumps of pig-iron statuary, twice man-size. The flight of steps split into teak-railed galleries united by a terrace. A plate-glass wall overlooked the central quadrangle, half an acre of uncultivated flower-beds and sparse lawns pricked with signposts and industrial artwork. The chapel's dome and silo-like spire were dwarfed by the flying buttresses of the college pool and gymnasium.

'Do you have kids?' Ryan asked.

'Two girls,' Lindsay replied.

'Are they students here?'

'One's married, in England; the other one's a hairdresser in Lannerburn.'

'You didn't encourage them to benefit from higher education?'

Lindsay shrugged. 'They're happy as they are.'

'My daughter,' Ryan said, 'is set on being a teacher.'

'She'll be coming up to college here, then?'

'Not if I can help it. I'd rather she took the degree at an established university.'

'This place will get the charter soon.'

'The charter's only a bit of paper,' said Ryan.

45

'Where does your lassie want to go?'

'Here.'

'Aye,' said Lindsay. 'So it's you that fancies the cap-and-gown charade for her.'

Ryan dropped his cigarette into a sand-bucket.

Lindsay was as sharp as a dirk; the cap-and-gown charade was exactly what he fancied for his daughter Jean; the snobbish pride of seeing her receive her scroll from the hands of an eminent academician under a vaulted ceiling four or five centuries old. It wouldn't be the same in this modern degree-factory.

'We'd best find the Principal,' said Ryan curtly.

The Principal's office, nerve-centre of the college, was out on the south-east corner of the quadrangle; a large room, warm and well-lighted, free from the remembered stinks of learning, the inky, chalky, tobacco-reeking dens of the head-masters of Ryan's schooldays. Bookcases were lined with paperbacks and thick glossy-covered textbooks. Curtains were printed with bright eccentric designs; the furniture deep and comfortable. Lindsay and Ryan seated themselves in block chairs before the desk. Scammel, the Principal, stayed on his feet. He had the restless manner of a man who operates best in motion, and carried the weight of his authority as lightly as a boy totes a fishing pole. He was not so old that the few flecks of grey in his hair meant any-thing, and the hair was longish, curling a little over his collar. His hacking jacket was clean but rumpled, the Daks had a mod flare over the chukka boots. Shirt was pale blue, the tie pricked with the college emblem. His face was thin and almost elfin, and his neck long. He had no air of dis-tinction; if Ryan had been on the County Education Com-mittee he would have voted this man no higher a posting than the woodwork room. Within five minutes, though, Ryan of the open mind was willing to revise his opinion.

McDowell's file lay on Scammel's desk, but the Principal didn't have need of it. The facts it contained were already committed to memory and he had even anticipated some of Ryan's questions. Briefly he gave the detectives a break-down of McDowell's student record, and an opinion of his character gleaned from teachers and tutors. None of it contradicted the portrait which Ryan had already begun to form of a young man of dull wit, who would have made his way in life quietly. Scammel outlined the structure of

46

the degree course in architecture; Ryan knew what the Principal was on here, telling him indirectly that, as several classes were shared with students from other faculties, McDowell's circle of possible acquaintances would be large. Lindsay transformed the report into neat shorthand, outlines which in transcription would contain no nuances whatsoever.

When Scammel finished, Ryan said, 'You didn't know McDowell personally?'

'No.'

'You wouldn't know what his extra-mural activities were?'

'Only those listed on his file; he was a paid-up member of the college film society.'

'And?'

'No "and" : that's all.'

'None of the sports clubs?'

'McDowell doesn't appear to have been athletically inclined.'

'Politics?'

'The political unions haven't got a grip here yet.'

'Tell me about the film society, please.'

'A somewhat unsocial body,' said Scammel. 'They hold one meeting per month from October through May; half fill the college theatre to watch a double bill of flickery Continental movies and disperse again, presumably uplifted by their contact with European culture.'

'You don't approve?' asked Ryan.

'I don't disapprove,' Scammel replied. 'I'm a Spencer Tracy fan myself.'

'Oh!' said Ryan. He paused, then asked if Tom had any special cronies in the college.

'Two in particular,' said Scammel. 'I asked them to be on hand. A girl and a young man.'

'Names?'

'Ruth Oliver and Robin Laurie.'

'Yes, we know about them,' said Ryan. McCaig, that morning, had made mention of this pair. 'Is the girl . . . I mean, was the girl attached to Tom in any way; his . . . his sweetheart?'

'Bird,' said Scammel. 'They call it "his bird" now.'

'Was she?'

'I couldn't say.'

47

Ryan nodded. 'Sorry to eat into your time like this, Mr Scammel, with you being so busy with the opening of term.'

'I'm only sorry it's necessary, Inspector,' Scammel said. 'Still, I have had it fairly easy here so far, barring a few minor squabbles.'

'With students?'

'With staff : the students have been embarrassingly well-behaved. Gathering their strength to give me a hot time this second year, I expect. Naturally this drug slur worries me. It reflects badly on the reputation of such a new and un-fledged establishment.'

'It may have no connection with the college.'

'I hope not,' said Scammel. 'On the other hand, if it does have a root here then I'll do absolutely everything I can to help you unearth that root. You needn't fear that I'll block the police, Inspector, try to cover up for the sake of the college's reputation. I'm not that kind of fool.'

'Thank you, Mr Scammel,' Ryan said.

'Is there anything further I can do right now?'

'Have you a room we could . . .'

'Use this place,' Scammel said promptly. 'I can work from my secretary's office for a while. Shall I send in the girl Oliver and Robin Laurie?'

'Please,' said Ryan. 'One at a time, though. The girl first.'

Scammel went out and, a moment later, Ruth Oliver entered the office.

Dent came into the kitchen and placed his bag on top of the refrigerator. He went at once to the sink to wash his hands. For the life of him, McDowell could not imagine what the doctor had been up to in the guest bedroom which necessitated such a thorough ablution; even scrubbing his nails with a small stiff-bristled brush. McDowell set down his coffee cup, left a slice of buttered toast untouched on his plate and lit a Rothmans from the pack which Laura had thoughtfully provided. He could hear Laura moving about behind the high divider, the crinkle of her apron and the faint dainty padding of her ballet-like slippers. A kettle clinked on the hotplate and the teapot rattled. Dent would not drink coffee, even at breakfast.

'How is she, Martin?' McDowell said.

Dent ripped off a strip of paper towelling from the roll above the sink, dabbed his hands on it. He was of middle height, but his stooped shoulders made him seem short. Greyish-blond hair formed a feathery chaplet over his ears and brow. The shirt was the same Viyella country check he'd been wearing yesterday.

'I told her,' Dent said.

He folded the soiled towel and posted it deftly into the waste unit by the sink. The Menzies' kitchen was a perfect square, patterned in red and white; everything was red and white, right down to matching breakfast cups. Seated in the dining-nook, McDowell's arm stretched along the back of the padded bench, his knees drawn up beneath the folding table. Dent seated himself on a stool, penning McDowell in. The clash of the toaster made McDowell start slightly.

'About Tom,' said Dent. 'I told her about Tom.'

'Was she strong enough?'

'Yes, yes,' said Dent. 'She's had a good long sleep. Best to get it over with, don't you think? I deemed it wise to tell her myself. I take it you don't mind?'

'On the contrary,' said McDowell. 'How did she take it?'

'Better, actually, than I'd anticipated.'

'Did she believe you? I mean, did she comprehend?'

The doctor unclenched his fists and leaned back, swaying as he discovered that the stool was backless. Quickly he grabbed the table's edge and brought himself into balance. Laura came around the divider and put a tray in front of him; egg cup with a brown egg in it, toast rack, little tea-pot, sugar and cream.

'I'm not really hungry,' the doctor said.

'Eat it, for God's sake,' Laura told him.

Dent glanced from the woman to the man, then back to the brown egg. Lifting a spoon, he cracked the shell and, with the delicacy of a surgeon, picked shell particles from the white jelly.

'Did she really understand?' said McDowell.

'I think so.'

'Aren't you sure?'

'Yes, yes, she believed me.' Dent trepanned a core of yellow meat and put it in his mouth. 'I'm surprised she's in such good shape. Mildred's tougher than you give her credit for, Frank.'

'What did she say when you told her?'

'She thanked me.'

'*Thanked* you!'

'Sedatives,' said Dent. 'Sedatives aren't all that potent, you know. Mildred hasn't been *completely* kaput for the last forty-odd hours. She's had a little time to think, to ponder, to ask herself questions and generally tune up her nerves for coming out of it. Obviously, it occurred to her that Tom hadn't been in a road accident.'

'But did you tell her about the drugs?'

'Yes, yes.'

'And she realised what you meant?'

'Good God, Frank, she's not a child.'

'Just what did she say?'

'Asked me if he'd suffered much?'

'What did you tell her?'

'The truth; that he just drifted off to sleep.'

'*Is* that the truth?'

'Near enough,' Dent said. 'I also spoke to her about the police. She asked me if they'd found the person responsible. That sort of reasoning speaks well for her innate stability, don't you think?'

'What else?'

'Told her the police might wish to question her. She asked if it was McCaig. It seems she used to know McCaig's wife quite well.'

'Yes,' said McDowell. 'She did.'

Dent buffed sticky egg yolk from his teeth with his tongue, then bit into dry toast. 'She wants to see you first, though, Frank.'

'I'd better call McCaig.'

'I'll call McCaig,' Laura said, from behind shelves of herbs and spices. 'Go in there and see your wife.'

'I've left her a couple of things,' Dent said. 'When she feels she's had enough, or if she shows signs of cracking, make her take one; just one. It'll slip down easy with water. Keep the other in reserve; give it to her later tonight.'

'What things?'

'Capsules,' said Dent. 'To help her rest. I'll call again later in the day.'

'Shall I keep her here?' said McDowell, adding, 'If you don't object, Laura.'

'Yes, yes, keep her here,' Dent said. 'She's comfortable, and it's best to have a woman around, isn't it?'

'Laura's been a brick,' McDowell said.

He drank coffee and nibbled smoke from the filter cigarette. 'Are you sure she's strong enough. You know what I mean?'

Glancing up from the solid curve of albumen which he had finally separated from the shell, Dent said, 'How are *you*, Frank?'

'What?'

'Are you all right?'

'I'm perfectly fine.'

'Then go and see your wife,' Dent told him. 'She's waiting for you.'

McDowell laid the cigarette in the ashtray. He did not grind it out, but carefully placed it along the furrow as if to signify that he planned on being back before it could burn away. He got up, eased his stomach round the table's edge. Dent held the tray with both hands, silver teaspoon stuck in his mouth like a thermometer, nodding approval. McDowell shifted out into the middle of the big kitchen. He looked at Laura. She was too neatly dressed, even for a middle-class *Hausfrau*; all feminine in her best apron with frills and cerise flowers on it. Her fingers were at her throat, picking the pin of the Celtic brooch. She stared back at him sombrely but sourly, almost as if some sort of betrayal was in process of being committed.

'I'd better see Mildred,' he said.

'You'd better,' Laura said.

He went into the hallway and crept to the door of the bedroom which snuggled under the steep pitch of the stairs. He knew what the room was like; a glory-hole turned into a pretty place with an open fire and a miniature Tudor window and a sloped timbered ceiling, like a tiny Swiss chalet. He stood outside the door, listening, hearing no sound at all. Perhaps, he thought frantically, the sedative had taken hold of her again, tugged her back into sleep.

'Frank?' The voice did not sound feeble. 'Frank, is that you?'

'Yes, Mildred.'

'Come in.'

He took a deep breath and pushed open the door.

The girl was good-looking. Full-breasted, full-lipped, round dark eyes. She was the tweed skirt and blazer type; a sensible and stable sort, Ryan reckoned. Even her emotionalism hadn't set her off kilter. She answered his questions quickly and articulately. Ryan felt sorry for her, and relieved that he'd stumbled across somebody who had not only known Tom McDowell but had liked him too. In spite of her willingness to co-operate, Ruth Oliver wasn't much help. She'd known Tom for a long time, since they'd shared a desk together in primary school. The picture she drew of her friend was of a very average young man. She was unable to throw light on any particular issue. Ten years back, Ryan might have supposed the girl to be a clever liar, bent on covering up her own involvement. In the course of his career, though, he'd run up against real experts in the false-hood field, from projectors of tiny white ones to icy per-jurers on the grand scale, and experience told him that this girl spoke only the truth. He led her through background and character questions, before zoning in on Saturday's events.

'It was just an ordinary Saturday,' the girl said. 'We trooped down to Glasgow to watch the first college match of the season.'

'Soccer?'

'Rugger,' she said. 'Against Jordanhill.'

'How many?'

'One regular supporters' bus, carrying about thirty, and a fleet of cars. I went with Robin, Robin Laurie, in his car. Tom came after in the Sabre.'

'He was alone?'

'Yes.'

'You left Thane together?'

'We usually meet at the Elrig, have a shandy and a bite to eat, and leave at approximately the same time. That's what we did last Saturday.'

'What did Tom drink?'

'Tomato juice. Tom wasn't a drinker.'

'All right.'

'We went out and got into the cars and the bus and drove to the Jordanhill grounds.'

'In convoy?'

'Not actually, but the Sabre was right behind us most of the way.'

'When did you reach the ground?'

'About half past two.'

'Tom was with you during the match?'

'All the time.'

'And after the match?'

'We hung about for a while talking, then went to a pub.'

'In Glasgow?'

'Yes.'

'The name of the pub?'

'I don't know. Robin will be able to tell you.'

'You didn't have a regular haunt in Glasgow?'

'No. It depended where the match was being played, you see.'

'Tom was still with you?'

The girl nodded.

'How many others were in the group?'

'Perhaps ten,' the girl said.

'All New College students?'

'Yes.'

'Anybody wearing a Cagoule,' said Ryan, 'one of those . . .'

'I know what a Cagoule is,' the girl said. 'Nobody was wearing one.'

'Any garment in orange or light red?'

'No.'

'Are you quite sure about that, Miss Oliver?'

'Quite certain.'

'Do you recall who the other students were, their names?'

'I think so, most of them.'

'Good,' said Ryan. 'When we've finished here, would you be kind enough to dictate a list of the names to the college secretary.'

'Of course.'

'Now, in this pub – west end, I take it?'

'Yes.'

'In the pub, did Tom stick with you?'

'He did.'

'All the time?'

'We had a big corner table. He didn't leave.'

'Was anyone drinking heavily?'

'Not in our group, they never do. Just lager and shandy.'

'Did you see much of Tom during the summer?'

'He came down to the tennis club occasionally, but he didn't play. In any case, I was in France the whole of August.'

'Did Tom have a girl-friend?'

'No.'

'You seem sure of that?'

'He didn't have a girl that I know of.'

'You weren't his . . . his girl-friend?'

'Heavens, no.'

'Back to Saturday,' said Ryan, quickly. 'What happened when you left the pub?'

'Robin and I went to a twenty-first birthday party in Giffnock. Robin's cousin's party. Tom was invited, too, but he didn't come. He told us he had to go home.'

'Did this surprise you?'

The girl glanced sharply at Ryan, wondering, perhaps, how he had read her reaction so accurately. 'Yes, it did surprise us,' she said. 'Tom wasn't madly keen on parties, you know, but he did tend to just drift with the gang. I couldn't imagine what reason he had for going home on a Saturday evening.'

'Did he know Robin's cousin?'

'They'd met a few times, yes. It wasn't shyness which put him off.'

'What was it?'

'I don't actually know,' Ruth Oliver said. 'It's hard to say why, but I got the impression that he . . . he had something else to do.'

'When did you leave the pub?'

'Not until after seven.'

'You all left together?'

'We did, Tom too.'

'Was he alone?'

'Yes.'

'You're sure he didn't hang around after you'd left?'

'No, we all went out into the street together and Tom got into the Sabre and drove off.'

'In which direction?'

'Towards the Great Western Road.'

'He didn't appear to be in any particular hurry, though?' said Ryan. 'Didn't keep glancing at his watch, looking at the time?'

'No.'

'You and Mr Laurie went to Giffnock?'

'We did.'

'When did you get back home?'

'Two o'clock, or a little after.'

'With Robin, of course.'

She gave the ghost of a smile. 'Of course.'

'How?'

'In Robin's car, an Alpine. He didn't have much to drink.'

Ryan was even willing to take her word for that. He would question Laurie soon, but didn't somehow anticipate that Laurie's account would differ significantly from the girl's. He'd get the name of the pub from the lad; it would have to be checked out.

'How did Tom strike you on Saturday?'

'No different from usual,' the girl answered. 'He was normally quite quiet, you see.'

'Withdrawn?'

'No, not withdrawn, just . . . just quiet.'

'Quieter than usual on Saturday, would you say?'

'Perhaps just a little.'

Easy, Harry, Ryan told himself. Don't push the lass, or put words into her mouth. It's her impressions you're after, not a playback of your own ideas. He could always come back to her later to check out points.

'Miss Oliver, has anybody offered you drugs?'

'Never.'

'You're sure?'

'I wouldn't forget something like that.'

'Have you ever heard of any of your friends being approached with an offer of drugs of any kind?'

'Absolutely not.'

'Tom didn't hint?'

'No. The subject never came up in conversation; not that I can remember.'

'Miss Oliver,' said Ryan, standing, 'you've been very helpful. If you think of anything that might be of interest to us, I'll be around the college for a day or two.'

'Yes, I'll let you know if I do.'

'The list,' Ryan said, 'in the secretary's office.'

He opened the connecting door.

He said, 'You liked Tom, didn't you?'

'I liked him a lot.'

She was crying, gently and without fuss. She had no fear of Ryan or what he represented, was without guile or guilt, just wanted to understand what had happened to Tom

McDowell, worried, perhaps, that she, for all her innocuousness, might fall into a similar trap. Ryan looked round the corner of the door and saw a dark-haired young man come quickly off the bench behind the typist's desk, moving to the girl, comforting her. Robin Laurie, no doubt. Strictly speaking, Ryan knew it would be better to bring the boy in now. But what the hell; if they cooked up a matching story, were hiding something, then they would be too smart for him anyway. He closed the door and retreated into Scammel's office again.

Lindsay looked up at him, raised his eyebrows.

'Next witness?' he asked.

'In a minute,' Ryan said.

Mildred McDowell's pale, portly features topped a pale portly body wrapped tightly in a dark Paisley-pattern shawl. She occupied the bed like a wheatsack, plain, except for the grotesque tarting of scarlet lipstick on her mouth. Her eyes, very bright, were fixed upon him. On the bedside table was a vase of roses, a carafe and water glass. Light emanated from the tubby bow window, striped by the stems of a climbing plant. The woman's hands were folded in the hollow of the quilt, and the bump of her feet came midway down the bed.

'You wish to ask me questions?'

'If you feel up to it,' said McCaig.

'Do sit down.'

McCaig perched himself on the edge of a cane-bottomed chair.

'How is your wife?' Mildred McDowell enquired.

'Muriel? She's well, thank you.'

'Got tired of living in the county, so I'm told.'

'She's staying with her sister in England.'

'In England?'

'Lytham St Anne's.'

'It's so nice in Lytham.'

'Yes.'

'Do give her my regards, will you?'

'Yes.'

'We used to be quite good friends, you know.'

'I remember,' said McCaig.

The woman reached out, clasped the water glass, brought it steadily to her mouth and sipped. When she replaced the glass on the table, the rim was marked by the print of her lipstick.

'Now,' she said, 'about Tom.'

'Yes?'

'I can tell you all you'll need to know about Tom.'

'Mrs McDowell,' said McCaig wearily, 'you do know how Tom died?'

'Drugs.'

'Heroin, to be accurate.'

'I don't for one moment believe that Tom was an addict, do you?'

'No, frankly, I don't.'

She twitched the corners of her mouth and smiled to thank him for his generous hypocrisy.

'Tom was a good boy and a good son to me,' she said.

McCaig had heard many such statements, uttered in all sincerity, by the mothers of convicted rapists, arsonists, housebreakers, by the wives and fathers of vicious extortionists, pimps, blackmailers, killers and congenital thugs. It was true, of course; a villain could be a better son than most, home and mother a refuge from the evil sibling who inhabited his body. His hooded eyes gave no hint of scepticism, were sympathetic.

'Did you know that Tom took drugs?' he asked.

'Tom didn't take drugs.'

'Was his behaviour of late any different from usual?'

'Not in the least.'

'How did he spend the summer?'

'Studying.'

'He didn't find a summer job, then, like some students?'

'Tom didn't have to.'

'I thought, perhaps, he'd served a stint in one of Mr McDowell's shops.'

'No.'

That answer was curt enough.

McCaig said, 'So he spent his time at his books?'

'It wasn't easy for Tom to keep up with the course. He was a very sensible boy. He knew he had to work very hard to make up for his slowness.'

'He was . . . slow?'

'A little.'

'Did his father *make* him work?'

'No,' the woman said. 'Tom knew he had to apply him-

57

self. He knew that, understood that his talent lay in discipline and perseverance.'

'Where did he study?'

'In his room.'

'Surely he didn't spend all his time up there?'

'He went out with his friends.'

'Which particular friends?'

'The boy Laurie, and a girl called Ruth.'

'Others?'

'I don't recall their names.'

'Did he bring his friends to the house?'

'No.'

'Why not?'

'Frank didn't like it.'

'You mean, his father forbade it?'

'Let's say that Frank didn't encourage it.'

'Tom was a big lad to be under his father's thumb.'

'He wasn't under his father's thumb. He wasn't under anyone's thumb.'

'Where did Tom get the drugs, Mrs McDowell?'

'I know nothing about drugs,' the woman said. She turned her head slowly, very slowly, as if it were being laboriously cranked on a spindle. 'Perhaps you should ask his father.'

'Oh, really! Why's that?'

'You've seen the motor.'

'The Ayer Sabre, you mean?'

'The Sabre!' Mildred McDowell said. 'Yes, Frank foisted that thing on to him.'

'Didn't Tom like it?'

'Tom said it was dangerous. He wasn't a confident driver.'

'Then why did he continue to use it?'

'He needed some sort of personal transport,' the woman said. 'All boys do, nowadays. He asked his father for money, a birthday gift, to buy a little secondhand Morris he had his eye on. Frank insisted on buying him the buggy instead.'

'Didn't Tom refuse it?'

'How could he? Nobody refuses Frank.'

'Did your husband know how Tom felt about the Sabre?'

'Oh, Frank didn't care. I had words with him about it, but he felt it was the right sort of car for a young man. He wouldn't listen to me any more than he would listen to Tom.'

'Mrs McDowell, I don't see what this has got to do with how Tom died. He didn't meet with an accident, you know.'

'It's all connected.'

'How is it all connected?'

'Your wife would understand.'

'I'm sure she would,' said McCaig thinly, 'but she's too far away for me to ask her. Won't you try to explain it?'

The head cranked away again. 'I think I've said enough.'

Inwardly McCaig cursed her. He couldn't quite decide if she was raving, or if some sort of complex truth lay behind her confusions. He said, 'Did Tom stay home all summer?'

'We all stayed home. Frank was too busy with the shops – this being the tourist season – to go away.'

'Didn't Tom fancy going off on his own?'

'I think he probably did.'

The idea of a nineteen-year-old having to apply for permission to take a vacation was patently ridiculous. At best, it was an anachronism; lots of things about Tom McDowell seemed old-fashioned.

'Tom didn't even go off on his own for a few days?'

'No,' said Mildred McDowell.

'Was he ever away from home overnight?'

'No.'

'Did his father . . . discourage that too?'

'Frank wouldn't have minded. Tom just didn't seem to want to go anywhere.'

'I see.'

'Tom loved us, and loved his home.'

Oh, bloody hell! She's slipping her cogs, thought McCaig. Grief took women in peculiar ways. Really, he preferred wailers. Mildred McDowell was just too controlled; the interview was proving effortless enough, but it was sour and basically infertile. He didn't doubt the veracity of what she told him, only the tone was decidedly off-key. He would have to pick and choose carefully from his stock of questions, to fish from her slightly addled brain only facts which he could check elsewhere. He asked her about Saturday, built up from her simple answers a time-table of Tom's movements. Apparently he had left home

59

in mid-morning and hadn't returned. It took him five minutes of gentle probing to elicit the facts from her. Definitely, she was wandering, sliding into a strangely formal mood, like an old dowager reminiscing about the distant past.

'You don't believe me, do you?'

McCaig cocked his head. 'Believe you?'

'You don't believe that Frank is responsible?'

'Responsible?' said McCaig. He was lost now.

'Tom would tell you, if he were here.'

'Tom can't tell me, though; so you must.'

'You have a son too, don't you?'

'Yes.'

'I'm sure you prefer him alive.'

'Of course, I prefer him alive.'

'You see!' said the woman, archly.

End of interview. He could no longer give credence to anything she might tell him. Leery of his own dislike of Frank McDowell, listening to this woman would only cloud his judgement with personal sludge. He got up, not too quickly.

'Thank you, Mrs McDowell.'

On the bedside table was a single capsule, a bullet of red and black gelatine; one of the doctor's wonder drugs, no doubt, probably luminal, or a similar barbiturate.

'Yes, I'll have it now,' the woman said.

McCaig hesitated. 'When did you take the last?'

'Not since last night.'

'I think I'd better send your husband . . .'

'No. Thank you. You may pour me a little water.'

No doctor would be daft enough to leave a capsule close to a patient unless it was permissible to take the capsule. McCaig decanted water, watched the woman lift the capsule, lay it on her tongue, sip water and swallow. She replaced the glass on the table, leaned back against the pillows and placidly waited for sleep.

She closed her eyes, opened them, stared at him.

'Don't forget,' she said.

'Forget?'

'To pass on my regards to your wife.'

McCaig backhanded his hat on to the rack and moved into the security of his office. Before he had properly settled

60

himself behind the desk, Sheila put her head round the door.

'Inspector Ryan's on the phone, sir.'

McCaig nodded, lifted the receiver.

'Chief?'

'What've you got?' McCaig asked.

'Not really very much.'

'Is Scammel co-operating?'

'No bother there,' said Ryan. 'We've interviewed the Oliver girl and Robin Laurie. They seem to have known Tom better than anybody, but even they didn't come up with that much. Whatever McDowell was into they didn't know a thing about it. They're just kids, really, nothing out of the ordinary for their class. They were in a bar in Glasgow last Saturday. I've got the name and location.'

'I'll have it checked.'

'McDowell wasn't a boozer, and doesn't appear to have been much interested in chasing skirts. On the whole, he's coming over as a bit of a prig.'

'I don't think so,' said McCaig. 'Dull, maybe, but no prig.'

'One interesting thing did emerge,' Ryan went on. 'McDowell left the bunch in Glasgow about the back of seven o'clock and drove off on his own. He didn't say where he was going, or what he planned to do, but both the girl and the Laurie boy got the impression that he wasn't just drifting, really did have some place to go.'

'Didn't he give them a clue?'

'Nope; told them he had to go home.'

'What about the driver; any word on him?'

'Not a chirp.'

'Right,' said McCaig. 'Send Lindsay back here to draft his reports. I'll have the pub covered.'

'What do you want me to do?'

'Pitch camp in the college. Check with Scammel first, then start to chip at the students. Best prepare a standard questionnaire : work from those who hung about with him, through his class-mates, and out on to the fringes. Have a word with staff members. Don't forget the janitors or porters, or whatever they call them up there now. And the cleaners, too. You never know what the cleaners might have found.'

'All this on my own?'

'You'll have Lindsay back shortly. I'll find another couple of men. You can brief them yourself.'

'You don't feel we should search the college?'

'I thought about it,' said McCaig. 'But it's a big place. Besides, I'd rather keep Scammel sweet and the press boys off my back. If I descended on New College in force, you can just imagine what they'd do to me.'

'Worried about your reputation, Chief?'

'I need the public,' said McCaig. 'Find me a better mouthpiece, and I'll be delighted to use it.'

'When is the inquest?'

'Friday.'

'What'll we get?'

'An open verdict,' said McCaig. 'Unless we have luck before then.'

'Hm!'

The sounded offended McCaig.

'What's your grouse, Inspector?'

'No grouse,' said Ryan. 'I'm just not happy, that's all. I don't feel I'm . . .'

'Christ, stop havering, man,' said McCaig. 'Happy! None of us are happy with this routine. Go on, get on with it.'

'Yes, Chief,' Ryan said, flatly.

McCaig hung up and, in the same sweep of the arm, switched on the intercom.

'Sheila,' he said. 'You can issue that description of the driver of the Ayer Sabre now. It's not much but it's the best we have. Trick it out with details of the buggy and a picture of Tom McDowell. Put it to all stations.'

'In what connection?'

'Just the usual vague crap, assisting the police of Thane County . . . you know.'

'Shall I mention drugs?'

'Not necessary; anybody with five new pence to spend knows what it's all about.'

'I've a batch of reporters in the basement, Chief. They want to know what's happening.'

'Nothing's happening.'

'Shall I tell them you'll keep them informed of further developments?'

'Aye, the soft answer turneth away wrath. Right, Sheila, tell them that.'

He switched off the intercom.

He shifted the file to the centre of the desk, opened it to a photocopy of Jebb's autopsy report. Certain paragraphs he'd already marked with ink. The report was an odd mixture of fact and hypothesis, not in the least like the didactic cut-and-dried prose which Willy Rudkin submitted. McCaig did not doubt Jebb's competence, and the report was valuable in its thoroughness.

Clearly the case would not be a simple one. Ryan was whining because there was no passion to trigger off his best hunting instinct. He should have learned by this time that violence isn't always shaped like a razor, and that the epitome of passion isn't necessarily rape. A hollow needle could be the tool of a different kind of violence, another variety of passion. Ach, but youngsters were too impatient to dedicate themselves to the tasting of life through life, now; wanted it in capsules, instant release. How could they ever hope to learn to endure the periods of emptiness between those vital moments which left sediment in the memory? How could they hope to collect sensations which the mind so quickly silted over? Too much of it and the nerves atrophied and you died; they called it God's Mercy in the old days, and carted you out in a box. No, the process was not one to be hurried. What could he do to kill off the spectre of Mildred McDowell's tainted sanity, to bury the fancy of Muriel in the bed in the room in Mossburn, and to exorcise his disgust at the pathetic Frank McDowell? It was hard for a man to mourn something he had never loved; McDowell must learn to do it, McCaig supposed, with guilt instead of tears.

At least, as a policeman, he was corseted with procedure. He would dispatch men into public houses, bar-rooms and cafés, into college classrooms, dance halls, discothèques, and riverside folk clubs, into youth centres, bungalows, farmsteads, into the elegant middle-class mansions of Mossburn and Armitage. He would carry questions to students and mechanics, to pharmacists, doctors and veterinary surgeons. He would systematically trace the threads of McDowell's recent descent back from the accident of dying, across the acres of the county, into the heart of the city if he had to, to docklands and alleyways, the flats of friends of seamen and airline pilots and hostesses. Personally, he would work closer to home, though, hard against the enigma of a sick household, with party-givers and the round of guests – the Binghams, the Menzies, George Johnston and his blind date. He would scrape up gossip, tune in to tattle-tales, murmurs from the underworld, the helpful cheeping of some officer's pet canary, all the time knowing that when he did track down the driver he wouldn't find viciousness or passion, only the weaknesses of a cripple, somebody inwardly maimed. Beyond the weakling, of course, would be a supplier, a manipulator. Like as not, however, the big man would be the bag of the Marine Division or Edgar Pomfret's Customs' Special Branch. He was not important enough to be in at that kill. He had quite enough to do to cope with crazy women and petty-minded men. In spite of himself, he was gradually approaching the conclusion that Tom McDowell had killed himself. Suicide, however fascinating a subject for those of philosophic bent, was small beer for a copper and a dismal chore for the law. Where the hell was the harm, and where the drama, in such foolish mischief? Where it touched those too weak to suffer loss, perhaps. Weakness again; always weakness.

McCaig lifted his eyes and glanced at the expensive new raincoat hanging in his shape behind the office door.

Good God! Was this Ryan's syndrome?

Was indifference contagious after all?

PART TWO

Motionless on the high-board podium, in a pocket of twilight close to the vaulted roof above the college swimming pool, Yule waited. Doors slammed softly in the dungeon dressing rooms. The pool cooled to a sheet of opalescent silk. The only vivid sound in the whole vast damp cathedral was a subterranean trickle of falling water. Night sky curtained the plate-glass wall. Below it, blurred by mesh screens, the corridor was clamped into the darkness like a cathode tube. Yule moved lightly out from the railing on to the board. It dipped submissively under him, rubber pustules gripping his feet. On the limit, he stopped. Pressing gently, toes curved over the edge, he felt the board's eager collaboration. He bent it, testing its exact resilience, glancing at it behind his heels. He was cautious, unafraid. Straightening, he let his breath out, then trod the board. He rode it upwards, pumping to catch its energy, swooped down and up again and parted from it on the spiral of its thrust. Back arched, he was transcendently suspended for an instant, then shot down towards the pool. His body split the membranous surface like a scalpel blade. A constrained echo of the sound, ripping through the empty bleachers, was gone before Yule surfaced. He drove up out of the water, raising his torso high on the parabola of the dive, skull sleek, black-capped, droplets dancing on his lashes. He was so filled with pleasure in the exercise of his skill that he did not immediately notice the figure standing by the stairwell wall. As the young man stroked towards the bar, Mulligan stepped out of the shadow, came close to the pool's edge, and let himself be recognised.

Yule swarmed to the railing and, with hardly a break in rhythm, gripped the metal, planted the sole of his foot against it and came lunging up out of the water, already reaching for the little man's lapels. Mulligan had no chance to retreat. Fists closed on cloth and he was yanked up on tiptoe.

'Hoy!' Mulligan said, indignantly. 'Mind the bloody gaberdine.'

'What in Christ's name are you doing here?' Yule demanded.

'I was worried.'

Mulligan's moon face was laced by a thin ginger moustache. He was more than twice Yule's age, and only a little more than half his size. He flapped his short arms, fingers splayed out like cocktail sausages. Yule held him as easily as if he'd just fished him out of the pool and had half a mind to toss him back. Their voices hissed in the metal vault. The splatter of pond-water from the pouch of Yule's trunks was abnormally loud.

'Listen, Greg,' Mulligan said. 'I got no bleedin' way of makin' contact with you, have I; have I now? I took a chance on findin' you here.'

Yule pushed him and he skidded, knees buckled, bounced off the barrier in front of the benches. The young man was on him again at once, jerking him to his feet.

'How did you get in? They wouldn't let you past the turnstile without a student's card.'

Mulligan's eyes creased, slits full of sly humour. 'Came in the back an' through the boiler room.'

'Were you seen?'

'Nobody saw me, son.'

'You realise the fuzz are all over the campus?'

'Sure,' said Mulligan. 'Doin' what?'

'Interviewing everything that twitches.'

'Done you yet?'

'Yeah, but I gave them nothing. Christ, I didn't even *know* McDowell.'

'That's what I came t'fine out.'

'You don't imagine I'd anything to do with it?'

'We can't talk here,' Mulligan said. 'Best get dressed before you catch your death.'

'What about you?'

'I'll come with you.'

'You can't,' said Yule. 'The porters are everywhere.'

'Mulligan, the invisible man.'

'Come on, then,' Yule said. 'You can hide in the cubicle. Most of the lights are out, anyway. It's better than letting you roam round here.'

'Whatever you say, son.'

66

Gregor Yule went forward to the tunnel mouth, listened to the sounds from the underground changing room, then gestured to Mulligan to follow him. Rolling like a drunken seacook, Mulligan trailed the young man down into the corridor, defined now only by a glimmer of light at its nether end. They hurried along it, passing the open doors of empty cubicles, ducked into one just as the elderly porter appeared at the corner. Mulligan hoisted himself on to the seat and pressed himself behind the hanging garments. Towel in hand, Yule stood outside, insolently facing up to the porter's authority. He stared defiantly back at the man in the red wool shirt, and languourously worked the towel over his intimate parts. After a minute, the porter went off again. Yule entered the cubicle and closed the door. He reached down clothing from the peg, exposing Mulligan's face. Mulligan grinned and watched without embarrassment as the young man finished the drying process and began to dress. Yule was all hard, honed muscle; even in the days when he'd followed the fortunes of heavyweights round the city's gyms Mulligan hadn't seen a finer, stronger body on a man.

'I gave you explicit instructions, Mulligan, not to follow or contact me, or even show your mug across the county line,' said Yule quietly. 'What am I going to do about you?'

'I didn't know the McDowell lad. I didn't flog him nothin'.'

Yule glanced up. 'Then who did?'

'Don't ask me, son.'

'You know your clients. Which one off-loaded the shit on McDowell?'

'You know's well's I do, I don't feed them enough for them t'go sellin' it.'

'Then how did McDowell pick up a big enough snort to do for himself?'

'Look, son, I've always played it straight b'your rules. Six hand-picked clients an' never more. That stuff never come from one of mine. Maybe, it wasn't our shit that done for McDowell, at all.'

'And how many horse-traders are there in this part of the world?'

'Jesus, Greg . . .'

'If Charlie hadn't picked you and given you the okay, I'd suspect you of being at the fiddle.'

'Charlie knows better'n that,' said Mulligan. 'It's been a grand wee partnership up t'now.'

'So now some fink coughs it, and you panic and come calling at the college.'

'I never panicked. I read about it in the papers, an' though they was maybe on t'you.'

'Not a chance.'

'What do the blues know about us?'

'*I've* no inside source,' Yule said. 'Listen, until last Monday, I didn't even know this guy McDowell existed. He wasn't on my course. Three thousand students in this establishment. I know, on nodding terms, about forty of them. The others are ciphers, blanks, man. If I didn't even know him, how come he laid his paws on our shit?'

'Maybe Charlie . . .'

'Christ, Charlie's been at sea for five bloody weeks. Anyway, Charlie never trades.'

'But he takes the biggest risk, don't he?'

'Meaning?'

'Nothin'.'

'Then keep your bloody tongue off my brother,' said Yule waspishly. 'This's our problem, not Charlie's.'

'Aye, an' it's bad. I don't like the smell of it.'

'Mulligan, you know who hawked the stuff, don't you?'

'I swear t'God I don't.'

'Lying git,' Yule said. 'Come on, let's get out of here. You by the boiler house, and me by the turnstile. I've my card to collect. I'll meet you round back.'

'Okay,' said Mulligan. 'Okay.'

At the end of the corridor, they parted.

Though he would not admit it, even to himself, Yule respected the little crook's ability for stealth, and was without concern that Mulligan would be caught, or even spotted, in the college grounds. What worried him was that Mulligan professed to know nothing of McDowell, or of McDowell's source of supply. He returned by the exit corridor, exchanged towel and trunks for his student's card and pushed out into the deserted quadrangle. Still a little activity up in the main block, stragglers from the evening classes wending towards the staircases. Inside the chapel a single crystal light burned, sonorous tones of the pipe organ booming against the stillness as some ardent musical nut dusted his knuckles on the brand-new instrument. Gregor

Yule considered such pastimes as the height of folly. No profit in that kind of music; he scorned young men who devoted themselves to a subject which had no reckonable end product. Commercial incest wasn't his bag. He worshipped only things which could be tabulated on a Burroughs; cash, capital, stocks, bonds, settlements, investments, all of which could be made to multiply under the right conditions, like tissue cultures in the watch-glass trays in the biology laboratories. Organ notes fattened, a bass voluntary leaking through the ventilators, seeping from the lead-strips which held in place the jigsaws of stained glass, the music too lead-heavy and similarly opulent. He rounded the buttress and gable corner, jogged down the narrow path behind the chapel and pool building, to the half acre of gardeners' sheddings and fuel stores where Mulligan would be waiting, hidden. Beyond the back gate, kitchen windows of middle-class bungalows showed, die-stamped against the darkness. Mulligan slid out of nowhere and fell into step with him. They walked briskly towards the open gate.

Yule said, 'I didn't know McDowell. You say you didn't know him either. So it *must* have been one of the customers.'

'You told me not t'overfeed them,' said Mulligan. 'An' I don't.'

'You've been cutting the stuff.'

'Wouldn't know how.'

'When do you make the drops?'

'Saturdays, usually.'

'At set times?'

'Don't be bleedin' daft, son.'

'Last Saturday?'

'Aye.'

'In the county?'

'I don't peddle the county.'

'Balls.'

'I flog the stuff in the city – you know that fine.'

'No clients at all in Thane?'

'Nope.'

'Then McDowell must have picked it up in the city.'

'Dunno,' said Mulligan. 'But I've got the feelin' we're in trouble, son.'

'All right, then, call the bloody thing off.'

'Can't,' said Mulligan. 'I got six suckers bleedin' hooked

Sure, none of them know me from Adam, or how t'contact me direct-like, but if one of them fishes starts gaspin' an' flaps off t'the blues, then the blues'll find me quick enough.'

'Yeah,' said Yule. 'You don't have to underline it for me.'

'It'll be me the law'll come after, not you.'

'How much of the batch do you still have on hand?'

'Enough for one more round. I thought Charlie was due back last week.'

'He was, but the ship got held up, engine failure or some bloody thing. He's running at least ten days overdue, maybe more.'

'Jesus,' said Mulligan. 'What'll happen if we fall short on stuff?'

'We'll worry about that when it happens.'

'I mean, what'll we do?'

'Vanish,' Yule said.

'Son, we can't quit, 'specially right now, with the scare on. Listen, this driver the blues are howlin' for, he might even know about us.'

'Why should he?'

'I wish we knew what the police've really got up their sleeves.'

'We don't, though, do we?'

'Couldn't you find out, like?'

'Haven't *you* got friends?'

'Not friends like that,' said Mulligan. 'The blues're goin' crazy all over. Jesus, if a breath got out t'a singer, I'd be done for proper.'

'Pull out.'

'Wish I could.'

'Let the clients get caught.'

'Sure, okay, sure!' said Mulligan. 'I'd be willin' to risk it, if I was certain it weren't one of the clients what knobbled McDowell.'

'And if it happened it wasn't?'

'Then I'd quit the caper right now.'

They walked down a short driveway, fenced off between the neat lawns of the bungalows. Over the high ground above the strath, the sky was vast, a chain of lights on the Mossburn heights across the township contesting the hard surface of the stars. The swirling wind had a keen edge to it.

'Why not do it anyway?' Yule suggested.

'Son, get it int' your nut this's not like floggin' furry monkeys on a string. I spent two months cultivatin' the perfect market, and five months sellin'. The poor bastards're good and hooked. They depend on me. If I don't show up regular, then they'll pop off, the whole bleedin' lotta them. *They* don't know how to lay hands on the hard stuff. They only know me, not any other generous pushers. Jesus, *I* don't know any other pushers m'self. If they get desperate enough t'start crawlin' round the Trongate beggin' strangers for a snort, then the law'll nab them double quick an' we'll be right in the clag.'

'I thought you controlled them?'

'The junk controls them; I control the junk; an' the junkies control me. It works all ways, see.'

'You mean you're going to make Saturday's drops?'

'Got no option,' said Mulligan. 'The clients'll be worried enough, like, with all this bleedin' guff fillin' the papers.'

'What if I told you, ordered you, just to chuck in the hand?'

'Can't do it,' Mulligan said. 'I'm snared. I mean, if I knew for definite who yon driver was, and how the McDowell kid got his shot, an' none of it pointed in my direction, then I'd give up right now.'

'And Charlie?'

'Write him : tell him.'

'Not sure I can,' said Yule.

'Try.'

'It's the profit you want, Mulligan.'

'Eh?'

'You don't want to sacrifice the profit.'

'Sure, it was a sweet wee caper while it lasted, but any way you look at it, son, it's over. It was over the minute that bugger McDowell stuck a spike in his arm.'

'Your pickings have been fat, Mulligan. You must have enough stashed away to make a run for it.'

'Ach, Greg, be your bleedin' age. I've a record near as long's your arm.'

'For breaking and entering, not for pushing drugs,' Yule said. 'Listen, you could be in another country before the fuzz even started to identify you.'

'I got three thousand quid in my kitty,' Mulligan said. 'Good money, but how long'll it last me abroad? About ten bleedin' minutes. Anyhow, why bolt if you don't have to?'

'Think consistently,' Yule said. 'Make up your mind.'

'The blues would nail me before I got's far's the Clyde ferry,' Mulligan said gloomily.

'Not if you go now.'

'I'm not in a position t'go now. I got t'make them drops on Saturday. You've got t'find out if the coast is clear. If it isn't, then I'll scarper.'

'Are you threatening me?'

'How?'

'Are you saying that if they nail you, you'll blow the works on me and Charlie?'

'I never said nothin' like that.'

'The implication was there.'

'I'm no yellow linty,' said Mulligan. 'I've never blabbed an' I never will; not on you, not on nobody.'

'Tomorrow's the inquest,' said Yule, softly. 'They'll bring in an open verdict, probably, and that'll put a lot of pressure on the fuzz. If they do get you, Mulligan, they'll crack you like a peanut.'

'But they're not on t'us, far as we know.'

'We don't know enough.'

'Bleedin' right, we don't!' said Mulligan. 'An' it's for you to find out. I'm strung, can't do it; so you've got to. You're thinkin' fine, Greg, an' I agree with you. I think we should chuck it, while we're up. But I can't risk havin' a client blow. The blues're prayin' for a break like that. When'll Charlie be back with another batch?'

'He may not bring another batch,' sad Yule. 'You were told when you took on the selling, that Charlie can't guarantee a batch every trip.'

'He never let us down yet, though.'

'There's a first time for everything.'

A bus appeared over the brow of the hill, grinding into sight inch by inch. Mulligan stiffened, inclined towards it as if it was a tramp steamer bound for a safe harbour, and all he had to do to be quit of the mess was sprint ten yards to the stop. Firmly Yule clamped his hand on the little man's shoulder and drew him back into the shelter of the privet hedge.

'It'll do no good to panic,' Yule told him. 'There may be nothing at all to worry about.'

'Remember, I'm the bleedin' front runner,' said Mulligan. I'm the johnny with the record.'

'We'll organise a defence,' Yule said.

'Sure, okay, sure. Go on, then, organise.'

'Let me think about it,' Yule said. 'I'll contact you on Sunday, if not before.'

'An' the drops?'

Yule hesitated.

'Make them as usual,' he said.

Whitehouse found the tube while rummaging in an old potato box. Perforating the soft end with his thumb-nail he squeezed out a wriggle of bright carmine. Pure and wet, the colour excited him enormously. He rushed across the basement with it, trampling over the litter to reach the broken dinner plate which served as a palette. He blobbed out the paint until air bubbles told him it was all gone, then tossed the gnarled tube over his shoulder like a peasant appeasing the devil with a pinch of salt. The little turd of colour on the plate's rim affected him deeply. For days he'd been dabbling with browns and muddy blues, all out of high primaries, now he had redeemed something worth having, though, even thinned with turpentine from the bottle in his battledress pocket, it wouldn't go far, go large. Impecuniosity was still nudging him back into delicacy, and he was bored silly with water-colours, inks and cheap gouache. Carefully hugging the plate, he took it to the easel, under the naked bulb. The canvas was a jute sack stretched between staves sawn from a herring box. Scaly stink of fish, earthiness of jute, and the medicinal odour of primer paste lagged over the sack would perhaps become the hallmark of this period in his career, a tell for posterity's experts, protection against future forgers who might crib the style but would never be able to reproduce the stench of a genuine White-house '72. Holding the plate in his left hand, Whitehouse crouched in front of the canvas and seriously contemplated its stark, white virginity.

Landscapes evolved in his mind, like smoke in a Mason jar, sensual substances of childhood, the blissful age of perception. He had been reared in a cottage by a loch on the edge of the distillery holding. His father, a blender, had worked in the distillery, and the distillery had worked on Whitehouse junior, mixing the fecundity of barley and the peat tang, the smugglers' thump of casks on the ramps of the trucks in the dark, the natural geometry of vats and kettles, hoppers, silos and slate-roofed bonds. The early influences had been complicated by more recent impressions of the city of Glasgow, which had in turn mingled with a harvest of impressions from a long summer in a tent on a green beach in the western isles, after they booted him out of art school for welching on his year's bill for materials. The decaying landscape, sec-scalloped though it was, had elements of the city in it, one imagistic panoply pleated to another, each queerly enhancing each, until he had become so sensitive and so aware that he could hardly bring himself to paint at all. Now though, confronted by black primed canvas, there was an urgency, a desperation to track an uncharged brush over the whiteness, dry-run for another frustrating trip.

Outside, the tolbooth clock clanged eleven flat notes; Whitehouse hardly heard them. All the familiar sounds which drained through the bars on the basement windows were subconsciously processed, and no longer interfered with his thinking. He told the time by them as much as by the clock, interpreting the traffic lulls, the boozy exodus of the patrons of the Majestic Bar next door, the lively staccato of high heels and the honking of impatient cabs when the Majestic Theatre across the way absorbed or disgorged its nightly audiences. Urban occurrences, seeping through the ground, were easy to ignore; more difficult the presence of Vikki Harcourt in the kitchen next door, waiting for her tithing of attention. She would be slumped in the armchair by the grate, impatient and irritable as always. Why should he squander valuable working time by going out there to pander to the cow's inexhaustible vanity? After all, what the charming Vikki wanted he could not provide. Tactics! Would it be possible to sidle over to the connecting door and shut it accidentally, excluding her? He was keen to get on with utilising that blob of carmine oil paint, yet wary. He felt sure that closing the door would bring the bitch storming in on him, stripping his concentration with her tongue the way a blowtorch peels varnish from a post. Locking the landlady out of her own basement was not the proper method of handling the situation, particularly since he didn't even pay the rent. He had long since drawn his lines of compromise with landladies, even gave them an occasional civil word in exchange for being left alone. He would not, however, paint their bloody portraits, or sketch their favourite poodles or pussycats, and he definitely wouldn't roll in the hay with them, not even those who were crude enough to fancy the likes of him. Thank God and Alfred Munnings, Vikki Harcourt had no fleshly designs on him. She used him not as a stud but as an unpaid babysitter, a chore which he rather enjoyed. He liked Vikki's kid, could talk to her and amuse her with doodles of a felt-tipped pen on old magazines or scrap paper. Mummy was the problem, the old hag sprawled in the kitchen, rasping her thighs and breathing alcoholic fumes all over. It was only a matter of time before she carried through her scolding, offended because he could so easily pretend that she did not exist. Even by men they openly despised, women just had to demand notice. He wished that Greg would come home.

Whitehouse was as spare as driftwood, scraped down to the bone by the brine of his own dynamic energy. Grey, brittle and lean, skin pitted and scalp scurfed, he gave the impression that, should human sacrifice ever come back in vogue, he would be the ideal offering for the scrag-end of a bad year. Robbed of buttons and insignia, his rough khaki battledress had been weathered to the shade of horse dung. A single leather bootlace held the waistclip together. Brushes, pencil stumps and swabs of rag, leaves of charcoal, crumbling pastels, fingers of sponge stuffed the tunic's pockets, making them protrude like little breasts, as if he was becoming a hermaphrodite for Art's sake. Whitehouse wore a soldier's dress because it had cost him next to nothing and was warm. Tennis shoes, moulded to his toes, would see him through the winter. His hair was cropped short and his jaw clean-shaven, mainly because he could not bear to go to bed with himself shaggy as an archetypal artist or a Slovak water-ghoul, both of which entities had haunted the dreams of his boyhood.

Whitehouse, you bastard! I'm out here, y'know.'

Jewel of red paint: snow-white vista of doctored jute. He willed the bitch to give up on him and snort off to her lair upstairs, tune up her telly or uncrate another dozen cans of the brown stout she drank when she couldn't find a man mug enough to stand her gin. Old Hogarth would have made a meal of Vikki Harcourt. Whitehouse laid out the etching in his mind, dispersing the formation of other clotted images.

'Bleeder, I know you're in there.'

Whitehouse sighed, unsquatted, laid the plate on the trestle, changed his mind, lifted it again, whipped a blunt hogshair from a jamjar and fitted it between his teeth like a freebooter's cutlass. For a surprising moment, he actually tasted the elements of his craft; found them nauseating, and spat thickly into the rubbish. Still sucking his teeth, he sailed into the kitchen, twirled and bowed.

'Victoria,' he said, diction impaired by the brush in his mouth. 'Didn't heah you arrive.'

'Where's Greg?'

'Cleansing his pores, of course.'

'Come bloody off it, Whitehouse.'

'Swimming.'

'Wha' for?'

'Don't ask me.'

'Take that thing out of your mouth.'

Obediently Whitehouse removed the brush. He wiped his lips on his cuff.

'Louise sleeping?' he asked.

'Says she can't.'

'You shouldn't give her coffee for her supper.'

'She's my kid,' Vikki told him. 'Anyhow, she likes coffee.'

'Well!' said Whitehouse. He paused. 'Well, back to work.'

'I'm here for the rent.'

'Ah!'

Vikki's accent, Lancashire or Yorkshire he couldn't tell which, thickened in ratio to her drunkenness; he reckoned she was about halfway gone tonight. Not cut enough to con.

'As you know, Victoria darling, Gregor handles all my financial transactions; and Gregor isn't here at the moment.'

Greg always had spare cash; he'd shell out to the old moo. She wasn't really that old, thirty-six or seven. Greg would give her what she really wanted, which wasn't the rent at all. Hard to credit that such a leathery piece of slag could have mothered Louise. Maybe Louise would grow up, change, become hard and ugly through self-indulgence too. The prospect saddened him. The child's father had been a casual mate of Charlie Yule's — so Greg told him once — and had flitted briefly through the Harcourt house eight summers ago. He had travelled, spawned and gone back to the ocean like a cock salmon. Vikki herself, not reticent about her lost lover, was for ever dropping hints as broad as the Kingston Bridge about him, enlarging the fellow, his private parts in particular, into legendary proportions. The truth of it was that the seaman had been a forty-year-old deck-hand, standing five feet dot in his seaboots, who had taken almost an hour to coax up an erection. Vikki could hardly recall his name now.

She slouched in the wooden armchair like a Lautrec whore, with that same full, flushed, sodden look to her. A pair of fibrous black stockings or a pink chemise would complete the reference perfectly. Whitehouse regarded her studiously; straggling off-blonde hair, massive saggy breasts, high cheekbones, raked nose, eyes sullen as bruises – not Lautrec, more Rouault. She liked having him stare at her, but must have picked up the aura of his deliberations, the silent insult.

'Hey, Whitehouse, stop . . .'

Whitehouse blew out his cheeks as Gregor Yule swept back the heavy blanket which served as a curtain at the bottom of the stairs and took command of the situation. Big, sun-browned, and confident, he seemed to fill the entire corner nook. His hair was still damp, the soft ringlets, which on any other male might have seemed girlish, just beginning to coil. Yule was so aggressively masculine that he could have worn a rose behind his ear or frilly knickers and still not have seemed pansy.

'Something wrong?' he asked.

'Vikki wants rent,' said Whitehouse. 'In twain.'

'Wha'?' the woman said.

'Wants it now, does she?' Yule asked.

'Shouldn't wonder,' Whitehouse said, quietly.

Yule put a hand up to the pole on which the curtain hung, and leaned forward from it. The quilted jacket in Prussian blue fabric made him appear even broader than he was. He grinned crookedly at the woman.

'Be a luv, Peter,' the woman said. 'Nick upstairs and keep an eye on Louise.'

Whitehouse glanced at the dinner plate. The bright red spot had already acquired a curdled skin. He might argue with the woman but he was in no position to argue with Gregor Yule. Being a parasite had its disadvantages. He

77

placed the plate on top of the locker by the basement door and went out of the kitchen, closing the curtain behind him. Vikki was already sniggering lewdly, like a farm tractor stuck in gear. Whitehouse didn't want the child to hear. Resignedly he went upstairs, closed the door there too and, with all his visions fading, entered the bedroom to talk to the little girl.

They lay under a blanket in the truckle bed in the corner of the warm basement kitchen. The room was lit only by a pinpoint lamp over the desk and by the lick of flames in the coal-dross in the grate's belly. Vikki was on her back, knees drawn up to hold in the dew of satisfaction, Yule on his side facing into the room, eyes open, relaxed but alert. He had coolly feigned a climax; pill or no pill, he had no intention of risking a pregnancy with this woman, especially at this difficult time. She was a stupid and calculating enough bitch to reckon on trapping him by the age-old trick. She didn't know him well enough, however, if she thought she would play on his sense of fairness, the quality of being a gentleman, a young man of honour. All that was only the front. If it ever came to it, he would either set her up with a decent abortionist, or promptly decamp. He wasn't ready yet to make a move. He had two years still to run on the Management degree course, and would cruise to a usefully high academic mark there. In addition, his capital was mounting, thanks to Charlie and the five kilos of horse his brother had so far managed to smuggle into the country by the obvious, undramatic manœuvre of walking ashore with them in his dunnage.

Charlie was unmarked, had no record, was just another undistinguished merchant seaman and one of the thousands who steamed into the port of Glasgow every month. It was long odds that he would be searched by the overworked waterguards. The incident of McDowell's death, though, had shortened the odds considerably. Yule mulled over the notion of sending Charlie a coded cable through the shipping offices, but it might be too late for that. Besides, Charlie was shrewd, totally aware of the risks and hazards, had weighed them all up before welding a tentative contract with the man in the bar in Palermo and investing – gambling, really – all their life savings on the tin of heroin, a small quantity of a powder of indeterminate strength and quality which, luckily, had reaped them four hundred per cent clear profit. Charlie didn't worry him; Mulligan did. And McDowell.

Gregor Yule was convinced that Mulligan was responsible for feeding McDowell the lethal dose of heroin, though not necessarily by intention. It could be that Mulligan had been at the fiddle, increasing the number of trading clients over the stipulated six, then cutting the junk to make it spin out, keeping the additional profit for himself. Or it could be that one of Mulligan's addicts had introduced McDowell to the needle. Or it could even be that Tom McDowell had found himself another source of supply altogether. Yule worked at the problem with unhurried logic, breaking it down into its components. Six addicts were maintained on a controlled dependence ration; not likely that they'd waste some of their precious supply on an unfledged youngster. Besides, none of the six were that young, and none of them poor, and all of them were intelligent enough to understand exactly what they were into and that they would be cold turkey without a regular drop. Yule devoted no mental energy to the motivations of the group. Finding reasons for their habit was not important; sooner or later, demand would increase; Charlie had allowed for a rise in tolerance level, had measured out the last kilo batch to cover the eventuality. If ever Charlie failed to make a pick-up in Palermo, then he, Greg, and Mulligan too, would simply drop out of sight; the addicts would be left stranded with no kick-back at all. The organisation had been carefully structured to cover such possibilities; and it was the organisation more than the smuggling run which had yielded such fantastic returns so far. Gregor had planned it all. He had boned up on the subject, read everything he could lay hands on, then applied the precepts of two years' college training in Management and Administration to construct a faultlessly simple system of distribution. A masterpiece of marketing, it had the inbuilt safety device of Mulligan. Only Mulligan ever made direct contact with the clients; as middle-man, Gregor did no more than prepare the heroin and pull in the lion's share of the profits. Everything had gone smoothly so far – except for the enigma of Tom McDowell. Mulligan was entitled to worry, and he was entitled to worry about Mulligan.

'You ought to get rid of that feller,' Vikki said.

Yule glanced at her sharply. 'Who?'

'Whitehouse. Don't know why you keep him around.'

'He's all right,' Yule said.

'You don't even like him.'

'Yeah, I do.'

But Vikki was right; he didn't really understand why he put up with, let alone supported, Peter Whitehouse. They had roomed together for almost two years now, Whitehouse in the chill squalor of the long underground studio and he in the cosier kitchen; two years and he still couldn't figure out what Whitehouse had which made him different. Pride would not let him admit that he relied on Whitehouse's friendship. He didn't like the woman to talk of it, didn't like the woman to talk of anything much, except sexual matters. From ignorant whores like Vikki, and fools like Whitehouse, he would soon escape to the ranks of the new gentry. Horse trading would give him a flying start. He was no mere social climber, though; long ago he had pinpointed where the money grew, and devised how best to get among it. In recognising lines of demarcation between the classes, in defiance of the fashionable idea of a classless society, Yule reduced his objectives to forms as fundamental as the round coloured bands on an archery target. For the eldest sons of a family of ten, fathered by a man intent on drinking himself to death on a woman so witless that she could not sign her name to the family allowance forms, Charlie and he had done well for themselves. The eventual goal was the establishment of Yule Enterprises. Already they had moved towards it by seeding out the profits from the four runs of horse. Soon there would be no more murky basements, no more ageing sluts, petty scufflers like Mulligan. Soon Charlie and he would set up their penthouse apartment, modest office in the city, employ a girl to take dictation and answer 'phones, hire an accountant, a corporation lawyer and selected brokers to found the team. Soon too he would shape a life-style in which pleasure and profession were one and the same, and the partnership would be well on its way to success. He was determined that nothing and nobody – alive or dead – would stand in the sunlight of that dream and block him from it.

The woman said, 'You hear any more 'bout that junkie?'

'Nope.'

'Thought the fuzz was in the college?'

'They are,' he said.

'You know him?'

'Who?'

'The feller?'

'Nope.'

'I heard the coppers was close to making an arrest.'

Yule put no faith in coincidence. Did Vikki have an inkling that he was connected in some manner with McDowell, or was it that he was now receiving the left-overs of a conversation which had started earlier that evening? It wouldn't do to betray too much interest.

He said, casually, 'Got inside lines in the cop shop, then, Vikki?'

'Heard it round the Deacon.'

'From whom?'

'Bridget Jackson.'

'And how did Bridget get her news?'

'From somebody in the know. Bet there's things go on in this county you wouldn't believe. Bridget says McDowell's running a stable.'

'Tom McDowell,' Yule said scathingly, 'wouldn't know a whore from a hole in the road.'

'Not the boy, the old man; got himself a business in young chicks.'

Yule laughed aloud. 'You're hard stuck for patter.'

'Take it from me, he's just the kind. Respectable front, and dirty work back of it. I mean, how'd the boy get the stuff, otherwise. His old man kept the hems on him.'

The woman pressed her flanks against him. She wore only a pantie girdle. Her brassière, unclipped, hung across her shoulders. Her breasts were heavy and coarse, the nipples wrinkled and brown. She laid her chin on the crown of his shoulder and breathed booze into his nostrils. Yule permitted her to rub and stroke her belly against his buttocks.

'Bridget's making it up,' he said.

'Nah, she's not,' said Vikki. 'She's got contacts.'

'Like hell she has.'

Yule debated with himself, considering the possible authenticity of Bridget Jackson's theories. He knew Bridget, older than Vikki, and a show-off. Bridget dabbled in what passed among women as the black arts, read cups and cards, attended spiritualist meetings, and gathered gossip the way a vacuum cleaner gathers dust particles, nothing too small for her to suck into the sack she used for a brain. Bridget also rattled on nineteen to the dozen, and would invent any sort of lie to hold attention, to gain the awe and admiration of stupid cows like Vikki Harcourt. For all that, it occurred to him that he had unwittingly found himself a possible source of the kind of information which Mulligan had requested or, at least, a starting point. What had been beyond his abilities, out of sight, an hour ago, now seemed vaguely within his grasp.

He said, 'Bridget doesn't have . . . ?'

'She knows McDowell's cleaner, for one thing; Jessie Harrison. Lives down Riverside, too. And she knows this girl who works in the C.I.D. and knows everything that's going on, like.'

'What girl? Some canteen cook, likely?'

Vikki pushed her chin adamantly over his ear. She was irritated at his jocular irreverence towards the local prophet, and his impeachment of her honesty. 'McCaig's personal secretary.'

'Who is McCaig?'

'The boss, the big cheese.'

'Yeah, I think I've heard of him,' said Yule. 'But who's the bird, then, and how come Bridget knows her?'

'Bridget chats her up down the laundromat.'

'Laundromat?'

'In Fitzgerald Street.'

'What's her connection?'

Vikki's finger wormed rudely into his crotch. 'That's her connection, you can bet, right in there.'

'And she talks?'

'Yer.'

'What does she look like?' he asked. 'Have you seen her?'

'Yer; she's not much. Blonde, glasses, walks with a limp.'

'Christ!'

'Yer; that copper can't have much taste.'

'Maybe she has hidden talents,' said Yule.

'Like me.'

'Get off,' he said. 'You've had your ration.'

He pushed her fingers away from his body, and shifted from her. He did not leave the bed yet, however, and was only concerned with keeping her mind off his sexual organs and focused on the subject of the girl in the laundromat. It was worth thinking about, this opportunity which had dropped to him like a plum from a tree. Not so extra-ordinary after all that Vikki should have fitted him out with a possible contact. Though Thane was not exactly a small town, not like Lannerburn, it had a small-town mentality, difficult to keep too many secrets in it or to confine choice scandal to a particular area.

'What's this bird's name?' he asked.

'Sheila something. What you asking for?'

Yule shrugged. 'Curious.'

'Bridget says old McDowell keeps his chicks on the hook with drug addiction.'

'What else does Bridget say?'

'Bridget says he gave drugs to his boy to get rid of him.'

'Ballocks!'

'Bridget talks a lot to Jessie Henderson, and Jessie's up at the McDowell house every day. He doesn't give that wife of his the life of a dog.'

Yule frowned. All this luke-warm rumour must be digested with large pinches of salt. Was there any truth at all in the Harrison woman's wild surmises, or was Bridget just building up gossip on no foundation? Hard to tell. He recalled the indifference of the fuzz in the college; the one called Ryan, who'd pulled him out of the corridor and, reading from a sheet, had slid a dozen desultory questions at him. It had been in his mind then to needle the snoop a little, to ginger him into giving out pointers as to how the case was shaping. But he knew better, said nothing, answered the simple questions politely and got out again, surprised that his heart rate had increased during the three or four minutes he'd been in the office. He had plugged in to the talk around the college, of course, but found nothing there to clue him up and did not dare get close to McDowell's mates, the Oliver girl and Laurie, whom he did not know at all. The fuzz would be sensitive just now. Sweat beaded his armpits and shoulder blades, more than the dampness of sexual exercise had incurred. He swung himself out of the bed, and heard her moaning in dis-appointment behind him.

The streets outside were quiet now, late. There was no sound from upstairs. Whitehouse would have hypnotised the kid into sleep, would be asleep himself perhaps, propped in the wickerwork chair by the bedside. He thought of the girl from the cop-shop, the one who washed her smalls in the laundromat in Fitzgerald Street and blabbed to tattles like Bridget Jackson. If the girl was whore to the police chief of the whole damned county then she would be stuffed to the chops with information. It did not even occur to Yule that he would not be able to contrive a meeting, that chance or coincidence had any part in the formulation of the plot which was cooking in his skull. Though he was still staring at the woman, at the intimate fleshy regions of her exposed body, he no longer saw her, pupils blank.

'Greg.'

He blinked, shaking his head a little as if he had just emerged from the depths of a cold green pool.

'Greg?'

'What was that name again?'

'Uh?'

'McCaig's bint, blonde, glasses, a crip; her name?'

'Sheila something. Why?'

'No reason.'

He lifted his pants and sweater from the floor. He dressed, going nowhere at this hour, only giving her the hint that it was time to push off.

Ten minutes later he was shot of her. Standing with his buttocks to the stove, he rocked on his heels and thought about his plan, wondering if it was worth the effort and the time. He was standing in that lordly pose when White-house shuffled through the curtain, yawning.

Immediately Yule smiled.

Pointing an index finger at the painter, he said, 'Peter, I want you to do something for me.'

'What? Now?'

'No,' Yule answered. 'Beginning tomorrow.'

'Will it take long?'

'I doubt it.'

'How much is it worth?'

'A fiver.'

Trained by vocational hardships, Whitehouse shrugged.

'Okay,' he said. 'Done.'

The turn in the weather rubbed home the fact of his impotence and the insupportable irony of accepting Tom's burial as a man should, with tears held back and his eyes full of the bright red and yellow flags of the late autumn shrubs which flanked the Oakfield cemetery and gave him a measure of tranquillity which friends and neighbours who did not know him well confused with dignity and masculine strength. The impressions of that afternoon would be pinned to the atlas of his mind forever, like brass markers, polished at first, slowly losing their shine. Before they rusted and fell out, he too would be dead.

McCaig had placed the highland detective among the mourners, but did not have the gall to attend the interment in person. They were all there, though, all the others, none shirking duty, all his acquaintances and associates, councillors and managers and buyers and craftsmen from the cottage industries with whom he had commercial dealings. All *his* friends, droves of them, as if it was *his* funeral and not Tom's. At the back of the crowd were the youngsters who had come not out of curiosity or responsibility but to pay a last goodbye to the boy; the Oliver girl and Laurie, and four or five others, looking fresh and young in the convocation of middle-aged and elderly people, too young even to be sincere in their grief. Below in the street, under the caul of the spruce trees, infants released from school ran free down the pavements, little groups and cliques of children, boys in red blazers and billed caps and girls in green, hand in hand with nannies and mummies, and with each other, passing the long line of black limousines, without even a glance at them, too small and innocent to fear the predatory significance of the parked cortège. After the service they had returned to the Oakfield Hotel and had eaten a meal, drank liquor, and passed an hour, stiff, sombre and formal in spite of murmurous chatter and the cheerful pall of cigarette smoke in the large room. Unable to bear it, Mildred had retired. But he had endured it alone, soaking up commiserations and speculations and expressions of horror, sucking in the inquisitive questions of those too rude to let the chance pass, until he felt as bloated as a sponge saturated in viscous liquid and, curtly, left too, alone.

Through the wine-like air of the afternoon, through the dusty slanting blue shadows which the low sun cast across the streets, he had driven the Stag, driving nowhere, round loops of council houses, through the schemes of Thane, by the ripple of the river weirs, the old locks of the canal, all sharp and solid in the waning sun, like rocks cast up through green verdure by the summer's ebb. He wanted nothing then, felt himself as cool and faded as the long grass on the perimeter of the playing fields, released from all desire or anxiety, irritation or guilt. He drove thus for two hours, into the twilight, by the lanes and back roads which latticed that quarter of the county, skirting little townships and fringes of the town itself, circling, hands on the wheel, not so much steering the Stag as taking hold on it as it went its own way, letting it choose the route for him. He had no volition of his own. With the lessening of the egotistical weight that was in him came a unique tranquillity, akin perhaps to that which Tom had experienced as the heroin flowed into his bloodstream and infiltrated his brain, claiming him, tugging him sweetly into the careless state of death. What Frank McDowell experienced though was neither mystical nor religious in its origins; the serenity was really a vacuum, a void where all the things he had been until that moment had been stored and which had drained like a fuel tank on a craft driven at too furious a rate. Nothing replaced them and, sooner or later, he would be obliged to suck them back into him again; those foibles, fears and urges, were what made him alive. It would have been better for him if he could have found the strength to take control of the wheel, fist it once or twice – out of the circular by the Galtway road, for instance – turn due south, or north even, increase the pressure on the pad of the gas pedal and push the car out of Thane, and all that it held, forever. But he could not do it; in his mood, in the peace of it, was no such temptation. At dusk, on low beam, earth dark and sky clear, he drove sedately into Rodale Avenue and swung into the short steep gravel drive which led him home.

What had sustained him yesterday and cocooned him to the shock of the funeral and on the morning after the inquest, would not protect him for long.

The sound of the television set was turned low and the images had become distorted through some atmospheric quirk, herring-boned and grotesquely elongated. Mildred was not in the room. A sewing case lay by the armchair, a tea cup on the circular table. Serenity, the last of it, trickled out of him. Quickly he got to his feet. He did not really know if he had been asleep or merely in that relaxed and trance-like state again. Mildred had left the lounge in silence and in stealth. No creaking came from the ceiling, no whisper of plumbing in the bathroom or the understairs toilet, no clinking china in the kitchen. Panic squalled across his mind. He leapt for the door, yanking it open, dragging himself by the newel-post on to the stairs, rowing himself upstairs in long gliding bounds. Vigour had returned to him, an angry fright. He burst through the door of Tom's room like a madman.

She was standing by the stripped bed, hands clasped at her breast and eyes unseeing. The room was devoid of the presence of the boy now, bedding, clothing, books all gone, yet Mildred seemed to be emulating a crazy medium, striving to make the aura of her son tangible in the chill empty air of the room. Was it possible that Tom *would* come to her, quietly, as he had inhabited this house, spectral even in life, so quiet that at times he had seemed less solid and real even than the furniture.

He shouted his wife's name, and reached out for her.

'No,' she said. Her tone was firm, not fey. 'No, Frank.'

'What are you doing?

'Nothing.'

'Then get out of here.'

'Why should I?'

'I tell you to.'

'Frank, are you ill?'

'I'm not ill.'

'Shall I fetch you something?'

'Mildred, will you . . . ?'

He looked at his hands, clutching his wife's arm, found the puckering of her flesh suddenly abhorrent, released her and sank his knees on the edge of the mattress.

'Why did you do it, Frank?' she said.

'Do . . . ?'

'Take it all away so quickly. Couldn't you have waited just a little while?'

'No.'

'It was all I had left, you know.'

'We'll go away.'

'You can't,' she said. 'You can't leave right now.'

'Of course we can.'

'I don't particularly want to.'

'We *must* go away.'

'Run, you mean.'

'It's not . . . not right.'

She smiled at him, and tried to touch his arm. But he shifted position, standing on the opposite side of the bed from her. In scouring the room he had forgotten something; a Christmas bauble from a cake, a tiny plaster duck, dusty yellow, set, for some inexplicable reason, in a corner of the window frame. Tom had taken the duck from the cake at Christmas, put it in his pocket and brought it to his room, had put it where it was now. How long ago it seemed since the boy had been young, a child, gawky as a bullock. The cheap trinket appeared to glow, to radiate a malignant force. McDowell plucked it up and held it in his fist, smothering the emanations with both hands.

'You didn't notice Alouette, did you?' the woman said. He wished she would stop smiling. 'You forgot about her?'

'Who?'

'The little ducky. He liked it,' she said. 'Give it to me.'

He held it tightly, closing his fingers, until, in the depths of his palm, the bill cracked audibly and a chalky dust soiled his hand.

Mildred sighed. 'It doesn't really matter.'

Why had the configurations of the duck epitomised for the boy all that was good about Christmas? Why had that particular Christmas – he could not even remember it now – merited the storing of a keepsake? He didn't know, and had no inclination to dip into Mildred's prodigious store of trivial memories. That she would recollect every detail was unquestioned. He put the remains of the trinket into his trouser pocket, brushed his hands together and blew off whitish crumbs. You did not see the shifts and progressions, the changes wrought by laziness and cowardice and the other manipulations of circumstance. It all just happened; then it was as it was now, the presentation of a complete fulfilment, a finished thing – Mildred fat and dewlapped and his own waist thickening and the boy dead. He was left only with what he had become; with Mildred and what he had made of her too. Enigmas had no merit in easing this realisation. McCaig was as remote from it all as the person or persons whom the detective pursued. McDowell was astonished to discover that of all the sundry hatreds suppurating in him none could be classified as a lust for revenge. He did not know nor care how Tom had come by the drug which had killed him; or who had corrupted the boy, or the form the seduction had taken. He had no curiosity at all. Yet he would not be saddled with the past, with Tom, when Tom no longer existed. If only he could be rid of Mildred too, then he might still find what it was that he sought and longed for twenty years ago, and the ideals and longings might serve as an elixir to stave off the long decline, the same foul withering process which had paralysed his own father and mother.

Mildred smiled at him. He recognised not inanity, but kindness, sympathy, as if she had the strength and he was the weakling. She was an old woman now, though in years, fifty months younger than he was himself.

He licked his mouth and rubbed his hand across it, tasting chalk.

'At least we know he didn't suffer,' the woman said. 'We have that; and we know where he's buried. We have that too, don't we, Frank?'

He flung open the door and went out on to the landing.

Behind him she was alone in the bare room, held immobile in refined light like an exotic ugly beetle in a cube of amber.

He went into the bedroom, switched on the lamp by the canopied bed and unlocked the drawer in the dressing table. He took out the dark brown bottle which Dent had given him in the hour before the funeral, unscrewed the lid and shook two capsules into his palm. They were different from the first pellets, slimmer, leech-like, of soft muddy gelatine. Dent had instructed him to allow Mildred two before bedtime. Two capsules lay in his palm. He put one by the water carafe on the bedside console, and held the other between finger and thumb. From his breast-pocket he removed the stout leather cigar case and unsheathed the inner from the outer part. The tube-like recesses held no cigars, only five coated pellets, three of red and black, and two dun. He added a sixth, closed up the case and returned it to his pocket. He went back to the dressing table, locked away the bottle, then went out on to the landing.

Mildred was still as he had left her, alone in the vacant bedroom at the top of the stairs. He looked at her blankly and she smiled her faint, brave, sad, sympathetic smile.

He touched his hand to his breast and, holding the leather case in place, went downstairs once more.

The clock above the doors told him that it was after seven. Sketching was beginning to bore him : even so he continued to swirl the soft felt pen across the pad, glancing at the shapes of women along the bank of machines, or grouped by the coffee vendor in the alcove. The light was too harsh, too arctic; the geometric background of washers and spin-dryers and institutional rows of plastic seats did not inspire him. Still, he stirred the pen around, blocking in shadows, his eye caught by the stoop of a shoulder, the fall of a headscarf, the aggressive stance of a young matron as she thrust her family's dirty washing into a vault as if it was a furnace which would burn up all evidence of her wedded state. Four fulsome strokes and a crescent of cross-hatching reduced her buttocks to scale. She moved back, pushed the door with her shoe; Whitehouse fixed that ani-mated motion too in a single flowing stroke, individual and urgent and not quite legible, like handwriting. He hooked the pen into the brass catch of the jerkin and reached be-neath the bench for the coffee container, sipped the chemical liquid thoughtfully. He'd been in the laundromat most of the afternoon. Nobody had challenged him, or betrayed more than a passing curiosity in him. The com-ings and goings and fitful labours among the electric suds somehow excluded him. He hadn't sketched from the life for years now, not in public, but in student days, hours spent, pad on arm, in court galleries, railroad stations and bus terminals, had made his fingers so facile that he could scribble out a fair likeness of anything, human or animal, which the retina of his memory retained.

Darkness was down now in the October street, artificially tinted by lamp-standards and the flat sheen of the super-market frontage. The laundromat would close at nine. It did not occur to him to jack in his vigil early. Whitehouse was loyal and patient, rudiments of character which his craft had stiffened into habit. He sat quite still, coffee carton to his lips, pad on his knee, left hand dangling passive between his thighs, only the grey scrupulous eyes active. In the last hour the place had filled with a motley assortment of housewives, bachelors and bachelor girls from the flat properties of Craigton, students from the hostel round the corner, and one elegant gay gentleman with a dinky collection of silky drawers in a Pan-Am bag under one arm and a woolly miniature poodle under the other, a caricature of sophisticated perversity, advertising his choice of style by banal symbols.

More of the same tomorrow, Whitehouse reckoned. If the stake-out ran on into next week he would sting Yule for an extra quid per day. Of course, he knew what he was looking for, but asked for no explanation; enough to be burdened with the knowledge which tenancy of the basement made unavoidable. Yule was at a fiddle of some sort, but Whitehouse could think of no line in vice which would oblige him to forsake his secure billet in outrage. What Greg was up to and how he made his loot was not his concern.

It wasn't unpleasant in the laundromat; he had the sketch pad for cover should the caretaker become curious. He put the carton under the bench once more, unhooked the pen, and, for absolutely no reason, fashioned a string of Chinese characters down the side of the page.

When he next looked up, the girl was already unpacking the carrier. Greg's description was spot-on. She was unmistakable – blonde, glasses, a fairly pronounced limp. Involuntarily the felt-tipped pen created a likeness on a corner of the pad; then he closed it, got slowly to his feet and sidled out of the laundromat into Fitzgerald Street.

Walking rapidly, it took him fifteen minutes to reach home and, a little breathlessly, report the girl's arrival to Gregor Yule.

Seated on the laundromat's only wooden chair, Sheila Summerfield watched the laundry lap and swirl behind the plexiglass window of the washer. Sudsy foam smoothed their rotary beating, slithering tongues of greenish water across the interior of the pane. For some reason, some devious distortion of the brain cells, the sight fascinated her and invariably made her think of her father. In spite of her imperfect vision and a stunted leg, legacy of the polio epidemic of '53, her father had always been proud of her. He would have been even more proud of her if he had lived long enough to see her established as a member of the civilian staff in the Chief's office. On the other hand, if her father had lived, no sympathetic breeze would have blown rumours of her ambition to McCaig's ear and most probably she would still be slaving away in the Electricity Board's typing pool. On the whole, her career with the C.I.D. was a monument to her father, who had assiduously dinned into her the realisation that knuckling under to adversity is the one major sin a person can commit; he advocated the principle of relentless persistence as the taproot of character. His death had been his final object lesson in that belief.

Though Duncan Summerfield was neither dynamic nor dramatic, he'd died a hero. Eighteen at the time, Sheila had been quite old enough to accept the dreadful circumstances as a natural culmination of her father's refusal to accept defeat. Watching the water in the washer dash the glass, she thought of it all again, dreaming, not melancholy and, with such recollections, not at that moment lonely.

She was at secretarial school when it happened, but later made it her business to search out every shred of evidence, every detail, of the action which had won her father his medal and taken him away from her. His ancient Morris Oxford stood where he'd left it on the humpbacked bridge. Spate waters boomed over the bastion, the sound seeming to indicate that, given another hour of rain, the river would storm the parapet of the bridge too. Rough-handled by steep banking, the river swarmed over the concrete slab of the weir, converged into deep, narrow channels under the span itself, then fanned out into a large rock-tusked pool above the first of the series of falls. In flood, as it was that morning, the current was cruelly squeezed by the invisible rockery and, in turn, exacted its spite on the banking, dragging trees and shrubs from the crumbled clay. Sergeant Summerfield was lucky to be on the spot, visiting an ailing colleague in one of the white cottages which hung their lawns over Millikan Ford. The press called it an amazing coincidence. Sheila could imagine the door of the Morris wide open, raincoat and rubber boots on the cobbles, cottage doors opening as her father hopped on to the parapet. He was drawn into danger by the sight of a jerry-built raft spinning out of the upstream salmon pools. Down the long milk-maned channel, swirling and rotating towards the scales of the falls and the boiling white water beneath, it came. Clinging to the raft were five children. If the raft had swept cleanly through, even her father could have done nothing. On the rim above the falls, though, the raft grounded on the big rocks which posted the river's normal course and the end of the dry walk of an anglers' pier. So her father leapt on to the parapet and poised there, his arms back and fingers spread. Rain still spattered from the smudged clouds. The rearguard of the night's gales shook the trees. The children clung desperately to the tilted raft, numbed by fear. The spate pounded them and smashed away timber and shoddy ropes and rusty oil-drums from which, in foolish adventure, they had constructed the raft. Old women out of the cottages – no men at home at that time of day – danced helplessly as the sergeant plunged into the torrent and struck out for the half-submerged raft. There was nothing they could do, and could not later be blamed for negligence. One by one the policeman plucked the children from the mass of débris, lifting them like rabbit-skins, his shoulders braced against the submerged shelf, arms and head raised, grabbing at the bundles of panic, hauling them across his back to the willow trunks, pushing each child in turn up on to the mud, then floundering round and fending his way again out into the roaring water. He brought in four of them, saved their lives without a doubt; yet Sheila knew that her father would have considered himself a failure. Four out of five was not a good enough tally for him, not a winning percentage. Success must be total to have any worth.

The last child, a boy, would not release his hold on the ropes, trust himself to the sleek-haired swollen-featured adult in the copper's uniform who wallowed out of the mad water. The child could not open his eyes to the fact that he must, for his safety's sake, put his faith in a police-man's strength and judgement. The women told Sheila what happened next, sparing her nothing; told how the sergeant struggled to mount the angled planks, to haul himself over the bucking oil-drums to reach the little boy; told how the raft exploded – that was the word they used – exploded; told how the child, welded to his pinewood slat, had pitched and surfed down the scoop between the rocks into the foam of the falls. Duncan Summerfield should have let it go at that; but he was a father himself and the boy was very young. Quite deliberately he had gone after the child, kicking away from the rock shelf, plunging belly down.

93

The river had swallowed him as it had swallowed the boy; both were lost at once. The bailiff's mother, an old water-witch a century on the riverbank, added the touch that Sheila could not have imagined, told the girl how through it all the salmon, hungry for the spate, leapt and twisted upward, a mighty flock of them, blinded by primal urges, big fish, the woman said, and strong. In the dark of the evening a team of frogmen netted the bodies nine miles down at the Griddle Pan under the viaduct where the township of Lannerburn begins. Sheila was there, and McCaig.

So, a couple of years later when he was the boss, McCaig's elephantine memory had brought him to her and in part he had paid dues to her father by offering her the post he had created, a kind of personal secretary, in the heart of the department. She jumped at the chance, asked no questions, reckoning that McCaig would get his money's worth, even if most folk in that part of the county put his altruistic act down to sexual motives. She didn't much care what they thought; her mother, living happily enough in Grangemouth with a married sister and her clan, was well out of range of the gossips.

Sheila had no illusions as to what she was – an ugly, shortsighted girl with a limp. She soon got over her envy of the strong good-looking policewomen with whom she came in contact, and recovered from shock at the nature of the work, most of which touched her only by proxy. Her respect for her father and all guardians of social order increased enormously during the months of her employment in Thane headquarters. She liked most of the officers, Harry Ryan in particular, and felt sorry for McCaig. The Chief was hardly the sort of man a girl should feel sorry for. In spite of his toughness, however, she could sense the core of loneliness in him, and in loneliness she was fated to be an expert. She had no man of her own, perhaps never would. She'd read in a magazine once that a girl is as beautiful as she feels, but she could never bring herself to feel beautiful, to put herself through the laughably inadequate processes of trying to make herself into a silk purse when any male with half an eye could see that she was nothing but a sow's ear. In any case, she hadn't the income to buy fancy clothes, nor had she contact with nice respectable men outside the crews of the Force. Her work divided her from other environments, set her slightly apart, made the groups and cliques where she might have found companionship seem naïve. She wasn't a virgin. In the last three years she had had five different men, would have others too if she could meet them in the right sort of situation. Without guilt at her promiscuity, she told herself that she was only being sensible in taking what she could when it was properly offered to her. She could do without men, was highly selective, but, holding herself in no great esteem, experienced no loss of self-respect in taking a man to her bed if the opportunity presented itself favourably. What her mother would have said if she had known of her daughter's occasional pleasures didn't bear thinking about; Sheila was careful and discreet.

The laundry roiled and slopped soundlessly in the humming cubicle, splashing foam upon the glass. She watched it, unseeing, lost in casual thoughts.

'Pardon me.'

The voice did not intrude. She hardly heard it.

'Excuse me, please.'

She looked up.

The young man was standing over her.

She peered at him through her spectacles, wondering if her vision was playing her tricks again. Never in her life had she seen such a handsome male; square jaw, curly dark hair, well-muscled body under the quilted jacket. Not the aggressive maleness of the hard man or the athletic hippie, though; he had charm too, and neatness, and he was shy. She could see the blush under the tanned skin, though he spoke firmly and without hesitation.

'Yes.'

'I wonder if you have any new pence,' he said. 'Change.'

'What?'

He grinned at her, and held up the silver bit.

'Coins,' he explained. 'For the coffee vendor.'

A little flustered, she was reaching for her purse before she knew it. She zipped open the purse and spilled coins into her palm, picking them over. She felt strange, harried, not herself. Glancing up, she was relieved to see that he hadn't gone away.

'Ten?' she said.

'Fine.'

Clumsily she counted out the coppers.

Under the rally jacket, he wore a spotless white nylon

shirt, and she could discern the scrolling of body hair on it, and the tint of his flesh across the broad chest. The tie was embroidered with the insignia of New College; a respectable young student. Not quite so young, either; maybe her own age, give or take a year. His eyes were piercing, merry, a dark blue, like agates, or was it opals. He looked incredibly clean-cut and healthy.

He put the silver piece carefully into her hand.

He bowed slightly.

'Thank you.'

He went away, two paces, then, hesitatingly, returned.

'Would you . . . care for some?'

'No,' Sheila said. The tightening of disappointment at the corners of his eyes made her change her mind immediately. 'Yes, please. White, no sugar. Thank you.'

There was a churning in her stomach, like a miniature of the wash-tub. She watched him go down the aisle before the machines and ease his way to the vendor. He moved beautifully, relaxed and rhythmic. She began then to wonder what casual motivation has caused him to ask her for change rather than one of the other women. Making a brisk survey, she scanned the rest; a couple of them were better looking than she was, smarter, prettier. She darted her attention back to the young man, afraid that he would slide away and be lost. He stooped to lift the filled cartons from the delivery tray. She wondered who he was, what he studied, whether he had a regular girl, and, defensively, reminded herself that he was only being kind. Kindness, though, was a rare quality, not to be confused with charitable pity. He hadn't seen her limp. He couldn't know; yet he had come to her. No, she insisted, it's only fortuitous; a fellow as good-looking as that couldn't want me.

Could he?

He handed her the carton.

'Watch it,' he said. 'It's hot.'

'Thank you.'

She was still looking up at him, waiting.

He blew over the surface of the coffee, then, as if it had occurred to him before but he had been too reticent to ask, he said, 'Do you mind if I sit down?'

Sheila looked at the empty chair beside her.

'Please do,' she said.

96

She pulled the pink dressing gown around her, her mother's garment, patched, stained and far too large for her thin frame. Under it, shrunken cotton pyjamas gripped her legs below the knees. She tucked her legs under her. She would have long legs, dancer's legs, in a year or two. He had made her comb her hair, and the back-light of the lamp shone through the fine edges, making a soft radiance, like gold leaf rubbed into calfskin; hazier, diffuse, but still retaining the perfect, subtle shape of the little skull under it, In the light, the child's thin face was very pale, shadows giving it elfin pointedness. The nose was not quite formed; it would not be as sharp as Vikki's. Whitehouse put the top of a stalk of peppermint rock between his molars and snapped off a chunk, rolling it, sucking loudly, into his cheek. The child emulated him, her face swollen with the sweetmeat.

He had four sticks of rock, and four pounds and eighty pence in his pocket. Tomorrow morning, early, he would buy colours.

'Tell me, kid,' he said. 'What does rock taste like?'

She didn't question his right to ask, and was not in the least perturbed by the nature of the problem. She thought about it, then said, 'Toothpaste.'

'Try again,' Whitehouse suggested.

'Gingerbread?'

'Gingerbread! Never!'

Louise licked the blunt end of the candy experimentally. 'New clothes,' she said.

'Better,' said Whitehouse. 'You're right; it does taste like new clothes.'

The fact that he hadn't worn anything new-bought for six or seven years didn't trouble him; he could remember the feeling from boyhood. Noisily he drained the sugary effusions from his cheek pocket.

'Rose Madder told me she thinks it tastes of crocuses,' he said.

'What else did Rose Madder tell you?' Louise asked eagerly.

'It does taste a bit like crocuses, don't it?' he said.

'I don't remember what crocuses look like,' the child said.

'Good God, kid, you're not old enough to start forgetting things like that.'

'Doesn't Rose Madder forget things?'

'Not her; she remembers everything.'

'Wouldn't like that,' said Louise.

'Sure; it's okay for the likes of Rose, but it wouldn't do for us, would it?'

'Did her red hair grow again?'

'Of course,' said Whitehouse without hesitation. 'Overnight.'

'I wish my hair would grow again.'

'Red hair grows faster.'

'Why?'

'Because it's red.'

'Why?'

'Because it's . . . a fast sort of colour. Flames grow fast, don't they?'

'Traffic lights don't.'

'Pillar-boxes don't grow at all, come to think of it,' he said, 'but you're just being difficult, kid.'

'What colour is Rose Madder's hair?'

'It changes,' said Whitehouse. 'Like sunshine changes.'

'Sunshine's yellow.'

'Not usually. When it's young in the morning, and old at night, sunshine's red, golden red, red like fire, you know.'

'I wish my hair was red like Rose Madder's.'

'No, you don't,' said Whitehouse. 'I like you the way you are.'

'But you like Rose Madder too?'

'Yeah.'

'As much as me?'

'Not *quite* as much as you.'

'I'm not sleepy.'

'Maybe not, but I am.'

'Don't put me to bed yet.'

He looked at the clock on the iron overmantel over the smouldering fire. The lounge was drab, yet it too had all sorts of warm colours hidden in it which the muted lighting of the lamp revealed. In daylight, and in the full light of the ceiling bulb, it was one of the dullest rooms he'd ever been in, but on the autumn nights, like this, with the fire and the lamp and shadows creeping out of the ivory-yellow cornices, it had a certain profound appeal. But the smell of Vikki lingered, and a few scraps of visual evidence to remind him that he did not belong here and was not ulti-

mately responsible for the child. Tomorrow he would paint.
And tomorrow night – it being Saturday – he would blow
some of the lolly and take the kid to the movies. There was
bound to be a Disney on somewhere. And when he came
home, perhaps it would be like this in the house, with Greg
out and Vikki out; or, perhaps, it would be Vikki's turn to
have the gang round, her poxy sister and a gaggle of slag
and their men-friends and, if she was lucky, Greg too. He
would sit with Louise, protect her from the ribald screams
and alcoholic laughter and the blundering, lumbering
strangers who might stumble into her bedroom to vomit or
have intercourse in the darkness on the dusty carpet by the
side of her bed. He sheathed the wet end of the candy in
paper, finished it with a little twist, and held it out.

'If you don't go to bed in two minutes,' he said, scowling,
'the fuse will burn down and blow us both sky-high.'

'You haven't lighted it.'

'Don't have to,' said Whitehouse. 'I'm secretly Dynamite
Dan and everything's automatic.'

Louise evened off the rock with her teeth, wrapped the
end as he had done, and held it out. 'An' I'll blow up
Dynamite Dan.'

Whitehouse got to his feet, and crowned her very lightly
with the candy. 'You can't,' he said. 'Dan's only made of
paper. He'd just waft away, far away.'

'An' I'd never see him again?'

'Probably not.'

He sensed immediately that he had said the wrong thing.
The trouble with kids was that you never quite knew what
would strike into the softness of them, hurt them. Louise
stared at him, her large eyes moist at his careless winding
up to the fantasy. Well, that was how it was with fantasies,
not just with kids. The wee girl was learning; soon she
would appreciate that deprivation isn't always imper-
manent. Her under lip was tucked under her front teeth.
He grinned and put his arm round her shoulders.

'Here, now,' he said. 'You don't think Dan would desert
you?'

'I won't blow him up.'

''Course you won't,' said Whitehouse. He stooped and
lifted her, cradling her knees and the small of her back.
Her arm went round his neck. 'Even if you did, he'd be

sure to drift back some day. That's how it is with paper people.'

'Is Dan made of paper?'

'Yeah!' said Whitehouse.

'Rose Madder's not?'

He pushed the living-room door with his shoulder and carried the little girl across the hall into the bedroom, negotiated back the sheets and blankets with one hand, and slid her between them neatly. She lay on her back, still in the outsized nylon robe, the rock in her hands like a sceptre. He kissed her, something he did not do often, and drew up the clothes.

'Rose Mad . . .'

'No, kid,' he said. 'Rose Madder's just as real as you.'

'*You* won't go away?'

'I won't go away.'

Softly he pulled out the wickerwork chair and, sighing, sat down.

The Northcote Library, principal city branch of Glasgow's network of free public lending libraries, was bathed in sunlight, ruled and scissored by the crenelated architecture of the fine Victorian blocks which towered over it and patterned the building and dusty macadam of the little square. Saturday morning; a mite too early for the heavy influx of weekend shoppers, normal congestion shrunk to a partial emptiness which reminded Mulligan of pre-war years when portions of Glasgow had been as handsome and dignified as any city in Europe. Mulligan was trim in a pale shortie raincoat and pork-pie hat, brown shoes gleaming, jaws flushed with the scrape of the razor, moustache vibrant on his upper lip. Stoutness and rolling gait gave him the cheerful air of a man of leisure. At the door to the basement reading room, which opened earlier than the lending department, he slipped on the fine leather gloves and entered the library. His heels made no sound on the thick floor covering. He smiled at the girl assistant behind the counter and moved on into the long low-ceilinged room. Reference volumes were shelved in deep bays to his right. Glass-topped tables, chairs set regularly round them, took up the centreway, while to his left were the sloping lecterns and brass rods which held the fresh daily and weekly newspapers. The only sound was the purr of the fan-heaters and the rustle of pages. From under the brim of the pork-pie hat he surveyed the room. Two shabby men, not together, browsed over the literary supplements of the *Herald* and *Scotsman*; a tall gent in a black overcoat and bowler was flicking over stock-market reports in the *Financial Times*; a pair of sharp young clerks, out of a shipping office perhaps, were bowed over a massive directory at one of the tables. At the far end of the room, on the last table of all, lay a pair of spectacles attached to a filigree chain, a small floral handbag, and a single white cotton glove. Even as he spotted the items, the woman came from the shelter of the bay, an odd-shaped volume in her hands. Her floppy-brimmed flowered hat hid her face completely. She was not young, hair white, features thin and pale, eyes lack-lustre; still, she carried herself with an uprightness which Mulligan considered to be the hall-mark of the aristo-crat. He knew what the book was; he'd seen it in her hands before. It was early, very early; often he didn't get around to Miss Graham until after lunch. Being a real true-blue lady, of course, she never showed impatience or anxiety no matter how late he was. As she did not expect him, she did not notice his arrival until he was adjacent to the table. The open volume on the glass; the musical notes prancing across the oblong pages were totally meaningless to Mulli-gan, like the notation of some deep mystery, a spell to increase his awe of Miss Graham. She reached for her spec-tacles, loose sleeves of the pale cerise coat trailing, ungloved hand grotesquely contorted, like a claw carved out of knotty hardwood. Even the simple action of picking up the glasses and fitting them to her nose seemed to strain her dexterity to the limits and give her pain. Unhooked, the slender chain hung from one ear, spilling on to her collar. She saw him, stared at him for a moment, her expression giving no hint of the relief she must feel, or surprise at his early appearance; then she plucked up the white cotton glove and fiddled it over the bent and swollen hand, modestly hiding its nakedness, its ugliness.

Mulligan made small show of reading the indices taped to the sides of the bookcases before he entered the bay. A heater surmounted by a green metal shelf projected from the wall under the shuttered window. He scanned the cases, picked out a heavy book on Scottish surnames, carried it to the green shelf, opened the book at random, removed his hat and laid it, crown down, beside his elbow. He looked at the list of names on the pages, without being aware of them. A minute, or minute and a half, passed like an eternity. His nervousness was particularly acute; he wished that the day was over. Holding the music book to her bosom, the lady came slowly from the table, Hearing her footsteps, halting, he admired the coolness and authenticity of her performance. Of all his clients, Miss Graham was least likely to explode.

She came in front of the shelves to his right, and cut the corner diagonally. He fastened his gaze upon the printed page, on the names, read them, made his lips move: ERYGTONE, ESDAILE, ESHIELS, ESKDALE. The corner of his eye caught the blur of the white glove and lilac-tinted envelope, the buff-coloured envelope too. His hat tilted, the glove vanished, footsteps continued. A waft of sweet perfume drifted across his nostrils like a ribbon of fine chiffon. He went on reading: ESSIE, ESSLEMONT, ESSLINGTON, ESSON, ETHERSTONE, then gently closed the book, tucked it under his arm, and glanced swiftly over his shoulder. Miss Graham's back was to him, spine like a plumb-line, flowery hat tipped back. He could see the corner of the score on the table, but no sign of the buff-coloured envelope with the six small glassine pouches inside. In his field of vision was only the woman. Slipping the lilac envelope from the bowl of the pork-pie, he pushed it into his raincoat pocket, stuck the hat on his head, returned the book to the shelf and strolled out of the library without looking back.

He climbed the steps from the reading room and sucked the cold air gladly down into his lungs, letting it slacken the tensions that were in him. It was a fine bright morning, indeed, and no blues lay in wait in Northcote Square.

He headed west, through the arches, turned south into the broad shopping thoroughfare of Christopher Street, bound for his next rendezvous in Swanson's department store.

One down, and five to go.

Mildred would be at home in bed in the room with the curtains closed. In the kitchen, Mrs Harrison would be drinking her ninth cup of tea, smoking a cigarette, and keeping a sympathetic ear cocked for sounds from upstairs.

Prompted by the bonus he had promised her, the cleaner had readily assumed the role of nurse. As he had prowled the Stag down the driveway and set off for the round of his properties, he had experienced a lightening of the heart. Managers and staff would not expect him; the projection of his image as a boss who kept his finger on the pulse of his concerns would be enhanced. They had all been at the funeral, of course, four managers of four shops, some senior assistants, too. But none of them had dared approach him with problems of commerce on that afternoon; protocol demanded that they now await his emergence from the gloomy chamber of mourning. How many appointments had Miss Crombie been obliged to cancel during the last week? How many representatives of trinket firms and fey bargainers from homecrafts industries, many of whom he represented in lucrative foreign markets, had been stranded? Too many at this season, when the last rush of tourists had gone and, with stocks depleted, every major trader in Scotland was stocking up for the Christmas catalogue trade. He would have to scratch around for lines which would sell well, try to forecast which new designs in tartan-wear, pottery, staghorn and deerskin, or in the field of the poster and the plaque, would become the season's fancy.

Automatically he registered the *No Limit* sign at the beginning of the country straight, squeezed on the throttle and boomed the car up to eighty along the Lannerburn Road. Cross-winds, coming over stubble fields in the basin, flicked at the black hood; he wished that he had taken trouble to furl and pack it away, make the ride open, let the wind burn his cheeks and whip away the troubles which blackened his life like ergot on barley.

The land was clear and horizons distant, hills like quilted deerskin, drystone walls like horn. He passed trucks from the farmsteads and farmers' bangers wending into Thane; drove faster into the long curve by the Kettles, through the esses under the banking which raised up to the ridge of the Eswick woods; drove faster still, hands tight on the dished wheel, tautness spreading across his shoulders into his neck, into the small of his back, transmitted into thighs, calfs and ankles, until he felt that he was built from a dull metal less flexible, less resonant, than the material of the car itself. He could not escape. Like whorls and flowers, butterflies, faces, galleons, encased in the solid translucence of paperweights, beautiful, cold, heavy and smooth, the calculating madness lay deep at the heart of his composure. He could have gone on like that, until the Stag wriggled, leapt over the verge and crunched into the trees and shock and fire cauterised the part of him which lay too deep to reach. Grinding his teeth, he gripped the fluttering ends of his will. He pressed the pedal, pumped it, and reined in the car. The needle dropped and sank swiftly to eighty, to seventy, fifty. Slowly he rounded the wall at the Smiddy and entered the tunnel between the dark conifers, travelling smoothly down the strath past the fences of Ottersford Hospital. He did not turn his head, could not, drove crouched like a hunchback, sneaking past the gates. By the time he reached the shop on the outskirts of the town of Lannerburn, twenty minutes later, he was trembling and exhausted.

Adam Scott, the manager, fed him coffee and a snifter of whisky from the flask in the drawer of the office desk. Shine of glass shelving and glitter of silver, the texture of fabrics in the outer aisle gave McDowell no consolation. He held the cup in his hands and drank in sips, like a convalescent, humiliated and ashamed that a man of his strength could no longer carry the burdens of personal grief. What Tom had done to him was not only unforgivable, it might even be incurable, too.

It was midday before he was ready to admit that he was in no fit state to earn his bread.

Wisely, Adam Scott insisted on driving him home.

With evening accomplished and the loud Glasgow night come down, Mulligan had supplied four of his six dependents. Mulligan's power over these superior people was manifest in their willingness to wait long hours for him. Not supercilious in his attitude towards them, he still felt it reasonable to ask them to run to his clock, changing the order and hour of the drops each week in a naïve method of self-protection. He looked at his watch; just after seven. Outside in the station, trainloads of soccer fans were returning from a game up in Fife, shouting in the jubilation of a victory, blowing bugles, chanting catch-phrases. A dozen of them swarmed raucously into the railbar to stoke up with food before an evening's drinking.

Quietly Mulligan folded his newspaper, and departed.

He walked slowly up Queen Street, turned into Buchanan Street, crossed to the Underground and caught the tube to Kelvinbridge. From there, still walking steadily, he threaded his way through back streets to emerge opposite the Argyll cinema, a big barn-like dump which soon must give in to Bingo or close its doors. It was cold out now, night air pinching his cheeks, making his ear-lobes tingle. He read the hoarding: two sex pictures, both Swedish. Thank God, he wouldn't be committed to peering at the murky nudes, trying to spell out sub-titles for long. He paid for a balcony seat, climbed a narrow staircase and yielded his ticket to an usherette. Except for a few couples cuddling in the back row, the upper tiers were almost empty. At that moment there was sufficient light from the screen to outline the heads. The usherette lazily allowed him to pick his way to a seat. He loitered motionless at the bottom of the shallow steps until his eyes adjusted to the gloom, then climbed up towards the beam of the projection box, his right hand counting rows. He counted six, peered along that row, then shifted into it, holding up his belly with his forearm. The girl was in the tenth seat. He crushed past her knees, looking down to make sure. Her features were just distinct enough to assure him that he wasn't about to make a clown of himself by accosting the wrong bird. Grunting, he lowered himself into the seat by her side, removed his hat, laid it on his lap, and looked at the screen.

To his surprise, her hair brushed his cheek. She seemed to be leaning her head on his shoulder as if he was some young lover. She had never been demonstrative, and never impatient, before. 'Give it to me,' she hissed, caressing his ear.

He could hardly remember what she looked like.

His opening contact had been with her husband. He had only seen the girl clearly a couple of times, once by accident when the house lights had gone up for an interval between features. She was fair and pretty and very young, by far the youngest of his clients. He wasn't even sure that Hilary *was* his client; the taciturn husband might be the eventual recipient of the load. Maybe, they both used it. He had first encountered Dennis Lawrence in the lavatory of a pub in Swan Street, not far from this picture-house. At that time, with Yule's list just under way, he had been tailing a small-time pusher of pot who, shortly thereafter, faded out from the Glasgow scene and returned to his runs in London. In the cubicle, Lawrence had been firing up a thread-slender reefer, filling the lavatory with the dangerous sweet scent of grass. Leaning against the bowl of the wash-basin, Mulligan waited until Lawrence, slack as a hank of wool, drifted out of the closet. He had made his approach from that advantage. It wasn't difficult. Within a week, Lawrence had been vetted, approved as a person of sufficient substance to support himself on heroin, and added to the list. Lawrence was as cagey as they come, and smart with it. Yule had not been happy with this particular arrangement, but had found no fault in it. It had worked well enough; the girl, the wife, never failed to show up to make payment and take delivery.

'Easy, lass, easy,' Mulligan murmured.

Was she setting him up for a copper's rap?

'Here's the cash. Give me the stuff.'

'Will you shut your mouth – *please*.'

Jesus! He'd never even crossed words with her before or heard her voice. Their argument was echoing round the damned cinema like part of the sound-track.

He put his hand across her chest, pressing his wrist against her breast. Nothing sexual in it, only a calming gesture, mildly threatening.

'Cut it out, girl.'

'It's . . . it's Dennis.'

'What about Dennis?'

Their heads touched again, but he did not withdraw his arm. She seemed much, much calmer now, and sorry for her impatient outburst.

'He's to catch a train . . . in an hour,' she said.

'Where's he going?'

'London.'

'For what?'

'To see his brother,' she said. 'He won't want to miss the train. And he wants to take the stuff with him. You've got it, haven't you?'

Mulligan said, 'I've got it.'

'Can I have it? I'm in a rush, see.'

'Didn't Dennis tell you to be extra careful, like?'

'What?'

'He must've read the papers.'

'What?'

'About the lad who . . . about McDowell.'

'Yes, I did . . . Dennis read . . . something.'

'Did your hubby know McDowell, by any chance?'

She did not answer him verbally, but he felt the shake of her head. Ah, sweet Jesus Christ : a smooth talker, setting him carefully up for the pinch. Coppers on the stairs, coppers behind them in the back rows, coppers in the foyer, coppers waiting to make the grab, nail him with hot marked money on him and the girl coming down to show them the shit in the envelope.

He drew in a long sloughing breath. Her story about Dennis and the London trip was scant enough to be true; naturally, Dennis wouldn't go without a good supply of horse. His brother might be on it and all.

Nothing to worry about.

On screen the slender boyish naked shape of the heroine flitted through what looked like a sail-yard, pursued by a rough-looking geezer in a matelot's sweater.

The girl by Mulligan's side said, 'Please hurry.'

He had to decide; even if he didn't complete the exchange, she could still shop him to the blues. He had all the envelopes on him, four full of money, two full of sachets of pure bloody heroin. For the first time since he had become Yule's pusher, Mulligan realised the enormity of the risk. Until that moment in the Argyll picture-house, he had not been fully aware of it, and just how damning would be the evidence against him if he were caught in the act.

'Give me the money,' he said.

He took the envelope from his raincoat pocket and laid it in her lap. In turn, she laid a long manila envelope in his lap. He felt it with his fingers. The girl shifted. He gripped her thigh, pressing down.

'Me first,' he said.

'All right, if you must.'

He stuffed the manila envelope into his pocket with the others, put on his hat and sidled out of the row. He descended into the aisle which separated the balcony from the circle, and cut left towards the exit alley. When he reached the upper foyer, bleak, uncarpeted and completely deserted, he didn't make for the next flight of stairs. Instead, he climbed upwards again and entered the lavatory at the neck of the stairs just outside the balcony's back entrance. Yule would have been gratified by Mulligan's precautions. Months back Mulligan had cased this cinema more thoroughly than he had ever bothered to case the cribs he had cracked in his days as a b. and e. man. The lavatory was a single crescent urinal, stinking and unbleached, a closet and a blocked basin. A metal-framed ripple-glass window opened out from the rear of the closet. The metal was leprous with rust. It took Mulligan a couple of minutes' work with his penknife to flake off the red scum and prise open the window hinges. High up on the front wall of the Argyll, the window overlooked the canopy of the main doorway and the lamp-standards of the busy street. Supporting himself on his elbows, he leaned out and inspected the pavements. Parked cars were all empty; no paddy wagons, no snoopers' carts that he could see. He stiffened. Two blues marched down the opposite pavement, big men, tall. He watched them, saw them laugh, slow moving like trained bears. Obviously they'd just come off duty in the substation further up Springthorp Street, and had absolutely no interest at all in the Argyll cinema. Mulligan sagged his gut against the window ledge, still keeping scout.

After a couple of minutes, the girl stepped from under the canopy, hesitated, then moved to the pavement's edge. Though dazzled by the light from the standard below him, he could make her out plainly enough. She stood on the kerbstone, looking up and down Springthorp Street and across into Orion Street. Mulligan's heart thudded against his ribs. She stepped off the kerb, and raised her left arm high in the air, signalling.

The cab zoned in on her, and stopped.

She climbed in and closed the door.

The cab took off down Springthorp Street in the general direction of the city.

Mulligan blew out his cheeks, and let himself slump back off the window ledge. Diligently he closed the window, used the urinal, then wended his way down the stairs to the entrance, and out into the street.

Only the Englishman remained unsupplied now. Mulligan was sorely tempted to let the Englishman sweat for his fix. Dregs of loyalty, and an artisan's pride in a job well done, prevented him quitting before it was through. He walked back to the Underground, took the tube for two stops, and disembarked in the heart of Glasgow's west end.

In his right coat pocket was the last bag of narcotics, in the left were five envelopes of different quality and sizes, bunched bulky, containing an aggregate close to three hundred pounds.

However strained by the travels and exertions of the day, Mulligan could not deny that the weight of all that loot made the effort seem worthwhile.

They left the Odeon in Mill Street, Thane, at ten-thirty and walked through the cobbled alleys and quiet lanes. If he had been at all like the others, Sheila would have invited him up to her room that night, but Gregor was different; young, for one thing, fantastic-looking for another, and – the reason which stayed her eagerness – boyishly shy. All evening she had waited for him to declare himself, to begin fumbling under her skirt or in her blouse; he had behaved himself like a perfect gentleman. In spite of his gentleness, there was a strong animal force in him. Uncertainty was the worm in the bud of her happiness. What should she do to keep him?

When they reached the bottom of the close to her flat, they halted.

She said, 'Would you like to . . . to come up for coffee?'

He seemed startled by the suggestion.

'No,' he said. 'No, really.'

'Come on,' she said.

'No, I'd rather . . . not.'

'Why not?'

'It's late.'

'It's not late,' Sheila said. She would have said more but she did not want to give him the impression that she was forcing herself upon him. The problem was delicate; truth was, she *was* forcing herself upon him. Whatever Gregor wanted from her she was fully prepared to give.

He smiled, shook his head firmly. 'Not tonight.'

'Oh!'

'I'd . . . like to see you again, though, if I may.'

'All right.'

'When may I . . . ?'

'Any time,' Sheila said. 'Unless I'm called to work.'

'Would . . . would tomorrow evening be pushing it?'

'I shouldn't think so,' Sheila said. 'Tomorrow afternoon if you like.'

'I'm afraid I have to visit my mother in the afternoon.' Sheila giggled. 'Actually, so do I.'

'Would seven o'clock be too early?'

'No.'

'Where?'

'Anywhere,' she said. 'Here, if you like.'

'No, I . . .'

'Call for me,' she said. 'Top floor. It's the done thing, Gregor.'

'What is?'

'To call for a young lady.'

'Well, then,' he said, with a grin. 'I suppose it'll be all right.'

Acting on information received, Inspector Sellars led members of the newly formed Drug Squad into the premises of one Angus Thatcher at twenty-two minutes past midnight, Sunday, October 23rd. There, members of the squad took possession of a quantity of the drug cannabis, and duly charged the said Angus Thatcher under Section 5 (a :1) of the Dangerous Drugs Act 1965, and the Dangerous Drugs (No. 2) Regulations, 1964. Four other occupants of Thatcher's flat were also charged under various sections of the Act Amendment, 1967 which amounted to a charge based on the Third Regulation, Unlawful Possession – with some additional frills flung in to give Sellars and the Stipendiary Magistrate a bit of practice in presenting the case.

Thatcher was twenty-four years old, an erstwhile student of dentistry in Edinburgh, currently unemployed. Of the four others, three were girls, aged sixteen, seventeen and eighteen. The second male at the tea party was Angus Thatcher's cousin, James Thatcher, a grocer's assistant in Thane. Angus Thatcher had resided in the single room and kitchen for four months, paying rent, but leaving all other domestic bills outstanding, up to the time of his arrest. Close interrogation of the Thatchers revealed that cannabis had been obtained from Robert Hennigan, also an unemployed former student of dentistry in Edinburgh, now resident in his parents' home in Leith. Hennigan had sold cannabis – a quantity which even Sellars admitted was almost microscopic – to Thatcher's former girl-friend, aged sixteen, piqued in no small measure at being left out of the party. Of the three girls charged, two had never taken any sort of drug before, and the third had smoked pot only once – in a house in Edinburgh in company with Angus Thatcher and Robert Hennigan. None of the persons taken into custody had previous convictions and none, through tears of contrition and wails of fright, could dredge up anything which might have pushed McCaig and Ryan closer to a solution of the McDowell case.

Privately, Sellars thought it all a farce. Hell, he'd seen more licentious behaviour at Police College barbecues. Nevertheless, he looked forward to his next raid. Crusading in the name of the law was turning out to be bloody good fun.

Sticky with sweat, the track-suit clung to his body. He did not jog, but ran, ran hard for four miles. His route came out of the centre of Thane, round the corner by the Tolbooth to quieter back roads lined by warehouses and into more open country over the river. He crossed the disused canal at the lock, arms out like a wire-walker and feet, in the rubber-soled shoes, turned outward like a dancer's. He ran with his arms held loose and his head back and his eyes squinting a little against the ball of the afternoon sun which hung like an orange over the tiers of the houses at the top of the town and, save for the stillness and the colours of the leaves, turned the calendar back from the imminent onset of winter. He did not leave the town completely, doubling back on his trail several times in the allotted stretch, crossing the river and then the canal again by roadbridge and footbridge, holding to tracks and paths in the vicinity of the two winding waterways, one natural and one man-made. At length he emerged at the rear of the millhouse on a section of the canal where dank undergrowth and stunted trees gave way to the rufous mountains of the old mine coups, monuments of open-face workings which, for half a century, had made the village of Drury on the outskirts of Thane a rich but dirty outpost of the Industrial Revolution. Drury was the limit of the boundary of Thane now, absorbed in part into the burgh, yet in the wilderness along the canal and the volcanic ranges of the slag-heaps, retaining its own unenviable individuality. Yule took to the tow-path by the rank, reed-fringed canal, the

111

water stagnant, the colour and texture of crude oil. He slowed his pace almost to a walk.

The end of the hand-made bamboo rod was balanced in Mulligan's palm. A plastic tray lay on the grass by his side together with the match-box in which he kept such gear as he felt he needed to fish the canal. Reel and line and spinner were expensive, only the short rod itself cheap. Buried in the weeds behind him was the gravestone of Jocky, horse of the water-carrier who had lived – horse, not carrier – to the incredible age of forty and had died in the traces in 1924. The place was known to boys and worthies of the town as Jocky's Fall. Mulligan leaned his back on Jocky's stone and delicately spooled in the line. The spinner twirled up from murky depths and showed glinting copper just under the surface.

Yule, hardly even panting, stopped by Mulligan's feet and, hands on hips, looked up and down both banks. Directly opposite, half a dozen kids played a military game on the shoulders of slag, explosive shouts and mouthfuls of ricochets thin and faint in the warm lazy stillness. Mulligan brought the spinner to the bank and tipped the rod into his fingers. He wiped a thread of weed from it, checked the hinges and, with a short practised sweep of his right hand, cast it far out into the canal again.

'There's nothing alive in that sewer,' said Yule.

'Aye, but there is,' replied Mulligan.

'Like what?'

'Pike.'

'Pike? Get off.'

'Used to be some grayling too, a while ago.'

'Pike need food,' said Yule. 'Like everything else.'

'They eat the rats,' said Mulligan patiently. 'Rats swim over from the shale bings scouting for grub, and the pike eat the rats.'

'Ever caught one?'

'Sure, but not lately. Used to come here with my father on push-bikes. He was a great one for the fishin',' said Mulligan. 'He'd take pike when there wasn't nothin' else t'take in season. Variable beasts, though. Sometimes they give a grand fight and sometimes you can just drag them in.'

Yule shook his head and sat on the grass. He mopped sweat from his face with the sleeve of the tracksuit.

'Any problems?'

'Nup.'

'You got the money?'

Mulligan changed hands on the cork of the rod, reached into his jacket and brought out an envelope. He tossed it on to the grass by Yule's track shoes. 'Three hundred and twenty, less a hundred.'

'You had trouble?'

'No trouble.'

'Weren't the clients shy?'

Nup.'

'Did any of them mention McDowell?'

'Nup.'

'I told you you didn't have to worry.'

'I'm still worried,' said Mulligan. 'Worried about the blues.'

'Leave the blues to me.'

Mulligan jerked the rod with thumb and forefinger and rotated the handle on the spinning wheel. 'You heard something?'

'Not yet,' said Yule. He leaned back on his elbows and gazed out over the motionless surface of the canal. 'I will, though. I should have some inside word tomorrow.'

'How?'

'Never mind.'

'Y'heard from Charlie?'

'No,' said Yule. 'Probably won't either.'

'You're lettin' him bring in another load'f the stuff?'

'Depends on what I hear.'

'You're a nutter, Greg.'

'You're the one who advocated holding the bloody deals open.'

'Aye, I suppose I did,' Mulligan sighed.

'How much have you left?'

'Enough for one more drop – just. If Charlie's comin' he'd better be here by Friday week, or it's all off. Once the clients start to pop, at least one of them'll pop good.'

'What's the argument?'

'The argument is we're committed to go on.'

'If Charlie gets the shipment through, you mean?'

Mulligan chewed his moustache. 'I dunno.'

'You can be replaced, Mulligan,' said Yule. 'I could easily find another runner.'

'Maybe y'should do that.'

'Chicken?'

'Aye, a bit.'

'Supposing I get strong word that the fuzz have nothing at all on our operation, would that make you feel any better?'

'Aye, sure it would, but it wouldn't change the problem,' said Mulligan. 'It's that lad gettin' killed, that's the problem.'

'No connection with us.'

'I wish I could be certain, Greg.'

'You think one of the clients was in on it?'

'I . . . no, none of my herd.'

Yule got to his feet. He slid the envelope into the breast of his tracksuit top and tugged the draw-cord tight about his waist. The spinner hung limply in the water, near the edge. In spite of Mulligan's remembrance, he did not believe that there still was life in that water. Pike, rats even, couldn't survive in such pollution.

'I'll be in touch,' he told the older man.

'Frank! Come in.'

'Where's Brian?'

'As a matter of fact he went golfing with George.'

'Golfing?'

'He . . . he needed a break.'

'Quite!' McDowell said. 'I don't blame him.'

'And Mildred?'

'At home, of course.'

'Does she know you're here?'

'No.'

'How are you?' Laura Menzies asked. 'I heard you weren't too well.'

'Nothing wrong with me.'

She wore a caftan over orange-patterned lounging pyjamas. The caftan had Aztec designs printed on it and was heavily fringed. He could not recall having seen the garish trousers before. He put his hat on the telephone console and his driving gloves inside it.

'What is it, Frank?'

'I thought . . .'

'What?'

'The boxes.'

114

'They're upstairs.'

'Fetch them.'

She hesitated, then did as he told her. He watched her sturdy buttocks under the clinging material as he took off his overcoat and tossed it too on to the console. He followed her upstairs into the bedroom. She was standing on a low stool reaching through the open doors of the built-in wardrobe, to rummage behind hat and shoe boxes on the top shelf. The single beds had Casa Pupo overquilts, plain and warm-looking. The drapes were not fully drawn and the reflection of the late afternoon sunlight made the room seem summer stuffy. She brought down the boxes, the plastic one first, the larger one of polished wood last, and held them, balanced, out to him. He took them and put them on the bed, her bed.

'Have the police . . . ?' she began.

He opened the wooden box and took out a neat miniature slide projector, uncoiled the cable and stooped to fit the plug into the distributor by the bedhead.

'No, Frank.'

He paid no attention to her protest. She had closed the wardrobe doors again, and stood against them, hands behind her back.

McDowell flicked open the plastic box, picked a slide at random, and held it up to the light.

'Frank, I said not to do that.'

'When did Brian leave?'

'About . . . about three o'clock.'

'He won't be home before seven.'

'You bloody . . .'

He held the slide between finger and thumb, and stared at her in surprise. 'Bloody what?' he said. 'What am I?'

'I won't stay here, if you . . .'

'Yes, you will.'

'What's wrong with you, Frank. Haven't you any feelings?'

'Now, move over.'

He rested the spar of the projector on the end of the bed, slotted the slide into place and switched on. Blurred coloured outlines blinked on the white-painted doors of the wardrobe. Laura flinched away from them. He screwed up the fine focus and made the image sharp. He preferred the clarity and lucid colours of the single frame. He had tried movies but the quality was unsatisfactory; besides, there was something disruptively amusing in the wallowing antics of the participants, an intrusion of reality. The slide held a moment of passion in repose, every detail perfect, posing not feigned but cleverly abandoned. Though excellent, the scene was not one of his favourites. He switched to its companion, a detail taken with the camera closer to the bodies, showing damp strands of hair, beads of sweat.

'Please, Frank, not yet. I mean, not today, not now.'

'Laura, it's important to me.'

'I won't do it, Frank, not so soon.'

'Soon?'

He dropped the discarded slide into the tray, and selected another; an interesting variation, two men and one woman enjoying each other thoroughly. Aggression without cruelty. He did not take pleasure in cruelty or outright perversion. He recalled the patience with which he had made his choice. Not for him the risks of pornographers' catalogues, plain wrappers which every postie could recognise a mile off. Four times in all he had gone in person to the shop in Edinburgh, had given the password which George Johnston, that juvenile satyr, had passed on to him 'in case'. He had been admitted at once to the room above the innocent floor with its cases of cheap cameras and photographic equipment, and had there made his choice; made his choice with great care, thinking not only of himself but of Laura and her limited imagination, her inhibitions, and her redeeming willingness to learn. He had used the slides only in Laura's company, not alone. He was too old, too mature for that sort of wishful wastefulness. But with Laura the blown-up and explicit photographs had added to the sense of adventure, and to the grossness of their love-making here in her bedroom in the afternoons. Adultery was a simple matter if one was discreet; heightening adultery to an obsession which would not become bland and routine, took constant care. Grasping quickly the nature of his needs, she satisfied him by buying special underwear, black and tight, knickers of French silk with tiny buttons like seed pearls fastening from belly to crotch, a corset of scarlet *crêpe de Chine* scalloped with black lace. What she did with these appurtenances, where she hid them, he didn't know. He trusted her sufficiently to be sure that Brian, prudish and dutiful but no longer interested in pleasuring his wife, would not discover them. And on the wall, always, the colourful extensions of opportunities which they were content to limit to each other, ruminating over the possibilities of being part of this group or that, comparing the breasts or thighs and the rigid organs of the males, speculating on the degree of pleasure which special positions might bring, as if the colours on the painted door had become flesh and blood and they themselves were only by choice incorporated in the larger group.

'Put it out, Frank,' she said. 'Take them away and destroy them. I don't ever want to see them again.'

'Nonsense!' he said. 'Why don't you lie on the bed and enjoy it.'

'Good God!'

Was it so evil to keep the spark of desire alive as long as possible? Laura would probably be the last. Switching slides again, he remembered other women he had known. He had gained more from them than the casual satisfactions of sexual release. With all of them he had conducted what could only be described as an affair. Denigrate intercourse, cry immorality, and you have the mob on your side. To revel in expressions of the body, to crystallise the appetites of youth and preserve them, and call it by any other name than love would be a rebuttal of all that he believed in. Or was that yesterday? Today, this week, it did not seem to matter; the philosophy had weakened. Today what he required of Laura was not access to her heavy breasts or her soft vaginal regions, but something less strenuous; what he wanted was not in the ritual, was new, could not be named or described, even properly defined. The habit of loving her with his penis, abetted by the debauchees on the wall, was all that he had ever had to help him. He could not break that habit now, because of what happened to the boy on the back road at Ottersford. He was in no way to blame for that.

Why couldn't Laura understand?

To keep separate the elements of his personality was all that he could hope to do and, having taught himself the knack long ago, he could see no sane reason why it should fail him now.

Laura was one of the prime ingredients in his self-administered therapy. He must not allow himself to change.

He propped the projector carefully, and came to her, caught her arm, shifting with her across the sparring couple

117

on the white door, through areas of colour, disrupting the spectrum. On Laura's face was no pity and no desire, only disbelief.

'Why not?' he said. 'I want you.'

'Frank, please, not . . .'

He increased the pressure, drawing her inexorably towards the bed.

Gentleness was over. She fought him. She swung one arm like a club and struck him across the head, beating him. He caught the blow, shook himself, reached out for the edges of the caftan, gripping bunches of tassels as if they were the fleece of a shaggy animal. He stripped the garment over her body, shrouded her head with it, gathered the folds again in one hand, pinning her. She kicked out at him. He stood to one side. Motes and grains of colour danced across her, staining the orange suit. He aimed directly for her breasts, kneading them, tugging her across the room. Holding her suspended over the quilt-cover for an instant, back arched and her thighs spread, he threw her across the bed, then fell on her with all his weight.

The projector tilted, spread its scene upward on to the ceiling, the body of the woman in the picture misshapen, her belly curved over the junction of ceiling and wall, as if, in transports of erotic sensation, she had begun to float heavenward, out of the confines of the frame.

Still buttoned into the worsted suit, waistcoat and all, he did not endeavour to free himself, or bare any part of his body. His hands were the sole medium of sensation. He groped and rolled at the woman below while she passed through a paroxysm of rage and terror – could he have made her fear him so much? – then fell limp and utterly passive. The movements of his hands became less and less frantic and, as if taking cue from Laura's limbs, dropped around her, no longer pawing but cradling her, protecting her.

He let go the pinch of the caftan and with a snapping motion bared her face. Her hair, in disarray, swirled on the crochet of the quilt-cover, her throat veined and creased, her lips open. Her belly rose and fell in great gasping sobs. Whatever had been between them was no longer there, as if a single act of uncalculated violence had destroyed the integrity of their relationship. In her acquiescence he recognised not disgust but shame; and the shame was in

118

him too, like the transference of an infection. How close, how very close, he had come to loving her; too close. Against that flaw each had deliberately set the elaborate actions of sexual play. No play now. He lowered his head to the strip of flesh between her brassière and the hem of the lounging pants, rested his mouth there, dry flesh of his lips against the faint moisture of the woman's diaphragm. She did not push him away, but she did not touch him; only gave in to the gesture not, as she gave in to all his gestures, willingly, co-operatively, but in melancholy recognition that Frank McDowell, like his son, was dead.

After a time, he rose gently from her. He was more drained of power than if they run the gamut of titillation and ejaculation, more solicitous – though he said nothing – than he had ever been in the past. She did not move, splayed out in the position into which he had thrust her, her legs heavy and open, pants tight, her breasts thrust up through the orange stuff below the swaddle of the caftan at her throat. It was as if he had killed her, like some medieval romantic, to avoid the anguish of parting.

Briskly he filed away the slides, tapping them into the plastic case. He unplugged the projector, and fitted it into its box, cable coiled tightly round the lens cap. He tucked both boxes under his arm.

Still he said nothing. Still Laura did not move.

She watched him out of blue pupils filmed by a slight moisture which freshened their innocence and slumbering intelligence. Perhaps, all along, she had known what it meant, and had waited patiently for him to realise it too. In the placid course of a life unaltered, it would never have happened. He slipped out of the bedroom and went downstairs. Carrying the boxes openly, he left the house, knowing that he would never come back.

Gregor Yule's moderation might have proved annoying, except for the fact that he was such an intelligent and interesting person. Her mother, correctly, would have called him ' a good conversationalist'; meaning that he had learned how to listen without interrupting. Sheila found herself talking at great length about many facets of her life which had remained within her for years. With little or no embarrassment in his presence, after the first fifteen minutes or so, she even quit trying to persuade him, by various wiles, to make a direct sexual advance. Now, late in the evening, she had fallen into traditional poses, had become in effect the kind of girl her relatives supposed her to be and the kind of girl her upbringing had made of her, modest, friendly, almost extrovertial. In an objective corner of her mind, she knew what was happening, and was astonished at her garrulity; but she could not stop. Now and again Gregor would interject intelligent questions, which proved that she wasn't boring him with her chat.

There they were then, in her small parlour, gas-fire purring, aroma of coffee and tobacco smoke, low sounds of voices, and a feeling, not of physical intimacy – though that was part of the undertow – but of communion, friendship and mutual understanding. Sheila quickly retreated from the hard line she had planned, instinctively played out the night in the right way. From companions at college she had heard of such jolly evenings, boys and girls and coffee and conversations, but had considered the implications as naïve. Now, she could not see them so. Perhaps the opportunity had arrived to make up the part of her life which had oddly got lost in the aftermath of her father's death.

'So,' Greg said, 'that's how the police department works.'

'That's it,' Sheila said. 'Some of it, anyhow.'

'Fascinating!'

'It isn't so fascinating when you're in it, on the spot.'

'Routines, you mean?'

'Yes, all the time.'

'You must find some of it interesting, though, Sheila?'

'Oh, yes, quite a lot of it.'

They were drinking their way through a second pot of coffee. A plate with hot buttered toast stood on the low table between them on the hearth-rug. Gregor had taken off his jacket. He looked very relaxed, lying back in the squeaky armchair, long legs crossed.

'It must be murder for an inspector,' he said, 'when he's got to ask hundreds and hundreds of people the same questions?'

'A house-to-house?' said Sheila. 'Beat coppers usually do that, though rankers will help out if there's a really big scare on.'

'In a case like this . . . this . . .' Greg snapped his fingers, summoning up escaped memory. 'The drug-addict fellow, what's his name?'

'McDowell.'

'That's the one; yeah, the police spent a week at college, just trudging round asking everybody the same questions. I mean, what could they hope to gain from that?'

'Catch somebody out.'

'But how?' said Gregor. He shifted, leaning forward, resting an elbow on his knee. 'It would seem to me that if some fellow in the college did know something, he'd just lie about it, and they wouldn't be able to tell the difference.'

'They might,' said Sheila.

'How?' said Greg. 'I mean, surely policemen aren't that astute?'

'It depends on the circumstances, and the nature of the inquiry.'

'I find it hard to credit that a policeman could find out *anything* at college,' said Greg. 'Unless from a friend of McDowell's?'

'Well, in this particular case,' Sheila said, 'we *didn't* find out anything. But that's just in this case. Did you know Tom McDowell?'

'Never met the fellow,' said Greg. 'I feel sorry for him, though. Imagine having to take drugs, like that.'

'Yes, it's strange,' Sheila said.

'The police will eventually find the . . . the . . . person who gave him the drugs, I suppose?'

'The pusher,' Sheila said. 'We haven't a clue so far.'

'Really! That's interesting. You'd know. I mean, you'd be in a position to find out?'

'Of course.'

'I don't envy you your job,' Greg said. 'What's he really like, your boss?'

'Good,' the girl said. 'Damn' good.'

'He'll be worried about this thing in the county?'

'He's worried about what it might mean.'

'Hm?'

'A big drug panic.'

'Surely not, not in Thane?'

The girl shrugged. 'Too early to tell.'

'That's really *most* interesting,' Greg said. 'I mean, I wouldn't have thought the police would go after users in general, just McDowell's connections.'

'Tip of the iceberg, and all that.'

'Yeah, I see it now,' Greg said. He frowned. 'Amazing

how efficient the police are, when you think of it. Surely, though, they *must* have a lead to follow? I mean, they can't just work in the dark, can they? That's not the way it happens in the movies.'

'Unfortunately, it's the way it happens in real life,' said Sheila. 'We had forty men working on the McDowell investigation all last week, and we'll hold that strength for another week or so; then cut back, I suppose.'

'This is the Drug Squad you talked about?'

'No, the Drug Squad is a separate entity.'

'Confined to the county?'

'More or less. They'll work out some sort of collaboration with customs and police generally, just like they do in other spheres of criminal activity, but mainly their concern will be with Thane.'

'How's it going?'

'Sellars – he's in charge of it – has pulled in one or two.'

'Junkies?'

'Smokers, nothing very wicked.'

'Not connected with McDowell?'

'No, not connected with McDowell.'

'You really don't think that McDowell's pusher will get clean away, I hope?'

'He might,' said Sheila. 'In fact, the talk round the office is that McDowell wasn't an addict at all.'

'Really! But the papers said he died . . .'

'The papers,' said Sheila, disparagingly.

'They don't tell the truth?'

'Some of it, twisted a bit. The press can be a damn' nuisance.'

'Inventing sensations?'

'Exactly,' the girl said. 'More coffee?'

'No. No, thanks.'

She talked until well after eleven, his quiet expressions of interest stirring her to confidences which did not strike her as being indiscreet or disloyal to her department. Many policemen talked quite openly about their occupation; only a few remained tight-lipped and secretive about it, as if there were masonic secrets involved which could not be trusted to members of the open society. The detective was less forthcoming than the blue, but he had certain techniques which were valuable and ought not to be divulged. No copper would talk openly of his informers, not even to colleagues.

There was nothing at all in the McDowell case or in the nature of her employment which put the seal of caution on her.

Greg left at midnight. He thanked her for her hospitality and for giving him such an interesting evening. She was glad that he found her interesting, that they had something in common. In the closet-like hall she helped him into his overcoat.

'Sheila,' he said. He touched her lightly on the shoulders with his fingertips. 'I hope you didn't mind me talking to you like that, in the laundromat, I mean?'

'Why should I mind?'

'Well, it might have seemed . . . forward.'

'No, Greg, I'm glad you did.'

'I don't make a habit of . . . of picking up girls.'

'No.'

'May I see you again this week?'

'Yes.'

Frank McDowell checked into the police station at Lannerburn, informed the duty sergeant that he intended to enter his shop at 158 Main Street in approximately five minutes, and that the sounding of the burglar alarm would not, therefore, signify a raid upon the premises. He explained that he wished to pick up a set of account books, and showed proper identification. The latter gesture was hardly necessary as the desk sergeant had recognised him the moment he came through the station door. The sergeant thanked him for calling, reminded him to re-set the alarm system when he was through, and bade him good night.

McDowell drove the Stag five hundred yards down Shepherd Street and turned past the hotel into the upper section of Main Street. Not yet ten o'clock, the automatic time-switches of the street's tourist shops hadn't dimmed out the window displays. He drove the remainder of the strip past the cottages to the last sandstone block in town. The block housed a Gas Board showroom and offices, and the bright, packed store of McDowell's most lucrative property. On the inside of the plate-glass an alloy grid defended the window against vandals and drunks. A matching gate barred the doorway, and made the place look a little like a bank. He sprung two of the padlocks on the gate and inched it back enough to allow him to squeeze through, pulling the briefcase behind him. He fitted his keys into the door-locks, turned them and pushed the door open. Though he had expected it, the clang of the alarm startled him and made him hurry across the central aisle to the closet where the setting device was housed. He fumbled the appropriate key from his pocket, pulled open the closet and switched off the mechanism. The dull ringing lingered in his skull for several minutes after the sound itself had been cut off.

He flicked the bar of the lighting system, and filled the front of the shop with light, closed the main door and locked it from the inside. Lugging the briefcase, he made his way carefully between laden shelves and counters to the store-room at the rear. He lit one bulb only, and moved on round the stacks and racks to the staff area against the far wall. Here Adam Scott's precise influence showed itself. Raffia matting, four canvas chairs folded and stowed neatly against the shelving, trade magazines and newspapers piled by the stove. The stove was stone cold, of course, but ashpan and belly still contained dregs of the previous morning's fire, coke clinker and a few small ends of kindling. Squatting, McDowell cleaned out the centre of the grate with the poker, packing the cinders back, making a vent to give it draught. From the broom cupboard, he took out two paraffin blocks and a handful of woodscraps from a bucket, built them up in the stove and lit the little pyre with a match. Leaving it to ignite and develop heat, he returned through the shop to Scott's office, and opened the small steel safe with a duplicate key. He removed Cash Book and Day Ledger and laid them on the desk. He closed and locked the safe, lifted the receiver of the phone on the desk and dialled Scott's home.

An ardent, almost fanatical philatelist, Adam Scott would almost certainly be poring over his catalogues or his collection even at this hour of a Sunday night. He took several minutes to answer McDowell's call, but did not seem unduly irritated at being interrupted.

McDowell explained that he had called for the firm's books, and asked where the Stock Record Book might be.

Scott had it at home, together with other documents. Did McDowell want him to bring it round to the shop, or would he collect it?

No, it wasn't all that important, McDowell assured him. In the pause, he sensed Scott's curiosity and perhaps anxiety. McDowell forced a chuckle.

124

'It's all right, Adam,' he said. 'Nothing's wrong; I just felt the inclination to put on the harness.'

'Ah!'

'I'll have the books back by tomorrow.'

'Good,' said Scott.

'Good night, Adam.'

'Good night, Mr McDowell.'

The shop smelled of sandalwood, the musk of skins, and mild heather perfume from the samplers on the counter. It was so silent that McDowell could hear the crackle of the kindling in the stove in the storeroom. He closed the office and carried the ledgers back to the rear chamber, put them into his briefcase, and took out the projector box and the plastic container in which the slides were filed. Gloved fingers grasped the container and tipped the slides out on to the matting. A large handkerchief buffed the plastic, cleaned the plastic thoroughly in all its parts and dusted over the projector case. The cased projector and the empty slide receptacle were returned to the back of the stock shelves, packed behind assorted cartons of similar photographic equipment and the square packets of Highland views.

McDowell knelt on the matting and stirred the stove gingerly, coaxing up flames. One by one, he fed in the little frames of cardboard with their delicate coloured miniatures, watched the heat char and melt them, bubble the pin-points of lurid flesh, wrinkle and reduce each square to identical nubbins of crisp brown, like the chrysalis of a tiny insect, which the card frames released, smouldering and flaking into ash. Adding more kindling and a few marbles of coke to invigorate the tired fire, it took him the better part of half an hour to destroy the fifty slides and break them down into cinders beyond all recognition. Save for a scab or two of glossy residue on the inner grid of the grate, the dross was indistinguishable from the domestic débris of Saturday's fire. Delicately he broke it down with a poker tip, and smoored the smouldering coke. Making sure that it was safe, he closed up the stove again, took off his gloves and dropped them into his briefcase with the books. He looked carefully round, found no trace of his activity, no telltales. He went out of the building, switching off lights, activating the alarm, securing all locks behind him.

Under the street lamps, as far as he could see, the pavements of the Lannerburn suburb were utterly deserted. The

air still, frost-sharpened, carried the harsh up-change of a
fast engine from one of the flanking highways. He lowered
himself into the driving seat of the Stag, briefcase propped
in the passenger well. Firing the engine he nudged the car
into gear and nosed off in a northerly direction. Though he
had destroyed a tangible portion of his private guilt, the
bulk of it remained, immutable, indestructible, too diffuse
to be gathered and defined. Four miles north of the town
he swung into a narrow dog-leg and circuitous secondaries
which would carry him back to Rodale Avenue, avoiding the
strath past Ottersford, haunted as it was by the scarlet
Sabre and ineradicable memories of his son.

PART THREE

Under cowled spots viced to the iron crossbeams of the motor pool, the reconstructed Sabre gleamed whole again. Hosed and dried and polished by conscientious mechanics, it stood in isolation at the north end of the low basement, a monument of scarlet fibreglass, black rubber and brightwork. Harry Ryan leaned on the trolley and blankly contemplated the landcraft. A second after-breakfast Kensitas dangled from his underlip, and he looked rumpled and shabby, personification of a Monday morning drudge.

Only a week since Tom McDowell had blown in out of anonymity? Seemed much longer. Prospect of an early solution to the enigma of the lad's supplier had faded. In his opinion at least, it was more remote now than when they'd started. Okay for Sellars to play at being a wolf, pouncing on stragglers, enjoying it even, but with the college clean, and the driver still undiscovered, and the place where young Tom McDowell went that Saturday night still not located, the case was in danger of running out of steam.

On the high road out of Thane, the buggy shifting like a bullet through the sift of rain – he had that image in his noddle and he couldn't shake it.

The Ayer Sabre, a kit car; four fat tyres and a fast Ford engine strung together with semi-racing club goodies. Driver in an orange Cagoule and sports shoes, boy or man whom nobody could identify. Not one of Frank McDowell's friends – though the buggy had come out of Mossburn, out of the drive in Rodale Avenue – and not one of Tom McDowell's few chums, all of whom had cover stories which checked out to the letter. McCaig was becoming, not irascible, but reconciled. Press jackals pulling off and trailing Sellars now, sniffing for hot news about addiction and vice, more corroboration for the public trial of a whole generation. Edgar Pomfret silent as a garden gnome. Bewildering but not, *not* distressing. If he could only warm to the pursuit, view it as a pursuit at all, then he might be able to put something together.

That was what had been happening in the hiatus of his brain. Yes, that was it; he'd been putting something together mentally, linking two separate units, two things which didn't seem to fit together, which nobody had even tried to join. He couldn't recollect what the units were, let alone put them together. Dream of a bored and overworked law officer? Probably! Best things only occurred in dreams anyway, didn't stand up to the light of day, faded into uselessness like negatives exposed to the sun.

Damn it all, he *had* made a connection.

Outside the windowless basement, an autumn sun would be warming the air, melting the light ground frost and beginning to find angles into the rooms of the upper floors of eastern prospect. Due on duty in fifteen minutes, Ryan was conscious of the electric wall-clock slicing off seconds, slicing off slivers of his concentration too, like a grocer's guillotine carving cooked meat. What the hell was he doing here, this early? He could not quite decide. Obvious answer was, looking at the Sabre. But the obvious answer hid subtle conclusions and Ryan now knew that somewhere inside his skull, by fits and starts, an idea was worming its way to the surface. All he could do was encourage it. Buried faculties had induced him to do his brooding here. He had left home even before the children were up to face the beginning of another school week. Jean too was still in bed.

Work it out logically, Harry lad, he told himself. Briskly, and for the fiftieth time, he checked off the commonplace proceedings of police work, discarding the appeal to the driver; sporting goods shops checked out, petrol stations, druggists, chemists, students' haunts. At the termination of the process he was back at what he started with – the driver, the buggy and the shooting gallery.

Intrigue, possible collusion, were suggested by eyewitnesses who had marked the Sabre emerging from the driveway at 7 Rodale Avenue. Councillor McDowell was not his project, however, and McCaig had grumpily rejected the notion that the old man was directly involved. Ryan had heard rumours, wild hindsight inventions, that McDowell was a scurrilous old reprobate, but there was no whit of proof to substantiate them. Even McCaig, a great one for unravelling scandal, tossed them out as worthless and malicious lies. Depravity took time; McDowell was too involved in commercial and political affairs to be managing a vice ring on the side.

The clock repossessed another whole minute.

Ryan shifted position, put his knee on the trolley instead of his hind-end, and scowled at the Sabre. The headlamps tried to out-stare him, without success.

Contributions from the past had also to be taken into account. A recent case at Balnesmoor, for example, had hinged on deeply buried guilts and innuendo. It *was* possible that Tom McDowell had created a secret life for himself, not, like Walter Mitty, in the mind, but in reality, a parallel world to that middle-class prison in which he lived. Could that be accomplished in total secrecy? Perhaps!

Frank McDowell was the biggest frog in the Mossburn pond, not the wealthiest or the most aristocratic or the most cultured, but certainly the most notorious and the most potent. Compared to Frank McDowell, self-made and wilful and capable of making trouble purely as personal diversion, the rest of the residents of Mossburn were as nondescript as minnows. The whole district had beeen manned, quizzed, stirred up like a porridge pot. Even Sellars, as ardent in his hunger for young maidens as St George's dragon, had to admit that he would be hard put to it to rake up a villain in that stodgy lot.

Another minute fell.

Five years ago, this bothersome notion, whatever it was, would have popped into his head without a struggle. He experienced no excitement, only irritation at its tardiness and the premonition that it would after all be worthless.

He dropped the cigarette stub to the concrete, ground it out with his heel, lit another immediately, and took himself for a short perambulation round the beast.

Then he stopped.

Save for a slight widening of the eyes, his expression of moody fretfulness didn't change, only the tempo, the rhythm of his movements. The cigarette pinned between his fingers came jauntily to his mouth; a twitch of facial muscles cocked it. He put his hands behind his back and, pedantically stooped, took one more tour round the buggy. Emerging from orbit, he headed in a straight line for the far-away stairs. He had it now. The difficulty had been in recognising what the hell was what. He hadn't dreamed up one new idea, but two. Hypotheses, locked like mating wasps, rolled into his conscious mind.

'Give me that again,' McCaig said.

'I don't think it was a boy. I think it was a *girl*.'

McCaig drummed the fingers of his right hand on the cover of the magnum folder, glanced at the connecting doors, then back at the inspector. The aura of arrogance was something he hadn't felt from Ryan for a long time. The hunch-player in him, garbed in an executive respectability which would not admit the existence of such wayward faculties as instinct, was tickled by the ingenuous simplicity of the inspector's theory. It was, he had to confess, a new line, a line so obvious that he, or one of the scores of men employed on the McDowell case, should have come up with it a week ago. Trust bloody Ryan!

'You mean,' McCaig said cautiously, 'it *might* have been a girl.'

'Can you tell them apart?'

'Yes, of course, Harry. Now don't ...'

'Young ones?'

'I hardly know any young ones.'

'Surely, sir, you've *seen* them round here, in the Interrogation Room, at the desk?'

'All right! Yes, it's possible it *might* have been a female,' said McCaig. 'How does that radically alter ... ?'

'Tom's connection with the person who drove him into Ottersford Hospital eight days ago has always puzzled me.'

'A masterpiece of understatement, Harry.'

'Primary motivation, then, could have been sexual, rather than addictive. I mean, he could have fancied the girl, not the narcotics.'

'And where do we find the girl?'

'I'm not sure of that,' said Ryan. 'But if you'll excuse me, sir, I have another ... another idea which is possibly tied.'

'You've had a busy weekend, Inspector,' McCaig said. 'Go on.'

'There are probably hundreds of girls in this county, thousands if you take in Glasgow, who'd love to get behind the wheel of a big red monster like that Ayer Sabre.'

'I don't doubt it.'

'But how many could drive the brute at high speed, in the wet, at night, over twenty miles of road?'

'Yes,' said McCaig. 'I take the point.'

'Look at the time for the run.'

'Very fast indeed.'

'She must have been familiar, to some degree, with the handling of the Sabre, otherwise she'd have had it off the road.'

'Unless the gods were smiling on her mission of mercy?'

'Listen,' Ryan went on. 'We have it on the authority of his parents, that Tom McDowell was a quiet lad, no tiger, and that he didn't let his mates bomb around in the Sabre.'

'He was a bit afraid of it himself.'

'Out of hundreds of reports, not a single one spots Tom with a passenger.'

'That doesn't mean he didn't carry passengers.'

'No, sir, but it could mean he kept the girl secret.'

'Because he thought his parents would object?'

'Or because he was ashamed of her.'

'Or she was ashamed of him.'

'That's not likely, though, is it, Chief?'

'Not really,' McCaig admitted. 'He had a girl, then, on the quiet, and she was privileged to drive the Sabre. At least, she could shunt it along efficiently enough when the need arose.'

'Where did she learn to drive like that?'

'Anybody can learn to drive like that: the roads are littered with maniacs.'

'In Ayer Sabres?'

McCaig hesitated. 'Conclusion?' he asked.

'She drove the machine *before* it came into McDowell's possession.'

In a single instant McCaig appeared to change from restless scepticism to complete, almost sleepy passivity. A hand drifted out from his lap and touched the lever of the intercom.

'Sheila?'

'Yes, Chief?'

'Raise Frank McDowell for me. I'll take it on one.'

'Right, Chief.'

Blinking once, he tucked the beginnings of his dewlap into his collar, then regarded Ryan at length. 'Why did the buggy come from Rodale Avenue? Do you have a contingency to cover that too?'

'Not yet,' Ryan said.

McCaig lifted the receiver on the starboard wing of the desk. Left hand tugged back the cover of the folder and let it drop open at the star photograph of Tom McDowell. A family portrait, large, expensive and coloured, it showed the young man looking stiff and uneasy in front of the lens.

'Mrs McDowell?' he said into the mouthpiece.

'This is the ... ar, housekeeper.'

'Is Mr McDowell at home just now?'

'Ar, he is.'

'May I speak with him. It's Chief Superintendent McCaig of Thane County Crime Squad.'

'He's in bed still.'

'Awake or asleep?'

'How would I know?' the woman said.

'You could find out.'

'Wait a minute, then.'

McCaig filled his chest, let all the air out again, sagging further back into the chair. He took off his hat and laid it on the desk, sustaining the mood of relaxation. He could sense Ryan's eagerness, tension in the inspector's posture, like a coiled watchspring, or the bending of a bow. A responsive quickening was in him too, a match for Ryan's but of different temperament, manifesting itself in slackness and silence. As yet he did not wholly subscribe to the new theory of evidence, and during the long wait for McDowell to come to the 'phone, he thought of nothing, scrutinising Tom's portrait as if he had never seen it before and as if it was the face of a stranger – which in a way it was.

'Mr McDowell?' he said at length.

He held the receiver away from his ear so that Ryan, forearm on the desk, could stoop forward and listen to the councillor's replies.

'McCaig?'

'Yes, Mr McDowell. You weren't asleep?'

'No. What is it?' Frank McDowell's tone was rasping. 'Have you found ... found something, something I should know about?'

'Not so far,' said McCaig. 'Listen, you told me you bought the buggy, the Ayer Sabre, not as a kit but already made up.'

'That's correct.'

'Where did you buy it, from a friend?'

'Of course not.'

'Where then?'

'From a garage?'

'Which garage?' McCaig asked patiently.

'In town here, not far from you.'

'The name of the garage, please.'

'Why do you want to know?'

'Merely another avenue of enquiry,' said McCaig. 'I doubt if it'll yield anything, but we do have to keep . . .'

'Yes, very well,' said McDowell. 'It's too early to listen to your excuses, McCaig.'

'What was the name of the garage?'

'Brander Park Garage.'

'Where is that exactly?'

'Near Brander Park – as you'd expect.'

'You don't have the address?'

'Not offhand, no. It's not difficult to find. On the river side of Brander Park, between the old Brander Bible Hall and the new block of flats.'

'In the square off-shoot?' Ryan whispered.

'In the off-shoot?' McCaig relayed the question.

'Yes. Why are you . . . ?'

'The Sabre was there, and for sale?'

'I told you.'

'How did you pay for it? Cash, or cheque?'

'Cheque.'

'It's been passed, I assume?'

'Naturally, it's been passed. McCaig, do . . . ?'

'Was Tom with you when you bought the buggy?'

'No.'

'Did he know it came from Brander Park Garage?'

'He was with me first time we saw it.'

'When was that?'

'I can't be sure; towards the end of August, or a little further back into the month. Say the middle of August, about the 20th.'

'Who actually sold you the car?'

'The proprietor of the garage.'

'Did he tell you where it came from; who built it?'

'It was built, apparently, on the premises.'

'You were the first owner?'

'More or less; it had been driven around a bit by the proprietor. He built it for himself, I believe.'

'Why did he sell it?'

'I wouldn't know.'

'Didn't you ask?'

'I wasn't interested.'

'Didn't the fellow, the mechanic, give you any information about it, chat to you about it?'

'I never met the husband.'

'The what?'

'Husband.'

'Then who clinched the deal?'

'His wife.'

McCaig could not resist the temptation to look at Ryan. The inspector twitched his eyebrows evocatively.

McCaig said, 'You only traded with the *wife* of the owner?'

'All the time. She's in charge of the place. I don't know where the husband is. She sold me the Sabre. I made the cheque out to her.'

'Not to the garage?'

'To her.'

'Didn't you think that strange?'

'Not particularly – I assumed she was up to some sort of fiddle with the tax authorities.'

'Her name?'

'Lawrence,' said McDowell. Yes, that's it. Hilary Lawrence.'

'Young?'

'Yes, surprisingly young.'

'Thank you, Mr McDowell.'

'Wild goose chase.'

'Hm,' said McCaig. 'I wouldn't be surprised.'

Promptly, he hung up.

Ryan was already on his feet.

McCaig reached for his hat, shifted it towards his head, then checked the action.

'No,' he said.

'No?' said Ryan. 'You want me to take Sellars?'

'Christ, no,' said McCaig. 'I don't want you to take anyone. It was your idea, Harry, you check it out on your own.'

'So if it *is* a wild goose chase, we won't waste valuable man-hours on it?'

'Right.'

'What was her name again, the owner's wife?'

'Hilary Lawrence,' said McCaig.

Ryan brought the Cortina in from the north, from the populous wedge of Brander, where a shopping centre and a complex of box-shaped flats piled against the railway embankment. On the far side of the park, however, the architecture had hardly changed and Ryan was brushed by a strange nostalgia for the place as it had been thirty years ago when he was a lad. In the little square which was now occupied by the garage, had been a conglomerate of one-man offices, a charcoal seller's store and, in the long loft, a printers' workshop. Though the structures remained basically the same, they were for the most part abandoned. The garage, drab and oily with three garish pumps drawn up in the yard like robot guardians, struck an incongruous note. Iron balcony and fretwork staircase were still fixed to the front of the building, though, and the windows of the printers' shop on the upper level were still curtained with rough hessian. The forecourt below the balcony was deserted. Ryan slowly bumped the Cortina into it, rolled it past the pumps and parked it by the blank wall out of the way. Seated in the car, he surveyed the lineaments of the garage.

Beneath the wrought iron was a small plate-glass office, unlighted, flanked by two weathered wooden sliding doors on which had been stencilled, some time ago, *Brander Park Garage, Repairs, Renovations, Body* : there the legend ended as if the painter had run out of whitewash, or enthusiasm at that point. Adjacent to Ryan, on the other side of the court, two battered cars were drawn up nose to tail; a Ford Consul, and a hybrid machine with piebald paintwork and a faint resemblance to a Vauxhall Victor of the utility era. A rack of partially worn tyres was chained and padlocked to a tubular frame by an antique air pump with a snaking black hose coiled round it. Leaves drifted round the corners; pigeons hunched along the ridge of the roof. It was quiet.

Quitting the car, Ryan walked across the court and peered through the plate-glass door of the office. It had been panelled in imitation pine, but was otherwise spartan; a narrow counter, a high stool, a cash register, a Pirelli calendar on the wall. The door was locked. He strolled along to the left-hand set of sliding doors, found the latch, put his weight tentatively against it, and felt the door move quite smoothly on oiled casters. Squeezing through, he entered a repair shop lit by daylight from an open double door in the rear wall. The area was large, much larger than he'd expected. Strip and hook lights were bolted to the beams overhead, and an inspection pit yawned in the centre of the concrete floor. On the ramps was an old Volkswagen Beetle, robbed of all four wheels. Its engine block hung above it on a drapery of chains attached to a primitive crank jib. Grease-stained work benches, accoutred with vices and a litter of fine tools, lined the shop, broken by bays of metal shelving which held oils and parts in a semblance of order. A lathe backed on to the gable of a sentry-box shed in a corner and the bulb above it was lit. Ryan went on again, passing out of the workshop into the rear yard.

The yard was rectangular, again larger than he'd anticipated, and crammed with the carcasses of discarded vehicles in various stages of dismemberment. A vintage Land Rover pick-up with a jib-crane in the back stood near the doors. Around it was a clearing in the débris which massed thicker and rose higher and jutted over the summits of the surrounding walls like an angry metal sea, a grand-scale tableau of the order of New College's pig-iron statuary. Feeling a little insecure, Ryan skirted the soaring waves of junk, treading lightly lest it slump and crash down upon him. He aimed for the nebula of the torch, peacock's tail of molten steel and the black sausage of the oxygen bottle. He found the girl there, on her back under the axle-tree of a flat-bed truck.

At first, Ryan did not know if the prone figure was male or female. He could see nothing but sawn-off rubber boots, thick fisher-knit socks and the wrinkled knees of coveralls. Sinuous in spite of the welder's mask and gloves and the spitting ball of the torch in her fist, she trundled out on the trolley and came on to her haunches, staring up at him. The mask cloaked the whole upper part of the body in matt-black plastic, but for a clear perspex visor over the region of the eyes. Through it he could see the faded flesh and the round colourless pupils. He could not regard her as an individual; clothed thus, the figure seemed utterly inhuman, a mobile figment of the whole scrapyard scene, less custodian than prisoner. The mask dipped, leather hands

136

finicked patiently with the turnkey of the cutter, and the bright silvery light and rush of ignited gases fizzled out and died. She continued to hold the nozzle in her hands, watching it, Ryan assumed, to make sure that it was dead; then, rising, attended to the pressurised bottle, killed it too and laid aside the equipment. Later, it occurred to him that she had known what he was and what his business with her would be and had not halted her labours out of courtesy or even curiosity but from that pocket of resignation which fuelled her as the tank of volatile gas fuelled the torch.

For a girl, she was tall, lean rather than slender, with a strong-boned frame and shoulders too broad to make her small breasts prominent. In movement she was less supple than limp, each action, even the simple mechanics of walking, seemingly thought out, calculated and deliberate. She removed the face mask and held it by her side. Though it was of no great weight, it appeared to drag her body out of balance, tilting shoulders and hip girdle, making her head loll, adding a wistful submissiveness to her stance. Ryan blinked; the flicker-card-index of his professional memory unwittingly presented the image of a suicide – first in a quagmire of dead things – which he had found in a cramped kitchen of a tenement on his beat in Machlan when his uniform buttons still had their storeroom shine; a dead girl, his age or less, hanging from a short length of brand-new manilla clothes-line knotted to a hook in the centre of the lintel of the doorway, the kitchen chair kicked away from her bare heels, her long, smooth, pretty, naked legs straight and the feet curved, trailing not more than ten inches from a coco-nut mat which said *Welcome*. Dress and hair and bosom and arms and hands swooped in downward curves too, and, for some odd biomedical reason, her eyelids were demurely lowered. He crushed the recollection, blinking again.

'Mrs Lawrence?'

'Yes.'

She had pale brown eyes – not quite hazel, not quite grey – a thin face and reddish fair hair, cropped short like a boy's.

'Hilary Lawrence?'

'Yes.'

'There's nobody out front, you know?'

'No.'

She didn't pursue the lead, even though he allowed her time to do so. She should have asked him what he wanted, feigned the belief that he was a customer, after buying petrol or spares; but she did not.

At length, Ryan said, 'Is your husband about?'

'He isn't here.'

'When will he be home?'

'I don't know.'

The accent wasn't local. Borders, perhaps, or Galloway or South Ayrshire; low, mild, correct, making the girl sound thoughful and educated.

'Tonight?' Ryan asked.

'My husband's gone off.'

'Ah!' said Ryan. 'For long?'

'He's just gone off,' the girl said. 'I don't know where he is or when he'll be back.'

'How long since he left?'

'Eight or nine months, I suppose.'

'And you haven't heard from him in that time?'

The girl shrugged.

Again Ryan paused; still she did not question his right to question her. In the square-cut throat of the coverall was a dark blue roll-neck sweater. The sleeves of the garment protruded below the press-studs at the cuffs of the coverall, ragged and oil-saturated, fringing the wrists, industrial gloves fanning out from them, showing quilting. Were there marks on *her* arms? he wondered, and wondered too, in the unity of thought, how Sellars would handle the situation – roughly, most like. He struggled on, reluctant to reach the climactic point of the questioning, to put it to her that not only had he finally found her but that as she had already capitulated to the inevitable fact of discovery, all forms of pretence between them would be wasted.

'You sold an Ayer Sabre to a Mr McDowell?'

She nodded.

'When?'

'August, I suppose.'

'Early or late August?'

'About the middle.'

'You will, of course, have a record of the transaction?'

She shook her head.

'Why not?' asked Ryan.

'It was private. I didn't put it in the books.'

138

'Private?'

'The buggy was mine.'

'Your husband's, you mean?'

'He left it.'

'And you didn't see any harm in selling it?'

'No.'

'When did your husband build the Sabre?'

'A year ago.'

'Himself?'

'I helped.'

'You have no assistants here?'

'Somebody comes down in the evenings to help out.'

'Who?'

'Some men.'

'How many?'

'Three or four; it varies.'

'Who are they?'

'That varies too.'

'Boys?'

'Not boys.'

'Who are they?'

'Chaps who like cars.'

'You pay them?'

The girl shrugged.

'Come on,' said Ryan. 'Do you pay them?'

'Yes.'

'But you don't stamp cards for them, or pay Employment Tax, or anything like that?'

'Casual labour.'

'They work on the cars you have here because they like it?'

'And make a bit on the side,' she said.

'All right,' said Ryan.

Skirting it, mumbling on as if he was an accountant on the fraud and embezzlement detail. Hilary Lawrence's failure to demand her rights as a citizen or the civility of an explanation, began to blister his credulity and his patience. It was like trying to out-stare a stuffed animal.

'I'm a police officer,' he said. 'Detective Inspector Ryan.'

She nodded.

'Do you know why I'm here?'

She shrugged.

'I'm here because . . .'

139

She waited.

God, what was wrong with her? Nodding, shaking her head, waiting, shrugging; not with the sullen defensiveness of a guilty person, or the nervous twitchiness of a dolt, each tiny gesture separated from the lank immobility of her body, like a nut unscrewed from a spindle. All the things that Edgar Pomfret had said came back to him. Hastily he shovelled them out of his mind; instinct, rather than perceived symptoms, told him that this girl was not only the key to the connection, a vital link in the McDowell case, but that she lived in the limbo out of which Tom had emerged, and which he had inhabited, temporarily at least, on that last Saturday night. The ending might be the rim of the lawn in the grounds of Ottersford Hospital, but the bloody beginning was here. Ryan reckoned he had found the shooting gallery.

He swung round and looked up at the back of the building. The square windows of the old printers' loft above the workshops were curtained too.

'That's where you live?' he said.

She nodded.

'Alone?'

She nodded.

'Nobody there now, I take it?'

She shook her head.

'Mrs Lawrence, I'd like to . . . see your apartments, please.'

It was within her rights to refuse him search without a warrant – even the most ill-informed citizen must be aware of that – but she meekly acquiesced to his request, nodding – naturally – and shifting past him, still gloved, still carrying the gigantic face mask by her side. Ryan followed her across the yard, through the repair shed to the forecourt and up the twisting wrought-iron staircase to the door of the loft on the balcony.

The attic flat consisted of two rooms; or, rather, a single long room with a cubicle chopped from the end by a cheap chipboard partition. The cubicle would be the bedroom; he could see an iron cot and a trail of bedclothes and more of the chipboard pinned into a closet or wardrobe against the gable wall. A tiny kitchen and an even tinier bathroom were set side by side with the bedroom. Big and musty as a barn, the living room was furnished with isolated clumps of second-hand and home-made furniture. Two electric heaters, the sort used in factories, were plugged into sockets on the long back wall, but the main source of warmth came from a peeling pot-bellied stove which put Ryan in mind of the bleak R.A.F. billets of his National Service. A trestle table with a plastic cloth was pulled up near the stove, breakfast dishes, packets and sauce bottles propped upon it, like a new-style chessboard. Angle-iron and chipboard shelves held motor manuals, piles of magazines, and a fourteen-inch TV set which looked like a Logie Baird prototype. Four bulbs with paper shades dangled from the flat whitewashed ceiling, an exercise in perspective which made the room seem even longer than it was. The stained pine floor was coated with a patchwork of dusty rugs, under-felt and odd lengths of rusty brown carpeting. Hessian curtaining webbed the windows and the wooden walls were decorated with posters of racing machines, vintage cars and a couple of unfriendly film stars in cream fire-proof suits and crash-helmets.

The girl – Ryan judged her to be, at most, twenty – stepped over to the stove, turned again and, with a sweeping gesture of the mask and another enormous shrug, indicated that he was free to make his inspection.

It would be here all right; a drug – pill or powder – hidden under the boarding or in a cavity in the walls or the ceiling, an aperture plastered over by one of the posters, in one of the car manuals, in a box or packet in bedroom, kitchen or bathroom. It might even be hidden below in the work-shops or in a waterproof container amid the tangle of junk in the yard. It could be about anywhere, the drug and the tools needed to administer it. Was she confident of her hiding-place, or, innocent of that particular guilt, not an addict or a holder at all? Not for a moment did Ryan waver in his trust of instinct, though he would firmly deny that such a thing was part of the police detective's equipment. After all, *he* didn't need to find the stuff; even if he did, there were innumerable ways in which the girl could be smoked out, watched, badgered, starved of whatever chemical essences she needed to keep herself in this particular state of being to stave off the drabness of her existence as a forsaken wife.

Christ, Ryan thought, what a bloody hypocrite you are! A real prime piece of Ottersford Women's Guild, middle-class smugness, to assume that because this girl lived in bleak squalor she should necessarily be unhappy. Perhaps all that car junk below gave her infinite pleasure. The passionate devotion of men to bits of machinery was a common enough complaint. It could apply to a girl, too; no reason why it shouldn't.

Moving gingerly round the room, and back, as it were, towards the crux of the matter, Ryan forced himself to resume his probing.

'How long have you lived here?'

'Four years.'

'Who owns the property?'

'Dennis.'

'Mr Lawrence, that is?'

'Yes.'

'Did he buy it, or what?'

'It was left him when his uncle died.'

'His uncle?' said Ryan, as if the word was new to him.

'His uncle owned the property; all of it. Dennis was working here with his uncle, as a mechanic, when the old man died.'

'And Dennis inherited?'

'Yes.'

'What age is your husband?'

'Twenty-eight.'

'No other claimants?'

'Beg pardon?'

'Did no other relative contest Dennis's inheritance?'

Clearly, she did not even comprehend the question, and contented herself by raising and lowering her shoulders twice.

'How long have you been married?'

'Three years, near enough.'

'Have you family in the county?'

'No.'

'Has Dennis?'

'No.'

'Why did Dennis walk out?'

She'll balk at this one, Ryan told himself; but she did not.

'He didn't like it here,' she answered.

'Wasn't it profitable enough for him?'

'It wasn't the money.'

142

'Another . . . another woman?' said Ryan, unable to frame it without cliché.

'No.'

'Did he tell you where he was going?'

'England.'

'Where in England?'

'London.'

'Does he have relatives there?'

'A brother, I think. Never met him. I think his brother lives in London.'

'You run this place yourself?'

'Yes.'

'Don't you find it hard?'

A shrug was the whole answer.

'Are you in . . . debt, Mrs Lawrence?'

Very pointed, and really irrelevant; he could have led the girl to any question and received an answer of sorts. She wasn't resisting him at all, not following a policy of obfuscation. Vagueness was inimical to her character, or to her condition. He could have asked her if she'd slept with one or more of the amateur engineers on her staff, and she would probably just have shrugged or nodded. Sexually, she was not unattractive, Ryan supposed, though she had no substance. The props of her unfeminine trade interlaced job and character, one shoring the other, until, even on short acquaintance, Ryan found that he could not imagine her in frills and fancies, only in kinky extensions of leather and all that borderline jazz, none of which seemed to suit her mild personality.

'*Are* you over-committed?'

'No.'

'Brander Park Garage is a going concern, then?'

'I can live on it.'

'Where are you from?'

'Galloway.'

'Where in Galloway?'

'You won't have heard of it.'

'I might,' said Ryan.

'New Castleton; just a village.'

'I've been there,' said Ryan.

White-walled cottages on an arm of a sea-loch, flat, green, sandy, sweeping country with cows in the fields, picturesque and, as he recalled it, completely unspoiled.

'You have folks there?' he asked.

'Yes.'

'You keep in touch?'

'No. Not for a while.'

'How long?'

Shoulders, a purse of the lips as if he had come quite close to annoying her.

'Five or six years,' she said.

'What do they do, your people – farm?'

'My daddy's a slaughterman.'

'You left home and went ... ?'

'Edinburgh.'

'As?'

'Beg pardon?'

'What did you do in Edinburgh?'

'Started training as a nurse, but I didn't like it, and I got out and went to Glasgow and worked there.'

'Doing what?'

'In a fish shop, serving.'

'Until you met Dennis?'

'No.'

'I ...'

It wasn't his questions which were beginning to wear on her wick, but his inability to buckle down to the leads. That was it; she was a bit bloody riled because he wouldn't come the strong-arm and clunk her, verbally, over the head. She was more anxious than he was to reach down to the dirt, to get it over with.

'How did you meet your husband?' said Ryan, casually.

'I went to work in a garage in Glasgow, in Pollokshaws, and they got short in the working crew and I did some of that, then I went to classes ...'

'Classes, what sort?'

'Motor mechanics, night school; I met Dennis there.'

'I see,' said Ryan.

By the simple action of opening her fingers, the girl dropped the mask to the rug. She dropped her hips too, bending back into a canvas-sided chair.

Ryan was sweating. It wasn't warm in the loft, but he was conscious of dampness down his breastbone and, like scent, behind his ears. He took off his hat and fanned himself with it. Hilary Lawrence was ten feet away from him, indistinct in the gloom. Her features were not so much blurred as faded, like a print on old parchment left in the sun.

All he had to do to establish the validity of his hunches,

was start down the main avenue. If she resisted him, then the detailed procedure which had become second nature to him and in which were blended not only the law's flexible formalities but tricks and traps of language and psychology, would come to his aid – and, his reluctance notwithstanding, Sellars' drug squad too.

'Mrs Lawrence, don't you want to know why I'm asking you all these questions?'

'You're a detective.'

'But why . . . ?' Ryan stopped fanning himself and put the hat back on his head. 'All right. Where were you on the evening of Saturday, October 15th, and in the early morning of Sunday 16th?'

'Here.'

'Working?'

'No.'

'Were you alone?'

'No.'

'Who was here with you?'

'Tom McDowell.'

'I see,' said Ryan, coolly. 'You drove him, drove Tom McDowell . . . ?'

'I took him home, but it was busy and I didn't go in.'

'You went instead to Ottersford Hospital?'

'Yes.'

'Why?'

'He was dying.'

'Mrs Lawrence, do you have in your possession any drug or narcotic compound which is prohibited by law?'

'What will you do?'

'Take you to C.I.D. Headquarters and ask you questions.'

'What will you do with the stuff?'

'Confiscate it.'

'And what'll happen to me?'

'Treatment.'

'I know,' she said. 'I knew that. Yes.'

'Where is it?'

'In the bedroom.'

'All right,' said Ryan. 'And where's the telephone?'

'In the office downstairs. Listen . . .'

'No,' said Ryan. 'Don't say anything. Come with me, show me where the telephone is.'

'I'm sorry he died.'

'Just shut up,' said Ryan. 'I mean, keep quiet. Come on, the telephone.'

'In the office . . .'

'Look, you've got to accompany me. I can't let you out of my sight, and . . . Never mind; never mind. Just do as I tell you and you'll be all right.'

She got out of the chair. Her manner hadn't changed in the least. She showed no signs of apprehension or of relief at having unburdened herself. Now Ryan wanted the consolations of the department, the uniforms and expertise of colleagues to take off the pressure of being alone, and vulnerable, in the company of a girl who had not only yielded herself into the hands of the law but, in the most tacit manner possible, had put herself under the direct protection of the law. She came past him, arms hanging by her sides. He opened the door and let her precede him on to the balcony.

The air was the colour of a beech leaf bleached by frost and sunshine and terrestrial swing, as if the atmosphere too dipped into seasonal sleep, wrapping the township in a mellow dream which, when the days darkened soon, would deepen into a state like death. Across the park, the walls of the flats were muted pink and the disused signal box at the Brander junction stood up against the faint mists of the town like a cardboard cutout of the prisoner's dock in the new High Court. The girl stepped away from him, cupped gloved hands over the wrought-iron rail of the balcony, pushed her belly against it, and lifted her head.

Ryan grabbed her.

Heels ringing on the iron, an unintelligible cry came out of his throat, loud-sounding and gruff in the stillness. He grabbed her by elbow and shoulder and spun her round, pulled her to him until he held her like a contrite lover, pressed against his chest. Below him, far below, through the intricate iron weave he could see the macadam of the forecourt, distance magnified by the enormity of his carelessness in the sick, hysterical moment when he thought that she had tricked him after all and jumped.

She did not lift her arms from her sides; she did not struggle. After a second, she laid her head against his chest. Confused, shaken, Ryan hadn't the temerity to push her away. He thought that she was weeping and even a detective, sometimes, will succumb to tears.

Then he realised that she was chuckling, not maliciously

and not at him, the sound as devoid of obvious source as was her horrifying indifference to detention. Ryan nudged her away from him, locking his hand across her forearm.

The gentle laughter seemed to rise out of her from a buried spring, like water seeping unexpectedly through a mountain of sand.

'No : not me,' she murmured. 'Not me : no, I'm not like he was. Okay?'

'What?' Ryan blurted out. 'Like who?'

'Not me, mister.'

'You mean Tom McDowell, don't you?'

The laughter died. The slight smile faded, no trace left on the blank anaemic face, not even in the eyes.

'Christ, you mean he *tried it?* said Ryan. *'Did he try it?'*

She pursed her lips, shrugged and, swinging away, tugged him towards the ancient iron spiral and the ground.

Complaint, coinage of all councillors and righteous committee-men, came wrapped in a package of Minutes and Agenda, intimation of the full council's monthly meeting, a work, packed solid and fastened with brass, upon which local Machiavellis fell like wolves. Progress, the dictum read, must be retarded at all costs – save the most expensive – and long-term policies must be geared to allow for maximum revision and general disagreement. The sixty-odd members of the Thane County Council who lounged in the tiered benches of the refurbished Surgeons' Hall – not counting employees and salaried advisers at the Convener's table – were thus steeped in negativism and only in matters of personal and party politics appeared sinewy with cunning. Approval of the Minutes alone was an opening gambit which could be prolonged throughout the morning, held over lunch, and dragged into the first session of the afternoon. When 'serious' issues were at stake, it might even be made to run into a second day, incorporating another lavish lunch at the ratepayers' expense.

Frank McDowell was rancorously acknowledged as a Grand-Master in the art of retardation, emulated by his foes, lauded by his colleagues, and secretely distrusted by his friends. He did his homework with a thoroughness which brought bile to the gullets of the opposition. It was not thought *outré* of Councillor McDowell to enjoy power; to wallow in it openly and with such arrogant relish, however, even the Independent Anarchist member considered a bit bloody thick. In three terms of elected office, McDowell had gone the rounds of most principal committees and sub-committees. In eight and a half years he had been instrumental in destroying the confidence of one Director of Education, the reputations of two County Road Surveyors, the marriage of a Director of Social Work, and the health of the now retired County Architect. As a permanent fixture on the Joint Police Council, his splenetic zeal had transformed that body from a lodge of smiling back-slappers into a spirited watchdog of the public's welfare. By contriving to make himself vastly unpopular with everybody in office, in obverse ratio, he had increased favour with his constituents and pumped up his majority at each election. While no man or woman in the warren of the County Halls was inhuman enough to gloat over the tragedy of young Tom McDowell, many harboured the not unnatural suspicion that the incident might mark the beginning of the end for the boy's father, and, like a tale from the Old Testament, in which staunch faith most of them had been reared, bring him to humility and eventual retirement. A more ordinary fate – car-crash, drowning, fatal illness – for his son, might have given rise in the long run to a quality of mellowness, have won Frank sympathy, a chance to demonstrate dignified resilience, and even more votes at the next poll. But, facts notwithstanding, the extraordinary circumstances of the incident cast a stigmatic shadow too deeply over Frank to be quickly erased, forgotten or ignored. Prophets, bowed over coffee cups or in the seclusion of their homes, hopefully predicted not so much a private withering as an apologetic public defeat. Even the most psychic of the inner circle – by general consensus, the Medical Officer of Health – could not have foreseen the sudden, dramatic end which McDowell chose for himself, or which the gods – more Greek than Hebraic – had chosen for him.

Perhaps it was fitting that his career should terminate loudly, in the setting where it had loudly projected itself so often in the past. If he had lived anywhere – and he had, he later supposed, lived everywhere where Mildred and Tom were not – he had lived most vividly under the cylindrical roof of the Surgeons' Hall and plush modern offices which grew out of it and, like dominoes upon a baize-topped table, fashioned lanes and corners of red brick across the sward of the 18th-century allotment of Monkscourt. Here, rather than on the corners of his ward, he had waxed plump on success, fattened himself with the sound of his own mordant wit and a sensitive awareness of his own cleverness. In the County Buildings, he was his own man, a party man, and behaved like a bachelor, indifferent to the routines in the home in Mossburn. Not to the trinket shops, then, or to the succession of women he had bedded, including Laura, or to Mildred and Tom did he give the best parts of himself, but to the *alter ego* who resided in Surgeons' Hall and its adjacent chambers.

Naturally, he had no intention of doing what he did. If he had had any inkling that he would be impelled to do such a thing, he would have committed himself to a private hospital before he would have packed his briefcase with the current copy of the Minutes and his portfolio of notes, and driven himself coldly to the meeting. The first twinges of irrationality worked on his mind with the sinister stealth of a cancer, hardly noticeable to the victim. There the analogy broke down; cancers did not burst full-blown inside the body as paranoia exploded inside his mind.

Merciful veils of amnesia cloaked the conclusion of the morning's misdeed. Even the preliminaries – chat in the bull-ring promenade, the sombre kindness of fellow-councillors were vague in his memory. It did not occur to him that he should not have ventured back into public life so soon.

The meeting was brought to order promptly at eleven o'clock. Schedules and introductions, delivered in the Convener's nasal whine, sang out through the hall like a Moslem call to prayer. McDowell was seated with others of his persuasion in the fourth row from the front of the north section. Papers and scribbled notes – all he had found energy to prepare – lay on the sloping ledge before him. Laird and Shaw, men of his stamp and vintage, flanked him, separated by a yard or more of padded bench.

The rigmarole began.

McDowell looked at the table, at the chairs and the men upon them, at the ranks of paid servants. To his astonishment he saw that *they were watching him.* Sunlight filtered through the ports of the roof and squared off the parquet, ruling subtle butter-yellow lines of demarcation which, now that he studied them, seemed to pen him in a lattice of dihedrals.

He screwed his eyes shut and opened them again.

Yes, it was undeniable.

They *were* watching him.

'Oh, stop it.'

He felt his lips move slightly, and the peculiar numbness of the mouth muscles, as if they had been treated by novocaine. He shifted his eyeballs. Head rigid, he darted a glance to left, then to right. Laird and Shaw too, heads screwed round, *were watching him.*

In the meaningless mumble of the words of the speaker time passed without consolation. Ordinary boredom, or a random declaration of contention, did not insulate him to the unflickering observation of the council. He could not understand it. Having left the house that morning prepared to dust himself off and pick up again the reins of office and reassume his dignity unimpaired by any implication that he *blamed* somebody for what had happened to Tom, he had become the focus of scrutiny. What did they want from him? Diversion? Brilliance?

Yes.

Old themes played on the fiddle of his reputation. McDowell's cadenzas.

He raised his head, found every eye upon him, waiting, watching, not hostile but expectant. Not so disconcerting, after all.

Above him, neck craned, he saw the vault, and blue sky through the clear concave glass, and an icing of cloud.

An African sky.

Go to Africa.

Pack and leave.

Set off for Durban.

Set off for Cape Town.

Johannesburg.

The Transvaal.

In bush shirt and veldtschoen, bare brown arms.

Mildred would not find him there. Tom could not.

Bent over the drawing board in the examination room with a brown wall and a green wall, knowing that his fingers were talentless and that his ability to cope with the intricacies of architectural theory, in terms of stresses and structures, could not be reconciled with soaring ambitions and visions of immortal edifices under a shimmering sky.

About him the business of the month went sonorously on.

Ashdown of the Finance Committee answered a barbed question which had popped out of the air. '. . . will no longer defray initial enquiry . . . extension of land option . . . government grant . . . loan.' Ashdown watching him, and his lips moving.

Ashdown down, and Dunlop up.

Mouthing.

Dunlop, bushy-haired and pug-dog ugly, swallowing his less informed phrases, sausages of sound trailing from his jowls. Mean, peering eyes on *him*. '. . . means to an end . . . deliberate sell-out . . . impractical and ill-advised at this juncture . . . not only prejudicial . . . vested interests at work.'

Counter-cheers.

Dunlop's man, Deputy County Architect, rising from the ashes of his predecessor's coronary affliction, suave and assured and indestructibly youthful : McElroy by name.

'In deference to . . . with due respect . . . not possible to evaluate long-term . . . flaws . . . intrinsic .. intensification of . . . put it to you, bluntly . . .'

McDowell experienced a pang of tension in his gut, clenched his fist on it, then it burst and released itself and he knew that his mouth was open and that he was snoring thunderously.

The voice ceased.

He closed his mouth, smiling broadly.

The voice of McElroy continued, muffled by uncertainty.

'Put it to you that irresponsibility . . . catchword . . . will not stand up to close . . .'

McDowell declared himself. *'Balls!'*

Silence, like a stone, hit the parquet, bounced once, and caught itself on the word. 'Balls !'

'Councillor McDowell seems to take issue with . . .'

'Councillor McDowell says *balls.*'

'Frank !'

'McDowell, are you . . . ?'

'Get him out . . .'

'Point of order, point of order . . .'

'Wait,' said McElroy. 'While one cannot but regret the crassness of the statement, everyone is entitled . . .'

'What the *hell* do you know about it?' McDowell rose slowly to his feet.

Laird and Shaw were leaning across space, propped on their hands, unsure.

Smug face on an autocratic neck-stem, confident of the triumph of rationality, now. 'You have a point to make, Councillor?'

'Stop staring at me, McElroy, you've seen me before.'

151

'Frank, please, if you'd . . .'

'Must ask for . . .'

'McElroy, you're a smug little shit, and you . . .'

'Out of here!'

'Suspend . . .'

McElroy's teeth parted and he yapped with pleasure, saying, 'Under the circumstances, Frank, of course I . . . understand.'

Before Laird and Shaw could lay hold upon his person, he went over the top of the bench, knee and sole lifting him. His hand found a grip on the hat of the lady directly in front of him; plaited straw and lace coarse under his fingers, her neck resisting, becoming stiff before it yielded. She screamed and yanked herself away. He trod on her shoulder, stepped over the backs of three benches and, travelling diagonally, leapt to the blue carpet directly under the well-shaft of sunlight. He ran for the table, screaming.

Younger men, servants of the electorate, were peeling off the benches and scattering from the carved table. Ladies of the company, his stepping-stone excepted, stood with their hands on their hats as if he had generated a hurricane in the chamber with the specific intent of robbing them of their millinery. Hambrough, eldest somnambulist in office, curled himself up like an albino squirrel, squeaking with amusement. The accountant whipped off his spectacles and held them behind his back. Hampered by the weight of official thrones, the chairmen were caught like a row of constipated invalids, half-doubled over.

McElroy crouched Cumberland style, papers floating round him, his cardigan now visible under the worsted waistcoat. He was too young to be afraid.

McDowell halted before the table.

He stood quite still. Behind him a dozen stalwart councillors of his own party congregated. Unwilling to admit that the position was, even now, untenable, they did not converge upon him and bear him bodily from the room.

He made them wait.

He buttoned his jacket, wiped his mouth with his handkerchief, and tucked the linen back into his cuff. Papers settled like flakes of snow in Brobdingnag.

McElroy wiggled his fingers and remained in readiness for combat.

'I wish to tender my resignation from this Council and

from all incumbent offices and posts,' McDowell heard himself say.

'No, Frank,' the Convener said, shaking his head. 'You're sick, man.'

'I'll put it in writing,' said McDowell, 'to make it official.'

He pivoted on his heel, nodded in semblance of a bow, then walked, unaided and unescorted, past the table and McElroy, down the short aisle and through the carved door into the sunlit corridors. Before anyone, friend or foe, could gather the will to come after him he had left the bull-ring by the back exit and stepped out of the limelight of public office for the first and last time in his life.

The girl was stored in the Interview Room on the ground floor. The view was to enclosed allotments with a few roses still in tardy bloom and a high wall of red brick which, within an hour of noon at this season of the year, would effectively slice off the sunlight. Still, one couldn't have everything : innocent and guilty alike shared the view and the table and the pleasant duck-egg blue of the décor. By this time, the girl would have been fed. McCaig glanced at his watch. Fifty minutes since Ryan had called in. Forty since Sellars had led the squad out; and just twenty-five since Ryan and the policewoman had returned with the girl in custody. No – McCaig reminded himself not to be hasty – she was not in custody just yet, though if a tenth of what Ryan had relayed turned out to be accurate, they had a case on several counts against the lady. It certainly appeared promising.

Corroborative proof arrived. Sellars knocked curtly on the door of the Chief's office. McCaig, pacing in unwonted impatience, barked at him to enter.

Sporting a trilby the colour of a cockpheasant and almost as feathery, Sellars breezed in grinning like a dairy-hand who's just had it off with the farmer's daughter and still feels the vibrations in his groin.

McCaig said, 'Got it?'

'Got it, Chief.'

'Give it here.'

Sellars handed over a plastic container. A label, thickly inked with details, was pasted to its lid. McCaig carried it to the desk and sat down. He held the box in two hands like an unexpected gift which had touched him deeply.

'Where was it?' he asked.

'Where she said it'd be,' Sellars replied. 'Under a floor-board, under the rug, under her bed. Some bed; just a cot, really.'

'Not well hidden?'

'Jesus . . . I mean, Chief, no; any raw copper could have found it. The board was loose and not properly fitted down.'

McCaig opened the box and looked at the contents with-out bothering to handle them. Glassine envelopes with a white powder stuffing, four of them.

'You checked this stuff?'

'Yes, Chief; it's heroin.'

'Are you sure?'

'Sure enough, sir.'

'Right,' said McCaig. 'And the hypo?'

'Used recently, I'd say.'

'How would you know?'

'Still wet.'

Twisting the box a little, McCaig peered more closely at the contents. 'No spoons or candles?'

'Not in the cache, sir, but there was a bloody big heap of spent matches around the place, on the floor.'

'Did you find the shoes or Cagoule?'

'Not a trace, Chief.'

'What are they doing now, the squad, I mean?'

'Searching the whole area.'

'You'll want to get back, then?'

'Well, I reckon they can do . . .'

'No, you'd better get back. We want a competent man on the job, don't we?'

'Yes, sir,' said Sellars. 'What about the prisoner, sir, the girl who owned this haul?'

'What about her?'

'Do we have her?'

'Well, Inspector, I didn't let her go.'

'No, sir, I mean . . .'

'She's downstairs; she'll be questioned shortly.'

'By Inspector Ryan?'

'No,' said McCaig. 'By Chief Superintendent McCaig.'

'Will that be all, sir?'

'Aye, that's all,' said McCaig. He offered back the plastic container. 'Labs and dabs on your way out.'

Sellars left stoically enough. He couldn't expect to have all the fun around the place. Besides, however efficient Sellars might be in certain matters, he was too aggressive to be much good at examinations.

McCaig took a cigarette from his packet, lit it and sat back. It was in his mind that if the girl *was* addicted to heroin, he could keep her downstairs long enough for withdrawal to commence. He could get anything he wanted out of her then, blackmail her. Not that he would ever stoop to such a lousy trick – but the thought was there. He would remember it; in fact, he would be haunted by it, taunted by it, during the course of the afternoon.

He lifted an outside line and rang Jebb's home number direct. Willy Rudkin was not the man to bring in on this, and if Willy saw fit to flaunt his right to precedent, it would be just too bad. For fifteen minutes McCaig spoke to Jebb on the telephone, eliciting much information, and a final promise, before returning the receiver to its cradle.

It was now ten minutes after one o'clock.

He lit another cigarette.

He had enough concrete evidence to charge the girl with being in possession of dangerous drugs, etcetera. He *could* make the charge before he began the questioning, warn her of her rights to call legal council, have her medically examined, and, up to a point, do what he wanted with her under the eye of her lawyer. He knew the rules, how to bend them and make them work to his advantage, and to the benefit of justice on that dim and distant day of trial which arresting officers weren't allowed to think about philosophically but, if they were shrewd enough, always did.

The decision was really already made; drugs and hypodermic were on their way to the various departments through which they would pass and from which, given a little time, reports would slide forth. Obviously, he would charge the girl with no crime and no misdemeanour. He would treat her as 'under suspicion' – and delay.

He flipped the switch of the intercom.

'Sheila, where's Harry Ryan?'

'Outside your door, sir.'

'And the Lawrence girl?'

'Room 2, sir, with Policewoman Greaves.'

'Stenographer?'

'Detective Constable Rice, sir.'

'Downstairs?'

'With Inspector Ryan.'

'Right, Sheila; you know where I'll be.'

'In Room 2, sir, with the prisoner.'

'Suspect,' said McCaig. 'With the suspect.'

He switched off and abruptly got to his feet.

The time was one-eighteen.

McCaig said, 'My name is McCaig. I'm Chief Superintendent, in charge of the investigation. This is Inspector Ryan, and the lady is Policewoman Greaves. The chap in the corner is a police stenographer, but you don't have to worry about him taking down everything you say. He won't be doing that yet awhile; though he may make a few notations, on my instructions. Do you understand?'

The girl nodded.

McCaig said, 'Are you comfortable enough, Miss . . . Mrs Lawrence?'

'Yes, sir.'

'You've had something to eat and drink?'

'Yes.'

'Fine.'

Ryan noticed the gentleness in McCaig's manner. It was almost as if the Chief were interviewing a child. Hilary Lawrence was seated on one side of the table and McCaig on the other. McCaig, though, did not lean his authority upon her, and Ryan, taking this lead, kept himself in the sunlit corner of the rectangular room, his back against the wall. Square, contained and in formal pose, Angela Greaves occupied a chair against the opposite wall and Rice was in the far corner. The room was large enough to hold them all without giving the suspect a sensation of threat or menace. Having changed during the waiting period, Hilary Lawrence was now dressed in a grey wool trouser suit and shiny block-heeled shoes. She seemed composed.

McCaig took two packets of cigarettes from his pocket and put them on the table.

'Help yourself,' he told the girl.

She took a cigarette from one of the packets and McCaig lit it for her.

She plucked in some smoke, held it, then said. 'You found the gear okay?'

'Just where you said it would be,' McCaig answered. 'When did you take the last shot?'

'Ten.'

'This morning?'

'Yes.'

'When will you need another?'

'I could do with one right now.'

'I take it that you really can't do without it?'

The girl smiled faintly, sourly, at his naivety, and shook her head.

'How long since you began taking drugs?' McCaig asked.

'Over a year, nearer two.'

'What sort of drugs?'

'Grass for starters then heroin.'

'Nothing in between?'

'No.'

'You've never taken hallucinogenic compounds?'

'No, never.'

'Where did you get the grass the first time?'

'Dennis got it.'

'Your husband?'

'Yes.'

'Where?'

'He brought it up from London one time.'

'Much of it?'

'No, just a wee block. He didn't flog it, if that's what you're thinking. We just used it ourselves.'

'You and your husband only?'

'Just the two of us.'

That might be lie number one, Ryan thought; he searched her expression for a sign, but found none. He expected McCaig to go for the jackpot, ask about the heroin and how she came by her supplies, but McCaig did not, switching back, a grasshopper in kid gloves.

'Miss . . . Mrs Lawrence,' said McCaig. 'I'm sure you realise that my principal concern is to find out what happened to Tom McDowell. You've indicated in pretty definite terms to the Inspector here that you may be able to throw light on the circumstances which led up to McDowell's death. Now, be clear on this point, I'm offering no deals or bribes of any sort. You'll certainly be charged under the Dangerous Drugs Act, but, at my direction, and with your co-operation, it is within my power to have you confined pending an appearance in court, not in a place of detention but in a hospital where you will receive adequate care and attention during what will be a period of withdrawal.'

'Cold turkey?' said the girl.

'Not necessarily,' said McCaig. 'There are other, less painful methods. None of them are pleasant, I know, but you've put yourself in this position, in defiance of the law and, so far as I can gather, have willingly relinquished yourself to whatever protection we may offer. Now, I don't pretend to understand it, but I have it on good authority that, with the co-operation of the patient, physical withdrawal and rehabilitation can be successfully effected. I repeat, this is not in any way a threat; you're here, you will be charged, and, probably, *probably*, convicted on one or more counts and sentenced to a period of imprisonment. In any case, you'll be confined to a cell prior to the setting of bail – *if* your counsel's plea for bail is successful, which isn't really likely under the circumstances. Are you with me so far?'

'I didn't have to tell you anything,' the girl said, matter-of-factly. 'It wasn't him,' she looked at Ryan, 'and it wasn't ... Listen, I understand okay what you mean. If I help you, you'll help me.'

'But be clear ...'

She showed a flicker of impatience, waving the cigarette like a piece of chalk. 'Yes, yes, mister, it's got to be *voluntary*. Think I'd be here at all if I didn't want to be? No, I don't want to be. *I don't want to be.* But I am.'

'You're frightened?' said McCaig.

To Ryan she did not appear frightened, but the Chief's conclusion was valid. McCaig was using a brutal kind of honesty with her, gentleness replaced by clear indications of necessity. The Chief would get what he wanted without sullying his conscience.

'Isn't that it?' said McCaig. 'Nothing to be ashamed of in being scared.'

'When I ... when I take it, just after the fix, that's when I'm scared. Funny,' she said, 'funny how it's then; even when I've got the whole of the score salted by and know I'll be okay for the next one and the next, that's when it gets me. It's about all that comes through. It doesn't mean anything; just keeps me right, you know.'

'Have you ever been without it for long?'

'Once or twice.'

'What did you feel then?'

'Scared too, but not about the same things. You can't think about anything else except how to get it. You're only scared in case you never do again.'

'Do you feel that way now?'

'I should, shouldn't I?'

'Do you?'

She considered the matter carefully, sounding down into the nerves and tissues of her body for an answer. 'Not yet.'

'Pardon my ignorance,' said McCaig, 'but I was under the impression that *all* that every addict ever worried about was maintaining a supply.'

'Used to be that way,' the girl said. 'With me, I mean.'

'What changed you?'

'Tom McDowell.'

McCaig licked his underlip, hesitating. 'Because he died?'

She nodded. 'When I'm turned on now, it isn't like it was at first. That's when I . . . no matter how bloody it gets sometimes, I can't get it out of my head that I'll die too. I don't want to kick it.'

'Kick?'

The word-play amused her a little. 'Kick,' she repeated. 'Kick the habit, or kick the bucket. I don't want to do either one, really.'

'But it seems it's one or the other?' said McCaig.

She shrugged.

'Tell me about Tom McDowell,' McCaig said. 'Tell me how you met him and what your relationship with him was all about and what happened to him on the night of his death. Will you do that, Mrs Lawrence?'

'Yes.'

'All right.' McCaig edged his chair a little closer to the table and folded his arms, not across his chest, but over the slight bulge of his belly. For a second or two there was silence in the room, then the girl began to talk, her tone even lower than before, very precise but the delivery faster.

She said, 'Mr McDowell and Tom first came to the garage back in July. They drove up in a Triumph Stag and asked for petrol. I hadn't seen either of them before. They got out of the car and went over to look at Dennis's buggy in the corner of the forecourt, and talked about it for a bit. Then they got into the Stag and drove off again.'

'Was the Sabre for sale at that time?' asked McCaig.

She shook her head. 'It didn't have a sale notice on it. But I was tight for money, and when I saw him . . .'

'McDowell?'

'Yes; the old man, Tom's father; when I saw him looking at it, it occurred to me that it would be okay to sell it and that I might be able to make a lot of cash on it.'

'Wouldn't Dennis be mad at you selling his car?'

'To hell with Dennis,' the girl said, without spite. 'He'd been gone a long time. Anyhow, McDowell came back about a week later, alone this time, and I'd got a notice on the Sabre saying it was for sale. We had some talk about it, and he said he thought he would want to buy it. He didn't quibble about the price, or anything, but he asked if he could take himself for a test drive.'

'You went with him?'

'No, I couldn't leave the garage. He took it out on his own.'

'How long?'

'Half an hour, forty minutes, something like that; then he came back and said he wanted it. I took the notice off it and drove it back into the shed. He came round four days later, like he said he would, gave me a cheque made out to cash for the whole sum, got in the buggy and drove off.'

'How did he come to the garage that day?'

'By taxi.'

'Right,' McCaig told her. 'Go on.'

'About ten days after that Tom appeared in the Sabre at the garage.'

'Where are we?' said McCaig. 'What month are we in now?'

'About the middle of September,' the girl said. 'It was late on Saturday evening and I'd . . . I'd been out in the afternoon. Nobody else was around the place. The chap who'd been looking after the garage had just gone home. I didn't want to be bothered with anybody right then, but Tom caught me coming out of the office, going upstairs to the house, you know. I told him the pumps were closed, but he said he wanted to talk to me. Tell you the truth, I didn't want to be disturbed.'

'You were on your way up to administer . . . ?'

She nodded.

'But you did stop long enough to talk to Tom?' said McCaig.

'To find out just what he wanted.'

'Which was?'

'To sell me back the Sabre.'

'Aye,' said McCaig. He glanced round, briefly, at Ryan; the inspector raised his brows. The revelations were diminishing now. Prospects for some grandiose mischief on the part of the boy receded. It was, Ryan realised, an act of rebellion on Tom's part, and must have required a certain

160

degree of anger. The little he had learned from McCaig about Tom's character and his relationship with the domineering old man helped put this piece of information in its proper perspective.

McCaig said, 'Did he give you a reason?'

'He was a lousy driver,' Hilary said. She peered up from her fingernails, and cocked her head again. 'He just was, you know. I mean, he couldn't drive for nuts. He kept having frights when the buggy would do things he couldn't control.'

'For example?'

'It wasn't a bad piece of machinery,' the girl said, 'but I could see his problem. He couldn't handle the shift, for one thing, and he would tramp the tyres without trying and his pedal control was all to cock, and . . . Anyhow, he wanted something else.'

'You said he wanted the money back?'

'That's what he asked for, but when I got on the chat with him he told me he would take a trade-in.'

'For what?'

'Pretty well anything, a Volks or an Anglia,' she replied. 'Like that.'

'In your opinion, Mrs Lawrence, was it only the difficulty in controlling the Sabre that made Tom want to exchange it?'

'It was too showy for him, too . . . what's it?'

'Ostentatious?' McCaig suggested.

'Okay. He was shy of it. He got flustered when people kept looking at him when he was parking or something, and he didn't like that.'

'He told you all this?'

'Kind of.'

'When?'

'Later.'

'You didn't brush him off, then?'

'No.'

'You were interested in making a trade for the buggy?'

She shrugged. 'I don't remember whether I was or not. Maybe I was. I could've placed him with a bodged-up box. He'd have been happy, and I'd have sold the Sabre to somebody else.'

'You reckoned his old man wouldn't like you doing that?'

'His old man was *his* problem : Christ, his old man really *was* his problem.'

'What do you mean?'

161

'He was hung up, Tom, I mean. The old bastard didn't give him a chance.'

'Did you . . . encourage Tom to trade-in, or sell, the Sabre?'

'Nothing I could do about it. He'd made up his mind. He'd made up his mind long before he came to see me. It wasn't up to the likes of me to try and make him see different.' The girl paused for almost a minute. She rubbed her nostrils with her knuckles, hard enough to transfer a smudge of oil to the tip of her nose. 'I told him to come back on Sunday night.'

'Why Sunday night?'

'Quietest time of the week.'

'Was there a reason for . . . for stealth?' asked McCaig.

'I dunno,' she said. 'I mean it, sir, I dunno why I did that.'

'No?' said McCaig.

She shook her head, the typical, repetitive gesture, wilder this time, signifying not merely denial but fretfulness.

McCaig said, 'Mrs Lawrence, what age are you?'

'Twenty-two.'

'Tom McDowell was nineteen; hardly young enough to lie on the other side of the generation gap, or to be considered a boy. We know, more or less, what he wanted with you. What did you want with him?'

More head shaking. She wasn't being evasive, Ryan decided, merely confused by the significance of complicated emotions none of which she could isolate and set in logic. McCaig seemed intent on running down motives. Ryan hoped that the Chief would not push the girl too far, tip her over into defensiveness or vagueness.

'Heroin's not cheap,' said McCaig. 'You had the money for the Sabre; how long would that keep you supplied?'

'Half a year,' she said. 'Maybe a bit longer.'

'Could it be that you saw in Tom McDowell a possible source of capital?'

'Beg pardon?'

'Could it be that you thought he was the type who would finance your habit, to some extent?'

Her face flared up, losing its gauntness, puffing out and reddening like some pretty reptile's. Her throat was very long and her fingers, inactive until that moment, writhed and knotted under the lip of the table.

162

'*I* didn't turn him on,' she cried. I wouldn't never do that to *anybody*, mister. *I* didn't turn him on.'

'All right,' said McCaig, placatingly. 'All right.'

'Look here, you don't know much about it, if you think the stuff's so easy to come by. I got just about enough to keep *me* going. I could pay for it and I could be pretty bloody sure of picking up more, regular, but I wasn't in the way of . . . of *sharing* with anybody, even if I was bitch enough to want to do it.'

'Why did your husband leave you, and a lucrative business in Brander Park?'

'He *loved* me.'

'Come off it,' said McCaig.

'One source of horse wasn't enough for two of us.'

'Don't give me the martyr bit,' said McCaig. 'I'm talking about heroin addiction. Shit and love, shit and loyalty don't mix.'

'Dennis . . .'

'What?'

'What's Dennis got to do with Tom McDowell?' she asked.

'I don't know yet; what about Dennis? Why did he bale out?'

'Mister, I don't . . .'

Ryan pushed himself away from the wall. 'Sir?'

Startled, perhaps irritated by the intrusion, McCaig gave him a terse, 'Yes?'

Ryan said, 'Mrs Lawrence, Dennis didn't take heroin, did he?'

'No.'

'What was his bag?' said Ryan, awkwardly. 'Pills, hash; what?'

'Both, anything really, but not whites.'

'He went to visit his relatives in London often?' said Ryan.

'Yes.'

'He brought back supplies with him?'

'Yes.'

'And fed some to you?'

'Yes, sometimes.'

'He wanted to pack in everything here and go to London?'

'Yes.'

'You wouldn't?'

'No.'

'Why not?'

'I wasn't hooked on . . . on his friends.'

'You went there, to London, and met his friends?'

'No.'

'Dennis got the heroin for you?'

'Yes.'

'In the hope that you'd be dependent enough to . . .'

'No,' the girl said. 'Well, maybe; but we didn't fight about it, or anything. He did it because he thought it would be good for me.'

'Why didn't he take to heroin, too?'

'I dunno. He didn't. He set up the contact, then he . . . he just drifted off to London. I didn't think much of it, thought he'd come back soon, but he didn't. The longer it got, me not having heard of him, the better . . . I mean, the easier it was to put him out of my mind.'

'He didn't even write to you, or ask for cash. It's *his* garage business, after all?'

'I kept hold,' the girl said. 'Look here, I kept hold on it.'

'Must have been difficult when you were on the junk?'

'It was,' she admitted. 'But I did it.'

'There was only you,' said Ryan. 'Just you, taking it, and hiding yourself in the garage? Nobody guessed, none of the part-time mechanics?'

'No; they didn't guess.'

'Did Tom guess?'

'No,' she said. 'He wouldn't have been able to guess.'

'You had some money and a source of supply. You didn't need Dennis and, in view of the fact that he didn't come back from London, Dennis apparently didn't need you. Is that a fair statement?'

'Yes.'

'Thank you,' said Ryan. He shuffled his feet and took up position with his shoulder-blades against the wall again, in the shadow which the failing sunlight cut out of the window corner.

'Yes,' McCaig said. 'I think that's clear enough. Did Tom return on Sunday night?'

'Yes,' the girl answered.

'In the Sabre?'

'Yes.'

'Though he was worried by the buggy, he continued to drive it?'

164

'He hadn't anything else to drive.'

'I see,' said the Chief. 'What happened on Sunday night?'

'Nothing. We talked.'

'Where, in the yard?'

'The office.'

'What did you talk about?'

'The Sabre, cars in general, and . . . about his father.'

'What did he say about his father?'

'I dunno, now. He didn't seem to like him. I think that was another reason he wanted rid of the Sabre; because his old man had given it to him. He was building up to something against his father. He was a sad boy – Tom, I mean. He didn't know what to do, because he'd never had much of a chance to find out what to do about, about anything. He was in that college place, studying something his old man wanted him to study. He didn't like it and he didn't get much fun out of the college because he had to work so hard to keep up. It's funny! He wanted to fail in a way, to force his father to pull him out of the college; then again there was something in him which was sort of persistent and proud and wouldn't let him start to fail. Funny!'

'Did he like you?'

'Yes.'

'Why?'

She lifted her shoulders, then, as if she could not complete the implied gesture of indifference, held them hunched, her head thrust forward. 'He wasn't scared of me.'

'How did he . . . treat you, Mrs Lawrence?' asked McCaig.

'He was sometimes nervous, and sometimes, when he forgot himself, very talkative. He didn't really know how to chat up somebody like me, though.'

'You'd say he wasn't experienced?'

'You could say that,' she replied. 'He wasn't experienced. It was . . .'

'Go on.'

'It was like me and the buggy had got tied together in his mind somehow. Funny! I mean, he wanted to flog or change the buggy to spite his father, to teach the old man a lesson, and he chatted me up for much the same sort of reason. He liked me as well, though.'

'You didn't exchange the Sabre?'

'No,' she said. 'But I hinted I might. I told him I'd give him lessons in driving it, and he said okay to that.'

'Why did you do that?'

'I . . . I liked him, I suppose.'

'He came back often?'

'Occasionally.'

'How many times?'

'Half a dozen.'

'That's more than once a week?'

'Yes.'

'You gave him lessons?'

'No.'

'What *did* you do?'

'Talked.'

'In the office?'

'Third time he came, I took him upstairs.'

'Why?'

'It was cold that night.'

'I see,' said McCaig. 'He was at his ease in your apartment?'

'No,' the girl said. 'He was always nervous.'

'Do you think he knew anything about you?'

'Only what I told him; not about the drugs.'

'But he knew you were married?'

'I told him I was separated.'

'He definitely didn't know you were an addict; the attraction wasn't towards heroin?'

'No.'

'Are you quite . . . ?'

'It was *me* he wanted.'

'Right,' said McCaig. 'Now we're getting somewhere. He wanted you, physically?'

'Yes.'

'Did he make advances?'

'He didn't know how to start.'

'Come off it.'

'It's true, mister, he didn't even know how to find out if I was willing or not.'

'Were you willing?'

A shrug was the answer.

McCaig said, 'Didn't you encourage him?'

'Why should I?'

'You tell me.'

166

'I dunno if I did or not. I didn't. I wasn't attracted to him that way, really. If he'd tried, I might have. I felt sorry for him.'

'But you still felt he might be . . . useful.'

'No.'

'That he might be useful if you ever needed help, financial help, say?'

'I didn't think that far ahead.'

'How far ahead did you think?'

'I just waited, not thinking,' she said. 'I imagined he'd get fed up and chuck it, or find himself another girl, or something.'

'Did he have another girl?'

'He said he hadn't. He told me, one time, he'd fancied a girl in college, some girl he'd known for years, but he didn't think she'd do that sort of thing . . .'

'What sort of thing?'

'Love . . .'

'Intercourse, you mean?'

'Anything like that.'

'Had he tried, do you think?'

'I told you, he didn't know how to try. That was the whole bloody trouble with him. He didn't know what to do about *anything*. He wasn't hardly even sure what he wanted; all he knew about it was all the things you're supposed to find out gradually. Not his sort of things at all.'

'You've lost me,' McCaig admitted.

'You think he was simple; well, he wasn't simple. There was nothing simple about him. He just hadn't ever been given the chance to find out what was really right and what was really wrong – because his old man rammed everything down his throat.'

McCaig pinched the bridge of his nose and made small rolling gestures with finger and thumb.

'When did it happen?' he said, muffled. 'When did he try it?'

'Saturday.'

'Saturday, October 15th?'

'Yes, that Saturday night.'

'Tell me, please.'

'I'd been out to pick up a wreck, out in the Land Rover. I got back late. He was waiting for me. He'd put the buggy

167

away inside the big shed and there was nobody there but him.'

'What time was this?'

'Close to nine.'

'Right.'

'He asked if he could come up. I told him no, he couldn't.'

'Why not?'

'I was in need of a shot, that's why. I was beginning to go over, even.'

'He noticed this?'

'Yes, but I told him I had 'flu coming on.'

'What did he say?'

'He said I should go to bed.'

'You mean he offered to put you to bed?' said McCaig.

'Something like that. I still told him he couldn't come up.'

'How did he take it?'

'He didn't seem any different from usual,' Hilary replied. 'But then I was having it bad, quite bad, and I wasn't that much interested in him. If I'd been okay I'd maybe have noticed how he was.'

'How was he, then?' McCaig pushed.

'Desperate,' the girl said. 'I think he'd made up his mind, and underneath he was determined.'

Ryan could believe it; it wasn't quite a 'classic' clinical description of a rapist, but it had certain positive connections. The warring elements of a strong sexual drive, a suppressed disposition and a characteristic inability to take the initiative, lay at the back of several cases he had handled, when otherwise respectable men – usually not so young as Tom McDowell – cut loose and committed some act of uncharacteristic stupidity and violence.

'What did you do?' McCaig asked.

'Left him in the forecourt,' the girl said. 'I told him he could come back on Sunday after tea; then I went upstairs into the flat. I thought that was that, but he followed me. I didn't even notice that he was following me. I went into the flat and right into the bedroom and took off my jacket and started to take out the gear. When I looked round he was standing in the bedroom door, watching me. I got the message, then.'

'How did you react?'

'Shouted at him, told him to get out. He wouldn't go. I didn't really think about him, or notice anything about him.

I was three hours past the time for the needle and starting to crawl for it. It wasn't *all* that bad – it would get worse – but the need didn't leave much room in my mind for anything else.'

'You knew what he wanted?'

'Yes,' she said. 'He wanted me, to have sex with me.'

'How did you feel about it?'

'If I hadn't been so far into the drift, I'd have given it to him just to get rid of him. That was all I really wanted, to get rid of him and get on with spooning out the fix.'

'He wouldn't go?'

'He asked me if I was ill, then he came right into the bedroom and shut the door. I was sitting on the bed, holding myself, shivering a bit. My nose was just starting to drip and my skin was crawling. The bloody medicine was right under my feet but I couldn't do anything about it. I mean, he'd been so polite, so shy and nervous and reserved and so . . . respectful up till then. The contrast told me, even through the sickness, that he'd made up his mind to do it to me, and it wouldn't have mattered if I was dying. It was a cruel streak in his nature I wouldn't have suspected. At least, I thought at the time it was cruel.'

'He didn't leave?'

She shook her head. 'He didn't say a word. He just came at me and pushed me, hard, and I fell on the bed. He started to . . . put his hands all over me, hard, rough, clumsy, sort of.'

'Did you fight him?'

'I was shouting at him.'

'Did he remove your clothing?'

'No,' she said. 'He got me on my back, and . . .'

'I'm sorry,' said McCaig, 'but you've got to tell me, at least the substance of what happened. Did he effect intercourse with you?'

Now, either the girl was lying her head off, Ryan thought, or Jebb had been incredibly negligent in making his report.

'No,' she said. 'He just . . . handled me.'

'And what did you do?'

'Lay there. After . . . after . . . I don't know how long, he stopped.'

'Was he excited?' said McCaig. 'Aroused?'

'I don't know. I couldn't make it out. I wasn't interested in him. I mean, when you shoot juice, you lose the other thing, the feelings. I got myself together and told him I'd do anything he wanted and let him do whatever he wanted with me, but he had to wait, to get out for ten minutes.'

'How did he answer?'

'He didn't say anything. He just stood back from the bed against the door. It's not a very large room. I got up and looked at him. Sitting on the bed, I was, and he was standing. I'd never done it in front of anybody before, except Dennis, and nobody, except Dennis, even knew I did it. I was desperate, okay, beginning to think I'd go right over the top. It wasn't really that bad, not really, not physically, but I imagined it was. I think I started to swear at him, then I got down on my knees and took the gear out from under the board and put it on the bed.'

'What did Tom do?'

'I dunno. I was shaking. It was hard enough to concentrate on the magic without watching him, too. I reckon he watched me. He must've done. I got it set up and put it in, a big one, and sat there on the side of the bed waiting until it hit me. It was the best I'd ever had.'

She closed her eyes at the recollection, but there was no memory of relief, of peace, in the twitching movements of her fingers, or her long legs under the table, or in the tensions which manifested themselves all over her. Ryan could not quite imagine how she felt, even though he deliberately borrowed the remembrance of the symptoms of illnesses from the past. He glanced at his wrist-watch; she couldn't be withdrawing yet, not seriously, yet the evidence of the first gradual erosion of her personality was visibly apparent.

'And afterwards?' said McCaig.

'Took only a minute for it to hit right through me. I felt like I always feel, only a bit more so.'

'How do you feel?' said McCaig. 'Lethargic?'

'Normal.'

'Oh!'

'Satisfied, very, very satisfied. I didn't want him around. I just wanted to be alone to enjoy it, you see.'

'Tom was still in the room?'

'Yes, still there, standing in the corner.'

'Was he shocked?'

'I dunno.'

'Come on,' said the Chief, 'you must have some idea. I

presume your faculties were functioning again in some sort of fashion. Did he say anything?'

'He didn't; I did. I said something about "now you know".'

'He made a reply?'

'Look here,' Hilary said. 'I know how he was; he was shocked, okay, but he was kind of glad too, in an evil sort of way. I can't explain it better than that. I lay back on the bed. I wanted him to leave me in peace, but I wasn't screaming mad at him. It didn't really much matter to me, you see. It was okay what he did, really. I didn't care what he thought of me. I mean, *I* didn't care. You mark that, it was me, *me, not Tom,* who didn't care.'

'All right,' said McCaig, with a faint trace of impatience. 'What happened?'

'He started to talk. He spoke funny; cold, like a recording of a voice, like one of those voices you get on the telly, all electronic and distant. He told me he wanted . . .'

The girl crouched forward on the chair, folding the ledge of the table's edge into her gut, leaning her arms upon it, her face down. Ryan could see the cap of reddish-fair hair and a single bead of sweat on the prominent cheekbone of her left profile. She closed her eyes. The voice dropped down another decibel or two, becoming so low and murmurous that he had to strain to hear it. McCaig did not ask her to speak out, did not interrupt. It struck Ryan that she was tugging the perfect memory of that evening out of her as certain patients in hypnotic trances dredge up the long-forgotten traumas of childhood or, if reports are to be given credence, of previous incarnations. McCaig was silent now, no longer leading her. Angela Greaves had stopped staring, shifting her gaze four or five feet to the left, fixing her attention on the blank pastel-painted wall. The stenographer chewed his pencil and admired the creases in his trousers legs, bent over in thick emulation of the girl's pose. The account came out of her without halt; long, sinuous strings of words conjuring up images which were simultaneously erotic and pathetic, spooling out of her lips like a continuous tape.

'He told me he wanted me to take off my clothes. He didn't touch me, come near the bed, just said he wanted me to strip. I told him not to be daft. He didn't threaten me, or anything, not with his fists. He just stood in the corner and told me he would report about the gear and the addiction if I didn't do what he wanted. He was worse, just then, than me. I'd got my shot. I could handle it okay. But he couldn't. It was too much for him. I saw it. It hadn't anything to do with being afraid of him or of him squawking on me. It was just the way he *was,* left me no choice. He was big enough for being a man, but his face, his expression, was like a kid's, a young boy's, really blanked out, except for the colour of the blood shot all through it. He was shaking, his hands on the ends of his wrists, and his neck. I kind of shrugged, and started to take off my clothes. I got the shirt off and my slacks. I had on panties, a bra and socks, man's socks. Funny!

'He watched me stripping. I wasn't showing-off, not really, but I thought if he wanted it, he wouldn't be happy unless he got it properly. Okay, so I put it on a wee bit, sort of. I let him see. I don't think he'd seen one before in the . . . really. I thought he'd come on then, into the bed with me, but he couldn't move. I don't mean he wouldn't, I mean *he couldn't.* He couldn't seem to move out of that corner. He said for me to take off the rest as well, to stand up and do it. So I stood up on the bed and took the rest off.

'I wasn't really hot or excited – because of the horse, I suppose. But it was coming through to me just enough to keep me going and not, that far, to mind too much about it. I felt . . . felt sort of powerful, for a while; scornful of him. But I didn't make fun of him. I could see it was the biggest thing he'd ever made himself do, or let himself do. He *had* to do it. He'd come to me and gone through all this because he thought *he* should do it and not have it done *to* him. It's like that with some men, even from the first. God, yes, I've had more than Dennis, before Dennis. Even a couple, or three or four, after Dennis and I got hitched. Dennis knew about it, about sex, and he'd been down there in London – never mind London, you can do it anywhere with a crowd – and nothing, nothing could shock me because I don't believe it *should* shock you. Anyhow, I'd seen it all before, okay, with men. It wasn't any more new to me than sticking in the needle, and meant less, much less. But not to Tom McDowell. It meant more to him than what I was showing him, or anything I might do to him with all the things I was showing him. It wasn't just a work-out he wanted, he wanted to be an aggressor, to show himself, not me, that he could . . . could go further, deeper, right into it.'

'But he *couldn't*?'

'You think I'm ignorant, don't you? You think I'm *dirt*. Well, I thought I was dirt too. Really! I thought I was smart because I had learned to exist on a tolerance dose of shit and could still work and had it all going good towards one purpose. It was as far between me and Tom McDowell as you can get, as far as the distance between here and China. But I thought I was dirt. I didn't care about me. What he was doing didn't matter. He didn't hurt me. He didn't whip me, or kick me; that was something, believe me. Okay, so I didn't argue with him, protest. I did what he told me to do, not excited, not more than maybe lukewarm, not really caring. In the back of my head, I kept thinking it was better me than somebody else, some virgin who'd only shout and get him into bother.

'So I did everything he told me to do. I don't know where he got his ideas – out of dirty books, likely – but he had some weird ones. I went through the whole programme, on the bed, on the floor, over the railing of the bed, wherever and however he wanted, and he looked at me and didn't touch me.'

'Wait,' said McCaig. 'He didn't touch you at all?'

'No.'

'Didn't he undress?'

'No. All he did was take out his . . . himself.'

'Penis,' said McCaig; the clinical term sounded harsh, obscene and unsubtle in the context.

'Yes. He took it out and let it . . . he didn't do anything, touch himself or anything, and he didn't touch me with it, didn't even try to.'

'Was his organ . . . erect?'

She shook her head. 'No, it wasn't.'

'Is that the truth?' said McCaig. 'He remained flaccid and impotent during all this . . . show?'

'Yes.'

'Christ!'

'I saw it too. After he'd had me put myself every way he had in mind, he got more and more . . .'

'What?' McCaig demanded.

'I dunno. I can't find the right . . . Look here, he got more panic-stricken and told me to do things to him. It wasn't normal. I mean, it wasn't like a man who had you in that sort of position would do it, tell you and force you to do it and enjoy it and come up, up hard. It was like there were two parts of him. One part had the knowledge without the meaning and wanted all of it; and the other part, the dangerous part, stopped it. None of it seemed to show, though. I mean, he didn't cry or shout or grunt and snarl at me, or anything like that. He told me what I had to do, like reading it out of a book. God, he hardly even knew the right words of the things, the parts.

'I did it. I wanted it over with, you see; so I did what he told me, and put my back into it, only because I wanted him to shoot and get it over. I . . . I mouthed him and touched him and put myself against him, even got rough-house with him and dragged him against me. I wouldn't have been like this at all if I hadn't not cared. I just wanted to be alone for a while. That was really all I thought about, though I didn't feel hurt or humiliated in my pride because I was doing nothing to get him up.

'He got . . . got *something*. I pulled him down on me, and he got frantic. He was lying on me, across the bed. I was trying to help him, but I couldn't help him, no matter what I did, which was more things than he asked. I mean, you can't do it with the body, just the body, no matter how desperate you are. I would have thought maybe you could, except when you're drunk or in bad need of a jag or something like that, sick or in mourning, but not normally.

'Lying across me with his thing on my belly, but no weight to him, as if he was beginning to be polite, or afraid of hurting me; that feeling was coming through him, and whatever there was in strength kind of died again. Suddenly I was sick-tired of it, not disgusted, just tired of it, and stopped trying.

'He got up off me, and went back into the corner by the door, with his back to me. I think, maybe, if he'd waited, if I'd started over on him slowly, it might have come to something. But I couldn't do it, couldn't shake it up, you know. He didn't say anything, nothing at all. I got up off the bed and asked him if he was finished, and he nodded. He seemed okay, not too bad, leaning against the wall, buttoned up. I didn't see any pain on his face, or if I did I managed to ignore it. I had enough of my own problems. I didn't realise what it was, what it was doing to him, and that I – *me*, not just my body, was part of it.

'Anyhow, I took my clothes and went out into the toilet. When I was in there, I began to think about it, to see that I'd been lucky. I mean, he hadn't a rubber, and I quit taking the pill ages ago. I could've been in trouble. Anyhow, I thought about me and about him and how, bad and all as it'd been, it had been *something*. I hadn't had anything – I don't mean sex – for a long, long time. But, but I still didn't . . .

'I thought I'd got out okay. I thought, too, I'd pull together long enough to give him coffee and keep him with me until he'd come round. I mean, I didn't want him going out in a bad state and maybe causing questions which would bring authority round to knock on my door. I was thinking about myself, that's all, just myself.

'How long I was in the toilet, I don't know. Ten minutes, a quarter of an hour, maybe even longer. Eventually I got dressed and went out into the living room and poked about, looked at the stove and filled up a pot to boil coffee or something. The bedroom door was open, but I didn't look in. I didn't really want to see him until he was ready to come out. It was another five minutes before I noticed him sitting on the side of the bed.

'First glance, I couldn't make it out, then he turned and looked at me, and I saw that he had his sleeves up and the spike in his hand and was putting it in. I ran into the room, shouting. I saw he'd watched me close enough to know how to fix it – though God knows how he ever got it into the spike and through the needle into his tubes. He'd messed it all up, spilling, bleeding himself a little, and had wasted fifteen grains out of five packets – okay, not wasted, because he'd put the spike into his arm four times and was sliding in a fifth when I got him. I didn't know how much had gone into him, how many grains. It's not hard to find the vein, so I guessed he'd got enough through to make it dangerous for him.

'I snatched the spike away. He didn't try to stop me. He just sat on the bed holding his arm bent, looking down at the spots of blood on his elbow. I didn't know what to do. I got him on his feet and started to walk him. I'd heard that was the right thing. I thought he might vomit it up, but I wasn't certain. I'm not like Dennis; I haven't had much truck with addicts. How was I to know what was an overdose and what it would do to him?'

'You realised it might kill him?'

'Yes, okay, I realised that much,' the girl said. 'I thought I should keep him warm, and put his jacket on him again. He wasn't saying anything, not a word. He wasn't doing anything much either, sprawled on the chair in front of the stove. I could see it coming over him, rising up like a wave or something, and I knew he was going right under. I didn't panic, didn't fluster, not just then. But I knew I had to get him out.'

'Why?'

'Don't be daft,' the girl said. 'He couldn't die in my place.'

'You could have called an ambulance.'

'I was stoned, still, and not going to have . . . Look here, I did what I thought was right. I put on some outdoor clothes.'

'What clothes?'

'I don't . . . Dennis's Cagoule, and a pair of his shoes, and . . . I don't remember. I went down and pulled the buggy out of the shed and brought it to the foot of the stairs, backed right up. It was quiet out. The court's not brightly lit at the best of times, except for the lights of the house on it. I went back up to the flat.

'He was lying on the floor. I got down beside him. I could tell now he was going into a coma or something. I asked him how he felt. His mouth was moving. I put my ear down to it, and he said something.

'You know what he said?'

'Tell me?' McCaig said.

'He said he was sorry.'

'*What?*'

'That's what he said; he said he was sorry.'

'Aye,' said McCaig. 'Yes.'

'You see?' the girl said. 'He wanted to tell me what it was, why he'd used the spike. I thought, until then, he'd wanted to cool it and make it work for him. But it wasn't that at all.'

Ryan was hardly breathing now. He could not for the life of him have maintained McCaig's apparent detachment. The girl sank back from the edge of the table. The bead of sweat was matched to its mate on the other cheekbone, both clinging, not viscous enough to trickle down her skin. She sank back and tilted the chair on its hind legs as if she would throw herself over backwards with it. Nobody in the room moved to prevent her. She held the chair in balance, her legs in the grey trousers wide open, and her arms slack by her sides. For an instant, the low voice became hoarse with an emotion which Ryan could not begin to define.

'Would you believe it?' she said. *'He was ashamed.'*

McCaig held the long pause, dragged it out by fishing a cigarette from his packet, putting it in his mouth and lighting it. Ryan was glad of the respite, the chance to bank down the sudden crackle of unanswerable questions which flared up in him.

'Yes,' said the Chief, sibilantly. 'Now please go on.'

The sun had gone from the garden, syphoning off all warmth. The lounging chair rested on the flagged patio which jutted between rosebeds from a base hard against the kitchen wall, baffled against wind – had there been a wind – by the frost-white metal of fuel bins and the conical tar-black drum of the heating system. The sun lay south-west, rimmed with flat cloud, and cool, touching only the topmost blooms of the ramblers on the wall at the foot of the garden, making the puckered bunches momentarily pink once more. Heels crooked and feet raised, back and neck supported by floral-patterned cushions, McDowell lay motionless, face lifted towards the faded disc above the wall's horizon. He was dressed in the grey-striped trousers of his business suit and a starched white shirt, informally open at the throat. As a defence against the encroaching chill, he had donned a cashmere sweater of pale lime-green. Gargantuan Polaroids covered the upper part of his face so completely that Dent could not tell at first whether he was awake or asleep. On the flagstone by his right hand stood a long-stemmed wine-glass, empty, and a deep wooden box of cigars, full save for one vacant slot in the upper stratum. A long brown butt, lobbed five yards out on the apron of lawn, spumed out gradual smoke which, so still was the afternoon, rose like a thread of fine copper wire high into the air above the house-top.

Discreetly Dent stowed the Gladstone bag behind the fuel bin and advanced, as softly as his fallen arches would allow, on the reclining figure of the councillor.

'Frank?' he enquired.

'What do you want?'

'I . . . just happened to be passing.'

'Who called you? Mildred?'

'No, no, as a matter of fact, it was Ronald Shaw.'

'Shaw,' said McDowell. 'Yes, it would be.'

'What happened?'

'Didn't Ronnie tell you?'

'What's wrong with you, Frank? Can I do anything?'

'No.'

'Frank . . .'

'Go away.'

'You must be frozen. It's no time of year for sitting out.'

'You've seen me. Now you can go.'

'Come into the house.'

'Stop it, will you?' McDowell said, wearily.

Dent squatted on the patio, heavy-thighed, grunting, a hand out to steady himself on the frame of the chair. He debated with himself the advisability of proceeding, then said, 'According to Ronald, you made quite a scene in the Hall. Everybody was most concerned.'

'Concerned about what?'

'About you, of course.'

'They needn't worry. I meant exactly what I said. I'm resigning.'

'Uh-huh!' said Dent, shifting his weight. 'Is that wise, do you think?'

McDowell gave no reply.

Dent said, 'Everybody understands. You're not obliged to resign because of what happened. Nobody will hold it against you. After a decent lapse of time, when you're yourself again . . .'

'I don't want to be myself again.'

'Why don't you take Mildred off for a holiday; a cruise would be nice, don't you think?'

'No.'

'Frank, you're just not yourself. It's perfectly understandable. As your physician, I really must insist that you take it easy for a while. Shock makes terribly strange inroads into a man. If only you'd . . .'

'No.'

'A change of scene, for Mildred's sake.'

'What has she told you?'

'Mildred? Nothing; not a thing.'

'Look, I don't need your help.'

178

'You're not sleeping, are you? You're not getting enough sleep.'

McDowell did not answer for a while, then he turned his head. Dent watched the lips moving, tried to peer behind the opaque greenish-tinted orbs of the glasses, to diagnose condition and degree through the pupils. He could not even make out the whites, only miniature reflections of his own visage, fretful and whiskered as a wolfhound's, framed in puddles of submarine sunlight. A chatter of starlings skimmed the grass, changing the sites of their foraging, lording off a yearling robin from his feeding by the last of the raspberry canes. Evening restlessness was beginning to affect the birds. Rooks cawed in unseen trees in the central estates of Mossburn, and a gull, sea-spray white and a stranger in the area, lofted itself briefly into sight over the attics against the sky, then slid away again with a single apologetic yelp.

'That's true,' McDowell said. 'I'm not sleeping well.'

'Quite usual, quite usual,' said Dent, on more familiar ground now. 'That, at least, I can cure.'

'I don't want your potions,' McDowell said.

'They're quite safe, Frank. I'm not daft. It's much the same stuff as I gave Mildred, and they did her nothing but good. You can't deny it. She's looking – and behaving – well enough, considering her trying time, don't you think?'

McDowell touched his middle finger to the arch of the glasses, pushing them back against the flesh of his face. He was still angled toward the doctor, but might have been staring past him for all Dent knew.

Strange, Dent thought, how far back into the past Tom now seemed. Great Heavens, he could hardly remember what the laddie looked like. How was it, really, with Frank and Mildred? Even if only an iota of what he'd heard by way of gossip – to which he gave unusual professional credence – and the sum of the incidents and actions which he'd spotted for himself were accurate, then it must be obvious to a medical man, even to one who is not also a friend, that the McDowells were going through the mill in more than one sense. Tragedy did that to people; he had seen sufficient of it to be certain of his judgement.

If he had been asked to define the spasm which had jarred Frank that morning and created in consequence such wild, lunatic scenes in the Council Chamber, he would have dubbed it simply as *Nerves*, result of loss and mental suffering, of stress, and let it go at that. He assumed now – as he had not assumed before Tom's demise – that the relationship between father and son, though low key and not demonstrative, was normal; that, however McDowell behaved to his wife, the family nest was snug upon its branch. Yet it was Frank, not Mildred, who harboured still the debilitating virus of guilt. To smother it, as he might have chemically smothered a germ of lesser order, Dent would resort to pills.

'I've just the thing for you, Frank.'

'Have you?' said McDowell. He rolled back into reclining position and rearranged his feet, heel propped on toe, as if to make a sight large enough to draw a bead on the sun.

Dent hoisted himself to his feet, crabbed back to the bin and lifted his bag. Using the bin-lid as a counter, he opened the bag, rummaged in it, brought out a dark blue bottle with a sanded-glass stopper. Carefully, he counted out six glossy blue pills, dropped them one by one into another small jar, and took it over to McDowell.

'One at a time, at night, with water, and you'll sleep like a top, Frank,' he said.

Reluctantly McDowell took the jar in the palm of his hand.

'What are they?' he asked.

'Don't worry about them,' said Dent, who never admitted patients to the mysteries of medical nomenclature. 'They'll do you no harm.'

McDowell put his tongue between his teeth, then closed his fist on the jar.

Dent nodded approvingly.

'And think about going away,' he said. 'I would, if I were you. Do you both the world of good, under the circumstances.'

'Yes,' said McDowell. 'I'll think about it.'

'A nice long trip,' Dent said, 'with Mildred.'

'Yes,' said McDowell. 'With Mildred.'

McCaig had detached a part of himself completely from the operation. It was another of those inexplicable tricks which some officers have to learn and others, tougher and baser in nature than he had ever been, are gifted with almost from birth. He had learned it thoroughly, though, and could remove the emotional skin from his mind as easily as a poulterer could pluck the feathers from a chicken. The watch, the cigarette, the fading light in the hollow room, the distant, motionless figures of subordinates, all helped in the process. Mercifully he found that he was no longer capable of being shocked or surprised by anything that the girl might tell him. Armoured, or its reverse, he would move into the second phase of the interrogation – the interview, to give it its polite name – as calculatingly as possible, sensitive now to facts and distortions of facts and not to the sophistry of motivations and the dead-ends of behaviourism.

He inhaled tobacco smoke. 'Yes. Now, please, go on.'

'I guessed you'd get to me sooner or later,' the girl said. 'I mean, it would've been a miracle if you hadn't. If you hadn't, maybe I'd have come to you.' She shrugged, lightly. 'I dunno : maybe I'd just have gone on. It wasn't him dying that scared me; it was him being ashamed. I didn't know it still happened. Something like that, like finding it, makes you wonder. I didn't want him to die on me.'

'What did you do to prevent it?'

'You know what I did. I got him on my back and out into the air, and down into the buggy.'

'Was he conscious?'

'Not really.'

'All right; you got him into the Sabre.'

'It was in my mind I'd take him home. I went into the office and looked up the book – I remembered it was Mossburn – and got the address and checked it out on the town plan on the wall. It was the nearest place I could take him – home.'

'What time was it?'

'No idea. I wasn't thinking about the time.'

'How long had you been together, upstairs?'

'No idea, either. You can't count it out, when things like that are happening.'

'Then give me an opinion.'

'Two hours, more.'

'Right.'

'I intended to take him home. I drove to his old man's house in Rodale Avenue, and even went up the drive. I was going to leave him in the buggy and ring the bell and get out, but I couldn't do it.'

'No?'

'Not with all them cars in the drive and the house lit up and full of people. I mean, it was likely they'd all be drunk. Tom told me one time about how they got drunk on Saturday nights, respectaby drunk. Anyhow, I wasn't leaving him there, not knowing what they'd do to him.'

'Explain that,' McCaig said.

'They might have thought he was drunk, boozed up, and started sticking fingers down his throat, or just put him to bed to kip it off, or something.'

'You could have waited.'

'Like hell, I could. I should've had more sense than to take him there in the first place. I should've taken him to a hospital straight off.'

'There are hospitals closer than Ottersford.'

'Yes, but right in the middle of town. I was still looking out for myself. I checked him over. He was in a coma. Anyway, Ottersford's supposed to be the best. Dennis used to tell me what it was like in hospitals, where'd they'd leave you waiting round empty rooms for hours while they decided where was the best place to treat you. The best place for Tom, and for me, was Ottersford. At least, that's the way I looked at it then.'

'Did you appreciate the urgency of the situation?'

'Yes. I was scared, too, by this time, and I drove fast. I nearly had the Sabre over three or four times. I've never driven *right* after a fix before, but it did funny things to me. I got him there in about half an hour. That wasn't bad, considering.'

'Why did you abandon him where you did?'

'I took the wrong gate,' the girl said. 'But I didn't abandon him. A doctor or somebody came running out right after I stopped. I wasn't hanging around.'

'As a matter of interest,' said McCaig, 'how did you get back to Thane?'

'I walked through the woods and found a bridge over the river, and got on to the road. I started to walk, don't know which way, then a car came and I thumbed it, and it stopped.'

'A car,' said McCaig, surprised in spite of himself. 'You got a hitch into town?'

'Yes.'

'Still wearing the Cagoule and the sports shoes?'

'I took the Cagoule off and wrapped it up small and put it

up under my jumper. If you want to know who was in the car, they were English.'

'Aye,' said McCaig.

'They were going home, driving all night, a man and his wife, not young. If they hadn't been lost, and if it hadn't been raining ...'

'What did you tell them?'

'I said I'd been out with a boy and he'd tried to get fresh and when I wouldn't have it, he'd ditched me. They weren't very sure of me, but they believed it okay. I directed them back to the Lannerburn Road and into Thane. The man, the Englishman, was driving fast to make up for getting lost. They'd been on holiday up north, and wanted to get on to the motorway before it got too busy with dawn traffic. He dropped me off near the Park; I told him how to get on to the Glasgow Road, and that was it. I was home about ... I think about one o'clock.'

'When did you find out that Tom had died?'

'Next day, about tea-time, on the telly.'

'Why didn't you come forward, then?'

'Nothing I could do for Tom, was there? He was dead.'

'But you thought we *might* trace you?'

'Fuzz aren't stupid. Dennis told me some things about fuzz. I thought you *might* find me, okay?'

'How did you occupy yourself last week?'

'Best I could.'

'You were short of the narcotic, you must have been?'

'I managed.'

'How?'

'Kept inside most of the time, told the chaps who work for me I was sick.'

'They – these part-timers – didn't have any idea that you were on junk?'

'No idea.'

'How did you disguise the fact?'

'I didn't, not really. I've been lucky. I've always had the makings and the cash to buy the makings. I got it fairly good; you know what controlled tolerance doses are?'

'A myth,' McCaig said.

'No myth, mister. I knew from the start if I stepped it up, it would either kill me or set me back so much I wouldn't be able to work enough to meet the payments. I had it under control. I knew what I needed, what I could take and get off with, and it was that much and never any more. Where'd you get your notions about horse, anyhow? The only expert's the chap with an armful of fangs, and it's between him then and what he's made of.'

'You didn't endeavour to contact your husband?'

'It wouldn't have done any good. Anyhow, I don't know where he is.'

'And the supplier?'

The girl hesitated. 'It was hard last week. I thought I was going right into it three or four times. I nearly chucked in the hand and quit, tried to register . . .'

'You can't register.'

'God, don't I know it. But I could've come to you.'

'Why didn't you?'

'I wanted to see if I *could* peg out; if I had the guts to do it. Anyhow, when I was thinking about not having enough and dragging myself from going to the gear and cooking up a fix, playing it out by the bloody clock even, I didn't have anything left to think about Tom McDowell with, or to worry about how close you were getting to me. I didn't even have time to worry about feeling sorry or ashamed or anything like that.'

'How long were you obliged to "peg out"?'

'Six days.'

'You obtained a fresh supply on Saturday?'

'Yes.'

'Didn't it occur to you that your contact might have become worried by all the publicity and closed his shop?'

'It occurred to me.'

'And if that had happened?'

'I'd have come straight to you.'

'But you didn't come to us; presumably your regular contact showed up?'

'Yes.'

'On Saturday last?'

'It's always Saturdays; every two weeks.'

'And always the same amount?'

'Always.'

'A very efficient organisation.'

'You want to know about it, I suppose?'

'Naturally,' said McCaig.

'I can't tell you much.'

'Just tell us what you can.'

'I'm not defending anybody; okay?'

'Right.'

'I don't know his name, and I don't know where he lives. I only ever meet with one man.'

'Where?'

'The balcony of the Argyll picture-house in Glasgow, in Springthorp Street.'

'That's always the meeting place?'

'Always.'

'What time?'

'Evening. I go there about six, up into the balcony and wait, and he finds me.'

'You've never diverted from that set-up?'

'Never.'

'Who made the initial contact?'

'The man did.'

'With you, directly?'

She shook her head. 'With Dennis. I didn't have the monkey then. That was how I got started, straight in. He met Dennis in a pub in Glasgow ...'

'Which?'

'I dunno; I mean, I *really* don't know. Dennis saw him twice, then arranged the regular pick-up. I was on my own about a month later, and it's been that way since.'

'What do you pay him?'

'One pound a grain.'

'Isn't that cheap?'

'I wouldn't know. Yes, I think it's cheap. Maybe it's cut.'

'Does the strength vary from batch to batch?'

'I haven't noticed.'

'How many grains do you take per day?'

'Four.'

'Don't you ever want or need more?'

'Yes, but I don't give in.'

'It takes effort?'

'Yes, but not so much as you'd think.'

'You have a routine?'

'I told you.'

'You pay this man what? Sixty pounds a fortnight?'

'Fifty.'

'He gives you discount?'

She shrugged. 'I suppose so. Fifty pounds in fives in an

envelope and he gives me twenty-eight shots made up in packets.'

'When are you due to make the next pick-up?'

'Saturday week.'

'How was he, last time, after Tom's death? Was he upset in any way?'

'I was. I couldn't get it fast enough from him.'

'You shot up at once, in the cinema?'

'No, I took it home, by taxi. I still had enough in me not to take the risk. The man knew it, too; knew I was desperate. I mean, I told him it was for Dennis. He doesn't know it's me who's hooked.'

'He must,' said McCaig.

'Maybe he does. It doesn't matter. He gave me the stuff as usual and I cleared out fast. Okay, now that I think of it, he *was* nervous. I'd made him nervous. Yes, he asked me about McDowell, if Dennis knew him.'

'What did you tell him?'

'I told him no. I just wanted the delivery, you see.'

'Is there usually some conversation?'

'Never; not a word.'

'Think carefully, Mrs Lawrence, has this man, or has your husband, ever given you any pertinent information about the extent of his operations, or where he obtains the heroin, or *anything* which might give us a clue now as to his whereabouts?'

'I can tell you what he looks like, that's all.'

'All right,' said McCaig. 'Do that.'

'He's Scottish – Glasgow, to go by his voice; he's small and dumpy, and about fifty, I think.'

'More?'

'Yes, he has a moustache, a long, thin gingery moustache.'

'How does he dress?'

'Smart enough. I haven't seen him in the light, except twice. He's fat, and wee. I don't think he has much hair on his head. He wears a hat like . . . a bit like that of yours there, and a short raincoat.'

'Is he always dressed in the same rigout?'

'It's dark in the Argyll, but . . .' She nodded. 'I don't remember him dressing any differently.'

'Are you sure about his age?'

'No.'

'Fifty?'

'Could be older.'

'Not younger?'

'He's fat, you see.'

'All right.'

So that was the pusher, a standard figure, no hunchbank, no villain in mufti, just a small fat middle-aged Glaswegian who sported a fancy hat and a gingery moustache, and had a money machine running like clockwork every other Saturday. The wires across the length of Britain would hum with the description and an identi-kit picture composed by the best police artist available. Record offices and the big computers in the London centres would heat up the information and perhaps put a finger on the man. Dennis Lawrence, too, would be traced, brought back north to be grilled and add his groatsworth to the portrait of the pusher. Mechanics now, for a while, complex mechanics right enough, but familiar. If the worst came to the worst, and the man did not pop out of the box, they could, perhaps, set up a trap for him in twelve days' time. Thinking of that last gamble, which he hoped would not be necessary, McCaig made a mental note to keep the press in the dark about Hilary Lawrence. He would have Jebb commit her, as a voluntary patient, to Judgehead or some less austere medical institution where she would be treated gently and kept hale and fit enough to play her part in the stake-out at the Argyll – if all else failed. It was an ace up the sleeve, an insurance policy, though he would need a measure of luck to keep the seepage in hold and prevent some rumour of Hilary's detainment leaking out to hungry newspaper men, and to the public of Thane in general. He must do it, though; attend to the garage, keep the machinations of search and drug squads as quiet as possible. Christ, Sellars was out there right now; and Sellars would not be skulking. Already it might not be possible to forge a pretence and keep the pusher in ignorance of the girl's arrest. Records and subsequent identification were the best bet. The long-term scheme for a trap at the place of the drop was no ace after all, only a lowly deuce which could be played as a final anxious bid to recoup a lost position. Still, he would call in Sellars, put the girl on ice without preferring charges, hush up the developments of the day as best he could.

Now, too, was the time to seek Pomfret's aid again. Impatience made him lose his objectivity and calm. He stood up, knuckles on the desk, and looked down at the girl below him. For a second she seemed quite unaware of his scrutiny, then, sharply cocked her head and squinted up at him as if into a strong light. She looked drawn now, McCaig thought, and with a furtive glint in her eyes which he had not detected before. It was bloody ridiculous that she should have held off so long and, in the end, capitulated with the fanciful precepts of conscience which had sprouted in her – she said – as a result of what had happened to Tom McDowell. What the hell did she care about McDowell? What the hell did any of them really care about the boy? He was only a cipher, a cryptogram for frustration.

'You won't be needed, Rice,' he said.

Without a word, the stenographer got up and left the office.

Greaves was scowling at him, less bewildered than angry. She had the morality of all hypocrites, setting her personal standards as the standards of everyone, inviolate in her righteousness.

'Harry,' he said, without looking round. 'Fetch Jebb. He'll be in Sheila's office, or the canteen. I want him at once.'

The girl was still watching him and Ryan's exit did not divert her attention. 'Look here,' she said, 'you told me . . .'

'I'll tell you now,' said McCaig, severely, 'that if you've given me less than the truth, I'll find out about it and I won't be disposed to uphold any sort of bargain you may imagine – I say, *imagine* – you've made with me. Policemen, even policemen in my position, don't make bargains.'

'You don't believe me?'

'Yes, I do believe you – as far as it goes. Trouble is, it doesn't go far enough. This is it, Mrs Lawrence; this is the crunch you knew had to come sooner or later. Listen, I'm *not* charging you, not yet. You will be charged with a drugs offence in due course, but I won't press for manslaughter.'

'Beg pardon?'

'You heard, manslaughter.'

'I didn't . . .'

'In the meantime, you will co-operate with us to this extent. Policewoman Greaves will take you to another room in this building and you will assist one of our artists in making up a portrait of the man you met in the Argyll cinema. You will also reiterate some of the pertinent facts, places, descriptions and names, which you've told us already. Inspector Ryan will guide you. This is not a statement or an admission of any guilt on your part, and these documents will not be used against you in any court of law. Understand?'

'What happens to me? I mean, tonight?'

'Doctor Jebb will examine you. He will, like as not, find you in need of medical attention and will *suggest* that you put yourself in his care as a voluntary patient. The one guarantee I will make you, Mrs Lawrence, is that you will not be ill-treated or broken abruptly from your dependence on heroin.'

'What about my business, the garage?'

'An almoner, working with any other authority necessary, will settle all matters relating to securing your business interests. You'll be consulted, of course.'

'And what more do you get out of me?'

'Help, assistance, whatever I may need to cut off the supply of narcotics and apprehend the pusher and his confederates.'

She nodded wanly, and rubbed her nose with the flat of her hand. Her pupils had changed colour, taking on the same reddish tint as her hair.

'And Tom McDowell, what'll happen about him?'

'Tom's . . . the McDowell boy died of an accidental overdose of heroin. The enquiry will bring home a verdict in accordance with the facts.'

'He killed himself.'

'No,' said McCaig, loudly. 'He did *not* kill himself; that's only your opinion, and the facts don't necessarily confirm it. Besides, you were in no fit state to judge his motives.'

'But he did, and what he did . . .'

'He experimented, foolishly, with drugs, and accidentally poisoned himself.'

'Mister, I'm telling you . . .'

'Policewoman Greaves, I'm sure you heard only facts in this room this afternoon, and those *facts* will later be put on record. Opinions and irrelevant material you will ignore as invalid.'

'Yes, sir.'

The embargo annoyed her. But he would come down with a heavy hand on Angela and on Rice to keep them from gossiping. Before now he had manipulated his facts, suppressed oddments of evidence in order that a man who was patently guilty could be successfully prosecuted. If he had come close to lying to ensure punishment for the guilty, surely now he could come close to lying to protect the innocent. Anyhow, the messiness of the case would only confuse the courts.

'You just don't want to admit it; okay?' said the girl. She shook her head, sadly. 'God, you won't even let *me* admit it.'

McCaig clenched his fists, temper burning on the tip of his tongue. He held it in check.

'No, I don't want to admit it,' he said.

She pummelled her nose with the heel of her hand. Her eyes were moist. 'You're all bastards sometimes. You really are.'

'Policewoman Greaves,' said McCaig, shortly, 'take Mrs Lawrence out of here. See that she does what she's told.'

Greaves's mouth was like a bill-hook, curved, rusty with lipstick. Her voice was strained with outrage at what this girl had done and, perhaps, what he, as a professional exponent of social order, had done too.

'You,' the woman snapped, 'this way.'

Sheila was late getting home. Her relief at finding that Gregor had waited for her was enormous. Tired and hungry after an afternoon and evening of frantic activity, she was only too glad of his company and his kind offer to cook supper while she bathed and changed her clothes and rested in the armchair by the fire. He cooked and served the mushroom omelettes very efficiently and, as was generally the way with men, whisked out all the trimmings, grilled tomatoes, toast, cake and tea in a scatter. He seated himself across the small drop-leaf table from her and, having passed her all the condiments he could find, began to eat heartily.

'Busy day, Sheila?'

'Hellish.'

'New case?'

'No.'

'How's the omelette?'

'Delicious.'

'Have some toast?'

'Thank you.'

Briskly and with a flourish, he buttered four slices of the warm brown bread and laid two of them on her side plate. He forked up the yellow egg, put a large helping into his mouth, filled the additional space with toast, and washed the lot down with tea. She enjoyed watching him eat; he did it with such relish. Gregor wore a white woollen shirt, open at the throat, clasped round his middle by a broad black-hide belt with a buckle on it which looked as if it had been hewn out of basalt; a pair of tight broad-cloth pants in moss green. His shoes were suède, with thick rubber soles and silky laces, and his socks were white. The image he presented was different, looser, more confidently masculine. Perhaps, now that he was becoming used to her, he was allowing his true self to show. She was sure that she would like it as much as the Sunday-School teacher bit. She was also sure now that part of her attraction for him had been physical, and the recognition made her glow and radiate in uncommon self-assurance. There was time now, though, time to let the friendship grow and ripen naturally.

'What was it?' he said, glancing up.

'What was what?'

'The big panic?'

'What?'

'In your office.'

'Oh, that!' she said. 'The McDowell thing.'

'Routine flap.'

'Worse than that,' she said, and immediately corrected herself. 'Better, I mean.'

'You caught somebody out?' he asked, smiling.

'Yes, yes, we did. Where did this cake come from?'

'I brought it,' he said. 'I'm very fond of madeira.'

'So am I.'

'They really do work you hard, don't they?'

'Sometimes.'

'Vocations can be bloody trying.'

'How was college?'

'Same as usual,' he said. 'Dullish. The pace won't heat up until class examinations begin in November.'

'What will you manage, when you're through?'

'I don't know. I might go to Harvard for a year, if I can wangle my way on.'

'And then?'

'My own business.'

'How ambitious!'

'An excellent failing – ambition,' Gregor said.

They talked casually throughout the rest of the meal. Promptly afterwards, he cleared the dishes to the sink and washed up. Sheila dried.

If she had known more of the intimate details of the

McDowell case, if she had been privy to the secrets which Hilary Lawrence had spouted out in the seclusion of the interview room that afternoon, perhaps the more obvious parallels would have stayed her and given her earlier warning. The Chief, though, had not seen fit to confide to Sheila more information than was necessary to assist her in doing her job; he didn't have time for one thing. What she knew of Hilary Lawrence was minimal, but fragments of news collected from orders, messages and reports gave her clear indication of the importance of the girl and her direct involvement with Tom McDowell.

Gregor lit a cigarette for her and then returned to the armchair – which she now thought of as 'his chair' – on the opposite side of the fireplace.

She was aware of her body under her clothing; of her naked breasts and their fullness against the sweater; and of Greg, too. It wasn't natural that she should still have these thoughts about him, not with such urgency. But she wanted it all now, before something happened which would end it. Though she was happy, she was not quite assured.

'You really do look exhausted,' he said. 'I won't stay late.'

'Stay as long as you like.'

'It's not fair on you,' he said. 'What time do you start?'

'Nine.'

'Another hellish day in prospect, I expect,' he said.

'Probably.'

'One thing after another, that's life. Will your boss make an arrest tomorrow?'

'I doubt it. He might.'

The food and the warmth of the fire made her feel sleepy, but pleasantly so, put her off guard. Later, she liked to defend her carelessness to herself by blaming the heat and the food and the long day. It would have been too much for her to admit that she had been taken in so thoroughly by him that she was not even aware of being pumped, furiously pumped at that, for the knowledge she held in her head.

'Who did you catch then?' said Gregor. 'Was it the . . . the pusher?'

'No.'

'I expect you'll get him now, though.'

'What makes you say that, Gregor?'

'What you told me about how the organisation works; once you get a . . . a lead, was it? Once you get a lead, the rest follows on.'

'Your precise managerial brain is over-active again,' she said, taking up the thread of an issue which had occupied them on the verge of argument on Sunday evening. 'All we have is a description of the man. We'll run it through machines all over the country and, in a day or two, if we're lucky, we'll find him.'

Gregor sat forward, elbows on knees.

'A description? How'd you get that?'

'From a girl, one of his addicts.'

'*Jesus Christ!*'

'Gregor, really!' she said in mock admonition.

'No, I mean, that's astonishing; that you managed to track down one of his clients, to know that it's one of his clients. Who is she?'

'A girl who knew Tom McDowell. She drove the car for him.'

'Car?'

'That buggy.'

'Yeah!' said Gregor. 'And she had the stuff which . . . ?'

'I assume,' said Sheila.

He seemed to think deeply about it for a moment, then smiled at her again. In spite of her laxness, she could see that the smile was forced and wondered at the reaction which the conversation had had upon him.

She said, 'You don't know this girl, do you?'

'You haven't even told me her . . . her name.'

'Lawrence, Hilary Lawrence, she's from the Brander Park area.'

'A local girl; good God!' said Gregor. 'What next? Thane'll be getting itself a very bad reputation, if we're not careful.'

The flippancy, too, was off-key, strained.

'The pusher, too?' he said.

'I don't know.'

'You mean, the boss doesn't know?'

'*I* don't know. Let's talk about something else.'

'Sorry, luv,' he said. 'Must be dishwater to you, but you can't blame me for being fascinated. Policemen have that effect, you know.'

'Talk about something else; tell me about Harvard.'

'Yeah,' he said, sitting back. 'Yeah, all right.'

But he did not tell her about Harvard. He told her very little about anything and appeared to have withdrawn into some private area of speculation which made him not only reticent but almost truculent. Within fifteen minutes, in spite of Sheila's protests, he had excused himself and was preparing to depart.

She said, 'What's wrong, Gregor?'

'Nothing,' he said. 'I just don't want to take . . . I mean, you're tired, and I don't want to keep you up.'

'It's not late yet.'

'No, but . . .'

'Will I see you again?'

He raised his brows, startled, giving the impression that she should not have asked the question.

'Yeah, sure,' he said. 'What makes you think you won't? You do *want* to see me again, don't you?'

'Of course I do.'

He put on the rally jacket and pulled the zipper up to his throat.

'Give me a kiss,' she said.

'Oh ! Yeah,' he said.

He kissed her on the mouth and left. Tonight the kiss left her more puzzled than dazed. She could not define what had changed between them, or what flaw in her had suddenly made itself felt. It was later in the week before she realised that she had committed no imprudence, but that, for him, she had merely outlived her usefulness.

Mulligan's dwelling was an anachronism, a cottage close to the heart of the city; not just an ugly brick throw-back to the days of miners' rows or the mean hovels of weavers, but a genuine shepherd's croft stowed away behind the tenements of the north-western slums. Mulligan had lived in the cottage – called, by some flight of fancy, The Fold – all his born days. He could go back to the time when he shared one of its two tiny bedrooms with four brothers, all of them long since fled Scotland to establish their own Caledonian commune in Seattle, U.S.A. The family had never been close. Whole chapters of life in the dark days of the thirties were firmly closed behind him, so that he thought not of still-births and tubercular sisters and the five white coffins which had sat, for one night each, on the parlour table; or of his father, too crippled by a bone disease to earn bread; or of his mother slaving in the lemonade bottlers' a mile up the road for next to nothing. He did remember the taste of the different flavours of soft drinks which she smuggled out daily in her tea-flask, giving her children their only real experience of sweetness on the road to adulthood. Then his sisters died, his father died and his mother died, and his brothers went abroad, and he stayed behind and served his country while the cottage stood empty feeding on its own rot until he came back from the war to reside in it again. Mulligan did not think of the harsh times, when a heel of bread and jam was a feast. He did not care to remember the hungers that were sharp and constant, only that their satisfactions had seemed more real than any he had known since. After the war he had worked in a carpet factory, lived with a barren woman, took up with petty thieves, robbed a few houses and offices and made a few bob – until the coppers caught him out. A process of trial and sentence, and prison, and release, and probation and then arrest again, started. The first woman left him; he took up with another, as sterile as the first, but shrewish with it, and went on in that seesaw of imprisonment and freedom until the former became the more pleasurable reality and the latter only the waiting time between.

What broke him from the pattern was ill-health and an infusion of horse-sense engendered during a spell in a prison hospital by the rumour that his shrewish woman was trying to sell off the cottage – for all it was worth – behind his back. Sentiment came to his rescue; a brief period of consultations with lawyers and do-gooders from aid societies firmed his resolve to pull himself together, get outside and stay outside before some sharp operator took away the one and only thing which mattered to him, sheet-anchor of his very existence – the wee house where he'd been born. Most maudlin Scots would understand his motive for going straight, and give him untold verbal encouragement. So, well again, Mulligan went straight. He bummed jobs with bookies, clerked for back-streets' chandlers, kept his lady-friends in their place and lived his own life in the damp cramped cottage under the high tenements like the curator of a musty museum. If the city planners hadn't put the kiss of death on the area and chalked it out for demolition he might have been lucky enough to die there. Decay was Mulligan's milieu; change, though, would kill him.

It was at that time, with the grand municipal plans in infancy, that he first met Charlie Yule and was led again astray. He was conned into a new kind of criminal venture by the temptation of enough profit to ease himself gently into an altered situation and prop up the crumbling promise of a peaceful old age. Ethics didn't enter into it at first; survival was all that mattered. Even with money in the bank, though, and a couple of good suits in the wardrobe, he was not content. The job had become a heavier sentence than any ever meted out by judge or magistrate; an open-ended term too, with no reprieve in sight. At least he was still in the cottage, though earth-movers had begun to move earth – slates, bricks and mortar, too – from the neighbourhood. He realised that he would be lucky indeed to still have his home when spring came again. The money, wealth gleaned from his twice-a-month round of clients, did not after all insulate him to pangs of loss. What did give him respite was not the prospect of a comfortable removal, but the nagging suspicion that once more he would be kitted in prison garb on a stretch so long that he would never need a roof over his head again.

On Monday night, Mulligan was seated in his father's chair, recently re-upholstered, with his feet on the hob by the fire and the small-screen television set on the sill by the door where the shepherd had once built a little altar to some saint and his own mother had kept the precious family medicines. The bed of a sewing machine served him as a side-table. On it were all the luxuries he allowed himself : cigarettes, a bottle of Talisker and a box of buttered brazils, a compote of tastes which Mulligan found irresistibly cloying. He crunched a sweet between his teeth, sipped whisky and put the cigarette back in his mouth. The sounds given off by the set were almost deafening – he was a little hard of hearing, lately – and he did not at first pick up the imperious clacking of the front door knocker. How long the caller rapped, Mulligan did not know; but, hearing and answering, he found Gregor Yule with arm raised and furious impatience knotted on his face.

'Didn't hear you,' said Mulligan, showing no sign of surprise at the appearance of the young man at this hour and this location; though, to the best of his knowledge, Gregor didn't even know where he lived and had certainly never called on him before. 'Come in, son.'

Yule was already in; through the narrow doorway and through the box-like hall and into the parlour. His height emphasised the crampedness of the room. His bulk seemed to fill it as if it was a small cage and he a large restless animal. Hiding his anxiety, Mulligan latched the front door and returned slowly to his armchair by the fire.

'Whisky?' he said, tapping the bottle.

Yule looked round at the entrance to the bedroom.

'Nobody here,' Mulligan told him. He didn't ask what the trouble was; Yule would tell him soon enough.

'The fuzz picked up Hilary Lawrence this morning,' Yule said. 'They've got her on ice.'

'Ah!' said Mulligan. 'Jesus!'

'She gave them a description.'

'Of . . . of me, y'mean?'

'Who else?'

'Aye,' said Mulligan. 'That's not so good, is it now!'

'How long will it take them to put a name to the description?'

'Depends,' said Mulligan. 'Could be minutes, or hours, or days, dependin' how smart they are in the Records Office. I should think, they'll not take over long.'

'How soon can you leave?'

'Leave?'

'Christ, you're not to sit round here and wait for them to pick you up. You can be out of the country by tomorrow morning.'

'Might be safer here.'

'Mulligan, are you out of your bloody skull?' Yule shouted. 'If they get you, they'll get the rest of us . . .'

'You'n'Charlie? Aye, they might at that.'

'I mean it,' said Yule. 'I went to a lot of trouble to keep in touch with fuzz developments, to give you a chance to make a clean break for it, and you sit there and tell me you're not going. Christ, you old bastard, I'm *ordering* you to go.'

'Don't panic, Greg,' said Mulligan. 'Findin' me is one thing, and provin' I was the lassie's connection is another. I know more about how the blues work than you do, remember, an' I'm tellin' you it won't be so easy for them to fiddle up a case, not on her say-so.'

197

'And the others; what about the bloody junkies?'

'They'll keep mum, if I'm nicked.'

'I want you out of here by tomorrow morning,' said Yule. He reached into his pocket, brought out a cheap plastic wallet and held it out to the man.

'What's that?' said Mulligan.

'Money; three hundred quid,' said Yule. 'I've kept it in cash on hand for an emergency.'

'What'll I do with . . .'

'Buy a bloody plane ticket,' Yule said.

'I've money in the bank.'

'And every bank in town might be supplied with your photograph by nine tomorrow.'

'No chance,' said Mulligan. 'Hell's bells, son, blues aren't that bleedin' efficient. No, no, I've a day, maybe more, before I really need t'sweat. They might turn up a tracer, but they'll have t'put it through a whole system before they can pin down bank accounts, an' that.'

'You want more?'

Mulligan sighed. 'It's not the money.'

'Then what is it?'

'When y'run, you've as good's admitted guilt. Scuffler's law, they call it. A joker who *walks* away stands a good chance of bein' let loose; the one who runs is nailed.'

'Not on this score.'

'She saw me in the dark.'

'Her husband . . .'

'Aye, that's true. I thought the shit was *for* her husband, right enough,' said Mulligan. He unwrapped a sweet, then seemed to lose his taste for it and set it in the ashtray, taking up the whisky glass instead. He downed the nip in a swallow and got to his feet. 'Dennis could put the finger on me. Did she turn herself in, or what?'

'No, they found her. I don't know how,' said Yule. 'But, listen, you've got to believe me, Mulligan. The heat's on you, been on you all afternoon. Christ, they could be storming up to that door right this minute.'

'I doubt it,' said Mulligan.

'Get out of the country while you can.'

'I wonder.'

Yule grabbed him, pulled him to his feet and held him high, hunched, then slammed him back against the mantel, making the oddments on it clink and rattle and, by a ghostly vibration, causing the door of the kitchen to lift on its latch and swing softly open.

'*You* were the one who wanted to quit,' Yule shouted. '*You* were the bloody one who advocated . . .'

'Son, easy; easy.'

'I'm not getting caught because of you.'

'I never said I *wouldn't* go.'

Yule released him.

Mulligan continued to lean against the mantelshelf, fat haunches broiled by the fire in the grate. His moon face was shiny, the flesh out of which his moustache sprouted sprinkled with sweat. The TV set was still spewing out music and canned laughter, though he had been oblivious to it since Yule had entered the room. He pushed himself away, pulled the plug from the side of the set. The silence was almost uncanny. He peered at Gregor Yule, frightened less by the possible advent of the law, than by Yule and all that Yule stood for, by the sudden suspicion that he might be driven out of Scotland not by fear of arrest and imprisonment but by Yule's selfish insistence.

Yule was right though. He *had* to go; had to pack up and head out into the wide world where everybody was a stranger. If only he'd stopped long enough to think about that before he got involved with Greg and Charlie Yule. It just hadn't come to him at the time that their dependence on him was as extreme as Miss Flowery-hat's, or the Englishman's or Hilary Lawrence's. *He* carried the weight; it wasn't enough to assure the Yules that he would carry it alone, right into a cell if need be. They wouldn't take his word for it; he couldn't blame them. No, it had to be emigration, and it had to be soon. He felt something like a vacuum inside him at the prospect. Better a Scottish prison than exile. For a fleeting moment he toyed with the idea of heading directly for Seattle, where at least he would have the consolation of his brothers' company. But that was a daft idea : the blues would have his next-of-kin on record.

'What'll I do?' he said.

'How much stuff do you have stored here?'

'None : it's all gone.'

'Where did you hide it?'

'In the back of yon clock.'

'In what?'

'A plastic bag.'

Yule went to the wall where the clock hung and took it from its hooks. It was of the kind which used to hang in railway ticket offices and behind post office counters; a sawn-off grandfather with a Roman face, fluted black hands and two holes low on the face for the winder; under it, a mahogany chest where the pendulum lived. The hands were fixed at five past eleven and had remained in that position as long as Mulligan could recall. Roughly, Gregor put the time-piece face down upon the table, heedless of the jangle of its parts. He unscrewed the wooden peg of the church-door portion at the rear, yanked it open, and peered inside. He ran his fingertips round the edges of the cavity, brought them out, sniffed and tasted them, and held them out to Mulligan.

'Get rid of it.'

'That clock was m'old man's.'

'I don't give a frig if it belonged to Bonnie Prince Charlie; get rid of it.'

'Okay,' said Mulligan, glumly.

'What did you wear when you made the drops?'

'Suit, coat, hat.'

'Ged rid of them, too.'

'Greg, son, I'll b'*wearin*' them.'

'No, you won't.'

'What's wrong with ... ?'

'That's how they can identify you, by the clothing. Besides, you could have a few crumbs of shit down in the lining, and that would be enough.'

Mulligan, not immune to intelligence, nodded.

'And shave off that moustache; not here.'

The old man's hand flew to his nostrils and patted the ginger growth lovingly.

'Where, but?' he said.

'You're getting out of this hole tonight,' Greg said.

'It's near midnight.'

'So what!' said Yule. 'Pack what you can carry, and go to a commercial hotel. At this time of year you won't have any trouble. Before you go to the hotel, though, you'll go to the wash-rooms in the station and shave off the moustache. Spend the night in the hotel, put in for an early morning call and then go to one of the big travel agencies and book a plane out.'

'What bleedin' hotel; a plane t'where?' said Mulligan, desperately.

'Get rid of the clock and the clothing first. Dump them someplace, tonight.'

'Where? I mean, how'll I . . . ?'

Yule had come close to him again. The clock lay on the table. The boy loomed over him. The little sill pressed against the nape of Mulligan's neck. Yule put his hands against the ledge and penned Mulligan in. Mulligan's gut contracted with a spasm of pure fear. He had felt no fear like it ever in his life before, and he ascribed it – as a method of clinging to the last vestige of his control – less to Yule's expression than to his sheer physical bulk, and his youth. It was the youthful quality, the invincibility of it, which lay deep at the back of his fear. Yule had the awful inevitability of an earth-mover, a ravaging, destructive thing which took no stock of sentiment or character or any other item, animate or inanimate, in its levelling drive. Even Charlie, older but much less strong, would have been easier to deal with than this brother. For a split second, in the very heart of his fear, Mulligan felt rage too, but it was soon swept aside and consumed. He waited for Yule to strike him, thrash him, but the boy did not lay a finger on him. The sudden cessation of his bullying and insistent demands heightened the older man's fears to terror.

'You can't do it, can you?' said Yule, gently.

'Aye, I can. Just show me . . .'

'Yeah, all right.'

The boy pushed himself away. Mulligan did not move, remaining like an obedient servant, or a lifeless dummy, where Yule had propped him. He watched Yule seat himself in the armchair, legs out and elbows on his stomach, fingers steepled before his mouth.

'All right, old man,' said Yule.

'Wha' . . . what?'

'I'll do it for you.'

'Greg, I'll . . .'

The boy pushed himself out of the chair again, lithe now and easy in his movements.

'Be ready, packed and ready, early in the morning.'

'You'll . . .'

'I'll look after you. I'll make the arrangements.'

'Where'll I go?'

'I'll arrange that, too.'

'Look, Greg, I'm sorry about . . .'

'Shave off that moustache, though.'

The boy pulled open the door and stood in the black box of the hall, listening. Mulligan shambled after him. He could not let him go like that, not with the shadow of his future in his pocket and no word to tell him what was what.

'Where?' he said.

'At the sink will do,' Yule said. 'It doesn't matter.'

'I don't mean the whiskers. I mean . . .'

'Tomorrow morning,' Yule told him, finally. 'You'd better be ready when I call.'

Defeated, Mulligan grunted his assent.

Yule was gone, leaving the low doorway to the lane vacant.

Snoring, Whitehouse lay in darkness, breathing up the sharp reek of anointed canvas, making small moist smacking sounds as if he relished the tastes and smells of the guddle of bottles, plates, tubes and brushes and found them, even in sleep, as appetising as *hors d'œuvre*. By daybreak, the mad bastard would be at it again, easel slanted towards an imaginary fall of light from grids which squinted up only to a slimy wall, railings and the undersides of pavements. The incomplete painting on its sackcloth screen would pose another problem to add to his already burdensome list. Whitehouse would cling to it now like a bluebottle to treacle-paper, wouldn't forsake it until whatever he saw as completion had been accomplished and the bloody master-piece set aside in favour of another.

Yule closed the connecting door and returned to the comparative order of his own room. Above the little desk a lamp was lit; on the desk were an alarm clock and a couple of sheets of plain foolscap paper. The fire in the stove reeked smoke and a few meagre ripples of flame where he had burned his stock of envelopes and containers which had tem-porarily housed his supplies of heroin. All gone now, he had scattered the dregs of the white powder grudgingly on the coals, mentally counting out the profit in pounds and pence. Unlike Mulligan, Yule was not afraid. Not that the plan was easy or without considerable hazard, but its effectiveness was commensurate with the risks and problems involved and he had full confidence in his own ability to pull it off.

What Charlie was up to en route from Palermo was the un-known factor in an otherwise watertight plan. It would be bad medicine if Charlie got himself nicked at the docks with a boxful of shit. Yule put it out of his mind; no sense in bothering with matters which he could not control. Anyhow, he trusted Charlie to find out for himself about the business back home; Rhinda Watson or some other member of the crew was almost bound to receive a package of newspapers from Scotland, or a letter or some similar source of informa-tion which Charlie would have access to. Charlie was not so stupid; he'd dump the stuff overboard before he'd run him-self into blue heat. They could afford the loss. Even if Charlie *was* nicked at the docks, he wouldn't peach—not if he had to take the whole fall himself. And when Charlie came out there would be the business, the firm, for him to step into, and the blues could do nothing about it.

Seating himself at the desk, he lifted his pen and checked off the items of attention on the topmost sheet, reading them over, lips moving soundlessly, before making the decisive tick which signified that he had memorised it, and devised the method of achieving it. The plan was complex, well con-ceived, difficult, balanced, and lethal.

Gregor Yule was in love with it already.

What could be done in practical terms had been done.

He mulled over sections and sub-sections, additions and amendments, until his head began to nod and the eagerness of his thinking became blurred. He pulled himself together, read through the material once again, then drew the pen in long strokes through each of the major headings, scoring out the names one by one—Whitehouse, Vikki, Mulligan.

That done, he burned the papers too, set the alarm for five a.m. and, fully dressed, rolled into bed to catch a few hours' sleep.

Judgehead Mental Hospital lay on the edge of the county, close to the long ridge which began in the north with the bump of Ben Brander and ran south-east, making a back-drop for green-belt estates which still thrived here, for com-muter suburbs, disguised as villages, and the older shabbier hamlets which the receding tide of open-cast mining had left high and dry in the midst of fields and grazing pastures. To look at, Judgehead was not unprepossessing. Until quite recent times, the building had been the family seat of the

Dukes of Brander and Thane, acquired by the nation under the terms of a trust which relinquished the big house and ten cultivated acres of ground in return for an iron-clad contract which protected the sprawling woods and farmlands from encroaching surburban developers and the possible greed of the late Duke's sons. However innocuous and unchanged Judgehead House appeared on the outside, the inside was just as sinister as any other asylum.

McCaig parked the Daimler and went up through the main entrance under the granite crest of the Family of Brander and Thane. Behind him, stretched out under the pearly autumnal mists, lay the city. On Judgehead's lawns the city's casualties stood or sat or lay, solitary and in groups, staring out at the urban panorama as if it was the horizon of a vast, unexplored and terrifying sea.

Hilary Lawrence was brought to him by Jebb. She still wore the suit in which she had been admitted and showed no signs of strain or distress at being in this place and, to all intents and purposes, a prisoner. A sprightly, well-set-up young man with jet black hair and eyebrows as arched and smooth as a matinée idol's, Jebb ushered in the girl then left again for the ante-chamber where, with a patience uncommon in his profession, he would await McCaig's call.

The Chief solicitously enquired after Hilary's health and welfare, received shrugs and nods in reply, then pulling out a chair from the table in the visitors' room, asked her to sit down.

From under the table he brought out a large flat leather attaché case, opened it against his thigh and laid on the table top a series of photographs all of uniform size but of varying quality and finish.

Twenty-three of them covered the table, in rows, like a parlour game.

'Which one?' said McCaig. 'If any?'

The girl leaned over her hands, frowning.

McCaig watched her eyes travel from left to right along the rows, slow, studied and methodical. The men looked back at her, full-face most of them, a sprinkling of ignoble profiles; pallid and lacklustre expressions with the flashbulb stares stamped identically upon them all. Widely differing types—fat, thin, gaunt, hefty, weedy, dignified, cowed —but all with that purblind stare and a carefully rendered blankness set into their expressions; McCaig could never really believe that these men lived and breathed and moved somewhere, in Bradford, Chiswick, Edinburgh, Aberdeen, Swansea, or in an anthology of gaols across the British Isles.

'Well?' he said.

'Him.'

'Are you sure?'

She nodded.

'This man?'

'Yes,' she said. 'No moustache, but it's him.'

'Wait.'

McCaig consulted the number on the back of the print, and delved into the case again. He brought out a stuffed buff-coloured envelope and slipped three files from it, opened one and extracted another set of photographs. Placing them on the table, he covered the documented details along the foot of each with the edge of the envelope and asked the girl to consider her choice again.

She didn't rush it.

'It's him, okay. I'm positive.'

'One more look at the others.'

He removed the files and envelope and the second set of prints and fiddled with a paperclip while the girl did her bit with the rows once more.

'No,' she said. 'No : none of these. The one you've got.'

'Thank you,' said McCaig.

'Who is he?'

'You'll hear in due course.'

'Have you found Dennis?'

'Not yet.'

McCaig placed the glossy portrait of the middle-aged, clean-shaven, rotund little man on the outside of the envelope, clipped it firmly, and stowed it in the upper division of the attaché case. He packed the others with less care, closed and locked the case and summoned Jebb. Jebb raised one expressive brow and McCaig, his back to the girl, winked.

'Good,' Jebb said.

'Keep her here,' McCaig said, then, turning, raised his hat and in the moment of departure thanked Mrs. Lawrence once more.

William Frazer Mulligan; born, January, 1921. No registered trade or profession. Royal Engineers, 1940-46, hon. dis. Serg. First arrest, 1950, guilty 4 chgs. b & e, one year Barlinnie. 1954, guilty 3 chgs. b & e, two years Barlinnie. 1959, guilty, burglary, thirty months Peterhead. 1962, while on prob, b & e, guilty, with recc., two years Barlinnie. No known aliases. Unmarried. Dist. marks, wen on root of lft. collar-bone; scar underside lft. arm. Kin: George Mulligan, 29 Clayton Street, Seattle, Wash., U.S.A. Bros., other, same U.S. area. Last known address: The Fold, Carradale Lane, Glasgow, N.W. And a chest infection, an ulcer at one time, and a ginger moustache. Not to mention a crafty shift from breaking-and-entering and kindred arts to a much more rewarding trade in narcotics. At least Mulligan wasn't given to violence, unless age had changed his character, or desperation and the pernicious influence of horse disposed him to treat the law less stoically than he had done in the past.

The uniformed constable drew the Jaguar up at the lane's end. Ryan got out of one side and Sergeant Lindsay out of the other. McCaig's Daimler, a burly sergeant at the wheel, glinted in the distance, blocking off the far end of the lane.

The sun was obscured by delicate tatters of cloud and a cauliflower of smoke sprouted from a kiln-like chimney to the east of the roof of Craigend Rangers soccer stadium. Ryan took the radio from his pocket and put himself in touch with the Chief.

'Come on slow, Harry,' McCaig said.

'Who's actually going in?' Ryan asked the box in his fist.

'I am.'

'Alone?'

'Christ, he's not going to shoot me.'

'Well . . .' said Ryan, dubiously. 'There's a gable wall, Chief, can we make it that far before you . . . ?'

'Yes.'

'Starting now,' said Ryan.

'Right.'

He put the box in his pocket, clipped it down and buttoned up his raincoat again. He swung round and gestured with his forefinger. Lindsay came up beside him.

'Up to the wall,' said Ryan.

The driver was leaning on the roof of the Jaguar, looking over the débris-strewn waste ground.

'Constable, when the Chief Superintendent hits that door,

you bring the Jag up fast and stop just where the wall breaks there.'

'Yes, sir.'

'Inspector Sellars is in Whitley Street which runs behind that warehouse. Keep the car line open directly to him.'

'Yes, sir.'

'All right, Sergeant?'

'Let's get at it,' Lindsay said

McCaig had already begun to walk slowly, almost ponderously, towards the cottage, keeping out in the middle of the lane. Ryan and Lindsay travelled faster, with short skipping steps, holding their coats against their thighs, and hugging the the protection of the broken wall on the cottage side of the vennel. They reached the blank gable a minute before McCaig reached the door.

McCaig drew himself up and stretched his left hand to the knocker, rapped. Through the wall, Ryan could hear the echo of the sound within the cottage; the quality of it, its hollowness, instinctively told him that nobody was home. Too tense to stand on such unmethodical assumptions, he did not relax his vigilance. Lindsay was leaning over a broken wooden gate and poking his head round to stake-out the ash-pit garden at the rear.

The Chief knocked again.

He used his left hand, his right hanging slack, elbow slightly bent, like a cowboy gunslinger covering his holster. His weight was nicely spread, Ryan noticed, so that he could either thrust himself forward or, in case of emergency, dive to his right.

In all these precautions was a faintly ridiculous overstatement of the seriousness of the situation. But, Ryan reminded himself, more than one branch had lost more than one officer through a measure of carelessness and a serious underrating of the quarry.

The *chap-chap-chap* of the knocker continued, making an echo now in the garden as well, changing to a rattle as McCaig tried his luck with the door-knob.

'Harry.'

'Yes, sir.'

'Windows.'

Ryan shifted out from the gable and, covering his temples with his hand, peered in at the low window. He saw nothing but the bed, an archaic wardrobe and a jug in a basin on a wash-stand. McCaig evidently found nothing more interesting in the adjacent window. A minute later, Lindsay came round the far side of the cottage, shaking his head too.

'Kitchen door?' asked McCaig.

'Locked.'

McCaig clicked his tongue against the roof of his mouth. 'Right,' he said. 'Summon up the beef and we'll force entry.'

Using the heel of his shoe to great effect, the driver of McCaig's Daimler shattered the lock with his second strike, and the three detectives entered the cottage.

In the living room they found the remains of a meagre breakfast, a half-empty bottle of Talisker, a box of buttered brazils, and a warm, unraked hearth.

In the bedroom they found empty drawers and two squares in the dust on top of the wardrobe where suitcases had been stored.

In the little kitchenette tacked on to the back of the house, they found wet soap and a sprinkling of ginger hairs in the sink.

What they did not find was William Fraser Mulligan.

William Fraser Mulligan, as the Chief succinctly put it, had flown the bloody coop.

PART FOUR

McCaig's frustration was the disease of a patient man whose body is clogged with bad air and excess of starch, coffee, stewed tea and nicotine. He could have been excused for crawling off home to bed – could even have excused himself for that – but he could not bring himself to leave the case as it stood. He badly wanted progress, something to happen; Mulligan to be brought in by the scruff of the neck, mainly, though he would have settled for news of the man's apprehension and appeased himself for the night with the promise of a settlement tomorrow. No Mulligan, though : no hilt nor hair of the man had as yet been found at any of the many standard exits through which the scared and the guilty run like greyhounds out of traps, chasing freedoms as artificial as mechanical hares. Presided over by an expert from the Glasgow Branch, in whose province Carradale Lane was situated and to whom, in politic deference, McCaig had referred the investigation of Mulligan's habits and home, the forensic detail had accumulated a trove of evidence to prove that Mulligan had actually existed – a fact which McCaig considered already proven beyond the shadow of a doubt. The hairs in the sink were what remained of Mulligan's moustache; the man was hiding behind a bare face again, obligingly returning to the visage recorded in his documents. Plumbing, dismantled, retained no traces of any known drug, but particle analysis of sweepings from the living-room floor had established a direct connection between Mulligan and heroin; microscopic amounts as damning as a landslide of shit would have been. Financial and documentary details, chains which bind all citizens, rich or poor, would be slower in coming, but McCaig was willing to bet that Mulligan had withdrawn his bundle, would be travelling laden with cash. Oddly, though, the local passport offices had no record at all of an issue to a man of that name and description. Was Mulligan holing out? Paying through the snoot for a refuge? Quite possibly; and quite possibly, too, that safe harbour would be with a friend or former acquaintance, or with some person intimately concerned with Mulligan's latest and last criminal venture, narcotics trading.

After a time, as dusk sifted down out of the silken sky and cold air sweated moisture on to the windows of the corridors, McCaig could not content himself with routine speculation. Shortly after eight, he gave in to his curiosity and to his spleen and, taking both emotions with him, like cocked fowling-pieces, went below to the motor-pool and checked out the Ayer Sabre.

The Daimler's automatic transmission and power-assisted steering had blunted the edge of his skill with hot cars. Though the Sabre could hardly be classed as a roaring dragster, its quirks and recalcitrant road behaviour absorbed all his concentration on the drive through the town to Mossburn.

McCaig steered the Sabre carefully, sitting high in the bucket seat with his toes on the pedals and the night air cutting his cheeks and ears like a winter blizzard. He muffed the gear-change and took the buggy jerkingly round the angle of the gatepost of 7 Rodale Avenue, stopped, started again and made a smooth ascent of the drive and a nice curving turn in the area before the front of the house.

Before he could apply the hand-brake and disembark, the front door of the house was pulled open and light flooded down from coach-lamps and hallway, making a lake on the gravel around the Sabre. McCaig turned and squinted into the light. McDowell wore a suède-fronted cardigan and slacks and red house slippers. He had the appearance of a man raked out of sleep by some thunderous noise, like an earthquake or a bomb-blast. His head was craned forward from the push of his shoulders and his legs straddled the threshold as if to brace him against the possibility of another shock wave. His expression was haunted, scarred by disbelief and an expectant horror.

'I'm sorry,' McCaig called out. 'I didn't mean to startle you.'

'Who . . . who is that?'

'McCaig.'

The Chief understood; McDowell's ear had identified the sounds of the buggy engine in the still night and, in some parabola of hope and superstitious fear, he had projected himself at the run from the lounge or dining room or bedroom to confront the origin of his emotional upheaval. Another sort of man might have scampered, cowering, for the shelter of the cellar or the darkness beneath the stairs. Trembling, McDowell came down the steps on to the gravel.

'What is it?'

'I brought back the buggy,' McCaig said.

'Why?'

'It's yours.'

'I don't want it.'

'Then sell it,' said McCaig. He climbed out of the driving seat and rubbed his hands to warm them. 'I brought you some news too, if you're interested.'

'News?'

'It'll be in the papers tomorrow, some of it, but I thought it only right that you should hear it from me.'

'Is it about . . . Tom?'

'Aye, it is,' said McCaig. 'Do you want to talk here, or can we go inside?'

'My wife . . .'

'It's up to you,' said McCaig.

'Wait.'

McCaig waited.

McDowell walked back into the house and reappeared a minute later with a heavy corduroy coat thrown over his shoulders. He still wore the slippers, though. In the doorway McCaig glimpsed the figure of Mildred McDowell, but she came no further than the top of the step and, after a moment's pause, closed the door on them and put out the light.

'How is your wife?' said McCaig.

'We'll take the Stag,' said McDowell. 'I'd ask you in, but . . .'

'I don't mind.'

McDowell led him round the side of the house to a double garage and again McCaig waited while the councillor entered the garage and drove out the low white sports car. McCaig got into the passenger seat, and McDowell took the car gently past the Sabre and down the driveway and turned left along Rodale Avenue. Something about the man had changed; it was too obvious to miss. He had the same sort of jerkiness of movement which McCaig had noticed in Hilary Lawrence, as if there was a lull between the brain's commands and the limbs' responses. McDowell also appeared untidy, unshaven and generally dishevelled. All trace of the introverted rage of a week ago had gone from him. He was, McCaig suddenly realised, vulnerable.

'Where shall we go?' asked McDowell.

'Anywhere,' said McCaig. 'It doesn't matter.'

'Towards Glasgow?'

'All right.'

'You . . . you say you have news?'

'You won't like this,' McCaig said. 'It isn't very pleasant. Perhaps you'd prefer to stop the car while I . . .'

'No,' said McDowell. 'I'd prefer to keep going. I'll be all right.'

McCaig said, 'What I'm telling you is in strictest confidence. You're entitled to know what I know of the truth. What I elect to release to the public, and to build into evidence, is really my business, and I'll keep as much of it back as I dare.'

'Why should you?'

'I told you, Mr McDowell, it isn't very edifying. I'm sure, when you hear me, you'll want to . . . to protect yourself from the sort of bloody gossip . . .'

'I'm not interested in protecting myself, McCaig.'

McCaig grunted. 'Suit yourself. You may change your mind.'

'Go on.'

'The girl, the owner of the garage where you purchased the Sabre . . .'

'Yes.'

'The heroin came from her. She didn't intend Tom to have it.'

'He took it.'

'I believe so,' said McCaig. 'The girl seems to have been straight with us. She's an addict. She's given us a description of the pusher. We're trying to track him down at the moment, but he's obviously taken fright and gone on the run.'

'Who is he?'

'His name's William Mulligan; have you heard of him?'

'No.'

'I didn't think you would,' said McCaig. He hesitated, then gave a carefully edited account of what had happened to Tom during the last Saturday and the weeks preceding it.

When he finished, he waited for reaction from McDowell, for some exclamation or declamation, but the councillor was wrapped up in his driving – or so it seemed – giving all his attention to the view from the windscreen, though the needle of the speedometer hardly topped thirty.

McCaig said, 'As far as you know, Mr McDowell, is the girl's account accurate?'

'Yes.'

'I take it you'd no idea that Tom was interested in her?'

'No,' said McDowell. 'He didn't say anything to me, not even when I . . .'

'When you what?'

'That time we went there together,' said McDowell, 'I remarked that the girl had a good figure.'

'Did Tom agree?'

'He was embarrassed,' said McDowell. 'He was always embarrassed when I talked about girls, even in the most casual way. I tried to get closer to him, you see. I tried to find out what happened to him, to discover if he was . . . unusual.'

'What did you say about the girl; can you remember?'

'Not really; something about her looking like a hot one.'

'Aye,' said McCaig. 'And Tom showed no interest?'

'None at all,' said McDowell. 'Why did he want to sell the Sabre?'

'Apparently,' said McCaig, 'he just didn't care for it.'

'He should have told me.'

'Didn't he tell you?'

'Of course not.'

'What would you have done if he'd come to you, asked you to swop the buggy for a Volkswagen, say?'

'I'm not sure.'

'You didn't have any dealings with this girl, with Hilary Lawrence, did you?'

The question did not seem to offend McDowell, though McCaig had put it warily, anticipating an outbreak of temper again at the challenge behind it.

'No, I didn't,' McDowell said, musingly. 'It may have crossed my mind, but . . . no, I wouldn't.'

'Wouldn't?'

'She wasn't my type.'

McCaig said, 'How many women have you had?'

'Too many,' McDowell answered. He glanced at the detective, blinked, then carefully drew the Stag into a lay-by by the side of the snaking back road, and cut the engine. He rested his hands across the top of the wheel, his elbows covering the spokes.

'What *have* you discovered, McCaig?' he asked.

'What I've told you, that's all.'

'About me, not about Tom?'

'About you?' said McCaig, surprised. 'I'm not investigating you, Mr McDowell.'

'Aren't you?' McDowell said.

'If you mean . . .' said McCaig, hotly. 'You can forget that. It's not important now, and it's got nothing to do with what happened to your boy.'

'You don't mean that, of course,' McDowell said. He sounded didactic, but not hostile. 'I *know* what you're thinking.'

'What?'

'You're thinking I encouraged Tom. I didn't. We didn't have much in common. Mildred really brought him up. I can anticipate your next question; the answer to it is that I loved him. I didn't know what the thing meant then, but I see now that I loved him. I didn't . . . didn't give him . . .'

'I didn't come here tonight for a confession.'

'You may as well have it,' said McDowell. 'Do you have a cigarette? I seem to have forgotten . . .'

McCaig gave him a Benson and Hedges, took one himself and lit them both. A white Hillman Imp cruised past; a courting couple in search of darkness and seclusion. Outside the Stag the landscape was pale and remote, still. He could smell the odour of McDowell's body, not rank or sour but musky. The scratching of his nails on his unshaven cheek was extraordinarily loud and rasping in the closed quietness of the car.

'I've given you a bad time in the past, McCaig. I don't regret it, you know.'

'I didn't come here . . .'

'No, you wouldn't abuse your authority. Why did Tom do what he did? I don't just mean why did he use that girl's needle. I mean, why did he do all that? Was he bored? Didn't he have enough? Did I let him down *that* badly?'

'Did you let him down at all?'

'I don't know,' said McDowell. 'Your boy, *your* son; did you give him any more time and attention than I gave Tom?'

'Perhaps not.'

'How did he turn out?'

'I ...'

'I knew your wife,' said McDowell, interrupting. 'Yes, I knew Muriel quite well. There wasn't anything between us, though. Have you ever wondered about that, McCaig? I expect you have. If it's any balm to you now, there wasn't anything much between us. I tried; I make no bones about it. Why bother lying, after such a time? I liked her, and I wanted ... She wouldn't. We talked about it several times, just the way you and I are talking now. But she wouldn't. I'd have taken her from you, McCaig, if that had been possible. But the old Protestant morality got in the way, I suppose. In addition, there was her son; your son, Derek.'

'Look, McDowell, I didn't ...'

'Of course not; but since we may not have the opportunity again, I think it's best to clear the air. I've been clearing the air quite a lot lately. Resigned from the council, you know.'

'I didn't know.'

'Resigned yesterday.'

'Why?'

'Why anything?' said McDowell. 'Muriel wasn't the first, or the last. Don't tell me you've never considered the possibility of making second chances for yourself, fresh beginnings?'

'I never thought about it.'

'Then that may be the difference between us, the difference which makes *all* the difference.'

'Have you been to a doctor lately?'

'Yes: I'm not sleeping well, that's all,' said McDowell. 'You've been very courteous, McCaig. Do you know, when I stopped thinking of changing what I'd got, things became much easier. I found that I had so little to trade with that it wasn't worth the sacrifice. Lost chances, lost opportunities, all the things that go down the drain, you don't miss them because you can always fool yourself that they are still, in some way, recoverable, that you can go back, fetch them, dredge them up again. You can't, sometimes; that's the ... Christ, that's the curse of it all. Why did he actually have to *die*?'

McCaig could not answer. It had never occurred to him before that such answers were available; answers to death, and the meaning of it. His concern was with facts, not with the sectarian meanings which made death mysterious and the mystery hurtful. Weakness imposed upon weakness; the strengths of one man bred out of the weaknesses of another. As in genetics, so he believed, the biological line towards normalcy is established over several generations, so the shadow of a father can cast itself over the son and, in time, the son's shadow stretch backwards and blot out all that the father thought himself to be. Temporality was not a static state but, like the mind of a schizo, could by degrees become fixed and immobile in its delusions, pass on its fevers without ever burning itself out. It was not important to discover what imagined treacheries Frank McDowell had found in himself in the late hour of his life; the existence of imagined bad faith was enough. Though McCaig would never know the facts and all the stems and roots of facts which, like a fibrous tumour, latterly clouded his reason, Tom, too, had found strength insupportable.

In an abrupt ending the boy had capitulated not with what he was but with what he had told himself to be. Another man's death did not diminish you in any way at all, but the guilt of indifference could be the basis of the most subtle erosions.

'Some of it will have to come out,' said McCaig. 'I don't quite know how much I can hold back yet, but . . .'

'The girl will come to trial?'

'She'll have to.'

'But it wasn't her fault.'

'It wasn't anybody's fault,' said McCaig, though he would never make this admission again. 'But she'll still have to come to trial.'

'What will happen now?'

'We'll just have to wait . . .'

'You tell me, McCaig. Do that much for me; tell me what will happen.'

'We'll track down this Mulligan character, sweep up a few more dealers in narcotics and put them behind bars for a while.'

'Will you?'

'Aye, we will,' said McCaig.

'Very well.'

He reached out and switched on the ignition and pulled the car out of the lay-by and turned it towards Thane again. He did not speak for a while. McCaig was aware of the silence as a man in the middle of the desert might be aware of an echo, a figment of the imagination, a trick of acoustics. In direct connection and in all hearsay accounts of McDowell, McCaig had known of him as a voice, a personality vocalised into experience; now he was mute. What McDowell had told him about Muriel was consistent with the facts as he remembered them. McDowell had offered her a second chance, too, but Muriel had been too cautious to accept it. Perhaps she had spent the next four or five years regretting her decision : or maybe she just didn't care for the man. It brought no relief to McCaig to learn the truth; brought nothing much of anything. Muriel had drifted out of his life in much the same way that Tom had drifted out of McDowell's. But there was a difference, a vital difference – Muriel was still alive, not beyond recall. All the bitterness and happiness, anger and contentment which they had shared still had some shape, held the possibility of a return and a new beginning, though in his heart McCaig realised that it would never come about. Were we all just the sum total of such opportunities, daydreams of relationships which, like junk in an attic, we did not want to use but could not quite bear to discard?

When they reached the proximity of police headquarters, McCaig said, 'I appreciate what you've told me tonight, McDowell.'

'Hm?'

'About Muriel.'

'Muriel; yes.'

'I'll do what I can for you – I would have, anyway.'

'There's nothing you *can* do.'

'I can hold down the publicity.'

'Mildred might appreciate that.'

The Stag came to a halt a hundred yards from the lighted front of the headquarters' building. McCaig opened the car door.

McDowell touched him on the shoulder.

'Did Tom love that girl?' he asked.

Startled, McCaig hesitated before giving his answer.

'He might have.'

'Might?'

'Given . . . given time.'

'Ah, yes,' said McDowell.

'What will you do with the Sabre?' asked McCaig. 'If you

wish, I can hold it up in our garage until such times as you manage to dispose of it.'

McDowell shook his head. 'Leave it where it is,' he said.

'Are you sure?'

'Yes,' McDowell said. 'Mildred would prefer it that way.'

McCaig got out. The Stag drew away slowly from the kerb and, at the same pedestrian crawl, went down the last hundred yards of the side street and swung at the lights out of sight.

McCaig walked along the pavement to the main door of the police block. He felt more relaxed now, less frustrated, though, in a sense, he had achieved nothing. Hat in hand, he walked through the corridors to his office. It was quiet now, Sheila and Ryan gone and Sellars in the throes of finishing a report at one of the portables in the Inspectors' Room. McCaig put his head round the door.

'Any word on Mulligan?' he asked.

'No, Chief,' said Sellars, hardly bothering to look up from the keys. 'No word yet.'

'Right,' said McCaig. 'I'm off home to bed.'

'Good night, Chief.'

'Good night,' said McCaig.

Already Mulligan was homesick. After all, he had devoted forty-odd years of his mortal span to learning certain routines within the confines of urban geography. He had taught himself that every wrench out of the groove could be borne with stoicism because endurance would in time restore him to where he belonged and felt secure. Even his term as a soldier had been like a walk down a long tunnel to a predictable daylight; and the periods in prison – Scottish prisons, with Scottish inmates and Scottish screws – had latterly come to seem more like extensions of the pattern of security than punishments. It was as if he was really the son of the long-dead shepherd who had spent seventy years in the narrow compass of Carradale Lane and had died in the same bed in which he had been born. Mulligan's father hadn't been a travelling man either. He had fought in France in the First War, and had been to Edinburgh a few times to consult specialists in rare diseases, all of whom had packed him off home again with the assurance that he didn't have a rare disease at all. Naturally, Mulligan had more scope than either the shepherd or his father, had frequently used trains and buses and motor-cars and accepted such amenities like a proper citizen of the twentieth century. But he didn't much care for them, and cared not at all for the prospect of boarding a liner or a jumbo jet which would whisk him off to an alien country.

In the cinema that afternoon he had watched, three times over, a garish documentary about Mediterranean resorts with something akin to dread, had built up a swift abhorrence for the brilliant blue skies and sun-tanned sands and their seal-like cargoes of foreigners. Even the main feature, which he had suffered twice, had plenty of scenes of foreign parts in it – Switzerland, Spain, North Africa. It unsettled him even more. Couple of days back, he would have enjoyed at face value the rattling tale of international crime, but now the film infected him with bleak panic at the thought that he might soon be out there, in person, amid sterile snows, fly-ridden mountains or crowded sinister bazaars. What had been a safe dimension suddenly transformed itself into a preview of terrible reality.

At seven that morning, Gregor Yule had winkled him out of the cottage. The youngster had dallied long enough to watch him shave off the moustache, had taken the clock and the pusher's suit and had disposed of them. Parked in the shelter of the gable wall had been a shiny motor-car, large, square and American-looking. Greg, so he said, had rented it for a couple of days. Even the ease with which Yule could acquire a car frightened Mulligan a little now. That real people could do such things, could find in society the means of doing such things, bewildered him and brought him dangerously close to a whole complicated, baffling area in which all of the things he'd witnessed on the goggle-box or read of in magazines might conceivably come true. Reality was austerity, confinement, stasis; now he was to be yanked out of it and flung, like one of those plastic starships, out into a galaxy of worlds which didn't really exist. Twenty years ago, when he was young and quite resilient, it might not have been so bad, and he might have found excitement in the project. But not now.

All morning Greg had kept him on the move, driving him round and round the outside of the city in an ever-increasing circle, stopping only once in a lay-by in the country to feed him ham sandwiches and coffee from a flask, eating with him, not saying much, not even letting him sit up front, but

219

confining him to the broad back seat where there was less likelihood of him being spotted and identified. Mulligan just could not believe that he was in that state known as 'on the run'. As a recidivist of long standing he had never been on the run before. All his worldly goods rattled in the boot – two suitcases and a brown-paper parcel. The money he had drawn from his four current accounts in four separate city banks between nine-thirty and ten o'clock that morning was stuffed into his pockets.

Then it was the cinema, an Odeon in the heart of Glasgow, big and modern and comfortable and thinly populated with an audience of pensioners, night-shift workers and bored men on the dole. Greg had told him which cinema, and which part of the house to sit in. Mulligan followed orders almost blindly – because he didn't know what else to do. It was weird to sit there with his pockets full of money, watching films, and waiting, hiding his face in his collar when the house lights went up for the sales intermissions. He dared a trip to the foyer, once, to buy hot-dogs and Coke, took them back to the same seat he'd vacated, and ate them, and did not feel appeased. At eight-thirty, Greg turned up. The cinema was not so quiet now, but the lad found him, sat beside him, and told him to get up and go out and turn right and right again and wait by the side door. He did this, found Greg already at the side door, moving ahead of him up the street, going into the rented car. Mulligan got into the car, too. Fifteen or twenty minutes later, he was across the boundary of the City of Glasgow, and heading through the rural night towards the county town of Thane.

Greg took him into a house opposite the Majestic Theatre, led him past closed doors and down a short narrow staircase into a basement. The suitcases were left in the car, the car parked in a cul-de-sac at the back of the building. The basement did not strike Mulligan, who was used to gloomy surroundings, as particularly opulent. It came as a disappointment to him. He had expected more from Greg's place.

'Your place?' he asked.

'Yeah.'

'How long'll I be here?'

'Not long.'

'An' where'll you take me next?'

'The airport.'

'Where am I goin', then?'

'Abroad.'

'But where?'

'Madrid.'

'Madrid? That'll be in Spain?'

'Yeah.'

'Are you comin' too?'

'Don't be so bloody stupid.'

'What'll I do when I get there?'

'I'll tell you when we're driving to catch the plane.'

'When's the plane due t'leave?'

'Midnight.'

'But it's after nine now.'

'We'll make it in plenty of time.'

'Oh, Jesus, Gregor, listen.'

'Calm down. It won't be so bad.'

'I've never been up in a plane before.'

'Nothing to it.'

'What about all this money?'

'Just take it through with you.'

'But what if the bleedin' customs ... ?'

'They won't bother you.'

'What if they do? Isn't there laws'r somethin' about takin' cash ... ?'

'Would I let you do it, if there was any risk?'

'What if I'm recognised?'

'It's not liable,' said Yule. 'It's too soon.'

'What did y'do with m'old man's clock?'

'Dumped it in a midden. Nobody'll find it.'

'M'suit too?'

'Yeah.'

'I wish I'd never got ...'

'Stop whining, Mulligan. I'm doing all this to keep you out of prison. You realise that you'd serve ten at least. You'd be an old man when you got out.'

'Son, I'm an old man now.'

'Stop whining.'

'Aye, okay,' said Mulligan. He seated himself on the edge of a chair before the stove and warmed his body at its faint heat. He was shivery with nervousness and felt strangely separated from his body. He had no curiosity about his surroundings now, thinking only of how awful the plane journey would be and wondering if it would ever arrive in

Spain or would crash, like the ones he'd seen on telly, into the side of a big bare mountain where they wouldn't even find his body until spring came, and would bury him over there to rot out eternity under foreign soil. He felt nauseous.

'You hungry?' Greg asked.

He shook his head.

'You don't feel well?'

'A bit ... a bit queasy.'

'You'd better eat something.'

'I couldn't.'

'You'd better,' said Greg. 'You'll really feel sick on the plane if you don't.'

'I thought they fed you on board?'

'Not on the night flight.'

'*Do I have t'go?*'

'Yeah.'

'Greg ...'

'Here, get this down you, and belt up.'

The plate was pushed against his hand. He took it. On the plate were two fresh bread rolls, middle-split, thick with butter and cuts of roast beef dressed with a yellow pickle. He put down the lid of the roll, listlessly.

'I'm not ...'

'Eat them,' said Greg.

Mulligan opened his dry mouth, lifted one of the rolls and bit into it. He chewed obediently, masticating bread, meat and pickle thoroughly. He looked up at the boy, who was decanting boiling water from a kettle into a tea-pot.

'What's in this?' asked Mulligan.

'Best beef; eat it.'

'Tastes a bit off.'

Impatiently Greg lifted the sandwich, sniffed at the fringe of meat critically, and put it back on the plate. 'It's fine. It's the pickle – or your bloody imagination.'

Mulligan thought of the jet aircraft and the lifting swoop of it. His stomach turned over at the prospect, and felt empty. He swallowed, bit, chewed and swallowed, tried to remember what it was they ate in Spain. Rice? Fancy omelettes? His chances of picking up a nice bit of Scotch lamb or a plate of mince and potatoes were about nil. Even roast beef would probably be a luxury. His spit was bitter with the acid saliva of misery. He masticated, swallowed, and felt his hunger increase.

The first roll went over his gullet. He struggled with the second. The taste and savour of it didn't interest him, or intrude upon his despair. He ate because he imagined he was hungry and because Greg had told him it was better to travel on a full belly. His mouth was sour with the pickle and his tongue burned. He drank tea from the mug which Greg gave him, strong tea, brown as canal water, and nearly as rancid. It too had a bitter harsh flavour. He had sudden longing for something sweet – a buttered brazil or a chocolate éclair.

The lamps of the basement burned and blurred on the edges of his vision. The firelight separated itself into colourful bands, like a straight rainbow. He shook his head, dipped his naked upper lip into the mug and supped deeply at the liquid, sighing with the hotness of it.

'What's the smell?'

'Paint,' said Greg, promptly. 'A painter lives next door.'

'Is he home?'

'No, he's out.'

'Upstairs?'

'Nobody to bother us,' said Greg. 'How do you feel?'

'Better,' said Mulligan.

Then, at that precise instant, he did not feel better. He felt worse, much, much worse.

The tea seemed to scald his throat, leaving a slime in his mouth like the oily blue slime on the top of a stagnant pool. The slime radiated heat. From throat to rectum he was filled with the sensation of boiling greasy fluid heat. Within seconds, the sensation increased, and changed. Buried under fat, the muscles of his gut cramped into a rigid spasm. The plate dropped to the hearth. He reared backwards in the chair. The chair fell and he fell to the rug, writhing. His hands clawed at the tightening muscles of his belly and groin as if they were chains which bound him, or gigantic bands of black rubber. The crushing coils strapped themselves over his chest and constricted his breathing. The organs of his body were squeezed and distorted by agonising forces. Involuntarily his buttocks jumped off the rug. Vomit flooded the back of his mouth, pumping up and sinking again like bubbles of mud in a geyser. Out of the strangled, gurgling gullet, he projected a single coherent sound, Gregor's name, all he could manage of a plea for assistance.

Above him, standing taller than ever, the boy was motionless, expressionless, staring down at the throes which racked him. With a slight curious tilting of the head, Gregor enquired, 'How do you feel, Mulligan? How do you feel?'

This time, this evening, Gregor did not wait for her. Slowly, Sheila let herself into her apartment. Somehow, throughout the day, she had known that he would not come that night. As she busied herself preparing supper, she thought about him, and about what she felt for him, and wondered if it could be love. In her book love usually equated with sentimental weakness, with narcissistic needs which had no part in her character. For all that she could not attribute her waywardness and the lack of commonsense to any other cause.

She cooked up a tin of Ravioli, spiced it with Parmesan and mixed herbs, and sat down at the little card-table in front of the fire to eat. The room seemed lonely tonight, less snug than ever before. She switched on the television set but, after fiddling with the dials for a minute, found no programme to her liking and turned it off again. She unearthed a back issue of *Harper's* from the magazine bucket, propped it against the sauce bottle and tried to focus her attention on the fashion pages while she ate. Daydreams of sophistication and elegance did not relieve her nagging boredom with her own company and take her mind off the pessimistic, reckoning that Gregor Yule had given her the heave for good.

Had she been too pushing for him?

Had she flogged on the pace of the friendship so fast that she'd scared him off?

Had he guessed that she wanted him, mainly, in bed?

Or had he just lost his sympathy, his initial impetus of pity when he had found out that she was tougher than she looked?

All daft speculations, dithery and self-corrosive as an old spinster's nostalgia.

He had come into her ken suddenly, and was fully entitled to take himself off again with equal abruptness. He owed her no explanations and no debt of courtesy. Besides – she tried to cheer herself up – he might come tomorrow or on Thursday. After all, he had his own life to lead and there might well be a very ordinary reason for his failure to call round tonight. As a student, no doubt he had notes to write up, class papers to prepare, perhaps evening tutorials to attend. Even so, she felt abandoned. She thought she might wash her hair. She thought she might go down to the Drovers' lounge and have a vodka and orange and see if any of her quiet steady middle-aged companions were there : then she thought that she wouldn't. Her present mood would make her bad company.

She cleared the table, washed the dishes, and sat down by the fire to drink a second cup of coffee and smoke a cigarette.

In that period of reflection she allowed herself to consider possibilities which, however improbable, lay beyond the realm of girlish selfishness, to enlarge on the uneasy suspicions which had taken her twenty-four hours ago, that Gregor Yule was not quite so wholesome as he pretended to be, and was using her for some devious reason of his own.

What reason, Sheila?

Sex, Sheila?

Gossipy rumours of the girl now stashed in Judgehead came back to her; Hilary Lawrence – a name she'd typed twenty times in the last couple of days. They said Hilary Lawrence was a pervert and a whore, as well as being a drug-addict. Outrageous tales had circulated in the canteen. You could sprinkle innuendo on any sort of tragedy and change its flavour, the way you shook Parmesan over pasta. Tomorrow she must ask Harry Ryan for a little of the truth.

Just what Hilary Lawrence's sordid life had to do with her own stillborn affair with Gregor Yule, Sheila could not define. Gregor had asked about the McDowell case, certainly, but lots of casual acquaintances expressed curiosity in the department's work, tried to wring inside information out of her to give themselves an edge in the public-house sport of one-upmanship. Not that she had ever told them anything.

She wasn't a blabber-mouth.

She wasn't . . .

Consider it carefully, Sheila; how much did you tell him?

Lying back in the chair, she crossed her legs and propped her ankles on the edge of the card-table, and set about a deliberate unpicking of all the threads of the conversations she had had with the young man. Just how much *had* she told him? What had been the topic to which he had returned unfailingly, circling it and appearing to avoid it but always coming back to it like a brown bumble bee to a tree hive.

Tom McDowell; her work on the case; her work in the Chief's office? It was to the facts of the McDowell case and its progress that Gregor had turned the conversation time and again.

In five days she had mapped out its whole development for him.

She sought for an outlet, an excuse to release guilt and funnel a growing awareness of her own dimwitted female stupidity into other channels.

It couldn't be; could it?

It probably wasn't.

But if it *was,* what had she told him that was so important that he had given up his search for current and secret news, had cut off the fountain at its source?

To admit that she had talked freely of matters under embargo, had given out information which could be detrimental to the police case, had betrayed the loyalty of her position, was more than she could bring herself to do. To cover up, though, at this stage, might involve a more serious sedition. Sheila knew only too well how detectives worked. Behind the vast apparatus of technology and scientific aids were still men who gathered intangibles and, by age-old processes of induction, saw the truth. Detectives worked like trackers reading invisible spoors, the broken stems of coincidence and crushed leaves of emotions. Allegedly it was supposedly a cut-and-dried, factual sort of profession – but it wasn't. Only the law courts demanded shape and pattern.

Besides, certain facts did fit – Gregor being a student at New College, living in Thane, seeking her out. Less than charitable towards him now that the glow of his personality had cooled for her, she found other signs and meanings in his behaviour which would explain, in the terms of her analysis, what it was that he had wanted with her all along.

It he had wanted that, what must his reason be?

Involvement, at one level or another, with the McDowell case; or – perhaps more likely – with Hilary Lawrence?

The bitch, Sheila thought.

She made no decision as to what she would do tomorrow, how she would confirm, or rebut, her assumption that she had been used by Gregor Yule and soiled by him as she had never been soiled by one of her casual sexual partners.

After a few minutes, she got up and washed her hair.

Shampoo, warm water and soft towels calmed her down considerably.

Tomorrow she would sound out Harry Ryan.

Really, Gregor might not be involved at all. She might be doing the guy, and herself, a dreadful injustice.

At this stage, a delay of a night and a day would make no difference to anyone.

The type and strength of the poison were unknown to Gregor Yule. He had found the packet, hardly used, stored amid a litter of bleach bottles, carbolic, holystone, and domestic cleaning fluids in the back of a neglected cupboard under the sink in Vikki's kitchen. By the look of it, it had been there for years. A kind of fungus had grown across the top of the substance which, in itself, appeared as lethal in colour and texture as anything Greg had ever seen. Curry's Killing Powder came in an old-fashioned dark-green cardboard packet, with a sabre-toothed rat silhouetted on front and dense blocks of print on all other surfaces. Advertising incentive consisted of dire warnings as to the death-dealing properties of the stuff. He read through the screed several times, but found no formula, and no indication that the compound would not work just as well on a man as on a rat. He assumed that its active constituent would be strychnine, not arsenic. The base material was not, as the label promised, a powder, but a lard-like lump the colour of tallow and blued by fungus. He deduced that it had deteriorated in the keeping but had no way of knowing whether its effectiveness had been increased or reduced by the change of state. He did not doubt, however, that a properly administered dose of Curry's Killing Powder would rid him once and for all of the nuisance of William Mulligan.

Poison needed no temper, no personal contact. He could perform the operation without soiling his hands or risking the possibility of funk at the crucial moment. The use of poison even made it all seem mildly tender-hearted, like euthanasia. When he had contemplated murder – as every man contemplates murder at some time in his life – he had considered it as an extreme form of defence, an ultimate weapon in the battles of the personality with society's pygmy armies. Greg was fully cognisant of the risks involved, but could not sanely equate the loss of what he had gained and the functions and fulfilments inherent in that gain with the intangible measure of a few extra years in prison. The odds for letting Mulligan live were not high enough to tempt him.

The preparation of the poisoned meat and drink was the easiest of all the chores he set himself to perform that day. The hiring of the car hadn't been too much of a problem, though it had taken time. Dressing himself in his best navy-blue suit and completing the image of a young executive by carrying his black leather attaché-case, he had journeyed by cab from Thane through the early morning darkness, out to the flatland of Renfrewshire where the City of Glasgow had built its airport. The desk clerk in the Hertz kiosk arranged the papers with practised efficiency and by seven o'clock Greg had become the temporary owner of a big steel-grey Ford Executive. Driving directly from the airport, he reached Carradale Lane by seven-thirty, shook up Mulligan, removed the tell-tale wall-clock and Mulligan's pusher-suit and strewed them piecemeal in the middens of the occupied tenements in the neighbourhood. With Mulligan in tow, he toured the city until the banks opened, dropped the old man, with full instructions, and picked him up again forty minutes later on the kerb outside the National Commercial in Beckett Square. For the next four hours he drove round and round the country backroads, weaving through four counties, crossing and recrossing the boundaries, until the Odeon opened for matinée trade at 2.00 p.m. With Mulligan installed among the audience, and safe for a while, he drove back into Thane, parked the Ford in a public lot on the outskirts of the town, and walked back to the house opposite the theatre to embark on the second phase of his schedule.

Adjusted to his student ways, neither Whitehouse nor Vikki were particularly surprised to see him at that hour of a Wednesday afternoon. He settled down in the kitchen and, in less than fifteen minutes, had planned Vikki's evacuation from the house in detail. He gave her money, suggested that she visit the Plantagenet, a garish new road-house complete with slot-machines, topless dancers and German keg beer, and led her to believe that he would join her there later in the evening. Naturally, Whitehouse was elected baby-sitter and, his demonic assault on his current canvas thus interrupted, was easily bribed into doing another little job for his patron instead. Shortly after the evening opening, Whitehouse was despatched to the Kettles lounge bar with orders to watch out for the arrival of a mysterious young lady whose description Greg, with the help of some old magazines, concocted in scrupulous detail. The stake-out was a hoax, of course, and Greg had been careful to create a female character who could have no possible counterpart in all of Thane. Loyal to the promise of another fiver, however, Whitehouse would remain at his post in the Kettles until fifteen minutes after the shout for last rounds. He would return by the 10.32 bus and wouldn't be back in the basement much before 11.00. Vikki would find herself a companion, and the possibility of her staggering home much before midnight was remote. By the time Whitehouse arrived, Mulligan, and all scraps of evidence pointing to Mulligan's brief tenancy of the basement, would have been swept away and destroyed. The only argument which Greg had all afternoon was over the welfare of the kid; Whitehouse was reluctant to leave her. Only Greg's repeated assurances that he would be at home all evening finally settled the matter. To Greg's way of thinking, this lie was too small even to take into account.

Shortly after seven, he furnished the kid with a packet of fruit gums and a couple of new comic books, told her to lie quiet in bed, and went out. When he returned with Mulligan, he installed the fat man in the basement and nipped upstairs to find that, as he had anticipated, the kid had fallen asleep. She lay on her back with a crescent of pastilles on her pillow, her mouth sticky and the comics glued to the quilt. Greg removed the particle of sweet stuff, drew the blankets over her shoulders and, leaving the bedlamp alight, went hurriedly below to deal with the old man.

In prospect, death by poisoning had seemed like a clean, sure method of putting down the old bastard.

Something had gone seriously wrong.

The strength of the paste had not been sufficient to kill him outright. Greg had visualised Mulligan rearing up from the table, clutching his throat and falling backwards, heavy and silent as a sandbag, already dead. With no previous experience of the science of murder, however, Greg was caught completely off guard by the old man's tenacity and refusal to knuckle under to the burning agony in his tripes.

The sight of him was horrible, fascinatingly horrible.

Moved by inquisitiveness, he asked hopefully, 'How do you feel, Mulligan? How do you feel?'

The features contorted into puckered ridges of muscle tissue, torn by the tendons below. Eyes popped, and the mouth was locked open, the protruding tongue like scorched leather, striving to wag him an answer. Flecks of froth and spittle hinged his lips. The croaking, cawing voice sprawled out obscene pleas for help and understanding, all unintelligible.

Shuffling backwards, Greg could not find the will to navigate himself out of the line of Mulligan's crawling progress. Primitive cells in the old brain hoarded cunning. The glass-bright eyeballs found focus on the horse-blanket curtain which hid the stairs. Greg reached it first, buttocks and shoulders sagging into the material. It was as if the man on all fours on the floor was a mad dog stalking him and he, cornered, was as hypnotised and spineless as a rabbit or a lamb.

The noises grew louder and more ferocious. Though no intelligible word yet formed out of the gabble, strangulated cries and anguished howls heaved out of the disintegrating gut. The sounds were pushed forward and amplified by the gullet's convulsions, to thicken in the mouth, clotting on vomit and the exudations of saliva in that gaping cave.

Yule could not believe that he had been responsible for creating this thing. He was paralysed by Mulligan's corrosion and filled with awareness of how hideous an entity death can be when it forces itself into the body of a healthy man. He jerked back from the sight. Parting the blanket, he tripped on the step and sat down hard on the stairs. Podgy fingers tore at the edge of the drape. Mulligan's face followed him, peeping up from the floor level, head balanced on shoulder, rocking on the distended belly. It appeared through the gap and vanished again, like the invention of a fiendish toy-maker operated by wires, weights and counter-weights. It came again. Greg lashed out at it. His shoe caught the soft cheek, skidded down into the mouth. The suppurating howls cut off. Bracing himself on his elbows, he hacked out again at the ghastly apparition. His heel struck bone, solid, real, frangible. The thing dropped and rolled and the claws retracted. The curtain wafted back and blotted it from view. Whimpering, Greg let his head drop backwards, exhausted by fear, but relieved that now, *surely*, it was over. Long, wavering scalpel-sharp screams cut into his eardrums, and jack-knifed him through the curtain, wild with rage.

Mulligan bore no mark of blood. Arms akimbo, he lay on his back, eyes screwed shut, screaming like a great fretful baby. Greg stamped on his throat. The scream broke into fragments, quick and fluid as mercury. Greg used his heel again. He drove in with all the strength of his body, transmitting it through thrusting thighs. He directed the blows consciously to the side of the dying man's skull, just above the right ear, and maintained the battery until all the sounds ceased.

Sweat coagulated on his brows and dribbled down the furrow to his nose. Absently he dabbed at it with his cuff. A series of spasmodic shudders passed along the deflated shape on the floor, shaking it vigorously from ankles to nape, making heels and head rap hard on the lino. Flabby arms slapped like flippers. Final vibrations of life passed along them like water through a hose until there was no more movement. The fatness of the man became heavy, the stillness fused with silence. Gregor knew that at last Mulligan was dead.

Motionless, he stood by the corpse. Shocked nerves twitched in him. In deep places, his whole metabolism had suffered shock. For all that, his mind soon regained its clarity. Within minutes he was thinking coldly and logically again. The shock would quickly pass off. Patiently, he waited until his system calmed enough to enable him to lift up his arm and look at his wristwatch. Black dial and broad white hands; he felt suddenly strong enough to go through with the rest of it.

Ten minutes to ten o'clock. In fifteen minutes the Majestic would void its crowd; the barman at the Plantagenet would ring the bell for last orders. Buried in the lounge of the Kettles on the other side of town, Whitehouse would give the clientele one last faithful scrutiny, disappointed that he had failed to find Greg's mythical female and earn his fiver that night.

Greg projected himself unsteadily across the basement to the sink. It occurred to him that he might throw up and he leaned over the sink in hope; nothing came. He washed his hands and face thoroughly in cold water, and massaged his skin until a feeling of warmth returned. He didn't feel too bad now, light in limb, clear-headed. From a hiding place in the cabinet, he removed a new clear plastic bag, unfolded it and stretched wide its mouth. Into the bag he dropped the remains of the meat roll, the broken parts of the plate, Mulligan's hat and gloves, and the dregs of the packet of Curry's Killing Powder. He washed out the mug which Mulligan had used, left the tap running into the sink to swill away all traces of sediment. Deliberately, he broke the mug on the sink's edge and placed the parts in the bag. From under the bed, he pulled out a cardboard carton stacked to the brim with back issues of *Management, New Society,* and *The Economist.* Under the magazines was a neat, smooth, red, builder's brick. Greg slid the brick to the bottom of the plastic bag, squeezed out all pockets of air, screwed up the mouth and bound it round with a length of nylon fishing line spooled from a reel in his pocket. Biting off the line, he tied two extra knots in it, weighed it thoughtfully, like a competitive angler with a salmon, then laid the heavy bundle by Mulligan's body.

Next, he exchanged his jacket for a garment of cheap black oilskin, knee-length, and fastened it to his throat. A pair of wash-leather gloves covered his hands. He got down on one knee beside Mulligan and rifled the man's pockets, removing bundles and packages of bank-notes, and all personal papers. He salted the money under the magazines in the carton and shoved the carton under the bed again; a purely temporary hiding place. Mulligan's documents he tucked into the pockets of the oilskin and studded down the flaps.

The tollbooth clock struck echoes from the flat, faded air of the street.

Ten o'clock.

Yule caught Mulligan's wrists. Touching the dead man's flesh caused him no alarm. He lugged the body through the horse blanket and laid it on its back against the stairs, hands and arms raised. Returning to the basement he straightened chairs and rugs, turned off the water tap, closed the cabinet, folded the towel and draped it over the rod below the sink. Lifting the plastic bundle in his arms, he picked his way round Mulligan, climbed the short flight of stairs and went out through the door at the top. A long, unlit, sour-smelling corridor led him to the kitchen. The fuel store door gave him direct access to the back yard of the building. At the close-mouth he hesitated, listened, heard nothing. He sauntered down the path and swung left to the patch of waste ground where he had parked the Ford. He unlocked the doors and boot, lifted the boot lid and stowed the bundle hard against the shell over the wheel arch. He shifted Mulligan's luggage – two suitcases and a brown-paper parcel – to the interior of the car, then, leaving the boot propped open, hurried back into the house.

The only light in the hall was the strip which showed from the bedroom door, and a faint fish-scale silvering from the panel of the front door. Yule went down into the basement. Turning, he presented his back to Mulligan's thighs. Stooped, he groped for the man's hands, found them, stooped lower still, then steadily drew himself upright, lifting the load from the stairs. When the weight of his burden was evenly distributed across his shoulders, he jigged round, trudged upstairs through the open door, and into the hall again. Mulligan's head nudged his inner arm. Yule kept his lips and nostrils closed against the bad smell from the dead man's mouth. Mercifully, Mulligan was so short that his feet did not scrape the floor, but the portly belly pressed against Greg's buttocks, throwing him off balance, straining him. Panting and sweating, he staggered through the kitchen and out into the yard.

Congested now in the region of the theatre entrance, cabs, buses and private vehicles hooted and rasped, ground-base to the faint fluctuating chitter of voices and footsteps. The tails of patrons' cars showed at the end of the lane. Greg unloaded Mulligan into the boot. The body fitted neatly, with room to spare. He folded up the stiffening knees, and jammed the elbows into the groin. He raised his head and glanced along the flank of the car, then round and up at the tenement windows. As always, they were curtained, and as blank as squares of blotting paper. He darted a dozen yards back down the lane to the corner of a wash-house where, earlier that evening, he had constructed a cairn of bricks and heavy stones culled from neighbouring yards. He transferred a dozen assorted bricks to the back of the Ford and built them against the body in the boot. That done, he locked the boot and returned to the house once more.

A last quick inspection of basement, stairs and hall satisfied him. He left, closing doors behind him.

In the driving seat of the Executive, he fired the engine gently. The car crunched forward, soft springs hardly recording the weight in the boot. Using only the radiance from surrounding buildings to guide him, Greg fed the vehicle slowly up the narrow lane, just in time to catch the departure of the last of the theatre traffic. A Wolseley pulled out from the space between the gables of Vikki's building and the Majestic Bar. Greg followed it. Switching on tail and side lights, he brought the Ford to the end of the cobbles at the kerb's edge, momentarily blocking the swarm of pedestrians from the bar. After waiting tensely for a suitable opportunity, he steered out into the main street. The Paddy-wagon, customarily on duty at the cul-de-sac beyond the junction, remained immobile in his mirror. It grew smaller and smaller as he swept uphill at decent speed and angled into the space between two tall buses.

When this moment of danger was over, Yule settled at the wheel. Methodically he ticked over all the things he had done. Minutes of concentrated mental effort steadied him still more. In a half-hour it would all be over, and he would be back home again. He had forgotten nothing, omitted nothing, made no mistakes. Even the bad deal with Mulligan, upon which he did not allow himself to dwell, had not disrupted his timing or seriously upset his schedule.

Mulligan would soon be well out of harm's way. The link would be broken, the connection sheared off once and for all, and he would be safe to go on as he had before; not trading horse any more, of course, but with all that profit, including Mulligan's three thousand, stashed away to be used when the time was ripe.

He felt very confident.

Nothing could tie him in with heroin, McDowell, or that bloody old bundle of guts swaying in the boot.

Nothing, and nobody.

The sheet gave scanty protection. Sounds came through it like globs of jelly through the tit of the cheesecloth when her auntie made jam out of brambles; big solid blobbing sounds which had no meaning for her and were all the more frightening because of their anonymity. Across her teeth was a film of sour raspberry stickiness from the fruit gums. Through a chink in her fingers she could see the corners of a coloured comic jutting under the sheet. She would have liked to have taken her hands down, catch a handful of quilt and draw it right over her head, made the darkness and downy folds contain her and keep her safe, stifle the noises which were coming in the door and up through the floor. How long she'd been awake, or what had wakened her, she did not really know. She couldn't think very clearly in her head. Her head seemed choked up with fright, the way your nose gets when you have a cold. But fright could not last at a sustained pitch. It lowered, and became confused with other stray thoughts and feathers of sleep, and with her own sticky fingers, her wrists, her tummy and the bump on the side of her nose which she could see when she shut one eye. When it was at its height, though, it made her sick and wet with sweat. It made her want the toilet, too, so that she closed her knees up and rounded her back, and lay there tiny, like a baby.

If Peter had been in the house, she would have hopped out of bed and scampered through the hall and shouted to him. Peter would have come bounding up the stairs, worried looking, with long knees and arms sticking out. He would have caught her with his hands and lifted her and held her against him, her ear pressing the spongy bumps of his chest, her legs dangling. But Peter was out; he had told her that he had to go out. Nobody else ever told her who was in or out, so that she never really knew how frightened she should be. He told her that Greg would be downstairs, and that if she wanted anything she was to call out to Greg. Greg had given her sweets and comics and tucked the clothes round her. But he wasn't the same as Peter. He didn't tell her he would be downstairs. He said nothing to her except to be quiet. She did not mind Greg when he was with Peter or Mama. But when he was alone he was just like other grown-up men who came and went. Some of them brought her things and smiled at her, even touched her, as if she belonged to whoever wanted her for a minute or two.

If she had a dog, it would come in now and put its nose under the covers and lick her hands. She would not be frightened to look out, would see it there wagging its tail. She would snap her fingers and he would come up and snuggle under with her and she would feel safe. If she had a dog, she would call it Bracken – which Peter said was an excellent name for some kinds of dogs. It would be warm and clean and large and lie beside her at night, or across the foot of the bed, with one eye open, to protect her from everything when Peter wasn't there. Peter said he would get her a dog, but Mama said she wasn't going to have a nasty dirty creature in her house.

235

She had a doll called Marigold. Marigold had a dark blue apron and a cloth face and cloth hair. She loved Marigold, but could not find her then to cuddle her and tell her how much she loved her. Marigold had slipped away and she did not dare move to find her in case moving started up the noises again. Peter would find Marigold when he came home. He would put Marigold close beside her in her elbow, because even dolls with cloth faces and no mouths to make smiles with like to be cuddled at night. She knew he could not be home yet, because he would have come up to her and kissed her and she would wake up enough to know it was him.

The sound came up out of the carpet. She could feel it as well as see it. She made a noise in her throat and felt wet in her stomach again. She could not breathe, waiting for a hand to pluck off the covers and get her. The sound itself was like a hand, a big claw, a monster's claw, curved and sharp to cut her in two. She waited for it, feeling it with her skin and her hair and her mouth, in the inside of her mouth even, while it changed its shape to screaming.

She wanted Peter, not a dog or Marigold. He would tell her it was all right, and would show her that it was all right. He would not be worried, because nothing worried Peter except what she did and how she felt. He would like to lie beside her and talk. The talk would be like the medicine her auntie brought for her once when she was sick. Soft and syrupy and sweet, it would trickle over her like the medicine trickled over her throat, and make the feeling go away.

But Peter was not in the house.

Peter was not down below, where the noises were.

Greg was down below, unless he had not come back from going out. He had gone out before, when she sat in bed trying to read the comics and taste the gums, thinking that the door was very far away and the roof high and waiting for the handle to turn.

'Peter,' she said.

She said it quietly because she wanted him to hear but not to let the noises know that she was in the house.

They came loudly again. When she tried not to listen, she found that she listened harder. She could hear them as loudly as if they were coming from right under the bed where the boxes were and the dust.

236

Something was screaming; then there were different noises, shouting. It wasn't like the noises Mama's friends made when they drank beer and whisky and had a good time in the front room. The noises were downstairs. There were never noises there, except when Peter shifted his easel or dropped something. Then she could hear him say 'Jesus' right after it.

She wanted to get up to the toilet, go running, shout for Peter. But the noises would be waiting for her. One of them would be at the bedroom door in the dark of the hall, waiting to pounce on her. She was not brave; she could not be brave anywhere, even lying in bed. She could not go and she could not stay. She closed her eyes and said Peter's name over and over again.

She was crying. She knew she was crying and held it in her nose, which made her eyes all the wetter.

Sounds on the floor, on the wooden stairs, in the hall outside. Things came from outside, from the dark of the coal-hole between the kitchen and the tunnel to the back court. The coal-hole housed a black hatchet and a hill of dusty black coal on which things lay, rotting. The sounds were like the hatchet flying in the air, coal tumbling and falling as if something was coming up out of it. She could feel heat between her legs where she needed the toilet. It distracted from her fear by the shame of thinking what Mama would do if she could not get up and go out into the hall to the lavatory. But the sounds were in the hall now. She could hear air outside, emptiness hissing. She did not know if it was coming in or going out.

Peter had said that when your fright got bad enough you did something about it, even if it was only running. Peter said that running in the right direction soon chased whatever it was that he was frightened of, except bulls. Before she could think about it she got up and ran over the long bare floor to the door. It was open a little.

She clung to the handle, the hotness in her tummy turned cold under her pyjamas.

The sounds came again like something climbing up inside the wall of the room, like the footsteps of the man with the big shiny boot who lived in the pub. The distance between the door and the bed was like the space in the sky above the curve of the close. She could not leave the door nor stop herself looking.

The hunchbacked giant shambled out of the darkness and crossed the light. He had two heads and feet sticking out of his back, white hands hanging as if they had been broken off and stuck on again in the wrong place. He did not look at her but went on down into the dark corridor. She could see him filling the door of the kitchen. She forgot everything, her coldness and her pee-pee. Everything was blotted out by the thought that the hunchback would come out of the coal when he had dug a place for her and would carry her off, drag her down through the coal into the black pit. She went back to the bed and sat on it, waiting, waiting for the sounds of his coming, creak of the door, limping thump of his shiny boot, his hand on her, his arms in the wrong place and feet growing out of his back, two heads.

She lay there, like that, with no ebbing of her terror; time stopped. The pee-pee was cold and swollen in her tummy. She closed her eyes.

He did not come slow and steady; he came running. The door did not creak but burst open. She knew that not only had he come for her but that he was mad at her too, and wouldn't wait to take her to the pit under the coal but would eat her alive here. She lifted herself up, swung from the knees, came off the bed on her knees, and landed on the floor. Peter was running towards her, stooped over to scoop her up. She had never seen anything like this face. Though it was not the face of the hunchbacked giant, it was mad. She thought he was mad at her. That was worse, far worse, than what she had seen and the waiting and the coldness of what she expected.

She opened her eyes wide, and screamed. The hot pee-pee clouded her legs. She looked down at it, still screaming, but could not stop it.

Peter picked her up. She knew it was him, broke, cried, clung to him. Her head was in his hand, her wet legs and pyjamas pressed against him. He didn't seem to care about it.

'*Who did it?*' he shouted. Then his voice was quiet but with a shout still behind it. 'Who the bloody hell did it, Louise?'

She cried.

He cradled her, rocking her, saying to her over and over again, 'All right, there now, all right, there now. All right, luv.' She could feel the sponges in his pockets and the brass

238

buttons and the roughness of the hair on his chin. Her mouth against his cheek, not alone any more, she wept.

Vikki fumbled with her doorkey, got the door open and backed, bum first, into the house. She wasn't nibbed with Greg for not turning up at the Plantagenet. She couldn't very well hold it against him when he'd shelled out all that lolly to buy her booze. She closed the door, took the key out and turned round.

'Greg-egggy?'

There had been that smart fella in the Plant who might have come home with her if she'd given him a tiny bit of encouragement. But she thought that she would rather have Greg, *would* have Greg, and there'd be none of the bother of getting rid of the fella in the morning. Some nights it was lovely to make it with a strange one, but you had to pay for the pleasure in the morning with natter, getting him fed and out of the house before daylight. Wasn't like that with Greg. He just gave her the heave when he'd had enough, and she went upstairs and to her own bed, and slept better for it. God Jesus, but she was a bent lady tonight; the carpet seemed to be moving away from her like a conveyor belt.

'Gregor-eeeeeee.'

When the bedroom door opened, her face sank into a peevish scowl. She thought she would see the kid there, would have to sober up enough to lead her to the loo, as if she wasn't old enough to go on her own. Nobody ever took *her* to the loo – fifty yards down at the bottom of the yard in a stinking shed – when she was young in Bradford.

'What the bleedin' hell . . .'

Whitehouse was leaning against the doorpost. He looked bigger, and less . . . less . . . she couldn't think of the word; just less.

On the painter's face was something she did not at first recognise. Only after she had come close did she see that it was the same look of blind, righteous fury which her own old man used to draw on like a mask when he'd got wind of what she'd been up to with the boys round the back of the mill. To recognise it at all she had to come within range.

Whitehouse's hand cracked across her jaw. A blizzard of red flakes danced over her vision. He hit her again on the other side of the face, making her neck twist sharply. Tilted on high heels, she began to fall. He pushed her shoulder with the flat of his hand to keep her upright and in target, and slapped her deftly four more times from cheekbone to the tip of her chin. She felt blood inside her mouth where the hinge of her dentures caught the lining. Too stunned to duck, she began yelling. He tackled her round the waist. She grabbed a handful of his filthy hair. It occurred to her that he had gone mad with repressed lust, that she was about to be entered and savagely raped right there in the hall. Alcoholic gases belched out of her as he squeezed her belly with his forearms and rammed her back against the door to the basement. It swung behind her. She went down, backwards, and fell with Whitehouse on top of her. The pain in her spinal column took away any fear, and anticipation, which she might have nurtured until then. She soared up into insanity, ripping him, pistoning her knees in the hope that she might disembowel the bastard. He was shouting too. She heard the word *Louise* repeated, but it didn't register. Whitehouse wasn't doing anything now, just laying on her, trying, in a vague kind of way to protect his genitals. He didn't seem to worry about his hands and face. She scratched and raked at all the exposed flesh. Then he pushed himself up. She went sliding downstairs and trying to save herself, lost adhesion completely and bumped and battered her way to the foot, where she lay groaning and moaning, thinking that he had killed her.

When she opened her left eye and looked up to make sure that Whitehouse wasn't coming on down to finish the job, she saw Greg above her in the doorway, his arm out to restrain the painter. Shouting, she started up, pointing her finger at Whitehouse.

'Get 'im out of my bleedin' house,' she screamed. 'Either that buggerahell goes or I . . . Get 'im out of my sight. Get 'im outa here, 'fore I kill him.'

'Vikki,' said Greg. 'Calm down.'

He leaned over, gave her a hand and dragged her to her feet. She went soft and limp against him. Whitehouse was still at the top of the stairs, bawling in a high outraged voice. She paid him no attention.

'What happened?' said Greg.

'He . . . attacked me. Unprovoked assault.'

'*Unprovoked nothing,*' Whitehouse shouted. '*You negligent bitch.*'

'I've a good bleedin' mind to call the coppers.'

240

'No,' said Greg, putting her at arms length. 'No, you don't want to do that.'

'It's my house; you wanna go with 'im too?'

'Go upstairs,' said Greg. 'Make tea, or something.'

He edged her upstairs towards Whitehouse. She would have gone for the bugger again, if Greg hadn't read her intention, got between them, and escorted her safely out of the basement into the kitchen. The big boy seemed harassed. She didn't know what had started Whitehouse off and she didn't care. She wasn't going to climb down now. For weeks she had felt his presence in the house as a threat, a living embodiment of disapproval. She had intended to find a method of being rid of him without offending Greg. Greg could stay; she wanted Greg to stay. It was very useful to have a man around the house. Whitehouse was no man, she hated his guts, and his dirty, haggard appearance, and all the attention he gave the kid. It wasn't healthy that a grown man should spend so much time with a kid, should think more of the kid than he did of the kid's mother.

She let the tears come. 'I mean it, Greg,' she said. He seated her solicitously at the kitchen table. 'I mean it, I want him out, tonight.'

'Don't be hasty, Vikki.'

'*Tonight.*'

'All right.'

'*Tonight: bag'n'baggage.*'

'I heard you.'

He slammed his hand down flat on the table beside her, disrupting her performance. She swung round to look up at him, uncertain if she had pushed him too far. He was gone, though, already out in the corridor.

She heard him say, 'You heard, Whitehouse. You've got to vacate; tonight.'

Then the door closed, and only the muffled sound of the voices came to her.

Five minutes later, still shouting like a tink on the end of a two-day drunk, Whitehouse hauled his gear through the hall and left.

Vikki wasn't sorry. Now she would have Greg all to herself.

It was breakfast time before Gregor Yule discovered what the brawl had been about. It had bothered him little during the night; the long day had exhausted him mentally and physically and the row had only put the cap on it. He spared a few minutes to placate the Harcourt bitch, assured himself that the barney had had nothing to do with what had gone on in the basement an hour before. He attributed it to booze, Vikki's usual skinful, and the effects of the Kettles' brew on Whitehouse. The blow-up had been looming for some time. Anyway, with the horse trading shut down, he could find no viable reason to retain Whitehouse. Whitehouse had been useful, though, and Yule would not have sacked him, or altered the pattern of their relationship in any way at that time, if it hadn't been for Vikki. He would have preferred to be rid of *her*; but she owned the house and he needed the basement as a convenient, cheap and inconspicuous seat of operations.

Breakfast with Vikki was a ritual he customarily avoided. She had to get up to see the kid off to school, making gestures over the frying-pan. Still blowsy and sick-looking, she was wrapped in a ragged peignoir which accentuated the fatness of her hips and the sag of her bust. She put her hair inside a net, and substituted a stroke or two of lipstick for a wash.

Greg waited until the kid had gone to school, then went out into the yard to study the weather. The morning was raw. Thick chill mist shrouded the streets and would drown farmland and towns alike. If the sun consented to make an appearance at all, it would not be until after noon. Mist would cloak the river too, folding over steep clay banks, draping the rocks, veiling the town's brick cliffs. It would cling to the water's surface like the ghosts of currents reluctant to leave the mother tide. The river would be still, stiller than the air, and black as Guinness in the bottomless pools by Worden and Penmore where factories spat out their effluents and the channel scored into bedrock and utilised for part of its journey the famous Worden fissure which made the potholes as fathomless as some highland lochs. His pockets full of stones, Mulligan was down there now, still softly descending perhaps, toes reaching for an eventual bottom, his large head lifted upwards. Bundle, parcel and suitcases, rock-laden, too, preceded him, touching nothing except other lumps of junk which had found their buoyancy level and hung suspended in the broth under the crust of the earth. Maybe there would be other bodies to keep Mulligan company; the bodies of unwanted infants, children missing and never found, suicides – a whole shoal of them, perhaps, in that best of all possible worlds to house the secret dead.

'You want this?'

'What?'

'Black puddin'.'

'Yeah, I'll have it.'

Vikki dropped the greasy meal-pudding from the end of her fork. It fell past his ear and landed on the plate, splitting the skin of his fried egg.

'Eat it, then.'

Greg took up his fork and listlessly ate a mouthful or two. He was dressed for college, collar and tie, hacking jacket and slacks, neat, not too new, conservative. He had already shaved, and groomed his hair. His first class was at ten. The Executive was parked in the lot behind the County Hotel. He would return it to Hertz later this evening. He would not, of course, ride to college in it.

'What happened last night?' he asked.

'That bugger molested me.'

'That much I know,' said Greg. 'Why did he go for you?'

'How should I know?'

'I thought maybe the kid told you.'

'Yer; well!'

'Whitehouse was none too pleased. Seems the kid was running round the house screaming her head off,' Greg said.

'She told me.'

'My fault, really,' said Greg, without contrition. 'I thought Whitehouse was home.'

'Where was he?'

'Out for a pint.'

'Where was you?'

'Here; studying. I went out for a walk, that's all. She was fine when I left. I wouldn't have left her, if I hadn't thought Whitehouse . . .'

'She told me.'

'Told you what?' Greg asked.

'Little bitch 'ad a nightmare, that's all. Nightmares at 'er age.'

'When?'

Vikki clapped down the frying-pan and kneaded her brow. 'How should I know? What's wrong with you? She 'ad a nightmare.'

'What sort of nightmare?'

'Saw a man in the house.'

'It might have been me. Was she out of bed?'

'You! Bleedin' hunchback she says she saw. She's 'ad 'er head filled up with rubbish from that bugger Whitehouse, if you ask me. I clipped 'er ear for 'er. She won't have nightmares again in a hurry, I can tell you.'

'What else?'

'Noises, sounds; you know what kids are.'

'Noises?'

'Had you a bird down here last night?'

Greg forced a grin. 'You're joking, of course I don't bring birds here.'

'Screams and shouts, that sort of thing.'

'Did she tell you this?'

'Yer.'

'Did she tell Whitehouse?'

'Tell 'im what?'

'About her dream?'

'Ask 'im about that, not me,' Vikki said. 'Good dose of salts that kid needs.'

'Yeah.'

'No right t'blame me, he hadn't.'

'I expect she'll kick up hell when she finds he's gone,' Greg said.

'She knows he's gone, but she thinks he's coming back.'

'She'll get over it,' Greg said, rising from the table.

'She'd better,' Vikki said. 'If she so much as mentions that bugger's name again, I'll kill 'er, so help me I will.'

'Yeah,' Gregor said, and went out to fetch his books.

The class was like the amphitheatre of a surgical demonstration room. Steep-tiered seats ascended from a platform upon which brushed steel spot-lamps fixed their shadowless beams. The classroom, like most of Thane New College, still smelled of fresh carpeting and paint. Lowered on steel rods from the curved ceiling above the podium, two massive television screens showed clear bright pictures of a nomadic tribesman, swathed in Lancashire cottons, leading a camel up a concrete motorway which seemed to stretch straight into infinity. The subject of the lecture was *Management's Role in the Development of Foreign Economic Environments*. In company with all but the most ardent student

244

conservationists, who muddled the basic premises, anyhow, Greg found it dull.

Above the music and the commentary, Swinstead, the dogsbody lecturer in the field, added his listless comments. The curtains were drawn, the morning thus blanked out, the overhead lights dimmed.

The classroom hardly existed for Greg. His mind was fixed with questing authority on the clues which Vikki had given him that morning, clues which required immediate interpretation. Though hardly conscious of it, his limbs were tensed to the point of rigidity, as if his mind was preparing his body for the execution of some superhuman physical task. In life – whether life be regarded as adventure or thrall – key scenes were not the result of sudden motor-responses. These sprang from tussles of the mind with the emotions, and the emotions with the will, and the will with a latent moral sense which, in Gregor Yule's case, was intricately linked with the fear of failure and discovery.

Greg worked it out logically, step by step.

Whitehouse had not been around the house long enough to have had much chat with the kid. Whitehouse might come back and have chat with the kid. The kid might talk. The fuzz might – though he could not see how – investigate his lodgings, and the kid . . .

The kid, the kid, the bloody kid.

He bit his lip.

Mulligan's removal should have been the end of it. Now the Harcourt kid had got herself involved. He could not determine how much weight to give her announcement or to the analysis of the reality of her nightmare. Did the fuzz take stock of such omens and arcane happenings; how much would the kid finally be able to put into words which would make sense in terms of what he had done to Mulligan? He rejected the nightmare altogether. The fact of the matter was that Louise Harcourt had been in the house and wide awake and had witnessed his business with Mulligan. *That was the solid fact.* She had seen and heard things which she could not define, but which an astute copper would be able to put together in no time flat.

The lights in the big sets faded as Swinstead switched off the power. The lecturer came to the edge of the platform, took up a control box, opened the curtains automatically and brought up the ceiling lights. Students shuffled and adjusted themselves and feigned some sort of attention. Swinstead began to talk about the film.

Greg covered his eyes with the palm of his hand.

How far could he stretch coincidence? As with Mulligan, he had made his decision. This time it would be harder, but, so his confused rationality told him, no less necessary and – if he could mount it correctly – no less viable. Ramifications extended outwards like the spokes in a wheel. He gripped them with his reason and tested the strength of each one.

Swinstead rambled on. The light outside the window faded over the concrete courtyard as the first winter-coloured cloud of the season surreptitiously leaned on the rooftops and the hidden hills beyond.

The child, too, Greg at length decided, would have to go.

In the next period, in the next classroom, after the morning recess, he would work out a way – an accident – which would be rid of her and leave him still in the clear on all counts.

But he must do it soon, very soon; like tonight.

Ryan came out of the Chief's office, nodded, and would have gone past her and through the door which led to the Inspectors' Room. Hurriedly Sheila got up from the typewriter. She felt flustered, untidy and disorganised. Harry, in a rush, would be curt with her, perhaps dismiss her interference as imagination or the disagreeable spite of a witless lover spurned because she was ugly and had a crippled leg.

'Harry,' she said. 'Can you spare me a minute?'

Both doors were closed. Through the glass partition McCaig's outline moved from the desk to the corner cabinet.

'Only a minute,' Ryan said. 'What's your problem?'

'I don't know,' she said.

'Well, if *you* don't know . . .' he said.

He came close to her. She took the pencil from behind her ear, put it in her mouth like a slender bone, then removed it again. 'Sorry,' he said. 'What's up?'

'Maybe nothing,' Sheila said. 'It might only be my nutty defence mechanism working overtime again.'

'Go on,' said Ryan. He propped himself on the edge of the desk.

'When you did the interviews up in New College, you questioned a . . . a young man called Gregor Yule,' said Sheila.

'I don't remember.'

'I know, you did hundreds of interviews last week; anyway, I checked the sheets and you did actually put Yule through the standard form.'

'What about it?'

'Last week, last Friday to keep it straight, Yule . . . Yule picked me up.'

'On the street?' said Ryan; he didn't mean it lewdly.

'No, in a laundromat. I didn't think anything about it at the time,' said Sheila. 'The place has more than a share of college students, and I . . .'

'What does he look like?'

'Tall, confident in the way he walks, but shy.'

'Sheila!' Ryan remonstrated patiently.

'He's dark and neatly dressed and polite; strong-looking. I would say he's handsome.'

Ryan nodded. 'Got him. He didn't know young McDowell, or claims he didn't.'

'He picked me up, and we got a . . . a little thing going.'

Ryan looked at the linoleum. 'How serious?'

'You mean, was it an affair?'

'You started it, Sheila,' Ryan said. 'I didn't. But if you've got something . . .'

'You're quite right,' said Sheila. 'It wasn't an affair. I didn't go to bed with him. But I've seen a lot of him in the last five days.'

'He made the running?'

'I didn't exactly discourage him.'

'You're not sure about telling me, are you?'

'I'm afraid it might be my imagination.'

'I won't laugh. I gave up laughing years ago.'

'We had long chats, soul-chats; you know, I was supposed to see him last night but he didn't show up.'

'That's surely not unusual?' Ryan said. 'You've only known him a wee while.'

'The trouble is,' said Sheila, 'I told him about Mulligan.'

'Oh!'

'See what I mean?'

'How much did you tell him?'

'Pretty well everything.'

'Yes, I see exactly what you mean,' said Ryan.

'What got me to thinking about him I really don't know, Harry. It just occurred to me that he was a bit *too* interested in what I did, in my job, and especially in the McDowell business. It's not right to blame him completely. You know what it's like.'

'You can't quite decide whether he was pumping you, or whether you just got carried away and talked out of turn?' said Ryan.

'That's it; I can't make up my mind.'

'Mulligan only blew that cottage a couple of hours before we got there,' said Ryan. 'That does make it look as if he was tipped-off.'

'The tip-off could have come from Gregor Yule.'

'It's possible,' Ryan admitted. 'On the other hand, Mulligan could have heard about Hilary Lawrence's arrest from some other source. Before McCaig put the blankets on, we were far too noisy about it. It may have nothing at all to do with your boy-friend.'

'But it might?'

'Yes, it might,' said Ryan, reasonably.

'What can you do about it?' said Sheila.

'Make a few enquiries.'

'You wouldn't tackle Greg outright; tell him that I . . . ?'

'And queer your pitch, Sheila?' said Ryan. 'I wouldn't do that.'

'I mean, it may be perfectly innocent on Gregor's part.'

'Scammel's the man,' said Ryan. 'He's very discreet. He'll be able to give me sufficient information on the lad to let us know if it's a lead worth pursuing.'

'I didn't *mean* to tell him anything,' said Sheila. 'I don't usually run off at the mouth like that. He was so . . . so persuasive, so nice.'

Ryan pushed himself off the desk. He had on a kindly smile, but Sheila did not know if it was part of the inspector's standard equipment, or whether he really did sympathise with her predicament.

'Nobody need know where my information came from,' he assured her. 'Don't worry about it, Sheila. All I have to do is ask questions. If your friend Yule *has* been up to something behind the scenes, then he's done us a favour by marking you as a soft target.'

'I'm a soft target, all right,' said Sheila. 'I'm a silly cow, that's what I am.'

'I'll drop in at the college later tonight,' said Ryan. He glanced at his watch. 'Right now, I'm supposed to be in

Glasgow talking to one of William Mulligan's less fortunate friends.'

'Where would Mulligan go?' said Sheila. 'Have you any idea?'

Ryan shook his head.

'Vanished,' he said. 'But we'll find him. It may take time, but we'll find him.'

Sheila had heard that confident line before, litany of coppers who, as days drift into weeks and weeks into months, encourage themselves with the assurance that nobody ever escapes the drag-net of the law. Ryan clapped her on the shoulder with his gloved hand, and leaned to open the door.

'You did the right thing, Sheila,' he said. 'Even if it means nothing, you did the right thing.'

'I hope so,' Sheila said. 'I wouldn't want to cause trouble for anyone.'

'I wouldn't worry,' Ryan said. 'This Gregor Yule probably has no more connection with this case than having a severe crush on you. You want me to arrest him for that?'

'Only if you give me custody,' Sheila said. But she did not feel flippant. She watched the inspector leave the office with a leaden premonition that she had started something which would do none of them any good.

Anger had gone out of Whitehouse, leaving restlessness and a sense of regret. As always when circumstances came at him with an unexpected uppercut, Whitehouse took himself home to the cottage under the green slopes of Ben Cairnoch, sniffed the autumn vegetation and the sour steam from Cairnoch Distillery where his old man worked, let his mother feed him up on stew and suet dumplings and dish him out a half from the house bottle in lieu of pudding. Like the hill, his mother never seemed to change. She was big and brown-skinned and passive. She did not berate her son for his errant ways or for ignoring her for months on end. Her philosophy was that he had his own life to lead and that she had never been educated enough to understand him or what he did and therefore was not entitled to criticise. Besides, she liked his paintings and was proud of them. Though by disposition a little more vain, his father had sense enough to take his son as he found him, which wasn't often, and let it go at that. Whitehouse gave no explanation of his abrupt arrival at the cottage door well after midnight. In dressing-gown and gum boots, his mother asked for none, fed him supper, changed the sheets in the cubby behind the kitchen, and let him sleep. If she sensed that her son had been hurt again, she sensibly reckoned that she was too inexperienced in the ways of his world to help him out of his difficulty. She cooked him breakfast, washed his shorts and shirt, cooked his dinner, and talked to him about his far-flung relatives. It was late in the afternoon before Whitehouse stirred himself from the soothing effects of being home again and, with the anger of the previous night all gone, went out into the landscape to do some serious thinking.

He began by thinking about himself. What would he do now that he had lost his refuge and his patron? He could stay at home indefinitely, of course, but there was no room in the cottage for him to create the sprawling muddle which he needed to work, and he could not fairly tap his family for subsistence and money with which to buy colours. He did not know quite what to do. Running quickly to the end of that line of thought, he shifted tracks to another, less practical, subject.

Walking at a loping gait down the track from the highway, he moved straight across the bottom of the Cairnoch plain. His eyes took in the pastures and oblongs of birch scrub, dense patches of pine on the distant ranges on the far side of the valley, all muted now under a sky like a wash of purple gouache on grey-tinted paper. Corn stubble held memories of sunlight, harshly forecasting imminent rain. The black rooks upon it were manic and foreboding, creatures of the mind, conditioned and created by the Dutchman's brush on the sand-coloured canvas of Cairnoch, as they had hung over the crops of Auvers, in another country and another time. Rain would come soon. The air was very cold now on his skin. He dug his hands into the breast of the jerkin and scowled at the sky.

It was to this place he came in occasional dreams. Dropping ten years of future time into the well of nothingness, Louise would no longer be a child. She would come to him through summer greenery, the skirts of her frock bending the frail poppies and yellow buttons of the buttercups. She would be eighteen; he would be older too, but not so old that he would not recognise her, and she him. Her innocence, her vulnerability, would be unchanged; she would be slender still, and bright and elfin. On the feathery wing of the hillside they would meet and talk like two new people. Chagall, he supposed, was behind the subconscious inventions. Last time he saw her she had not been a fragment out of a dream, more like the pathetic bellboys of Soutine, blotchy, red and ashamed. When he had lifted her and pressed her wetness against him, she had babbled and blurted out all the truth of a nightmare which she should not have been condemned to suffer alone. If he had not abandoned her she would have wakened, cried and found him in the darkness ready to comfort her and assure her that it was only a little rank bubble of fear bursting in her mind. In a rush and in detail she had divulged all the sedimentary horrors which the mind lays down in childhood, spoken of screams and shoutings, of bumps, of giants and gross figures in the hall. He had felt fury come up in him as it had never come up before. He did not regret beating Vikki Harcourt. He did not regret yelling at her, or at Greg. All he regretted was that he had gone so far they would probably not let him near the house, that he would not see Louise again.

It was not vain to imagine that Louise needed him. He was all the poor kid had, and he was worth little enough. How would it be with her now when the nightmares came, the desolation of knowing that she must struggle into adulthood on her own?

Paintings accomplished during his tenancy of the basement were less the products of Greg's handouts than of the strange, tenuous contact he had had with Louise. Now that it was broken, he realised that he could fill canvas after canvas with memories of the precious things the child had unwittingly given him. It would do his art no harm to discard her. But he could not simply finish with her, pack her into the past, as he could do with a slice of landscape or the sight of the sea beating on a green beach. Louise was not as constant as they were. She would alter and change all too swiftly. It was not sufficient recompense to fix her image on a treated jute-sack, and let it go at that – not if he could help it. Free board and lodging, the graft he shelled in from Greg's dirty little jobs, were all secondary to his feelings for the kid. She did not belong to him, nor he to her, yet she was unique in his experience, and too valuable to give up because of a stupid spasm of anger and disgust.

The facts of the nightmare were not rooted in anything he had told her. Yet they were *facts*, not fantasies; warpings of the callous men and thoughtless women who invaded the house and Louise's security; the screams and shoutings in the cellar, and the hobgoblin shapes in the hallway, the two-headed man. In his innocence he could not only understand them, but could even see them clearly in his imagination. The sensations of loss, of utter desolation, of panic, were very intense. Far across the plain under the cloud roof he stopped in his tracks.

Two kestrels hung on the eddy of the current, low above the quilted pasture, then, caught and unsettled by the first savage gust of wind, banked and plunged upwards and rushed away over his head. A single flake of sleet slashed his cheek. He touched it, rubbing it off with the palm of his mitten. Turning from the waist, he looked up at the hawks, but they were far, far off now, and high, almost indistinguishable from the grey tangle of the hill. In the dyke a mouse chirped and rustled, belatedly frightened; or maybe it was a weasel's pleasure sounds.

Dread intensified in him. He could not explain it. It was as if he had lost his sight, had become a prey to blindness, the affliction which he feared more than dying. Facing north again, towards the empty wedge of the glen, he watched the sleet shower gather itself out of the autumnal dusk. It quickened against his flesh, stinging him to awareness, awakening him.

As swiftly as the season's change, there on the plain of Cairnoch, Whitehouse's passivity gave way to a dark realisation of what Yule had done to him, how he had been made party to events which, without doubt, showed a cruel disregard for consequence. All along he had known of it, of course, but had deliberately blinded himself to his part in it, put down his indifference to a spurious neutrality, used his status as an artist as an excuse for all sorts of omissions and misgivings, for shrugging off the deprivations which humans brought upon themselves. Fear breathed upon him then, icy and raw, like the darts of sleet which embedded themselves in his hair and stung his skin.

He wheeled and ran, running hard back along the track. The blizzard, first of the winter season and eager, drove against his shoulders, cloaked the battledress, and laid a scum of moist whiteness across the surface of the track. His boots dug out a pale ephemeral trail, which thickening snow soon filled. By the time he reached the blacktop, thumb cocked anxiously at passing cars, his prints had been covered over and all record of his route erased.

Mildred McDowell believed that if only she could make Frank understand that nobody, ever, loses everything, he would begin to mend the broken parts of his mind which had fast disintegrated since the events of that council meeting and become himself once more. She didn't have the words for it. She wasn't bright or articulate enough to tell him anything, or close enough to what he had become— before Tom's death—to touch any part of him.

At night she would go early to bed, tired out with the unnecessary housework she had set herself to do as a therapy against her loss. He would come into the room in the dark and drop his clothes where he stood and put on his pyjamas, then he would lie beside her in the bed, not touching. He lay on his back with his arms folded over his chest and, even in darkness, stared at the ceiling until she fell asleep. She did not know when he slept, if he slept at all, nor did she try to comfort him; ingrained habits of reticence and apology would not allow it.

On this night she went to bed as usual, leaving Frank in the armchair before the fire. She would remember him as he looked then, not before, sprawled in the leather armchair, a scowl of hostile depression etched deeply into his features. It seemed well matched with the thick grey beard which coated his jaws and the thin brown cigar jutting out from his teeth, real now, yet not real, like a stranger, not Frank.

Without a word, she left him and went to bed.

She lay under the canopy and remembered Tom. It was a nightly ritual, like prayer. Before she had time to recall him out of infancy, she fell into a deep and dreamless sleep.

In the lounge below her husband stirred and rose from the armchair, crossing to the bureau in the alcove beyond the fireplace. From his key-ring he unhooked a tiny key which unlocked the pigeon-hole lid of a compartment at the back of a bureau drawer. Out of the chamber he removed a pill-box. Closing the lid and the drawer silently, he carried the cylindrical carton into the kitchen at the rear of the house. He put the carton on the dresser, filled the electric kettle and set it to boil. When it did so he brewed a cup of weak black coffee, cooled it to palatable temperature and carried it, and the carton, carefully upstairs into the bath-room.

He closed and locked the bathroom door.

He placed the coffee cup on the toilet cistern, took the top from the carton and tipped thirty-four capsules of assorted shapes and colours into the palm of his left hand. A few spilled, rolling away, escaping, like rubbery insects, to bounce and scuttle on the cork flooring. He let them go. Like a pony feeding on oats, he dipped his mouth to his hand and nibbled up a dry mouthful of the capsules. He washed them over his throat with coffee. They clogged in the hollow above his wind-pipe, a thick mass. He swallowed painfully and supped more coffee from the cup. The mass slid down, hot, raw and uncomfortable, into his chest. He fed himself a smaller mouthful, swilled it too down into his chest.

The window was a fretwork of tinted glass, catching light from the strip over the mirror on its amber bevels. Beyond its opaqueness he could discern the shadowy flitting of snow-flakes.

Four more capsules went into his mouth and down into his chest. He tried to weigh discomfort against the finality of the deed. In fact, he could hardly believe that it was happening to him. In his lassitude and rehearsed indiffer-ence, he could not ascribe to the imbibing anything more sinister than the satisfaction of an appetite, like smoking, eating or drinking alcohol.

Coffee dregs made the gelatine seem bitter. He drew a glass of water from the tap and drank it. It too lay heavy as mercury on the column which filled him from tongue to navel.

The first pain crept out of his gut, solid as an icicle, swelling and distending from the arch under his breast-bone into the cavities under his ribs, down into his bladder. Anticipated lethargy did not follow, rather a twitching restlessness which drove him noisily out of the bathroom.

In the dimness of the landing, he swayed, grabbed the balcony rail for support. The spasm passed. He made his way into the bedroom and, exactly as planned, stripped off his clothes and put on clean pyjamas. He buttoned them up, knotted the cord tightly round his middle, stealthily slipped under the eiderdown and stretched himself out by Mildred's flank. Folding his hands on his chest, he stared at the ceiling.

The quantity of material in him was no longer solid. It had liquified now, gurgled and heaved. Bile filtered into his mouth. He swallowed it. None of the reactions were what he would have supposed them to be. He felt aggrieved that the popular legend of a sleeping, effortless death should be so false. It should not be like *this*. Common law, the universal rule of the body, was failing him too.

Before his tissues had time to suck open the capsules and soak out their contents, his stomach expanded and he found himself, in a natural fastidious reaction, leaping from the dark bed and rushing through the upper hall back into the bathroom. With a final lunge he flung himself to the floor. Cupping the lavatory pedestal with his arms, he disgorged all that he had taken in. Warmth and passivity, a languorous passing had evaded him. He clung grimly to the toilet basin and wept at the humiliation of his failure.

When it was over, minutes later, he was admitted to that state which he had coveted, the feebleness of loss, the debility of despair. Crawling backwards, he left the shameful mess in the bathroom. Blind and undignified, he butted into Tom's room, seeking escape.

In the time which had passed since the boy's death and his cleansing of that room of Tom's possessions, he had avoided opening this door, looking into the emptiness. But the room was not empty. It had been recreated as it had been when Tom was alive : every item, every object, each book and stick and scrap of clothing restored, the bed made up with the patchwork quilt, the lamp over the board tilted just so.

McDowell flopped over, cruciform upon the side of the bed. His fists grasped the patchwork as if to hold himself upon a spinning wheel, which whipped and tossed his body round, and snatched all breath from his lungs.

That sensation too dwindled and eased, and he was floating free in the crowded room.

Kneeling, Mildred touched his brow.

'Frank,' she said. 'Are you . . . ?'

'I couldn't,' he murmured. His voice came from a long way down inside him. 'I couldn't hold it down.'

Fingers stroked his hair, brushed his beard. The warmth and heaviness of her breasts pressed against his chest.

'What more can I do, Frank? Do you want me to leave?'

'No.'

'Is it her you want? Would you be happier with Laura?'

'It isn't Laura. It isn't any of them.'

'Perhaps you would have been happy with her,' Mildred said. 'It may not have happened then.'

'No,' he said; it was not a denial or an agreement.

'It wasn't always like this,' his wife said. 'Do you remember how it used to be when we were young? It was good once, wasn't it? Do you remember how it was?'

'Yes,' he said, thickly. 'God, yes!'

She stroked his brow again, and held him tightly, giving him warmth until he slept.

Grinning, Yule filled up the glass and put it in her hands. He let his knuckles trail over the transparent cups of the brassière, rubbing flattened nipples, heard her croon and purr with pleasure like some mangy tabby cat poured milk and stroked about the ears. He had opened the buttons of the dress top to make her comfortable and give her something else to think about other than the quantity of whisky which he was intent on pouring into her.

They were in the basement. The kid was upstairs, eating fish and chips from a plate, cross-legged on the floor in front of the TV set in the living room. If he listened hard he could hear the jolly music of the cartoon show. Louise would not come down the basement steps—she knew better—and would not disturb them. He had planned it well, better this time for the weakness of his victims. The sense of horror, of conscience, which had almost caused him to muff the disposal of Mulligan, had gone.

In the afternoon, he had cut classes, gone through the dressing up routine, returned the rented Ford to a Hertz office in the city centre and bought two bottles of whisky to fill his attaché case. He had been home before Vikki, had changed again, and waited in the living room for the kid's return from school. Nothing was said between them. She was scared of him, though, he could sense it. She avoided him, evaded him, chose the dark kitchen as her hide-out rather than share the warmth of the living room with him. Something had made her change. Previously, she would follow anyone in the upper part of the house, follow them around like a puppy, not even trying to talk to them, just being close. He had always disliked that sneaky trait in her; but then he disliked most things about her, resented her very presence in the place which, upstairs and down, he had come to consider his own. He hated the kid worse than he hated Vikki. With Vikki he shared bed and booze and the experience of a relationship. With the kid he shared nothing. It was all too apparent that she connected him with the incidents of the previous evening. Soon she would fit the pieces of her bloody dream together, make them fit a pattern which the blues would be able to identify. Even if they didn't find Mulligan other threads might lead them here. Trained to think in logical possibilities, to predict disasters and potential dangers far in advance, he saw in Vikki Harcourt's child a potent threat to security which had grown increasingly precarious over the last two weeks. Cleverness and patience were no longer enough. It was time for direct action of the kind which had rid him of Mulligan.

The first manœuvre was to ply Vikki with enough liquor to put her under; that wouldn't take long.

Laughing, he splashed whisky into his own glass but did not drink it. Really Vikki had no head for the hard stuff. Already her mirth was becoming brittle, a cackle, her eyes turning glazed. She was talking about men again, about a man in the pub she'd met the night before, speculating on whether Greg would mind if she'd brought him home and, in veiled innuendo, hinting that a party with her in the middle might be a nice experience. Because the evening was young and he had tugged her into the drinking session without warning, she would not rush in yet. Like most women he had known, Vikki Harcourt could never discern the limits of her indulgence. She went from moment to moment with the thoughtlessness of a moth, taking drink when it was poured for her and men when they offered themselves, considering life all the easier for the somnolence of feeling brought on by the satisfaction of her appetites.

Greg was the anthithesis of somnolence. Even more so than last night his senses were lit up with a bright glow; all things, material and intangible, seemed more real and solid than ever before. It did not occur to him that, though he still had cunning and caution as watchdogs to his compulsion, consequences were less important to him now than the successful accomplishment of the act of killing itself. In the aftermath he would be confronted by blues and put through the verbal obstacle-course of an inquiry; that did not trouble him at all. He could cope with that. Young kids died every day; accidents happened. The blues were kindly and casual in their treatment of the people involved. Besides, he could have nothing to do with it. He would be here with the mother, her alibi bolstered by his own. Carelessness, indifference; the blues saw so much of it that they would accept, without much probing, the superficial appearance of tragedy. If Vikki cracked up and chose to blame herself, then that was her lookout, not his. Naturally, he would console her, stay with her, shack up with her even, to tide her over her loss and keep a roof over his own head for a term or two, then he would wriggle out and it would be over. He would have the money, close to ten thousand, counting Mulligan's legacy, and the knowledge needed to set up a solvent company, with Charlie home from the sea.

'Greg, you're te'bble.'

'What?'

'Yer, yer a te'bble guy.'

'Sure, Vikki,' he said. 'Still, it's all we've got, isn't it?'

'Never 'ad it so good.'

'Drink up, dear.'

'Gotter make tea.'

'Forget it : I'll make tea.'

'Gotter get the kid t'bed.'

'She's okay. Here.'

He poured from the bottle until her glass was full and whisky spilled over her forearm. She licked it, spilling more over her breast. Greg leaned forward, kissed the wet stain on the rising flesh. She grabbed his hair and thrust his head down, like a possessive mother with an errant child. He put up with it, hearing her guzzle from the glass above his head.

It was stifling in the basement, the fire roaring red. He put his arm around her, pulled her forward from the chair, played with her body lightly, waiting. She drank, crooned in her pleasure, then, with a suddenness which surprised even Yule, slumped across his shoulder. Every part of her was limp, except the wrist and fingers on the hand which held the glass; they were rigid, the glass and its precious load held upright as if in a toast. Greg lifted them away, and slid out from under her, supporting her with his forearm. Each phase of her inebriation was familiar. As he eased her to the floor, she came round again briefly, looked up at him out of the plaster of dirty blonde hair, mouth split wide in a beatific smile. He pulled open her dress. She whinnied and sighed and closed her eyes. Abruptly, her head wagged to one side, and she passed into a state of sleep or unconsciousness which would last for several hours.

Greg poured whisky over her hair, and dropped the glass by her elbow. The almost empty bottle lay on the rug. He filled his own glass half full and laid it carefully on the fender.

He dressed himself in the rally jacket and went upstairs.

The kid was lying on the floor, on her belly, her legs in the air. He could see up to the navy-blue crotch of her panties. She stared round at him and rolled over into a crouch, her eyes large and suspicious.

'Where's my mama?'

'Downstairs,' said Greg. 'She fell asleep. Listen, I've got a message for you from Peter.'

'Where's Peter?'

'Not here,' said Greg. 'Listen, he can't come here any more; because of your mama. She won't let him come here.'

'She will.'

'No, she won't. Listen, your mama won't let you see Peter any more. You want to see Peter, don't you?'

The kid nodded.

Greg said, 'I can't take you, because I've got to stay here with your mama. But you can go on your own, and be back here before she wakes up. How does that sound?'

'I'm not supposed to go out on my own.'

'You won't see Peter then. Peter's waiting for you. He's got a message for you.'

'Where?'

'It isn't far from here. You've been on your own before. You can find it, if I tell you how to get there. Sure, you can.'

'Mama'll give me a thrashing . . .'

'Only if she finds out,' said Greg. 'I won't tell her. I'll stay here and stop her finding out. If you run all the way, you'll be able to see Peter and come back. He says he wants to see you tonight. You wouldn't disappoint him, would you?'

'Where is he then?'

'You know the canal, the lock on the canal under the passage?'

'Why's he there?'

Greg clenched his teeth. 'Because he can't come here. Now, listen, do you want to see him or not?'

'Yes.'

'Then go up to the lock on the canal. You're sure you know where it is?'

'Yes.'

'He'll be there. Peter'll be there.'

'It's far, can you not take me?'

'It isn't far,' said Greg. 'And I can't take you because I've got to stay here with your mother. Go and get your coat on, and get started. Come on, Louise, you're supposed to be a big girl. Listen, Peter thinks you're big enough to go out alone to see him. If you don't show up tonight, he won't even try to see you again.'

She said nothing, walked across the living room, past him, and into the hall. She held herself upright, not cowed, with all the courage that was in her to make her immune to her fears of the dark hall and the kitchen passageway.

In a moment she returned, dressed in a stained school raincoat, a knitted helmet snug over her head. She wore gloves, too, black with grime, the left thumb bitten away, the fingers full of holes. She presented herself before him as if she expected him to approve of her.

'You know where you're going?' he said. 'The lock on the canal above Jockie's Fall.'

'I know where it is.'

He wondered about her. She did not seem like a child, yet she could not see through the simple subterfuge, the trap he had laid for her. For no other reason, not even to meet a Holy Saint, would she have taken herself out alone in the freezing night, or trusted him to steer her rightly.

In the door, framed against the pale golden glow of the gaslamp, she paused and glanced back at him; the small, pinched, waxy face encased in the woollen balaclava, the fists determinedly stuck by her sides.

She went out.

Yule tarried in the hallway, counting under his breath. When he reached one hundred, he followed her, closing the door and locking it behind him. He picked up sight of her as she turned the corner, hurried along after her, keeping her in view. She walked past the shop-fronts and into the road which wended its way towards the canal. She walked fast, not looking back.

Greg had no trouble in holding the loose tail, making sure that she would arrive alone and unmolested at the lock above the thick, oily water where, like several kids before her, she would accidentally drown.

'Oh!' said Ryan. 'Sorry to hold you back. Your secretary told me you were still here.'

Scammel unwound the scarf from about his throat and folded it, slipped out of the heavy tweed overcoat and tossed it with the scarf on the desk top. He sighed.

'Yes, Inspector?'

'I won't keep you a minute.'

Weary though he was, Scammel managed to be courteous.

'Take your time,' he said. 'It'll let some of the rush-hour traffic clear. God knows, the roads will be bad enough in this weather.'

Behind the plate glass of the huge window sleet thickened into snow, scoring the piebald darkness across the college grounds and whitewashing out the rooftops of the suburb. It seemed to be driving sideways, as if the Principal's room had been turned askew, and the long blast of the wind from the north-east had toppled the houses like cardboard models.

'October,' said Scammel, sighing again. 'Looks like being a long winter.'

Ryan agreed.

Scammel propped himself on the heater, back to the glass, and lit a cigarette. 'What can I do for you?'

'I'm interested in a student by the name of Gregor Yule; on one of your management courses, I believe.'

'Yule,' said Scammel. 'I know the chap, very bright.'

'Have you a reason for knowing him?'

'What? No, not really. He's an impressive-looking character. Represented the college at a couple of swimming galas last year, but gave up competing because he didn't have time to train. The coach wasn't too happy about it, but with Yule's academic record, who can complain if he puts a degree before the silverware.'

'He has a good academic record?'

'Excellent,' said Scammel. 'A mile ahead of his year.'

'A swot?' said Ryan.

'Comes natural to him,' said Scammel. 'He just has that kind of mind. What's your interest in him?'

'Casual,' said Ryan. 'Might I trouble you for a look at his record card?'

'Certainly.'

Scammel reached to the desk and used the intercom, but it stirred up no response from the adjacent office. He went out, returning within minutes with the green-backed post-card-size folder with which Ryan had become familiar during the college enquiries of the previous week. He took the folder, opened it, and studied the tiny clear-printed photograph at the top border. Out of the hundreds of students he had interviewed, it was a face he did recall. As Scammel said, the lad was impressive to look at. Largely ignoring the class markings and term reports, Ryan scanned the sections of information listed below. He looked up; he had made an error, had been negligent in his attention to detail, smothered, perhaps, by the dullness of routine. Good God, though, how *could* he have passed it up unchecked?

'His next of kin,' Ryan said.

Scammel leaned over his shoulder and squinted at the report.

'A brother,' said Scammel.

'No parents?'

'He's not obliged to list them.'

'Can he list who he likes?'

'Well, yes, technically. Actually, we have the parents' address over here.'

Scammel wet his thumb and turned a page.

'Obviously, if there was an accident or something of that nature, we'd notify the nearest set of relatives, which would be the parents.'

'What about his student grant?' said Ryan. 'Isn't that dependent on his father's earnings, or the household income?'

Another page :

Scammel said, 'No, look, the father is unemployed; family of seven, five children of school age or under. Yule, Gregor Yule, that is, has been scrupulously honest with us. See, he claims only a limited proportionate grant based on a support income from his brother, Charles Yule.'

'Isn't that unusual?' said Ryan.

'The honesty of it is odd,' Scammel admitted. 'It does happen. Sometimes the student has broken with the family, with the parents, and lists a sister or, as in this case, a brother as next of kin and person responsible for what we call "substance". What often happens is that the student registers the home circumstances—especially if they're

262

bread-line—to claim a heavy annual grant, and is in fact being supported by a relative or a friend outside the immediate family circle.'

'All right,' said Ryan. 'Yule hasn't done that. What's he losing by writing off his home?'

'A hundred and eighty or two hundred pounds a year.'

'Good God! Why?'

'I suppose he doesn't want to have *anything* to do with his folks,' Scammel replied. 'Why is this important, Mr. Ryan?'

Ryan let the pages drop back, tapped one line with his forefinger.

'The brother's occupation,' he said.

'Merchant seaman,' said Scammel; then, more warmly, 'Merchant seaman.'

'Two addresses listed; the first's the same as Gregor's, the second's care of Macdonald, Nair and Keating.'

'A shipping firm,' said Scammel. 'I understand the drift. Does this relate to the information on Yule which brought you here tonight?'

Ryan fumbled in his pocket for a memo pad, found it, and put it on the desk. Carefully he copied out the addresses, and a few other pertinent facts. He was stimulated now. 'Was Yule at classes today?'

'Wait.'

Briskly, Scammel went out of the office.

Ryan finished his transcripts, tucked the pad away, and continued to flip through the yellow card pages of the file. He was not unmindful of his promise to Sheila. Even now he would hold his enthusiasm in check and stifle the hunch that the girl had led him to another break. His hunches had been wrong before; he would not bulldoze his way to Yule—not yet.

Scammel came through the door.

'Attended this morning, but cut a tutorial this afternoon.'

'Yesterday?' said Ryan. 'Last week?'

'Off-hand, I can't go that far back,' said Scammel. 'Yesterday, he cut all three lectures, one in the morning and two in the afternoon.'

'Cutting's common, though?'

'Unfortunately,' said Scammel, 'but not, I think, for this particular student.'

Ryan got up.

Though he was not given to social gestures, he held out his hand. 'Thank you, Mr. Scammel.'

Scammel shook his hand briefly, and said, 'It would be, wouldn't it?'

'Would be what?'

'One of our best.'

'I don't know that,' Ryan said. 'Not yet.'

When he left, Scammel was staring out of the window at the snow.

Vikki opened one eye. It was gummed with sleep, as if the lid was glued to her cheek, like a slipped lash. Languorously she brought up her fist and rubbed the eyeball, and focused on the person who had wakened her. Whitehouse cupped his fingers over her shoulders, dragged her up from the rug and shook her violently. She was as limp as rubber. Her teeth chattered, but the cocoon of alcohol remained snug around her brain. She did not seem to recognise him and responded to the shaking with a fretful, childish petulance.

'*Where is she?*' Whitehouse shouted. '*Where's Louise? Where's Greg?*'

'Greg-eeee!'

'Come on, you cow, waken up. Where are they? *Where's she gone?*'

'Up.'

'*She's not in the bloody house.*'

Whitehouse tried to lift her clean off the floor, but she was dead-weight and he hadn't the strength to prop her on her feet. He had known drunks like her before. The crack of doom would not bring her round. He had no time to waste on reviving her. He hit her across the face, taking no satisfaction in it, too full of fear and panic now to harbour hatred for this wreck. She wept without waking. Jesus, she wept naturally in her stupor as she could not weep in sobriety, with an effortless flood of tears, make-up caked and blotched, lips parted. She looked like one of the mocked-up monsters the art school students used to make to ride the floats of the annual carnival parade; gross, tossed together, daubed with paint, and transient. He could no more rouse Vikki than he could have roused a dummy.

He dropped her, let his hands fall, pulled away from her, and ran upstairs three at a time, shouting the child's name.

In the living room, the TV set flickered light out into the

dark corners. On the carpet, before the smouldering fire lay a dirty plate and a few chips. In all the time he had been in the house, he had never known the child to be out alone after dark. He stooped and lifted one of the chips and put it in his mouth. Though the grease had congealed, the flesh of the potato was still faintly warm.

She wasn't alone outside; she was with Greg.

That was even worse.

Whitehouse went out into the hall, looked round, found the closet and empty hook where the coat should have been. Her woollen balaclava was missing too. He went into her bedroom. He felt as small as the child; crouched by the end of the unmade bed, listening, hearing the sounds she might have heard, visualising in his own terror the forms of her terror. He knew then for sure that she had not dreamed the sounds or shapes, but had been an innocent witness to some horrifying event, some enigmatic occurrence which had taken place in the house when Greg was alone with her and had supposed her to be asleep. He had known it for some time now, out on the plain of Cairnoch, in the van in which he hitched his ride back to the town, during the long loping lung-scalding run through the streets of Thane. He had known it, but could not be sure enough of the worth of the knowledge, until this moment when the certainty of it struck him down like a sudden fever.

Stumbling, he pitched against the bed-end.

The room had the smell of her, of her hair, her small warm body. Because of his dedication to a craft, to the useless skill of trailing paint across canvas in the tones and patterns of an imaginary world, he had spared no time to equip himself to deal with the reality of tragedy.

Whitehouse did not doubt that Greg had taken her, nor did he question his own sanity in ascribing to the incident a purpose so repugnant that his brain reeled at the concept. He felt dizzy and sick, but did not, could not, reject it.

Rising, he staggered to the door, made one more round of the ground floor apartments, closets, fuel store, and the dank passageway to the yard. Whiteness filled the sky. The houses stood against it, like an underpainting on a grainy canvas. The path which straggled acoss the unfenced yard was virgin, pasted over by wet snow. He ran back through the house and out into the close again by the front door.

In the street was the butt-end of rush-hour traffic, lights

and the slithering hiss of wheels. Bulbs under the marquee of the Majestic Theatre came alight. Heedless of pedestrians, he cupped his hands to his mouth and shouted her name. Town sounds swallowed up the cry. Even the air gave him no echo, no answer. He leaned against the fleur-de-lis of the railings at the step. Passers-by regarded him curiously and, thinking he was drunk, stepped out to the kerb and went past him quickly.

He began to weep.

The tears did not diminish his determination, or symbolise the weakness of capitulation. He found in them a cooling influence which reduced the surge of impotent, directionless energy which coursed through his body. Squeezing his eyes shut like a mystic oracle of a forgotten creed, he saw clearly what Greg would attempt to do to her.

He could not claim ever to think like Yule, but he had lived long enough in the man's company to have some of the knowledge he needed at that moment.

Springing away from the railing, as if the iron had charged him with cold current, he doubled to the right, and set off in the direction of the warehouse district between the banks of the river and the adjacent canal.

Sheila was unmistakable. Ryan decided that she had given up on him and, miserable in herself, had set off home in the hope that her beau would be camped on the doormat to tell her all was well. He took the Cortina on past the front of the headquarters building. She wasn't walking quickly, and the limp was pronounced tonight. Though her collar was up, she wore no hat or scarf and gusts of sleet feathered out the mop of blonde hair untidily. Cautiously he applied the brake, prowled the car in by the mush of the gutter, and opened the nearside door.

'Sheila,' he said, leaning across the passenger seat. 'Get in.'

She got in, and quickly closed the door.

'God, it's cold.'

'Aye,' said Ryan. He took the Cortina on to the end of the road and fashioned a slow skidding turn.

'Did you call on Scammel?' Sheila asked.

'I did.'

'What did he say about Gregor?'

'Not much,' said Ryan, cagily. 'Listen, Sheila, I want your

assistance for a half hour or so. Will you help me? It's un-
official.'

'It's Gregor, isn't it? You think I might be right?'

'His brother's a seaman. I checked with the shipping office.
He's been on roughly the same short-seas trading route for
over a year. One of the ports of call is Marseilles; another
is Palermo. In fact, he could have access to heroin in almost
any of the ports on the continent.'

'What about Greg?'

'He didn't show up at classes yesterday.'

'The day Mulligan went into hiding?'

'Yes,' said Ryan. 'But I'm still not convinced that he is
involved.'

'You're too trusting, Harry.'

'What I want you to do is this,' said Ryan. 'I'll drive you
to the place where he lives. Now, he's been careful not to tell
you where he lives, is that right?'

'It just never seemed to come up.'

'It's not far from here,' said Ryan. 'I want you to go into
the house, see him, talk to him. Don't tell him anything. I
mean, don't give him any indication that you've been sent.'

'Then what?'

'Come away again, just as soon as you can.'

'What if he wants me to . . . to stay?'

'Make an excuse.'

'And?'

'Come out and get into the car. We'll take the car down
the road a bit, hang on and see what he does. It's his reaction I'm after.'

'What if he does nothing?'

'Then I'll push him a little further,' said Ryan. 'I'll call
on him.'

'He'll know I sent you.'

'Maybe.'

The girl put her hands under the blow of the car heater
and kneaded her fingers together.

'Sheila?'

'Yes, all right.'

'It's the best I can do, lass,' Ryan said.

'I suppose so,' Sheila said. 'Have you told McCaig?'

'I may not have to.'

'But if Gregor *is* in it?'

'The Chief will understand.'

'And my job? I'll have to resign, won't I?'

'Resign!' said Ryan. 'Don't be bloody daft!'

She sat back in the seat, arms folded, and stared at the sweep of the wipers coping with the sludge of soft ice which pelted the glass.

Ryan felt the car slide slightly, and slowed still more.

'What a night,' the girl said. 'What a bloody horrible night.'

'As my grannie used to say—not fit for man nor beast.'

'Where are we?'

'Nearly there.'

Stone blocks which trenched the drop below the lock were thick and porous as cork. The massive oak shafts of the gates seemed more mineral in density than their supports, like toppled monoliths, bolted to iron stanchions and topped by fretted rods and saw-toothed cranks. Sleet drove across the lock bridge in shifting gusts, some gusts curved, some slanted in ruled diagonals, some in horizontal veils, back-lit by the gaslamps of the warehouse lanes, like arctic aurora. Enclosed deep below the ramp, the canal lay hidden, visible only to the south where it crept like an oil slick from rounded banks and bastions of pitted brick. Its colour there was darker than the night sky, scribbled with a single signature of bluish light, reflection of a neon bulb behind a cold-store on the opposite shore. Sleet vanished into it, flakes slitting the oily surface like a thousand tiny knives. In the stillness of the neighbourhood, the sift of the falling snow sounded loud, like the hiss of furry animals hidden in the hawthorn hedge. Louise stood with her back to the wall of the keeper's shed. It was broken down and roofless, the window holes boarded over.

From the alcove of the lodge Greg watched her. Long since abandoned the lodge, too, was smeared and blackened by the fires of tramps and local boys. He did not watch her long. He was wary lest her nerve cracked and she turned and ran for the populated streets a quarter of a mile away, disillusionment and fright too rife in her to make her wait for her friend the painterman. He watched her for a moment longer, examining her closely. She showed no sign of emotion, not outwardly. Her expression was sharp, alert, but bland, with a confidence in it which he could not fathom. In his ignorance he credited children only with outlandish expressions and pantomime displays of the emotional squalls which troubled them. He was pleased that he felt so cool. The familiar stirring of excitement in his nerve-ends was no worse than that which he felt on the edge of the high board before he thrust his body down against the spring and committed himself to soft air and hard water.

Hands in pockets, he sidled out of the shadows and crossed the broken cobbles to the packed earth of the tow-path which broadened before the keeper's lodge. The child's head clicked round. In helmet, close-skirted coat and knitted leggings, she resembled a soldier from Elizabethan times, a miniature guardsman.

'It's me,' Greg said, quietly. 'It's Gregor.'

'Where's Peter?'

'On the other side.'

'You told me Peter'd be here.'

'All right, don't shout. He's over there, on the other side of the lock.'

'Peter!'

'*Quiet.*'

'I'm going home.'

'Peter's over there,' said Greg. 'I forgot to tell you; that's why I came. I didn't want you crossing the lock-bridge on your own. Hell, your mama . . . Peter wouldn't like that. Come on.'

He was very close, looking down at her. Even now she didn't seem afraid of him, spread-legged, long-legged, arms straight by her sides, fists balled. The sharp little chin pointed up at him. Her eyes were as glossy as berries.

He offered her his hand.

'I'll take you, you'll be all right.'

'I don't want to. Can't Peter come here?'

'No,' said Greg. 'I *told* you, he instructed me to bring you to him. Now, come on, kid, we're wasting time.'

She gave him her hand. He closed his fingers about her wrist. The bone was prominent, cold, above the frayed cuff of her glove. Even as he took hold of her, she resisted him, not strenuously, but with evidence of sudden reluctance to trust him further. He tugged her, drawing her across the earth pad to the edge of the plank which adhered to the shafts of the lock, following them in a warped vee out over the close black waters of the canal. To the right, the surface lay knee-length below him, dammed against the gates. To the left was a long drop through air vivified by funnelled sleet, a confederation of eddies and upward currents which left the canal itself unsullied and jelly-smooth.

The cat-walk was two feet broad and unfenced. The planking was uneven and slippery. Greg put the girl in front of him, holding her by the belt of her raincoat. She had no choice but to pick her way along the walk, left hand out to hug the security of the lock-shaft. Already Greg had decided where he would put her over. He would drop her down the face of the gates into the depths where, even without flow, a gurgle of water seeped through an aperture in the barricade, and débris, trapped in the vault of the lower lock, gathered thickly. By no stretch of the imagination could she pull herself to safety from that prison.

Reaching the gap in the walk where the upper level lapped a broth of leaves and other sinister flotsam directly under her shoes, the child hesitated. She looked across to the far bank hoping to see Whitehouse, probably, then glanced over her shoulder at Greg. It was too bloody perfect, too neatly fortuitous.

He put his hands under her armpits and lifted her up.

She did not resist.

He lifted her into the air, and swung her.

Her legs flailed out and her hips bucked over the shaft. He bulled against her with his chest, then released her.

She did not fall.

She screamed, and scrambled on the slimy oak. He saw how her arm was crooked around the iron rod of the cranking mechanism. He stepped back.

Nobody around, only grey gusts of sleet patched by lights, warehouses' blank walls, a dark conglomerate of hedges. He cupped her chin in his hand and pushed. She had more strength than he would have thought possible. With fists and elbows too now, she clung desperately to the metalwork.

He raised his arm to strike her across the face.

The planking vibrated. His arm snagged in mid-air. He swayed dangerously, caught the rod, and dropped to one knee. His brow caught the flank of the lock-shaft. A boot drove into the small of his back. He went down, almost flattened, writhing to keep balance, head sliding out over the gap, over rank black water.

Whitehouse rode on his buttocks, reaching over him. Through spaces in the shapes of the lock mechanism, he saw the child's hands free themselves, her thin arms cocked, hands clawing. Then she was hard against the oak, screaming with piercing clarity, *'Peeeeeter – Peeeeeter!'* Then she was floating over him, held, as he had held her, under the armpits, travelling in a wide arc over the water. He heard the knocking of her shoes on the planking. Witnessing the sudden destruction not only of this part of the plan but of all he had worked for, killed for, he struggled up, pivoted on his knees and drove out blindly with both fists.

Safe behind the dung-brown wall of the battledress jerkin the child was beyond his reach. He could hear her screaming still, and Whitehouse, not shouting, telling her urgently, 'Run, run home, love, run home.'

Whitehouse was on his knees, holding her by the shoulders, staring into her face. Though he could not see the painter's expression, Yule sensed that he was smiling, as if the whole thing was some sort of game.

Yule snaked his arm around the lean throat and dragged on it. The child came into view, the back of her, legs and stockings, arms delicately held out like a little dancer's. Though she ran fast along the planking, the motion seemed to Yule as slow and lax as an idyllic dream, the staccato of her footsteps and her shrill squealings blanked out and deadened by his own fear and the wet winding sheets of snow.

Under the lamp, she paused.

Surging upward, Whitehouse broke the throttling grip.

'Run, kid, run,' he shouted.

She lifted her hand in acknowledgement, a signal of subtle rapport, as if, deep down, she understood it all; then she was gone.

Blindly, Yule hit out at the impediment.

Ryan had barely lit a cigarette, when Sheila re-emerged from the close and hurried down the steps to the Cortina. He climbed out of the car. 'What's wrong?'

'Gregor's not there. I think you'd better come in.'

The main door was open, the lights of the house lit; dim musty lights which served less to illuminate the hallway, rooms and corridors than to give shape to their drabness. Closet doors stood open and, in what must be the living room, a TV set spilled out voices.

'There's a woman downstairs,' said Sheila. She was close behind him, hanging on to his arm.

Ryan peered down the steep stairs. A blanket cut off most of the view but by its nether edge he could just make out the legs and feet of a woman. He went down carefully, not rushing it, gesturing to Sheila to stay where she was, waving her back. He parted the curtain and, with shoulders to the inner wall, dipped his head round the folds and took a snap survey. One more door, off to his right, flush with the stair-well wall; it was open too, a ribbon of darkness. The woman on the floor in front of the old-fashioned range was breathing sonorously. Bosom, bared, rose and fell with healthy regularity. Bottles and glasses filled in the story. Even so, Ryan did not enter the basement directly. He slipped through the curtain and, holding to the inner wall, crabbed to the connecting door, kneed it wide and, crouched to half his height, backed in against the post. His groping hand found a light cord, tugged it, filled the long bleak cellar with light. A cluttered studio, stacked with junk; an easel, a truckle bed in a corner, a table; no more doors and no closets. Rather sheepishly he got to his feet and went back to attend to the woman.

She was as drunk as a lord, as comfortably full of whisky as any woman he had ever seen, even in the distant days when he worked the slag-heaps of Thane and winkled meths drinkers and shambling winos out of their corrugated-iron tents. This woman wasn't sick, just drunk, and thoroughly used to the condition. Her semi-consciousness had a deliberate air to it, as if, like an addict, she had sunk herself to exactly this level and took a perverse pleasure in it. Her blubbery grin enhanced the impression; the obsidian glitter at the corners of her eyes was like secret laughter. Cautiously he took the bottle and sniffed the top. It smelled like the expensive product guaranteed by the label. He checked the woman's pulse rate and placed three fingers on her naked breast close to her heart. The pumping was as strong as a bass drum beaten by a big highlander.

'Is she all right?'

Sheila was staring round-eyed through the curtain.

'Happy as Larry,' said Ryan, ruefully. 'Smashed out of her mind on Bell's best, mind you, but glad to be that way. Do you know who she is?'

Sheila shook her head. She was curious about the room.

Ryan hauled the woman into a sitting position and set about the irritating process of bringing her round. He would simply have rolled her on to the bed and left her to sleep it off, if it hadn't been for the disarray of the house and the mystery of the wide-open door. In this area an open door was an invitation to robbery. Ryan surmised that somebody had searched the place, and had departed again in a hurry; such a search linked with heroin in his mind. He placed a cushion under the small of the woman's back, propped her up, and lifted a second glass from the rug, holding it by the rim. His nose told him it too contained whisky; indeed the bottom of the glass still held a fair quantity of the liquid.

'Did you know he lived like this?' Ryan asked.

'No.'

'I wonder,' Ryan said, 'who left in such a tearing hurry; your boy-friend . . . ?'

'I'd rather you didn't call him that.'

'Sorry,' said Ryan, sincerely. 'Was it Yule?'

Sheila did not answer.

'There's a studio next door,' said Ryan. 'Did Yule do a bit of painting, or was he sharing?'

'I just don't know.'

'Doesn't matter,' said Ryan.

'But . . .'

'I haven't a warrant,' said Ryan, 'but that doesn't stop me taking a look around.'

He pinched the woman's cheeks, and massaged the back of her neck. Her head hung forward. She snored gutturally.

'Come on, come on,' said Ryan. 'Look, Sheila, you do this. She won't bite you. Just keep her head up and slap her cheeks a bit.'

The girl got down by the prone form and did as Ryan had told her to do. The inspector rose to commence a systematic visual search of the basement apartment. He wasn't quite sure what he hoped to find which might throw light on the mystery of what had happened in the house that evening. He supposed that he was really in search of evidence which would tie Yule more closely to the McDowell case, and perhaps indicate a direct connection with heroin peddling. Containers, jars, drawers, matchboxes passed under the scrutiny of Ryan's practised fingers. He wore gloves and utilised such instruments as a pencil, a white handkerchief and a pair of pocket tweezers to help him make his search

273

both thorough and discreet. His delicate actions unearthed no clues at all. It was not until he reached the bed and pulled out the cardboard carton that he reached the point beyond which all possibility of Yule's innocence vanished forever.

Scooping up the bundle of magazines, slanting the carton to the light, he found a crumpled five-pound note. He laid it on the pillow, and, digging deeper, came up next with a handful of paper money of large size and high denomination. Grunting, he tipped the carton over.

Notes spilled out; a fortune, unbanded for the most part, in loose rolls and bundles. Ryan hopped in surprise as if he had uncovered a nest of vipers.

'Sheila,' he said. 'Go upstairs, see if there's a 'phone in the house. If not use the car radio; do you know how?'

'What is it?'

'It's money,' said Ryan. 'Lots of money; too much money for a young man to have come by honestly. Call McCaig.'

'What about her?'

'Leave her.'

'Harry,' the girl said, 'does this mean ... ?'

'It looks very much like it.'

'Damn, damn,' the girl said, viciously.

'Go on.'

Sheila got to her feet and moved slowly to the curtain. Ryan reached further under the bed, his palm flat on the floor, fingers groping.

When Sheila cried out, he ducked and rolled to one side, pushing her away from the bottom of the stairs. At the top of the flight, equally startled, was a large young man in the uniform of a police constable.

'Now then,' the constable said, with uncertain authority.

Ryan blew out his cheeks in relief, then, going up into the hallway, identified himself.

The constable remained puzzled.

'It's a wee girl, sir,' he said. 'We found her just round the corner, running in circles, you might say, not entirely *compos mentis*. She gave me this address.'

'What girl?'

'A child, sir, about eight years old. Had a bad shock, I'd say. She's not been tampered with, by the looks of it, but she is terrified. Not easy to talk to, sir; we managed to get it out of her that she lived here, and that she's just been up at the canal . . .'

'You're in a patrol car squad?'

'Yes, sir.'

'Where's the child now?'

'In the car, at the door.'

'What's this about the canal?'

'Somebody called Peter, and somebody called . . . sounded like Greg, were fighting up there. I can't make much sense of it. Since we were just round the corner, I thought I'd better check the home background.'

'You did say Greg?'

'That's what it sounded like.'

'Sheila,' Ryan called. 'Stay here.' Taking the constable by the elbow he steered him towards the front door, talking again. 'Leave your mate here with the child and the girl downstairs. We'll take the patrol car. Did the child say where on the canal?'

'No, sir, but she was coming from the general direction of the lock.'

'Right,' said Ryan. 'We'll try the warehouse district first.'

'Yes, sir,' said the constable.

Ryan crossed the pavement to the Cortina, flung open the door and plucked the transceiver from the dashboard. He tripped the switch. 'Ryan here; get me McCaig.'

Drumming his fingers on the instrument, he waited impatiently. His eyes lifted, watching in the mirror as the two uniforms escorted the weeping child across the pavement into the close; a small child, thin and broken, in a shabby school raincoat and a knitted balaclava.

'McCaig,' the voice said.

'Two cars and crews to the old lock-keeper's lodge on the Thane-Brander stretch of the canal,' Ryan said. 'I'll rendezvous there with them.'

'McDowell?' said McCaig.

'Yes, Chief, I think I've flushed the pusher.'

Only when he reached the cul-de-sac to the west of the river did Yule stop running. He could not clearly recollect where he had been during the last ten or fifteen minutes. The last thing he remembered with clarity was throwing himself off the end of the lock-bridge, and the jarring fall he had taken on the stones. After that – nothing; a blank. His body hurt : he could feel aching muscles, bruises and strains when he moved. Going on down the long dead-walled street, aware that it would lead him nowhere, he slowed from a fast sprint, to a shagging lope, to a walk, to a final shambling pace which brought him up to the fence.

The fence was high. Above it he could see an earth banking. He tried to reason out the position of the railway line in relation to river and canal. Yule stared at the sky-line; four posts, like gibbets, planted on the breast of the earthworks. The walls were totally smooth save for padlocked doors and slitted windows barred by iron and unlighted. The walls jutted out like the prows of battleships in adjacent berths. They seemed to curve outwards over him, threaten him; like that time when Charlie had taken him to the docks to look at cargo boats and tankers, and he had fought hard not to be frightened by them. He pressed his hands flat against the sodden wood, rested his brows between them, and let pain savage him and throb and die away. His knees were bleeding. A sharp stabbing pain afflicted his right hip. His spine felt as if it had been crushed. Braced as he was, it soon stiffened and cramped into an immobility which was symptomatic of his whole condition.

The wind had dropped, swinging eastward on the edge of the cloud-front, leaving the night air icy, ribbed sleet hardening in the gutters of Thane. Yule was conscious of cold, hugged his hands into his belly to warm them and contain the last of his volition. Now, he was being drawn back into the darkness, into the anxious, angry state of childhood. Of Mulligan, the Harcourt kid, or of Whitehouse, he did not think at all. Nobody could dismiss the past as he could. He did it now by habit, shivering and crouched in the dead-end street between the river, the canal and the high earth bank of the railway line.

The chiming of the clock sounded remote and hollow. It came to him and gave him a point upon which to fix his exhaustion. It ignited consciousness of his immediate position and how banal it was of him to give up everything and yield to merchants of order and so-called law. He still had a little time; not much, perhaps, but enough to work with. He stretched himself as if he had been asleep and, in control of part of himself again, padded up and down the wall of the cul-de-sac. In movement was an assurance of his own continuing strength. After a while, the wag of his mind took up where it had left off when Whitehouse's boot climbed up over his back. The pendulum of reason, rendered a fraction erratic, was in motion once more. Even so, it did not occur to him to turn and run out of the dead-end street. He busied himself with finding a flaw on the bulging staves which would give him access to the ridge above.

In the basement, in the carton under the magazines, he had salted three thousand pounds. That at least was safe enough. Even with the kid running loose around the town, it would be some hours before they wrung the truth out of her and got back to where his treasure was hidden. Pity about the bank accounts. More astute than Mulligan, he might even yet manage to pick the accounts clean and carry through the fiction of the escape he had plotted for the old man.

He thought hard about it.

He hadn't much time.

He had to do something; get the money and get out of the country.

An idiot could figure that out.

Charlie would arrive home probably tomorrow night. He doubted if he could wait that long, not even for Charlie. Charlie would understand the nature of the predicament, wouldn't blame him for taking off.

Three thousand pounds. Seven thousand pounds locked in the banks. How long had he been running? Twenty minutes, or half an hour. He did not even know where he was. Suddenly it occurred to him that the kid might obey Whitehouse's last instruction – just run home, hide under the bed, or lock herself safe in a closet. Vikki would be out cold as a mackerel. He could still redeem the situation. At least he could arm himself with the money, change his clothing, make himself neat and respectable. Better than that, perhaps even get out of the country in his own good time, with the ten thousand intact. Perhaps, if he could only contrive it properly, he might wait for Charlie and they could go together.

He would go back to the basement.

In the innermost corner of the cul-de-sac he hesitated. Pressure of earth had burst the staves here; rank grass and a scramble of dirt spilled out. The bricks were rough and broken. Above him, ten or twelve feet overhead, a tangle of rusty wire sprouted from the banking. A speculative humming sounded in his throat; not for the first time in his life he talked encouragingly to himself. He found a route up the corner and spurred himself to tackle it. It was easier than it appeared to be. Handholds and ledges for his insteps came readily out of the veneer of sleet. Groping upwards, his fingers soon discovered grass and, with a final lifting of his shoulders, claimed the wire. He tested it tentatively, found it secure. Kneecaps gave him pain as he placed them on the edge of the staves and, still clinging to the wire, drew himself up the soft banking on the track at the top; the branch line. South it curved sharply out of sight behind factory blocks; north it ran in a long arc towards the clustered lights of Brander Halt. The platform raked towards him, the single set of rails shining like silk ribbons on sleeper beds and pebble base. He took the middle of the track. Shortening his stride, he jogged towards the distant station, stepping on the sleepers and not the stones.

The high and unusual vantage point showed him perspectives of the town which he had not known existed; odd parallels of river, canal and railway line revealed between the dull giants of factories and furnaces, warehouses and older slum tenements. Cars and buses swam in strange isolation. Vistas of deserted streets opened below, brightly-lit, vacant supermarkets and drapers' stores. The walls lumbered slowly past him. He was treated to a tableau of the canal, some distance away but distinct in its puddle of darkness. The retreating haze of the sleet-storm skimmed across it, the sky over the open land beginning to bud with stars. He could even make out the gable of the lock-keeper's lodge, and the lock-gate itself cutting the level of the canal.

Nobody there; no sign of curious life.

He increased his pace, rounding the curve towards the station and access to the streets below.

It would be all right. He would make it yet.

The scene passed out of sight, blotted out by the cold-store's painted legends. A minute later he reached the ramp.

Constable Borthwick first spotted the bulging shape among the débris under the lock-gate and identified it as a body. His torch beam played over the surface. Pushed up by stirring gases in the mud, or perhaps in the corpse itself, the head floated surfaceward and hair spread out amid the trash of leaves, like weed fronds on a stone. At that same moment, the arms too lifted out of the oily depths. Drifting upward, the buttocks rose lazily. Leaning over the lock-shaft, Ryan saw that it was indeed a man.

Borthwick switched off the torch and hurried to the shed-dings in search of ropes. With distaste, Ryan remembered the four drowned things he had dredged up when he was Borthwick's age from this same canal. Returning with ropes, tackle, and a harness trace Borthwick set about preparing a belay from the old tow-rope anchor which was still bedded above the lower level.

Ryan called out, 'You don't have to do that.'

'Best to take a look at him,' said Borthwick. 'You never know, sir.'

'You need help?'

'No, sir. I can manage fine.'

Ryan nodded. The constable seemed completely self-sufficient. From ropes, leather traces and lengths of chain he improvised a secure double sling. Ryan crossed the plank-ing. Using a spare torch from the patrol car, he flitted a beam over the waters above the gates and on to the path which wound away from the bridge. Sleet had melted on the ash, then frozen; even so, he could discern no signs of a scuffle.

The town had drawn away from the fringes of the water-way, ebbing back until its housing schemes and principal industries lay along the flanks of the new highway, and the neighbourhood of canal, railway and river had gradually become neglected. If, Ryan thought, he ever wanted to plan a murder, this would be an ideal spot in which to contrive its circumstances. Strange, though, that he could as yet feel no shock at the discovery of the body. Stranger still that he should still be looking for Yule, when that thing floating below might be all that remained of the fugitive. He re-turned by the bridge, took up position by the anchors, giving added light to Borthwick who, abseilling down the facing, was hung out now directly over the corpse.

Ryan said, 'Be careful.'

He heard a splash and a solid Anglo-Saxon curse-word as the constable's boots slipped on moss and dipped him to the knees in the water. Ryan shifted closer to the edge, the torch beam steady. He watched Borthwick reach out and, paddling in the water, awkwardly fix a rope round the cadaver's chest and shoulders. After testing it, the constable dragged the upper part of the torso clear of the liquid.

It wasn't Yule. Poor light notwithstanding, Ryan was sure it wasn't Yule. The body was that of a young man dressed in some kind of khaki battledress jerkin.

'He's dead,' Borthwick called. 'We'd better bring him out, all the same, sir; wouldn't you think?'

Borthwick pendulumed, then, taking purchase, climbed up the lock wall. With Ryan's assistance, he hauled himself panting and dripping on to the stone. At that moment, a squad car siren echoed out of the warehouse canyons. A minute later, headlamps drenched the lock with light.

McCaig was out of the car before the vehicle had properly stopped.

Ryan held up the rope like a fishing line.

'Who is it?' McCaig demanded, peering over the lock. 'Is it Mulligan?'

'No,' said Ryan. 'I'm not sure who it is, but it certainly isn't Mulligan.'

'This pusher ... how did you ... ?'

'The pusher's name is Gregor Yule. That's not him down there either, sir.'

'Harry,' said McCaig. 'Perhaps you should ...'

Officers and uniforms debouched from the police cars. Directed by the capable Borthwick, the process of bringing up the body continued. Ryan and the Chief stood back from the edge now, as if under the auspices of a class rule which protected them from association with manual labour.

Ryan finished his explanation. 'Three thousand quid in a box under the bed.'

'Is this suicide?'

'No, sir : it's murder.'

'Are you sure?'

'No, but I'd wager on it.'

'And who do you think did it?'

'I think we'll find it was Yule.'

'The pusher?'

'Yes, Chief.'

'So we've got him on a big one, have we?' said McCaig.

'We haven't got him yet.'

'Near enough, though,' the Chief said. 'The bastard's out and running; all we have to do is spread the net.'

The corpse swarmed over the stone. Four uniformed

helpers bent to clear it. Hands lifted it, carried it away from the edge, laid it on a prepared layer of polythene sheeting on a straw-filled mattress. Flanking the body Ryan and McCaig stooped to ascertain that the state of death was complete. Headlamps cast crude light across them, cold as the air. Watching McCaig test for signs of life, Ryan thought how much more reality this death had than the death which had begun it all; how pitiful, how final it was for the floppy soaking thing on the sheeting.

McCaig got up. 'Mick,' he shouted. 'Respiration; old-style. Keep it up. Treat him properly. Jarvis, spell it out; mouth to mouth even if you only suspect you've got a flicker. Lindsay, I want an ambulance and full equipment here in five minutes.'

Ryan rose too and moved back, making room for the constables.

McCaig was shouting orders. Ten minutes ago this place had seemed deserted and oddly peaceful; now it was full of heavy uniforms, clatter of boots and the calling of voices – the chaos of procedure, a familiar and unpleasantly dispassionate drill of discovery. It was as if he had opened his hand and found all that he needed in it. Ryan was conscious of luck and the phrase of the instinct which had taken him, unwittingly, in the true direction. But it troubled him that in some way he had been responsible for bringing this second youngster to the grave.

'Chief, I'd like the use of a car,' Ryan said.

'For what?'

'If I was on the run, I'd probably have a go at recovering my stake money before I left.'

'Take the paddy-wagon,' McCaig said, 'and a couple of men.'

'Borthwick will do.'

'Which one's he?'

'The wet one,' Ryan said.

Travelling at walking pace, Yule toured the front of the building. Carefully he inspected the streets and alleyways which fed the main thoroughfare and, in passing, examined cars parked along the kerb. Not surprisingly, he found no lurking snoops or paddy-wagons in the vicinity. He did not connect the Cortina with Ryan. Rounding the back of the house, via the lane by the side of the Majestic Bar, he scrutinised the area there too. No hidden uniforms coming to light, he entered the close from the yard and tried the kitchen door. It opened. He went in, closed the door behind him and moved through the darkened kitchen into the hallway. Cat-like, quick and silent, he shifted across it, pausing to look back at the open closet doors. Panic struck him, and swiftly died; Whitehouse had been here, of course. The painter must have searched through the place for the kid. All would be not quite as he'd left it.

He looked at his wrist-watch. The glass was cracked, and a little rivulet of dried blood ornamented the strap, seeping from a graze at the base of his thumb. He had been gone only an hour and fifteen minutes. He peered into the living-room, almost expecting to see the kid lying on the carpet watching telly, but found it empty. Tracking back, he listened at the door at the top of the basement stairs, then, assured, went on down. He did not reach the bottom.

Halfway down, he stopped.

The blanket ripped back on its rings.

There was a copper below, a big guy, hatless, the dark uniform's silver chasing unmistakable.

Yule turned back.

At the top of the stairs was the girl.

He'd forgotten about her. For an instant he could hardly recall her name – Summerfield. Bloody Sheila Summerfield. She was the one who'd shopped him.

He sprang at her. She fell back. He stumbled into the hallway. The blue's fingers closed about his calf, the other hand grabbed at his wrist. Sprawled on his knees on the floor, he kicked back like a mule, struck something soft. The blue snarled in pain, and his hand slackened on Yule's leg. Yule drove up off the floor, struck the girl in passing, and dived for the main door. It was closed on the latch, but not bolted. He saw the empty gas-lit close outside. At once the copper lunged, bearing down on him even as he turned. He brought up his fist, hit the blue in the belly, and saw the judo pose freeze. The man sagged slowly, groaning, hands clutched downward into his belly. Behind the policeman Yule glimpsed the blonde cripple, at her hip the child, each holding each, both mute. No time to take revenge on them; the blue was hauling himself off the floor, unfolding in sections, beginning to consolidate and to mount another attack.

Yule ran out into the street.

The police van skidded – its fender missed him by an inch – and ploughed into the side of a parked car. Shouting dinned in his ears. Head down, he lifted his feet and ran with all the speed he could muster to the corner of Lauder Street. He was aware of another patrol car zooming over the crest of the hill, of shouting behind him and shrill whistling. In Lauder Street the pavement was slippery with sleet. He sprinted past padlocked shops and showrooms, flanked on the kerb-side by a perspective of parking meters and cars. Once he skidded, slid headlong, scraping his knees and elbows, bunching even as he lost balance and gathering himself up, winded but with hardly a break in his stride. The sing-song urgency of the patrol siren was bearing up on his left; he risked a quick flicking turn of his head. Behind him on the pavement two uniforms and the plainclothes snoop called Ryan were strung out in pursuit. On the road was a blue and white van which he recognised as the nightly watch on the Majestic Theatre and Bar. He was filled with deceitful exhilaration at the desperate nature of his position.

Stripped to its elements, the complex game had taken on the exact and simple pattern of a sport. All of it, all along, had been merely a sophisticated version of hounds and hare, now, at last, exposed for what it was. He welcomed the challenge in broad physical terms, running harder. As the van came abreast of him and braked, he darted behind it into the alley at the back of the insurance office. Under the wrought-iron archway of the executives' car park was a tarmac square completely enclosed by sandstone and Gothic windows, only a few of which were lighted at this hour. The blues, of course, would follow him. The paddy-wagon would circle the block to cut off his exit at the far end of the lane. That was what he hoped they would do. Four doors – janitors' doors – led into the square. He tried the first and found it locked. The second stood open and welcoming. A flight of steps folded round the dusty base of the lift shaft. He leaned on the weight of the door, felt it yield, and shudder into its sockets. He threw the vertical bolts, top and bottom. Ryan hurled himself against the outside and bawled at him to 'be sensible'.

'Fuck you!' Yule shouted.

Flight was now an escapade more reliant on cunning than on stamina. Somewhere in the building would be a janitor's flat. Front entrance was on Clayton Street. The building was seven storeys high, connected by fire-ladders to other blocks in Clayton Street. If memory served him right, escapes went down to ground level in three situations; one, he thought, into the well through which he'd just passed; two others on opposing buttresses, flanking Lauder Street and Ribbleside Street. Surely it would take the fuzz five minutes to obtain access to the building, and longer to cordon off the area. By that time he hoped to be out of the net, or over it. He cut up the steps from the lower level and emerged in the back ell of the main foyer. Dim inspection bulbs on steps and in corridors led him to the lift. Late-shift clerks would still be on the premises. Electrical power would not yet be beamed off at the circuit box. He listened, but heard no sounds from the upper floors. Pressing the red button, he watched tiny circular ports on the overhead panel come alight, numbering off the floors – three, two, one. The lift door glided open; he stepped inside. As he did so, he made out a babble of voices in the street, surprisingly audible. Somebody shouting *'Yes go on.'*

Glass shattered.

The lift door closed.

He thumbed the button for the seventh floor, felt the cage rise rapidly in the shaft. It occurred to him that if the fuzz were mad enough to resort to destruction of the ornate glass front door, they might also be smart enough to locate the elevator power source and trap him between levels.

The ride upwards became an unendurable agony of waiting, stretching his nerve and shaking his confidence.

The lift shot by the fifth floor.

His nerve broke. He jabbed the Halt button. With a sighing shudder, the cage levelled out at the sixth. The door grated open.

He ran up the steps into the top-floor corridor. It was carpeted wall-to-wall in a heavy pile Axminster. Unlike the fly-blown glass of the offices below, the doors which led off it were of richly grained wood, decorated by neat brass plates. This, Yule realised, was a penthouse office suite, eyrie of the upper echelon of the company who owned the property. It did not smell of carbolic and damp paper; had the luxurious effluvia of expensive carpeting and artificial air sweetener. Real flowers in a fluted vase stood on a little pedestal between two of the four doors. A burglar could probably make himself a tidy packet by breaking into these offices, appropriating

284

trinkets of success, table lighters and cigarette boxes, gold pens. For a wayward moment he was tempted to crack one of the locks – not to confuse his pursuers, just to see with his own eyes what the furnishings of power and successful endeavour were really like.

The lift doors closed. Slots of light behind them faded.

Yule found the steep flight of steps which zig-zagged up behind the shaft, gave access first to the elevator's mechanism, then, by a black-painted door, to the roof. The door lay ajar. Four cats on the bitumen surface scampered to him from their playground litter by the air-vent heads where fanned warmth from the rooms below had moistened the icing of sleet, and made a black tongue across it. He had two choices now; he could go round the parking square to the east and hope to find the connection which would take him to the Lauder Street escape; or he could fork to the west, a straight run along a narrowing wedge of the roof, and make his descent into Ribbleside. He rejected Clayton Street out of hand; that's where the fuzz would be. A breast-high wall contained the roof. Mists of lights and sounds from the streets below gave him a sense of location. Elbows on the brickwork, he rested his chin on his hands and peered down into Clayton Street. A police van was parked under him, but he could not make out its crew. Under a lamp across the street, a man and woman were caught in curious pose, swivelled to stare towards the entrance of the block. Two men came up Lauder Street, chatting to each other, casual pedestrians unaware of any unusual occurrence in the district. Traffic growled in the encompassing roadways; a Volkswagen, followed by a Vauxhall, tooled up Clayton Street and passed out of his sight behind the statuary of the façade, an Inca pyramid of sandstone slabs topped by the lion standard of the enterprise who owned the block. The cats had gone back to the warmth of the vent. Yule changed his vantage point, but the obstruction of the façade blotted out his view. Not knowing what lay below in Lauder Street, he chose the wedge and Ribbleside.

Height did not deter him. In fact he had to hold his recklessness on tight rein, not, as another man might, jig up his nerve to make the narrow crossing from one maze of rooftops to the next. Quitting the insurance block, he crossed over the fire ladder upright; insteps on metal plates, arms hooked over the railings which gave the bridge the likeness of a companionway on one of Charlie's ships. Right now Charlie would be tramping home, snug in his cabin or on watch in the darkness over the heaving sea, bringing more heroin, more produce for the clients, to earn more money. The deal was bust though; the clients would have to whistle for their shots, and Charlie fend for himself. Below him the passage seemed like a channel of milky liquid, an inviting sea-froth lapping from the walls, covering cool green depths. If he fell, it would not crush him on its horizontal solidity, but split before him and allow him privileged entrance to those secret deeps. Gingerly he stepped down from the final rung on to the roof of the General United property and ran across it to the inner balustrade.

The flight had lost its desperate quality. He had shed his desperation. Weary now, limping a little, his sharpness was giving way to welcome fantasies. Daring replaced caution; impatience throttled guile. No fuzz here to badger him, only open sky, a maze of little walls, and lakes of bitumen painted with the remains of the sleet shower. Metal vents, lean chimney-heads, relics of former decades; cowled entrances to the lofts and attics of commerce; power hubs, shuttered shafts through which discharges of air and electricity ran; gutters, drains like leaden flowerpots, and, here and there, lost to the aesthetes of the town below, a clover-leaf or a noble visage graven into stone. Trudging on, Yule sought diligently for the railings of the fire-escape which would carry him down to the safe and level earth. He dropped from the balustrade, and walked the diagonal past a concave skylight which, like a glass pond, lay below the level of the roof. He reached a corner by a shed-like structure. Behind it, rising up to an iron platform, he found the top of the escape.

Seated on it, side by side, were the cop called Ryan and a constable in uniform.

The blue got up, but Ryan didn't.

Ryan checked the constable's impetuous movement by stretching his right arm across the posts of the fire-escape's anchorage. He wore the same hat and overcoat that he had worn the last time Yule saw him and appeared no more anxious or ruffled than he had been on that occasion.

Yule leaned against the shed; a structure of thick metal lagged over with brown paint and bolted down under the layers of roofing.

'It's always a mistake to go high, Greg,' Ryan said.

His voice was very distinct and precise, like something stencilled in vivid white against the infinite blue-blackness of the sky.

Yule said nothing.

Now he understood that all sagacity, all forms of cunning and the wiles of an intelligent mind are relative only to primary functions imposed upon them by the zones in which they operate. He had thought himself unique. This bastard Ryan had taught him otherwise, had used the experience of a hundred ruses, a thousand evasions, to predict exactly what he would do.

'We'll take you down, Greg,' Ryan said.

A last spasm of vitality slackened the tension of defeat. He leapt to the side, pawing at the air.

Ryan, like a trainer, lifted his arm and released the man in uniform.

Too late.

Too late, you bastard.

Yule grasped the wall and vaulted on to it. Swaying, back to the street, his toes curled over the inner edge seeking grip and purchase. He could not limit himself, however, or rush through such a magnificent gesture of defiance. He had to pause, set himself up, transform it by a sporting ritual into something memorable. A breeze of medium velocity strayed up from the emptiness below, billowing the rally jacket, fattening him. He swayed again, raised his arms, and was still. His vision cleared. He looked down at the uniform, five yards from him, halted, like another wasted monument, carved not of stone but of coal.

And Ryan: Ryan was still seated on the platform.

Ryan hadn't moved.

Sweat dried and froze on Yule's flesh, crimping the skin, like lye.

'Ryan?'

'What?'

'Look.'

'I don't see anything,' Ryan said. He got up, walked three or four steps and touched the uniform's shoulder. He seemed to lean on it as if he was weary and cold and needed the constable as a prop. 'You don't see anything, Borthwick, do you?'

'Not a thing, sir.'

'Listen, you bastard,' Yule shouted. 'You're not going to take me.'

'I don't want you,' Ryan said. 'I'd rather see you jump, if you want the truth of it. I mean it, Yule; I'd far rather you jumped.'

'You're bluffing.'

'I can't be bothered bluffing. Jump if you want to jump. Come with us, if you don't. I'd really like to see you dead, son. That would suit me fine, and save the State a hell of a lot of expense.'

'*Listen . . .*'

'I'm listening.'

Yule opened his mouth.

It was a trap, he knew that. There was *no* drop behind him at all, only another level; or maybe a crew of salvage-men with nets and tarpaulins ready to catch him when he fell. Fell; not jumped.

He looked carefully under his armpit, and saw nothing; no ledge, no projection, no scuttling crew, no nets or snares or blankets. Ribbleside Street was empty.

'You see, son,' Ryan said.

The street was no longer fluid, but hard, the air vacant. Vertical lines of buildings converged mercilessly with horizontal dihedrals of pavements, and, by a trick of vision, marked out a shadowy cross on the spot where he would strike the concrete. Clouded and sick, the axis of his reason tilted him and made his body totter on its narrow perch. He was full of fear that he would fall, fall flat and final as a tin cat in a shooting gallery, never to rise again.

'Please,' he said. 'Please *help me.*'

After a while, a cruel moment, Ryan said, 'Constable Borthwick, bring him down.'

Crying loudly, Yule tumbled forward into the constable's ready arms.